P9-CDS-541

PRAISE FOR SHERRILYN KENYON

"Kenyon's writing is brisk, ironic, sexy, and relentlessly imaginative."
                                        —*Boston Globe*

"[A] publishing phenomenon...[Sherrilyn Kenyon is] the reigning queen of the wildly successful paranormal scene....just one example of arguably the most in-demand and prolific author in America these days."
                                        —*Publishers Weekly*

AND HER BESTSELLING DARK-HUNTER NOVELS...

BAD MOON RISING
"A skillfully written and entertaining tale...rich with complex characters, snappy dialogue, and sweet moments."
                                        —*Tulsa World*

ACHERON
"*Acheron* sucks you into Kenyon's world and keeps you there from the first page until the last."
                                        —*Midwest Book Review*

DEVIL MAY CRY
"An engaging read."   —*Entertainment Weekly*

DARK SIDE OF THE MOON
"A delicious balance of suspense and sensuality."
                                        —*Publishers Weekly*

MORE...

BAD MOON RISING

SHERRILYN KENYON

St. Martin's Paperbacks

This is a work of fiction. All of the characters, organizations, and events portrayed in this novel are either products of the author's imagination or are used fictitiously.

BAD MOON RISING

Copyright © 2009 by Sherrilyn Kenyon.

All rights reserved.

For information address St. Martin's Press, 175 Fifth Avenue, New York, NY 10010.

ISBN: 978-0-312-93436-1

Printed in the United States of America

St. Martin's Press hardcover edition / August 2009
St. Martin's Paperbacks edition / April 2010

St. Martin's Paperbacks are published by St. Martin's Press, 175 Fifth Avenue, New York, NY 10010.

10 9 8 7 6 5 4 3 2 1

ACKNOWLEDGMENTS

To my readers, who have taken countless trips with me and who have been begging for Fang's book for the last five years. Never have I felt closer to the Kattalakis brothers than I did here. I was finally able to speak for Fang and show all the depth of his character and all the beauty of one of my favorite wolves.

To my team at St. Martin's, which is the best in the world, and especially Monique and Matthew for letting me bend rules and have way too much fun. To Merrilee for all the hard work you do. Holly, who works so wonderfully behind the scenes, taking care of details.

To my friends who are always there when I need them: Kim, Dianna, Loretta, Sheri, and Ed. Thank you, guys, really, for keeping me sane. And to the best staff in the universe, Team Fabulous: Dianna, Erin, Kim, Jacs, Ed, Judy, Marie, Loretta, Sheri, Scott, Bryan, Julia, CiCi, Webbie, Alex, and if I forgot someone, please, please forgive me.

And last, but absolutely never least, my family. To Ken for being my anchor and support through all dark storms and for always being my best friend. My brother for being the best bro any sister ever had. And my boys, who fill my life with laughter and my days with joy. I couldn't make it through without any of you. Thank you.

THE BEGINNING OF
THE WERE-HUNTERS

Long before recorded history there lived a bold king. One who refused to yield before the wills of the Greek gods who commanded him. Like so many before and after, he made the mistake of falling in love with the most beautiful woman in his kingdom. A woman whose very smile was his life's blood.

Little did he know she bore the darkest of all curses. Because of the actions of her forefathers against the Greek god Apollo more than two thousand years before her birth, her people had been damned to die brutally on their twenty-seventh birthday. It was a secret she kept until the day when she, like all the others of her Apollite kind, began to decay and die.

In only twenty-four hours she went from a beautiful young woman to a crone, then nothing but scattered dust.

Lycaon was devastated by the loss of his love, but worse than that was the haunting knowledge that soon his own sons would join their mother and die every bit as horrifically.

Like her, they would die for something none of them had had a part in.

Unable to bear the injustice, he confronted the gods and told them to screw themselves. He would not stand by and watch his children die. Ever.

That very night, he began using the darkest of magick to splice the genes of his wife's people with those of the strongest of animals. Wolves, jackals, lions, tigers, panthers, jaguars, cheetahs, bears, hawks, leopards, even a rare dragon—those were his chosen few to be the saviors of his children.

When his experiments were complete, he'd created an entirely new species. No longer human, no longer Apollite nor animal, they were something else entirely.

The experiments turned his two sons into four separate beings. Two creatures who held the hearts of an animal and who lived as an animal by the light of day. And two who held the hearts of a human. By day, human would be their base form.

This was their gift.

And so was born their new curse.

From their mother's Apollite race, they inherited magick and psychic abilities. From their father's tampering they would live by day as their base form, either human or animal, and at night they would be able to switch to their alternate form. Man became beast and beast became man.

Under the light of the full moon, when their powers were strongest, not even the laws of time or physics would hold sway over them. From that day forward they would live for centuries, immune from the curse of Apollo.

The gods were not pleased. They demanded the king

slaughter all the creatures he'd made. How dare *he*, a mere mortal, be contentious enough to thwart their will.

But the king refused. "I will not allow my children to suffer for *your* vanity! You can all die for what I care."

So while his children were spared their Apollite curse, the gods gave them a new one. None of their species would ever be able to choose a mate of their own free will, only the Fates could assign them that. And there would *never* be peace between the animal Katagaria and the human Arcadians that the king had created.

Eternal enemies, the two races would become known as Were-Hunters because each would hunt the other. Throughout all time, they would battle and slaughter their own kind—forever suspicious. Forever angry. More than that, they would become the chosen food source of their own cousins, the vampiric Daimons who needed souls to live past their twenty-seventh birthday.

No peace. No succor. Their fate to suffer and to exist in spite of the gods.

Until the day the last two survivors kill each other. That was their prophecy.

And none were to suffer more than those who bore the name of the king's direct descendants. Those who bore the surname Kattalakis. . . .

CHAPTER 1

January 2003
Sanctuary, New Orleans

"So that's the infamous Sanctuary. . . ."

Fang Kattalakis looked up from where he was locking down his sleek Kawasaki Ninja to see Keegan eyeing the triple-story redbrick building across the street.

The pup was just hitting puberty—about thirty years old in human time, but true to their species and his Were-Hunter age, Keegan appeared around the human age of sixteen—which meant he was as excitable as an adolescent. Dressed in black leather to protect him while he rode his motorcycle, Keegan almost dropped his bike in his eagerness to visit the famed sanctuary that was owned by a family of bearweres.

Fang let out a long exasperated breath as he secured his helmet to his backpack. As punishment, he and his brother Vane had been assigned watch duty over Keegan and his twin brother, Craig.

Joy, oh joy. He'd rather have his entrails pulled out through his nostrils—whelp-sitting had never been to his taste. But at least they didn't have their leader Stefan along on this outing. That would have resulted in all-out bloodshed since Fang had no respect or tolerance for Stefan even on his best day.

And today wasn't even a "better" day.

The blond pup was all limbs as he started to leave, but Vane caught him by the scruff of his neck.

Keegan went instantly limp, which said it all about his age and inexperience. Even when he'd been a pup, Fang had *never* surrendered without a fight. It wasn't in his nature.

Vane released his grip on the kid's collar. "Don't leave the pack, whelp. It's a bad habit to develop. Wait on all of us."

It was why they were all riding motorcycles. Since "average" young weren't real good at teleporting until they were around forty or fifty years old, and because whelp powers tended to play havoc with even the strongest when being teleported by another, mundane human transportation was best.

So here they were.

Bored. Agitated. And looking human. What a disgusting combination.

Most of all, Fang was tired.

And since they were training the whelps to socialize and maintain human forms during the light of day . . .

Sanctuary had seemed the best and safest place to take them outside of camp. At least here if one turned wolf, the bears could hide it. Only the strongest of Katagaria wolves could remain human in daylight. If the pups couldn't learn to hold their alternate human forms under the power of the sun by the time they turned thirty-five, their leader would order the pack to kill them.

It was a harsh world they lived in and only the strongest of their species survived. If they couldn't fight and blend in with the humans, they were dead anyway. No need in wasting their precious resources on creatures who couldn't defend the pack.

Vane glanced over to Fang as if waiting for him to say something nasty to Keegan. Normally Fang would have some smart-ass comment about the pup, but he was just too tired to bother.

"What's taking so long?" Fury paused beside Fang, chafing at his delay. Not quite as tall as Fang, Fury was lean and vicious. With turquoise eyes, Fury had sharp features and everything about the wolf made Fang's hackles rise. His long white-blond hair was pulled back into a tight ponytail.

Slinging the backpack over one shoulder, Fang raked him with a sneer that said what he thought about the wolf—not much. "Locking down my bike, asshole. You want I should lock it to you so that I know it'll be here when I come back?"

Fury's pupils narrowed. "I'd like to see you try."

Before Fang could lunge at him, Liam, Keegan's much older brother, was between them. "Down, wolves."

In true wolf form, Fang bared his teeth at Fury, who returned the gesture. At Liam's insistence, Fury moved past him while the eight other wolves crossed the street.

He and Vane pulled up the rear.

Fang indicated Fury with a jerk of his chin. "I really hate that bastard."

"Don't kill him yet. He has his uses."

Maybe. But not enough of them that Fang wouldn't rejoice to mount Fury's hide to his wall. Not that he had a wall, but if he did, Fury would make a nice hairy decoration.

Fang turned his attention to his brother who was about an inch shorter—Fury's height. "So why are we really here? We could have trained the pups in camp."

Vane shrugged. "Markus wanted us to register with the bears. Since we have so many burdened females, we might need the help of their doctor."

Yeah, their sister Anya and half a dozen other females would give birth at any minute. Markus, the unwilling sperm donor for the three of them, had also wanted his "sons" out of his sight. Which was fine with Fang. He wasn't exactly fond of the old fart either. He would have already challenged him for leadership, but Vane and Anya kept pulling him back.

Since Vane was an Arcadian hiding in the midst of their Katagaria pack, the last thing they needed was Fang to be leader. That would lead to uncomfortable questions such as why Vane, his elder littermate who was their father's heir apparent and one they all knew had more magick strength than Fang did, wasn't the one fighting for leadership. But Vane could *never* do that. Because pain tended to make them involuntarily shift into their base forms, they couldn't risk Vane accidentally turning human in a fight.

It was why Fang had stayed up all night. Unconscious and badly wounded, Vane had been forced to sleep as a human. Their pack would kill his brother if any of them ever suspected Vane's true base form.

Yawning, Fang caught up to the pack that'd been stopped at Sanctuary's door by the club's bouncer. Bulkier than the wolves, the bear had long curly blond hair and wore a black T-shirt with the Sanctuary logo on it that was partially covered by a worn black leather jacket.

His blue eyes carefully scrutinized them. "Pack?"

Vane stepped forward. "Kattalakis Grand Regis Lykos . . . Katagaria."

The bear arched his brow as if impressed with their pedigree. Grand Regis meant that their father had a seat on the Omegrion—the council that oversaw and made the laws that governed all Were-Hunters. Since there were only twenty-three members (twenty-four originally, but one species had gone extinct), it was impressive to be one of them. "Any among you bearing the Kattalakis name?"

"Me and my brother." Vane indicated Fang.

The bear nodded as he folded his arms over his chest and took on a tough stance. "We're Peltiers. I'm Dev—one of a set of identical quadruplets so no, you're not seeing double or triple inside—and stay clear of the one who looks like me dressed completely in black—Remi's an irritable SOB. My mother, Nicolette, is the Katagaria Grand Regis Ursulan—so don't start no shit, won't be no shit. Quick rule rundown. No fighting, no biting, no magick. You break the rules, we break body parts and you're banned from here . . . *if* you survive." He passed a meaningful stare to the pups. "In short, come in peace or leave in pieces. You got it?"

Fang raised his hand to flip him off, but Vane caught his wrist before he could.

"We understand."

Hissing from the burn Vane was putting on him, Fang twisted out of his brother's grasp.

Vane glared at him. *Keep your mouth shut and your gestures to yourself*, he mentally projected to him.

I don't take orders from bears.

No, but you take them from me. Behave, Fang, or I'll kick your ass back to the Stone Age. Vane grabbed the sleeve of his jacket and dragged him into the bar.

Fang shoved him away. Unless he took him down with magick, Vane was nowhere near as strong as he was. "I'm not your bitch, boy."

Vane turned on him with a look that said he was one step away from taking his best shot. "Then do it for Anya. We might need them to help us if she has problems with her litter."

That was a low blow and it was the one thing Vane knew he wouldn't fight against. Anya was their lifeblood. For her, they'd do anything.

"Fine. I'm just irritable from lack of sleep."

"Why didn't you sleep?"

I was protecting you. . . . Some of the wolves had been on the prowl last night and Fang had feared them stumbling over Vane's position while he healed from his wounds and slept. So he'd stayed up to make sure Vane's injured scent and den went undiscovered.

But he would never tell his brother the truth. It would shame Vane to think his younger brother had protected him. "I don't know. I just couldn't."

"So who was she?"

Fang rolled his eyes. "Why do you assume it was a female?"

Vane held his hands up. "Didn't know you were fond of men. I'll file that under my special Fang folder."

Ignoring him, Fang glanced around the infamous

dark club that wasn't overly crowded in the late afternoon. A few humans sat at tables while more played pool and video games in the back. An empty dance area was set before a stage with the name "Howlers" spray-painted in dark blue and white on the back wall.

Craig and Keegan pulled three tables together in a corner to accommodate the ten of them. Some of the humans eyed them nervously which Fang found hysterical, especially the woman who put her purse in her lap as they passed. Like a wolf needed money. But then, they were a rough-looking bunch. Decked out in biker leathers, each of them was ready to fight if they had to.

The only one of them even remotely clean-cut was Vane, who wore jeans with a brown leather jacket and a dark red T-shirt. That being said, he had the longest hair of any of them. But with it pulled back into a ponytail and with a clean shave, he was passable. The rest of them looked like the feral beasts they were.

Fang dropped his backpack on the floor and took a seat to stretch out his long legs. Leaning against the wall, he adjusted his sunglasses and closed his eyes to catch a combat "nap" while they shot the crap among themselves. If he could just have ten uninterrupted minutes to sit and think about nothing, he'd be a new wolf. . . .

"There's a pack of wolves who just came in."

Her stomach sliding into her stomach, Aimee Peltier glanced up from the ledger where she was going over new orders. Their mother, Nicolette Peltier, froze at Dev's dry declaration.

She met Aimee's quizzical look as she pushed herself back from the large brown desk. "How many?"

"Looks to be eight Slayers and two pups in training."

Maman arched one blond brow. Though she was approaching eight hundred years old, she appeared to be no older than a forty-year-old human. Dressed in a fitted blue business suit and with her blond hair pulled back in a tight chignon, she looked prim and proper—unlike Aimee, who was dressed in a T-shirt and jeans and wore her long hair down. "Slayers or Strati?"

Strati were Katagaria warriors who were the fiercest of the bunch and usually quick to anger. The pups, due to hormonal shifts that were even worse on Were-kind than humans, were even more so. But they usually lacked the power and strength to back their egos. Slayers, on the other hand, were indiscriminate killers who slew any and everything that got in their way. Arcadians applied the latter to any Katagari soldier as a justification for why they needed killing.

If this group of wolves really were Slayers, their presence in the bar was like a keg of dynamite resting on an open hearth with a raging fire.

Dev scratched at the back of his neck. "They're technically Strati, but these are hard-core cases. Wouldn't take much to make them Slayers."

Aimee stood up. "I'll go wait on them."

Dev blocked her exit. "Cherise already got their orders."

She was aghast at his recklessness. "You trusted a human to wait on them?" Was he out of his mind?

Dev seemed unperturbed by his own stupidity. "Cherise is too even-tempered and sweet. I doubt even a true Slayer could be mean to her. Besides, I know how you feel about wolves and thought I'd spare you having to deal with them. We don't need any more drama here for a while."

It was true. Her encounters with wolves had never gone well. She couldn't explain it, but she shared her mother's distaste of their kind. Wolves were violent and filthy. Arrogant to the extreme.

Most of all, they stank to her "bear" sensitivity.

Nicolette stood up. "Aimee, go and keep an eye on them. Make sure they don't cause any trouble while they're here. I don't want another spectacle. If they so much as sniff in the wrong direction, throw them out."

She inclined her head to her mother.

Dev shifted to one side to let her pass. "If you need a hand, I'll be there with backup faster than you can say 'wolf stain.'"

Aimee had to stop herself from sighing in aggravation at her overprotective brother. He meant well. But there were times when she felt completely stifled by her family.

Even so, she loved them . . . warts and all.

Patting him on the arm, she walked down the hallway to the kitchen where humans unknowingly mixed with a Were-Hunter staff. They thought this was a normal bar and restaurant. If only they knew the truth. . . .

She grabbed her apron and tied it at the waist before she reached for her tray.

"Where have you been?"

She paused at her brother Remi's bark. Identical in looks to Dev, no surprise since they were two of the identical quads Maman had birthed, he'd inherited all the surly anger of his other three brothers combined.

Plus he barely tolerated her.

"With Maman, ordering food and alcohol. Not that it's any of your business."

Remi skirted a stainless-steel industrial table to encroach on her personal space in a way that made her want to knee him hard in his "man" pride. "Yeah, well, there's a bunch of wolves—"

"Dev already told me."

"Then get your butt out there and watch them."

She raked him with a sneer. "Nice attitude, Rem. Really, you should see about suing whatever asshole sold it to you."

He lunged at her.

Aimee caught him with her tray and shoved him back. "Don't, brother. I'm not in the mood."

He shoved her back.

"Remi!"

He froze as their father came into the kitchen. Over seven feet tall and well muscled, Papa Bear was a frightening sight, even to the children who knew he would never harm them. His long blond hair was pulled back in a ponytail that matched Remi's. In fact, he looked as much like Remi as Dev did and unless someone knew better, Papa could pass as an older brother.

"Leave your sister alone. Now go wash dishes until you cool down."

Remi glared at him. "She provoked me."

Papa sighed. "Everyone provokes you, *mon fils*. Now go and do as I say."

Aimee offered her father a reconciliatory smile. "It's

just a mild disagreement, Papa. Remi has this whole need to breathe in and out, which annoys me. If he would just stop breathing, I'd be fine."

Her father gave her a chiding stare. "Never say such to me, *chere*. I've already buried enough sons and you brothers. Now apologize to Remi."

Completely contrite, Aimee went over to her brother. Her father was right, she didn't want anything to happen to anyone else in her family. Even as surly as Remi was, she still loved him more than anything and would protect him with her life. "I'm sorry."

"You ought to be."

Aimee growled at his hostile personality. Why did he have to pick a fight with everyone?

She glared at her father. "You know, it's a shame Katagaria bears don't eat their young, especially the annoying ones."

Wanting to put distance between them, she headed out the door, into the bar area where the human waitress, Cherise Gautier, was filling drinks. Petite and blond, Cherise had the kindest disposition of any being Aimee had met in her three hundred years of living. Creatures like her were rare and Aimee wished she could be more like her.

Unfortunately, she had too much of Remi in her for that—another reason she couldn't stand her brother most days. They were two peas in a pod that together made an unsightly mush.

"Hey, Aimee," Cherise said with a bright smile that cheered her instantly. "You okay, baby? You're looking a little flushed."

"I'm fine."

Cherise gave her a gimlet stare as she covered her hand and gave a supportive squeeze. "You fight with your brother again, boo?"

There were times when she could swear that human had preternatural powers. "Don't we always?"

Unperturbed, Cherise returned to setting glasses on her tray. "Well, that's what family's for. But you know what I do. Anyone threatens you, Remi would have their posterior for dinner and you would do the same for him. That boy love you more than his life. Never forget that." Cherise started to pick up the tray.

"I got it." Aimee cut in front of her.

Cherise frowned. "You sure?"

"Absolutely. Besides, it's time for your break."

Her expression skeptical, Cherise stepped back. "All right then. I'll be just a shout away if we get busy suddenly. Those are for table thirty."

Aimee hefted the tray up and cursed at how heavy eight beers with iced mugs and two Cokes could be. It was a good thing she'd taken it from the human. As tiny and frail as Cherise was, she'd have had a hard time carrying it. But true to form, the human would never utter a single word of complaint. Cherise had never once bitched about anything or anyone.

Aimee carefully made her way from the bar area to the tables in front where the dogs had taken refuge. As she came around the corner, she let out an aggravated breath.

Sure enough, they looked like the dregs of the animal kingdom. Scruffy, leather-wearing brutes. She just hoped the younger two didn't try to hump the furniture or some human's leg.

Though as she drew closer, she couldn't help noticing that the one with the longer hair was extremely good-looking. His dark hair was made up of a myriad of colors. Red, mahogany, brown, black, even some blond. It was as striking as his dark eyes.

The only other one of them really noteworthy was the one wearing a black biker jacket, who leaned back in his chair with his incredibly long legs stretched out in front of him. His black T-shirt was pulled tight over a stomach that was rock-hard and flat. With short dark hair and an evident nasty attitude, he was hard to miss. His rugged features were covered with several days' growth of beard and his eyes were completely concealed behind a pair of opaque sunglasses.

There was something about him that screamed power. Something lethal. Deadly. Raw. The animal in her could appreciate how impressive it was to give off that vibe while completely at ease. It also set off her instincts and made her extremely wary of the whole group.

Yeah, that one wolf gave the word *Slayer* a whole new meaning. She glanced around the room to locate her allies. Her brothers Zar and Quinn were at the bar. Colt, another bear who lived with them, was having a drink in front of them. Their busboy, Wren, who was a tigard, stood in the far corner cleaning tables while his pet monkey, Marvin, poked his head out of Wren's apron pocket.

She was adequately covered if she needed it.

Putting off her own "screw you" aura, she closed the distance between them.

As soon as they saw her approaching, the wolves stood up . . . except for the one who looked the baddest of all. He continued to lean back with his arms folded over his chest.

"Fang!" the one with long dark hair snapped, kicking at his legs.

Fang came to his feet with a curse so foul, it actually made her blush. He had the one who'd barked his name in his hands before he seemed to realize what he'd done. "Vane?"

"Yeah, dick, let me go."

The long-haired white-blond wolf closest to Fang lowered his head threateningly. "Were you sleeping?"

Fang released Vane and passed the one who'd spoken a sneer that said he not only hated the other wolf, but that he thought he was an idiot. "Was I wolf or human?"

"Human."

"Then I wasn't asleep, was I, Scooby?"

She arched her brow at the insult. Wolves didn't like to be compared to dogs and to refer to them as a cartoon dog known for his lack-witted antics usually resulted in a fight.

The fact that the blond wolf didn't attack over it corroborated Fang's ferocity in a way nothing else did.

Fang shifted his weight and pulled his sunglasses off as if trying to be respectful of Aimee's presence—something that seemed incongruous to her and yet . . . these wolves were nothing like what she expected.

And his eyes . . .

They were a gorgeous brown with a hint of rust in them. Yet it was the pain and intelligence inside them that reached out to her. A pain that seemed boundless.

Yawning, Fang scratched at the thick whiskers on his face. "Though it wasn't for lack of trying."

The youngest wolf-pup came up to her. "Let me help you with that."

"I've got it," she said gently, surprised by how well mannered these wolves were. The ones she'd run into in the past had been from the lowest rung of the evolutionary scale.

As soon as the tray was down, they all took their drinks without waiting for her to hand them out.

Vane took her towel and wiped the tray dry before he held it out to her.

Aimee smiled at him. "Thank you." It was actually disconcerting to see wolves who appeared this rough having manners. She wasn't sure how to deal with them.

As she started away, the one named Fang stopped her with a gentle touch. "You dropped this." He bent down to pick up her pad that must have fallen out of her apron pocket.

As he stood up, she became aware of exactly how large a man he was. Not beefy like the bears she was used to, he was lean.

And he was ripped. Solid like taut steel.

"Thanks."

Fang couldn't speak as he looked into the clearest pale blue eyes he'd ever seen. They were set into the face of a blond angel. One who had just the smallest hint of a dimple in her right cheek when she spoke.

Her skin looked softer than velvet, and for some reason he couldn't name, he wanted to lay the backs of his fingers against her cheek to see if it was as soft as it appeared.

And her smell . . . it was lavender and lilac. Normally the scent of another species was repugnant to his wolf's heightened senses. But not hers. She smelled warm and sweet. So sweet that it was all he could do not to rub his face in the crook of her neck to experience more of it.

When her hand brushed his, his body erupted with heat.

Without a word, she put the pad in her pocket and turned away.

Fang had to catch himself to keep from following after her.

Vane handed him his beer, interrupting his attention. When he looked back, the female bear was gone.

"You okay?"

Fang nodded at Vane's question. "Just tired."

The moment he started to sit down, the bearswan was back. They all shot to their feet—something that was ingrained in them. Wolves protected their women stronger than any other Were-Hunter kind. Loyal and deadly, they were trained from birth to show respect to females, regardless of species. The fact that this bear was related to the ones who owned the bar made her even more honored.

The bearswan pulled her pad back out. "My name's Aimee. I forgot to take your orders."

Aimee . . . it was a beautiful, soft name and perfect for her. Even though he didn't repeat it out loud, he knew it would roll off his tongue like fine whisky.

"Steak," Vane said. "Rare as possible."

She jotted it down. "I assume you each want a couple?"

Liam adjusted his chair. "Yes. Please."

Aimee nodded and she bit back a smile over the

most favored request of their Katagaria clientele. All animals loved their meat only barely warmed by their human cooks who couldn't quite figure out why they had so many orders for it. "All right, two dozen house specials. Any chance one of you might want to live dangerously and try a vegetable?"

"Do we look like rabbits to you?"

Vane smacked the blond-haired man to his right on the shoulder. "Knock it off, Fury."

The wolf looked pissed, but reined himself in. As wolves, they all deferred to the alpha, even when it galled them to do it. Of course, they would also fight to the death at his command. No matter how much they fought among themselves, at the end of the day they were always united against any outsider. It was what made them so dangerous.

Wolves never fought alone.

They fought as a pack. Rabid. Cold. Lethal. And together they could kill just about anything that lived . . . or even those that didn't.

"Do you have anything sweet?"

Aimee turned her attention to Fang at his unorthodox request. Bears loved sweets, but wolves usually stuck to meat. "You have a sweet tooth?"

"Not me. It's for our sister. She's burdened and has been craving sweets."

This time she did smile as warmth seeped through her. "And you want to take something back to her?"

He nodded.

What a nice thing to do. It was something her— She froze at the stab of pain that thought caused. Even now that memory was razor-sharp and cut her to the quick.

She always did her best not to think about Bastien and Gilbert. Still, they snuck into her thoughts many times a day. "You got it. I'll toss in a couple of meats and treats for her."

"Much obliged."

For some reason she couldn't explain, Aimee wanted to stay and talk to the wolf. If for no other reason than to listen to the deep timbre of his voice when he spoke. There was a slight lilt to his speech that said he'd lived in England at some point in his life. It was really seductive. . . .

What is wrong with me? I hate wolves.

They were loud. Obnoxious. Smelly and always looking for trouble.

Yet there was something about this one that was compelling. And the fact that he thought of his sister . . .

At least he had a heart. That alone put him miles ahead of the others of his kind.

As she left them again, she couldn't resist looking back. Now he was smacking at Fury while Vane was separating them like a parent with two young sons.

Aimee shook her head.

That right there was why she didn't care for wolves. Something about canines, they were always nipping and sniping at each other and anyone dumb enough to come near them.

As she headed for the kitchen to hand her orders over, a boisterous group coming down the stairs made her pause. She cursed inwardly at the sight.

Jackals. Two females and four males. They must have teleported into the top floor that was reserved for that sort of activity—it was an area shielded from humans so that they'd never suspect what Sanctuary really was. To them it was just a club.

To Were-Hunters, it was neutral ground where none could be harmed.

And if there was anything she hated more than wolves, it was *those* canine cousins—the jackals. If being a jackal wasn't bad enough already, these were also Arcadian Sentinels and by the look of them they were on the hunt for someone.

Sighing heavily, she glanced back at the Katagaria wolves, wondering how they'd react to the Arcadian jackal presence.

The last thing they needed was for a vicious fight to break out between a clan of Sentinels and a pack of Strati, especially Strati with young to protect. That made them even edgier and more violent than normal.

She started back to the bar, but her path was cut off as one of the jackals teleported in front of her. He raked her with a sneer of disgust.

Aimee narrowed her gaze on him. "You can't use your magick in here. There are too many humans to see it."

He smirked. "I don't take orders from animals. Now tell me where Constantine is or we're going to tear this bar down."

Aimee refused to be bullied by anyone. "We are protected by the laws of the Omegrion, which you're obligated to follow. All are welcome, even your putrid selves, and none can be removed by force."

He grabbed her arm. "Fetch Constantine, or I'll make boots out of your hide, bear."

Aimee twisted her arm out of his grip. "Don't touch

me, or I'll mount your jewels to the wall over your head."

The jackals surrounded her. "We don't have time for this. He's here. We can smell it."

Aimee raked him with a sneer of her own. "You need to get your head out of your sphincter and stop smelling your own underwear 'cause the only jackals here, buddy, are *you*."

"Is there a problem?" For once she was grateful to hear Dev's deep growl.

Aimee looked past the leader's shoulder to see Dev with Colt, Remi, and Wren. Papa was making his way toward them too. "Yes. And I think it's time for our friends here to find an exit."

Dev reached for the leader, who spun on him so fast, she barely saw him move. With one fluid move, he had Dev flat on his back on the floor. Dev reached up and froze as the jackal held a Taser at the ready.

It wasn't the pain of a possible hit that gave them pause. One jolt and they'd lose control of their human forms for hours. For that matter, any hit of electricity would have them flashing from human to animal and back again.

Something that was hard to explain to human clientele who tended to get a little wigged-out whenever they saw it.

Aimee looked around at the number of humans in the room. They needed to dispel this as peacefully as possible.

And quick.

The leader looked past her and gave a subtle nod.

All of a sudden, the man behind her grabbed her hard and held a knife to her throat.

The leader's gaze glittered like ice. "Now take us to Constantine or I'll have your head."

Aimee passed a scared look to Dev who knew what she did.

They couldn't give them what they didn't have.

This was about to get bloody and she was going to be the one they drew first blood on.

CHAPTER 2

"Stay out of it, Fang," Vane said under his breath.

His anger snapping, Fang narrowed his eyes on the Sentinels surrounding Aimee. "It's a threatened female."

"She's not one of ours and we need the bears on our side. You break Omegrion sanctuary laws and they'll refuse to help us. Ever. They'll refuse to help *Anya*."

Fang heard those words and he was willing to abide by them. His sister was the most important thing. . . .

Until he saw the knife.

Vane cursed as he saw it too. Anya or not, it wasn't in their nature to let that go and since the bears seemed to be in over their furry little heads . . .

Vane's hazel gaze locked with Fang's. "I have the asshole in front, you take the one with the woman."

Fury lowered his head in agreement to their suicide run. "We've got your backs."

Vane inclined his head before they teleported to the fight.

Aimee considered the consequences of head-butting the jackal holding her. But he kept the knife tight to her throat, preventing it. She'd cut her own jugular if she even tried. She looked at her brothers and father, all of whom were standing back, too afraid to move for fear of causing her harm.

Tears of frustration welled in her eyes. She couldn't stand being helpless. The bear in her wanted to taste jackal blood regardless of what it cost her. Even death. But the human side of her knew better.

It wasn't worth the chance.

The jackal grabbed her by the hair and pressed the knife even closer. "Tell us where Constantine is. Now! Or else her blood flows like the mighty Niagara."

Papa opened his mouth, but before he could speak something snatched the knife away from her throat.

Aimee cursed as her head was snapped back and her hair wrenched. Unbalanced, she fell to the floor and landed on her stomach. Sounds exploded all around her as the jackals were quickly and painfully brought down by the wolves. Rubbing her throat where the knife had been, she looked to the jackal who'd been holding her.

Fang had him on the ground, slamming his head repeatedly against the floor as hard as he could. It was as if he were possessed by something that demanded he kill the jackal with his bare hands.

Blood covered both of them.

"Fang!" Vane shouted, pulling him away. "He's out of it."

Growling, Fang rose only to kick the jackal in the ribs. "Cowardly bastard. Pull a knife on a woman." He started back for his victim, but Vane caught him.

"Enough!"

Fang shrugged his brother off before he turned to

her with a look so anguished and tormented that it stole her breath. What demon had its spurs sunk deep into his soul? Something tragic lay behind that kind of pain.

It had to.

He turned for the jackal.

Vane spread his arms out to capture him. "He's down. Let it go."

Growling in true wolf fashion, Fang pushed past his brother. "I'll wait outside."

Before Vane could catch him, he got one last kick on the jackal's head on his way to the door.

Fury laughed at Fang's action as he twisted the arm of the jackal he held. "I really should break you in two. It might not brighten your day, but it would definitely make mine."

Vane shook his head at Fang's actions and Fury's words. Turning to Papa, he made his way slowly toward them. "Sorry we broke the covenant." He held money out to Dev. "We'll leave and never come back."

Papa pushed the money back toward Vane. "You don't have to leave. It was my daughter you saved. Thank you for what you did. So long as we have shelter, you have shelter." That was the highest honor a Were-Hunter could bestow on another. It was their oldest saying and only offered to another species as a show of eternal friendship.

No, more like kinship.

Vane seemed abashed by it.

Aimee watched as her family took the jackals from the wolves and led them away, no doubt to give them an even harsher ass-whipping out of sight of the humans.

"Are you all right?" Remi asked her as he helped her to her feet.

She nodded.

He glared at the one Fang had thrashed, who was still lying on the floor in a bloody heap. "Good, 'cause I'm going to skin me a jackal when he wakes up."

Aimee folded her arms over her chest. "I think the wolf already did."

"Yeah, but it's not good enough. I'm going to add my own head-pounding to him. That boy will have bear nightmares for the rest of his life . . . which just might prove to be a lot shorter than he ever dreamed."

Normally Aimee would have smarted back at him, but right now she was as shaken as the rest of them. It was rare anyone got the drop on her family, especially Dev, who was renowned for his fighting prowess. Never in all these centuries had she seen anyone pin him before.

A little beating on the jackals might go a long way in ensuring this never happened again. "What about the humans?"

Papa jerked his chin toward the tall blond who was walking around the crowd. "Max is wiping them even as we speak. It's why they didn't scream or move when the jackals attacked you. He heard the commotion and popped in."

She let out a relieved breath. Maxis was a dragon-were who had the ability to replace human memories. It was one of the reasons they kept him here even though it was hard to accommodate his large dragon form. His talents came in handy at times such as this and it meant they didn't have to kill humans who witnessed things they weren't supposed to know about.

"Should we go get Fang?" Keegan asked Vane as they started past her.

"Let him calm down first. We don't need him starting another fight."

Aimee held her hand out to Vane. "Thanks for the assist. I really appreciate it."

He shook her hand gently. "Anytime."

She smiled up at him and gestured with her thumb toward the kitchen. "I'll go put your orders in and have them out shortly."

Her father inclined his head to Vane. "And don't worry, it's on the house. Whatever you wolves need, just let us know."

"Thank you," Vane said as he led his wolves back to their table.

Dev grinned at her. "Never thought I'd say this about any canine species, but I think I like that group."

Aimee didn't comment as she headed to the kitchen where her mother was waiting.

Her features stern, Maman stepped aside to let her pass. "Constantine sits on the Omegrion as their Arcadian Grand Regis. I don't know him well, however I think we should find him and tell him where his friends are being kept—just to level the field a bit since they seem so eager to meet up with him."

It was a subtle way for Maman to say that she wanted the jackals dead and to be able to justify it to the Omegrion should anyone question her. After all, if the jackals were hunting Constantine so ferociously, it was only fair he know about it.

Aimee might have argued it was a harsh sentence, but given what the jackals had done to her, she was in the same sporting mood as her mother. "I'm sure Dev can arrange that."

Her mother's eyes darkened. "No one threatens my cubs. Are you truly all right, *chérie*?"

"I'm fine, Maman. Thanks to the wolves."

Maman patted her lightly on the arm before she headed back to her office.

Aimee went over to where a rare steak was already up on the order shelf. Handing her orders over to their cooks, she took the plate and grabbed a beer for Fang as she passed by the bar. "I'll be back in a few."

Her older brother Zar, who looked a lot like Dev with short hair, only taller and broader, stopped her. "Are you all right?"

At this point, that question was getting old. She wasn't a fragile doll that would break at the slightest wrong twist. She was a bear with all the strength and abilities inherent in their species. Her family, however, tended to forget that fact. "A little shaken and a lot of pissed off. I don't like anyone getting the drop on me the way the jackals did. But I'm fine now."

A muscle ticked in his jaw, showing her the anger he kept hidden underneath his calm exterior. "I'm sorry we didn't get to you faster."

Those words were haunting as they stirred memories inside her she didn't want to remember. "Really, it's okay, Zar. I'd much rather be the one threatened than to see you hurt." Again. She left that one word unspoken as she saw her own painful memories mirrored in the horror of his gaze.

It was a past they never talked about, but one that scarred them all.

"I love you, Zar."

He offered her a hollow smile before he moved away so that he could continue tending the bar.

Aimee headed out the back door to the alley and then across the street to where Fang was sitting on the sidewalk, waiting for the others. His features troubled, he reminded her of a lost child. Something completely incongruous with his tougher-than-steel aura. Not to mention his prowess at taking down her attacker without even scratching her. His speed and strength were unrivaled and frightening.

Even though he must have used his powers to remove the blood from his clothes, she remembered well the way he'd trounced the jackal.

But what surprised her most was the fact that she wasn't repulsed by his violence. Normally such overkill would have had her showing him the door.

Then again, she'd been the one with the knife at her throat. Personally, she'd like to kick the jackal around a bit herself. Yeah, that had to be it. She was too grateful to him to be angered over his actions.

Fang shot to his feet as soon as he saw her.

For some reason she couldn't name, she was suddenly nervous and self-conscious as she approached him. Hesitant, even.

How unlike her. She was always icy cold around men, especially when they were from another species. But with Fang . . .

There was just something different.

Fang swallowed as he saw Aimee pause across the

street. She was even more beautiful in the daylight than she'd been inside the dark club. The sunlight sparkled in her hair, turning it into spun gold and making his palm itch to touch its softness. She had to be freezing. All she had on was a thin Sanctuary T-shirt.

He shrugged his jacket off as she finally neared him.

"I wanted to say thank-you again," she said, her voice low and sweet. She scowled as he draped his jacket around her thin shoulders.

Fang lowered his head sheepishly as he realized why it bothered her. "I know I smell like a wolf, but it's too cold to be out here bare-armed."

She frowned even more as she looked at his arms. "You're wearing a T-shirt too."

"Yeah, but I'm used to being outside." He took the food from her. "So I take it I didn't get us banned after all."

She smiled, showing him that beckoning dimple that he would kill to kiss. "Far from it. Anyone who fights for us is always welcome here."

His features relieved, he nodded. "Good. I was afraid I'd have to listen to Vane's shi—stuff for the next few centuries."

Aimee stifled a laugh at the way he caught himself before he cussed in front of her. It was very sweet and charming and also unexpected. "You're not like other wolves, are you?"

He swallowed a drink of beer straight out of the bottle. "How do you mean?"

"I've never been around wolves who were so . . ."

He arched a brow as if daring her to insult him.

"Mannered."

Fang laughed, a warm, rich sound that lacked any hint of mockery. The expression softened his features, making him even more gorgeous and intriguing. And for some reason, she couldn't quite take her gaze off his well-sculpted arms as they flexed with every move he made. He had the best biceps she'd ever seen.

"Our sister's doing," he said after he swallowed a bite. "She has codes we have to follow añd Vane enforces them to please her."

"But you don't like them?" There'd been a note in his voice as he spoke.

He didn't answer as he cut the steak with his fork.

Aimee gestured back toward the bar. "You want to eat that inside with the rest?"

"Nah. I don't like being indoors and I can't stand most of them anyway." He jerked his chin toward the saloon-styled door where Dev was standing guard again. "You should probably go back though. I'm sure your brother doesn't want you out here consorting with dogs."

"You're not a dog," she said emphatically, surprised that she actually meant it. An hour ago, she'd have been the one to hurl that insult at him and the rest of his pack. Now . . .

He truly wasn't like the others and she really wanted to stay out here with him.

Go, Aimee.

She took a step away before she remembered that she wore his jacket. Pulling it off, she held it out to him. "Thanks again."

Fang couldn't speak as he watched her cross the street and head back into the bar. As he held his jacket against his chest, her scent hit him full force with a wave so strong he wanted to howl from it. Instead, he buried his face against the collar where her scent was the strongest. Inhaling deep, he felt his body harden to a level it had only done for one other female. . . .

He winced as old memories tore through him.

Even though they hadn't been mates, Stephanie had been his entire world.

And she'd died in his arms from a brutal attack.

That memory shattered the heat in his blood and brought him back to reality with a fierce reminder of how dangerous their existence was. It was why that jackal was lucky to be alive. The one thing Fang couldn't stomach was to see a woman threatened, never mind harmed.

Any creature cowardly enough to prey on a woman deserved the most brutal death imaginable. And if it was delivered to him by Fang's hand, then all the better.

Shrugging his jacket on, he picked up his plate and returned to eating.

Once he was finished, he took the dishes to Dev who thanked him again for saving Aimee.

"You know, for a wolf, you don't really stink."

Fang snorted. "And for a bear you don't chafe my ass."

Dev laughed good-naturedly. "You going back inside?"

"No. I'd rather stay out and freeze my ass off."

"I hear ya. I like it better outside myself. Too human in there for me."

Fang inclined his head, surprised that the bear understood. Anya had made him human enough, he didn't want any more housebreaking than that. Tucking his hands in his pockets, he headed back to the bikes to wait.

Aimee went outside at Dev's insistent grumblings that kept coming in through the earpiece she wore—all the staff wore them so that the Were-Hunters could appear more human whenever they used their powers to communicate with each other.

"What?" she snapped in the doorway.

He held out an empty plate and beer bottle.

"Oh." She stepped forward to take them from his grasp. Unbidden, her gaze went to Fang who was again sitting on the ground with his legs bent and his arms draped over them while he leaned against an old hitching post.

There was something very feral and masculine about that pose. Something about it that made her heart quicken.

He's not the same species, girl. . . .

Yet it didn't matter to her hormones. Gorgeous was gorgeous, regardless of breed or type.

Yeah, that was what she was reacting to. It was nothing more than the fact he was an exceptional specimen of male physiology.

"Something wrong?"

She blinked and looked at Dev who was watching her. "No, why?"

"I dunno. You have this dopey kind of expression that I've never seen from you before."

She made a sound of abrupt disgust. "I don't look dopey."

He snorted. "Yes, you do. Get to a mirror and check

it. It's really scary. I definitely wouldn't let Maman see that."

She rolled her eyes at him. "This from a bear who got his ass kicked by a jackal?"

His eyes flared. "I was preoccupied by the knife at your throat."

She gave an exaggerated laugh. "You were on the ground and pinned before I was held."

He started to argue, then stopped. He looked around as if afraid someone might have overheard her. "You think anyone else remembers that part?"

"Depends." She gave him a calculating stare. "How much you gonna pay me to back *your* version?"

His look turned charming and sweet. "I pay you in love, precious little sister. Always."

She scoffed at his offer. "Love don't pay the rent, baby. Only cold hard cash."

He gaped, his expression one of total offense as he held his hand over his heart as if she'd wounded him. "You really turning mercenary on your favorite older brother?"

"No. I would never do that to Alain."

"Ouch!" Dev shook his hand as if he'd burned it. "Bearswan got 'tude."

Laughing, she stepped out to give him a quick hug. "Don't worry, big bro, your secret's safe with me so long as you don't annoy me too much."

He tightened his arms around her and held her close. "You know I love you, sis."

"I love you too." And she did. In spite of their disagreements and quarrels, her family meant everything to her. Stepping away, she turned to glance one last time at Fang. Most likely she'd never see him again. A common occurrence, really, for their clientele, and yet for some reason this time that thought hurt deep inside her.

I have lost what three brain cells I have. . . . Bear, get your butt back to work and forget about him.

Fang stood up as he saw the pack leaving the bar. Vane was the first to reach him.

"Here." Vane tossed him his backpack, then handed him a bag of something sweet and rich. "The bearswan wanted to make sure you got that for Anya. She said there was something in there for you too."

That shocked him completely. No one ever gave him gifts. "For me?"

Vane shrugged. "I don't understand bear thought processes. Most days I barely understand ours."

Fang had to give him that—he didn't understand it either. He tucked the sack into his backpack as the rest of the wolves took up their bikes and headed out. They were silent the entire way back to the bayou where they'd made camp for their females to deliver their pups in peace and protection.

As soon as they'd returned, their father met them in his wolf form. Markus shifted into a human just to sneer at them.

"What took you women so long to return?"

As Fang opened his mouth to smart off, Vane shot him a warning glare. "I toured the clinic and have the contact information should any of our females require help."

Markus curled his lip. Even though he'd sent them

there, he had to be an asshole. "In my day we let the wolfswans incapable of birthing our young die."

Fang snorted. "Then it's a good thing we're in the twenty-first century and not the Dark Ages, isn't it?"

Vane shook his head while their father growled at him as if about to attack.

This time Fang refused to back down. "Try it, old man," he said, using a term he knew infuriated his father since Katagaria despised their human natures. "And I'll rip out your throat and usher in a new age of leadership to this pack."

He could see the desire in Markus's eyes to press the issue, but his sire wolf knew what he did. In a fight, Fang would win.

His father wasn't the same wolf who'd killed his own brother to be Regis of their pack. He was weak with age and knew that he didn't have many more years left before either Fang or Vane took over.

One way or another.

Fang preferred it to be over the old man's dead body. But other arrangements would work for him too.

It was another reason their sire hated them. He knew his prime was past and they were only coming into their own.

Markus narrowed his gaze threateningly. "One day, whelp, you're going to cross me and your brother won't be here to stop me from killing you. When that day comes, you better pray for salvation."

Fang's look turned evil. "I don't need salvation. There's not a wolf here I couldn't wipe my ass on. You know it. I know it and most important, they *all* know it."

Vane arched a brow at his comment as if taunting him to prove those words.

Fang gave him a lopsided grin. "You don't count, brother. I think more of you than to even try."

Markus raked them with a repugnant twist to his lips. "You both sicken me."

Fang snorted. "It's what I live for . . . Father." He couldn't resist using the title he knew made the old fart seethe. "Your eternal disgust succors me like mother's milk."

Markus turned back into a wolf and bounded off.

Vane turned on him. "Why do you do that?"

"Do what?"

"Piss off everyone you come into contact with? Just once, couldn't you keep your mouth shut?"

Fang shrugged. "It's a skill."

"Well, it's one I wish you'd unlearn."

Fang let out an irritated breath at the constant bitch-topic that had grown old three hundred years ago. He wasn't the kind of wolf to suck it up. Rather he gave as good as he got, and most times he gave better. "Against the grain is the only way. Stop being such an old woman." He turned and headed for the edge of camp where Anya had chosen to den with her mate Orian.

Fang always had to bite his tongue around them. He hated the wolfswain the Fates had picked for his sister. She deserved so much better than that half-wit, but unfortunately, that wasn't in their hands. The Fates chose their partners and they could either submit or the male would live out his life completely impotent, the woman infertile.

To save their species, most accepted whatever abysmal mate the Fates assigned them. In the case of his parents, his mother had refused and now his father was left impotent and perpetually pissed off.

Not that Fang blamed the old man for that. He'd probably be insufferable too if he had to go centuries without sex. But that was the only part of his father he understood. The rest of the wolf was a complete mystery to him.

Luckily Anya's mate wasn't with his sister. Anya was lying down on the grass in the fading sunlight, her eyes barely open as a light breeze stirred her soft white fur. Her belly was swollen and he could see her pups moving inside her.

It was pretty much gross, but he wouldn't insult her by telling her that.

"You're back."

He smiled at her soft voice in his head. "We are and . . ." He held the bag out toward her.

She sat up immediately and trotted over to him. *"What did you bring?"* She nosed at the sack as if trying to see through it with her snout.

Fang sat down and opened the sack to see what Aimee had given them. The moment he did, his heart quickened. She'd thrown in two steaks, baklava, beignets, and cookies. There was also a small note in the bottom.

He dug out the cookies and held them for Anya while he read Aimee's flowing cursive.

> *I really appreciate what you did and I hope your sister enjoys her food. Brothers like you should*

always be treasured. Anytime you need a steak, you know where we are.

He didn't understand why such a short, innocuous note touched him, but it did. He couldn't help smiling at it as an image of her drifted through his mind.

Stop being a head case.

Yeah, something was definitely wrong with him. Maybe he needed to see one of those pet psychics or something. Or maybe have Vane give him a sharp kick to the hindquarters.

"Do I smell bear?"

He tucked the note into his pocket. "It's from the Sanctuary staff."

She shook her head and sneezed on the ground. *"Gah, could they stink any worse?"*

Fang had to disagree. He didn't smell bear, he only smelled Aimee and it was a delectable scent. "They probably think the same about us."

Anya paused to look up at him. *"What did you say?"*

Fang cleared his throat as he realized how out of character it was for him to defend another species. "Nothing."

She licked his fingers as he held out more cookies for her.

A shadow fell over them. Looking up, he saw Vane standing there with a stern frown.

"Shouldn't it be her mate doing that for her?"

Fang shrugged. "He was always a selfish asshole."

Anya nipped hard at his fingers. *"Careful, brother, that's the sire of my pups you're talking about."*

Fang scoffed at her protective tone. "One chosen by a trio of psycho bitches who—*ow!*" He jumped as

Anya sank her teeth deep into the fleshy part of his hand. He cursed as he saw the blood dripping from the wound she'd given him.

She narrowed her gaze. "*Again, he's my mate and you will respect him.*"

Vane cocked him on the back of his head. "Boy, don't you ever learn?"

Fang bit his lip to keep from snapping at both of them. He hated how they treated him like their mentally defective distant relation. As if his opinions didn't matter. Anytime he opened his mouth, one of them told him to shut it.

Honestly, he was more than tired of their treatment. All they saw him as was the muscle they needed. A loaded gun to be used against their enemies. The rest of the time, they wanted him kept in a box, completely silent and unobtrusive.

Whatever.

Changing into a wolf, he left them before he said something they'd all regret.

But one day . . .

One day he was going to let them know just how tired he was of being their omega wolf.

Aimee paused at the table where the wolves had been. In the corner was a pair of discarded sunglasses. She bent down and picked them up only to catch a whiff of the owner.

Fang.

A slight smile hovered at the edges of her lips as she remembered the way he'd looked leaning back in his chair. Relaxed and lethal.

"What's that?"

She jumped as Wren spoke right behind her. Looking at him over her shoulder, she smiled at the young tigard. Handsome and lean, he had long blond dreadlocks with bangs that fell across his eyes, shielding them from the world. She was one of the very few people he ever spoke to.

She held up the sunglasses so that he could see. "One of the wolves left them."

He scratched at his whiskered cheek. "You want me to put them in lost and found?"

"It's okay. I'll do it."

He nodded before he moved on to bus another table.

Aimee closed her eyes and held the sunglasses tight. As she did so, she saw a perfect image of Fang in wolf form running through the swamp.

Someone sneezed.

She jerked, looking around quickly in fear of someone catching her using a power that no one knew she held. It was something only the most powerful of Aristi could wield and the fact that she had it . . .

It was as much a danger to her as a gift.

And it was a power that had cost two of her brothers their lives. For that reason alone, she could never allow anyone to know what she could do.

But today those powers weren't scary. They would allow her to find Fang and return his property to him. She checked the watch on her wrist.

In thirty minutes she'd be free to take a break and then she'd find the wolf. . . .

* * *

Aimee paused next to the cypress tree that jutted out of the water and twisted up toward the sky. The setting sun fanned around the branches, casting a majestic glow as it also reflected the cypress against the rippling black water. It was eerie and beautiful. Haunting.

Even though they'd lived in New Orleans for more than a century, she'd never spent much time in the swamp or bayous. She'd forgotten how beautiful they could be.

Smiling at the image, she manifested her camera and started photographing it. There was nothing she loved more than capturing nature in its purest forms.

Completely captivated by the complexity of the light playing against the tree, she stopped paying attention to her surroundings. The world faded away as she moved in a large circle, tilting the camera for better angles.

The murky water sloshed around her feet as she moved. Out of the corner of her eye, she saw a bird take flight. She turned to catch that as well, but as she moved, she heard something. . . .

A low, fierce growl.

Before she could react, a wolf attacked her.

CHAPTER 3

Reacting on pure instinct, Aimee dropped the camera and manifested a long staff. She crouched low, waiting for the attack. But in true wolf fashion, he didn't attack alone. He waited for three more to join rank. By their scents, she knew none of them were the wolves she'd seen earlier at Sanctuary.

These were feral and mean.

True Slayers . . .

And she was their prey.

Aimee twirled her weapon, bracing herself for them. If they wanted a fight, she would and could definitely give them one. Sometimes they ate the bear, but today the bear was going to take one juicy bite out of them.

Growling and snapping, they circled around her.

She shook her head at their bravado. "Trust me, guys, you don't want a taste of bear. This one bites three times as hard as you do."

It didn't stop the lead one from charging.

Aimee caught him against his side with her staff and sent him flying. The other two sprang forward. She planted her staff into the ground and lifted her body to kick one back before she twirled and used the staff to smack the other against his hindquarters.

He let out a vicious whelp.

"Cry to your mama, Big Bad Wolf. Little Red Riding Hood is about to serve your hide for dinner."

"You think you can take us?"

She turned to counter their leader. "Oh, baby, I can send you all straight to hell." At least that was her thought until four more ran at her.

Odds now . . .

Not so good.

Snarling and snapping, they moved in, slowly, threateningly. As she backed up, Aimee considered shifting forms to fight, but she wouldn't be as fast as a bear. They would have much better maneuverability and that would cause her to lose.

Losing to anyone was something she wasn't about to do.

No, she'd handle this as a woman.

"You know, a better weapon against them would be a gun. . . ."

She frowned as she heard Fang's voice in her head. Yet he wasn't near her.

The leader launched himself.

Aimee crouched and just as he reached her . . . just as she felt his hot, smelly breath on her skin, a large brown wolf intercepted him and sent him flying in the opposite direction.

Fang.

From the image she'd seen in her vision, she knew that this was him. He tore at the throat of the wolf that had initiated the attack against her. Aimee would have continued fighting, but the others backed away in confusion.

A large white wolf who put himself between her and the others transformed into Vane.

"Are you insane?" he snarled at the wolves. "She's one of the Peltier bears."

One by one the wolves turned human. Except for Fang and the one he fought.

"Stefan!" Vane snapped in anger.

Instead of standing down, Stefan went for Vane. Fang caught him in a vicious hold on his throat as the two wolves continued to fight and writhe. Aimee cringed at the savage anger that said the two of them hated each other passionately. Old memories surged as they growled and snapped, tearing at each other's flesh. The sight of it sickened her.

"Stop it!" She blasted both of them with her powers.

Fang yelped as a blast hit him hard in his tail. Sharp and stinging, it sent him reeling. He hated being injured and for someone to get the better of him. . . .

It spun him into a level of pissed off like nothing else could. Furious, he snapped to human form even though it was hard to hold it.

"What the hell are you doing?" he asked as he limped toward her, his rear cheek still burning.

Aimee narrowed her glare on him. "I don't like fights."

"And I don't like getting stung on the ass."

She didn't back down or back off. "Well, if you'd stopped when Vane told you to—"

"I don't take orders from a woman I was fighting to protect."

She held her hand up as if declaring war on him for those words. "Well, macho you. For the record, I didn't need *your* protection."

Fang scoffed at her misplaced bravado. "Yeah, right. They were about to take you down."

"I seriously doubt it."

Fang closed the distance between them to stare down at her as fury stung every part of him. He wanted her to fully understand the danger she'd stupidly put herself into. "This isn't Sanctuary, little girl. You're invading our territory and we have burdened females. What were you thinking? We kill you out here and no one blinks."

She screwed her face up in disgust. "Oh, get over yourselves. Like I give two snots about your den." She pulled out his sunglasses and shoved them toward him so hard that it forced him to take a step back. "I just wanted to return your property. So go stuff yourself."

Fang was stunned as her hand struck him in the center of his chest. Instinctively, he cupped his sunglasses as she vanished, no doubt to return home.

The only problem was, he didn't know what stung most. Where she'd shoved him on his chest, smacked him on the butt, or the blow she'd just dealt his ego.

"How did that bitch find us?" Stefan ground out between clenched teeth.

Vane gave him a droll stare that said he shared the same opinion of Stefan that Fang had—that Stefan was a first-rank moron. "She must have followed our scent."

Fang didn't speak. He was still too stunned at her anger toward him when all he'd been trying to do was make her understand the danger. How could she not know better? Had Stefan not called in for reinforcements and Fang not realized who it was they were grouping to attack, Aimee would have been torn into pieces.

Another few minutes . . .

His stomach churned over the images in his mind.

Vane snapped his fingers in front of his face. "Dude? You okay?"

Fang shoved at him. "Of course I am."

Stefan came forward with a grimace on his face. "What did the bear want with you anyway?"

Vane caught Fang before he could approach the wolf to attack and forced him away from Stefan. "She—"

"We don't owe him an explanation," Fang snapped, interrupting Vane. "He can kiss my hairy ass."

Stefan rushed at him.

Vane growled at both of them. "I swear to the gods that I am sick to death of breaking you two up." He pushed Stefan back. "And you—one more time and I'm not stopping Fang. One more insult, one more cockeyed stare, and I'm standing back and turning him loose to break ass all over you."

Stefan's nostrils flared. Instead of pushing the issue, he snapped his fingers for the others to follow him. Turning into wolves, they bounded back toward the den.

Vane faced him with a penetrating stare. "What *is* going on between you and the bearswan?"

"Nothing."

"Nothing? She came out here into the middle of nowhere to hand you back a pair of sunglasses for what purpose?"

To keep anyone else from being able to use his scent to track him. Aimee's kindness wasn't lost on him.

But if Vane couldn't figure that out, he wasn't about to clue him in. "I don't know. Since when do women of any species make sense?"

Vane's features softened. "Good point. All right then, I'm heading back. You coming?"

Fang nodded.

Flashing into a wolf, Vane took off. Fang was just about to join him when he saw something on the ground a few feet away from him.

It was a camera.

What the hell?

He went over to pick it up. The moment he did, he smelled Aimee all over it. He started to chuck it toward the water, but curiosity got the better of him. Turning it on, he scrolled through the digital pictures of the Peltier bears, sometimes in human form, other times as bears. He paused on one of the busboys he'd seen in the bar who was feeding a pet monkey peanuts. She'd really captured the way the neon light highlighted him and the monkey in a most unusual way.

But it was the landscape shots she'd made all over New Orleans that were truly breathtaking. The bear-swan had an amazing eye for light and shadow. Even a wolf like him could appreciate it.

Just toss the damn thing and let it go. . . .

He couldn't. It was as if he were looking at her private diary and he knew instinctively Aimee wouldn't want this to be lost. These were more than mere pictures. They were like a part of her soul.

Give it to Vane to return.

It was what he should do. Common sense told him to stay as far away from her as he could.

"Since when have I ever had an ounce of sense?"

It was true. Common sense had waved bye-bye to him a long time ago.

Tightening his grip on the camera, he flashed himself from the bayou back to the bar. He paused as he realized he'd managed to jump into the top floor . . . weird. It was hard to manifest into a place he hadn't been to before. The bears must have some kind of filter to direct them to a "landing pad" of sorts.

Which explained why the jackals had come from this direction earlier. Nice move on the bears' part.

Fang made his way down the stairs to the bar where Dev or one of Dev's identical brothers was tending it. "Where's Aimee?"

The bear tensed. "Who the hell are you?"

Definitely not Dev. "Fang Kattalakis. I'm returning her property, not that you have any reason for knowing that."

The bear raked him with a hostile glare.

Another bear with short black hair, one who was Arcadian if Fang didn't miss the tangy smell, nudged Aimee's brother gently. "Relax, Cherif, he's the one who saved her earlier from the jackals."

Cherif backed down, but not by much. "You want to run him back to her?"

"Sure." The Arcadian flashed a friendly grin at Fang. "I'm Colt," he said good-naturedly. "If you'll follow me . . ."

Fang did, but not before he gave Aimee's brother a go-to-hell glare.

Colt led him through the kitchen and past another Dev look-alike to a door that opened into a house that was decorated in a turn-of-the-century Victorian style. The walls were painted a soft yellow while the furniture was a mix of burgundy and black. The dark wood gave it a very regal appearance.

"Peltier House," Colt explained as he kept walking. "You weren't here earlier when Papa Bear toured your brother around. This is where the Were-Hunters who call Sanctuary home live when not working in the club. There are four floors of bedrooms total, but most of the Peltiers are on the second floor."

Colt headed upstairs. "Carson's the doc and vet and his office is here." He touched the first door they passed on the second floor and kept going to the end of the hall.

He stopped at the last door. Tapping lightly, he leaned close to it. "Aimee? You there?"

"Trying to nap, Colt."

"Sorry, but there's a visitor here who wants to see you."

The door opened so fast Colt almost fell in. Aimee looked surprised, then pissed to see Fang standing behind him. "What are you doing here?"

Fang shrugged. "Come to inadvertently insult you some more apparently. Who knew?"

Instead of being amused, which was what he'd been hoping for, she narrowed her gaze on him. "I really don't like you."

Fang leaned forward to smirk. "You're really not supposed to."

Colt's eyes widened. "Should I leave you two alone? Or stay and referee?"

"You can leave. I'm just returning this." Fang held up the camera. "And then leaving myself."

Without another word, Colt headed back the way they'd come.

Aimee snatched the camera away from Fang's grasp. "Where did you get this?"

"You must have dropped it."

She leaned out the door to make sure Colt was gone before she whispered in a low tone. "Did you tell anyone I was there?"

"No. Did you want me to?"

"No." She looked extremely relieved. "Thank you." Then, in the blink of an eye, she turned angry again. "Did you look at my pictures?" That was more an accusation than a question.

"Was I not supposed to?"

She screwed her face up. "Oh, you're such a pig! That's my privacy you've invaded. How dare you!"

Fang felt blindsided by her rapid mood swings. He was definitely going to need a signal light to keep up with her. "Are you always this high-strung?"

"I am not high-strung!"

"If you say so. But really, they need to put a collar on you that changes color with your mood swings."

She curled her lip as if his words disgusted her on the highest level. "Oh, you are feral."

"Yeah, duh."

She rolled her eyes.

Fang started to leave, then swung back around. "By the way, I did not overreact earlier in the bayou. You could have been torn apart."

Shaking her head, she blustered before she finally spoke again. "Enough already with your macho bull-crap. I am sick to death of men telling me how to run my life. In case you didn't notice, I have a whole bevy of men downstairs just dying to tell me how I don't measure up. The last thing I need is another one."

"Maybe you should listen to them once in a while."

"And maybe you should mind your own business."

Fang had never wanted to strangle anyone so badly in his life. Every part of him burned with fury and at the same time, he couldn't help noticing how beautiful she was with her cheeks glowing from her anger. The red in her cheeks made her eyes a sharp, vivid blue. "Maybe you should learn to say thank-you once in a while."

She closed the distance between them. "And maybe you—" Her hands touched his chest and the most primal part of him came alive.

Before he even realized what he'd done, he'd pulled her into his arms and silenced her tirade with a kiss.

Aimee couldn't breathe as she felt Fang's arms close around her body. Her rage died the moment his lips touched hers and she tasted a sweet, raw power the likes of which she'd never experienced before.

His tongue danced with hers as he fully explored her mouth. Every hormone in her body turned hot and she clung to him, wanting to devour every inch of his hard body with her mouth and hands. Both the woman and bear inside her turned savage and wanton. Never had she tasted or felt anything like this.

It was all she could do not to strip him naked and make him beg for mercy.

Fang left her lips to finally bury his face against her neck so that he could breathe in her scent. It was the most delectable thing he'd ever smelled. And it awoke something inside him that wanted to experience every part of her. Every hormone in his body sang with need.

And that horrified him.

Pulling back, he stared down at her dazed expression.

Her senses must have returned to her in that same instant. She balled her fists into his jacket. "You need to leave. Now."

He tried, but something about her . . .

Go!

Forcing himself away, he teleported himself back to their den in the bayou.

Aimee slumped against the wall behind her as she tried to steady her senses.

She'd just kissed a wolf.

A wolf.

Her family would kill him. Hell, they'd kill *her.* It was forbidden to dilute the bloodlines, especially when they were Omegrion members. Her duty was to maintain and purify their lineage. To strengthen it. As bears, they traced their lineage through the female and she was the only daughter in their clan. It was why her brothers were so protective of her.

Yet . . .

Aimee shook her head to clear it. She could never see Fang again.

Ever.

Never, ever, ever.

Ever.

And this time she was going to listen to her reason!

She hoped.

CHAPTER 4

Three weeks later

"Well?"

Aimee looked up from the book she was reading while lying on her bed to see her mother standing in the open doorway. Her stomach tightened in response. She'd been dreading this visit all day and hoping her mother had forgotten about it.

She should have known better. Maman had a memory that was second only to Aimee's.

"I felt nothing, Maman. Sorry."

Maman made a sound of disgust deep in her throat as she came fully into the room and shut the door.

Aimee got up to make room on the bed so that her mother could sit down beside her and set her book on the nightstand, taking care to not lose her place. She'd met with the other bear clan this afternoon, as hopeful as ever.

And as all the times before . . .

Nothing.

"I tried, Maman. I swear I did, it's just . . ." She

sighed wearily as she remembered the look of expectation on Randy's extremely handsome face. He'd wanted her to accept him as much as she'd wanted it, but it was followed by a look of extreme disappointment when she'd shaken her head at him. She'd felt nothing for the other bear.

Nothing at all.

"Maybe I felt the quickening and just didn't realize it."

Maman gave a low laugh. "No, *ma petite*. There is no mistaking the sensation. Every part of you is awake and alive. It burns like fire through your body. The urge to mate is so strong that there is little you can do to fight it. It becomes an all-consuming necessity."

Aimee looked away as a wave of terror consumed her. The only man she'd ever felt that way for . . .

Was a wolf.

"I shall tell their Regis that you're not interested. However, they may request a mating try."

Aimee cringed at the thought of bedding a guy she didn't really know and one she wasn't lusting after. "Randy was nice, but . . ."

"But what?"

I don't want to sleep with him. And there was more than just that. She also held a bitter secret that she dared not share with anyone.

Aimee bit her lip, afraid to tell her mother the truth. *I'm Arcadian. . . .*

She tried her best to say those words out loud. She'd been trying to say them for years. Yet once again, she choked on them. Her mother would be crushed to learn the truth. Aimee had been born Katagaria just like her mother. But during puberty, she'd converted over to Arcadian like her father.

It was the most guarded secret she had. Absolutely no one knew the truth of her base form.

No one.

For that matter, no one outside of the immediate family knew Papa Bear Peltier was Arcadian. The scandal of *that* had scarred her mother, and yet Maman had mated with him so that she could have the cubs she'd always wanted. So that she would be able to continue the Peltier seat on the Omegrion—a seat that had been held since day one by her mother's line.

It was the animal in her mother that pushed her to mate and procreate.

But the proud human in her rebelled at the thought.

Her mother leaned forward. "You are about to be in season again. For decades you have spurned suitors. It's time—"

"Maman, please. I know my duties." And she did. The problem was bears were different from the other animals. Even when in season, the female picked out the male. If he didn't appeal to her, win her over, as it were, there was no sex and therefore no chance of mating.

If they didn't mate, there could be no cubs.

Her mother's illustrious lineage would die out and another clan would take the Peltier place on the Omegrion—yet another reason her family was so incredibly protective of her. If Aimee could mate with a Katagari bear, then there was a chance she could have a Katagari daughter who could take her mother's place at the Omegrion when Maman grew too old for those duties. Then no one would have to know the truth about Aimee.

It was the only hope they had and the full weight of that responsibility was never far from her thoughts.

"I will keep trying."

Maman nodded. "There will be more Katagaria here tomorrow. This is a clan out of Canada. They have a dozen males for you to survey. I pray you find at least one of them worthy."

So did Aimee. "I'll do my best."

Maman nodded. "That's all I ask." Rising from the bed, she made her way to the door and left.

Aimee flipped the pages of her book as thoughts poured through her. What was she going to do?

It's not your fault. Her mother had mated to an Arcadian. No one could help that. Dev, Remi, Cody, and Kyle were all Arcadians and her mother knew about them and still loved them, regardless of their base form. Granted, her mother was in denial over it, but they'd never hidden the fact from her.

Only from the rest of the world.

She's your mother. She'd never hurt you.

Not entirely true. Her mother was a bear with the full instincts of one. To protect their den, her mother would kill any of them who threatened their security and well-being. It was the nature of their species.

Aimee never let herself forget that. Her mother had more compassion than most, but when Maman hated someone, such as in the case of Wren, there was no reasoning with her. Once Nicolette's mind was made up, she could never be swayed.

And that was truly frightening.

"What am I going to do?"

You will mate with one of those bears tomorrow and pray to the gods that one of them causes you to get a mating mark.

It was her only hope.

Otherwise . . .

No, she couldn't even contemplate that. Her clan's survival was all that mattered. Above her happiness and most of all, above her life.

She would mate with a Katagari bear even if it killed her.

CHAPTER 5

"Fang?"

Fang froze as he heard the seductive voice of what had to be the sexiest wolfswan in their pack. Petra. Tall, sultry, and stacked like a brick house, she stirred the hormones of every wolfswain who saw her. He'd never been an exception to that.

Until tonight.

He frowned as she closed the distance between them and rubbed herself against his side. Reaching up, she grabbed a handful of his hair and tugged at it.

She purred in his ear. "I'm in heat, baby. You want to help me out?"

Was that a trick question or what? Fang nuzzled his face against her neck, inhaling her scent. Normally that would have been more than enough to flame his lust to the point he'd be more than able to accommodate her.

C'mon, body, wake up.

But he only stirred a little bit.

What the hell?

She reached down to cup him like a pro. "Is something wrong?"

"No."

She pulled back to grimace up at him when he didn't get instantly hard. "You haven't mated, have you?" That would be the natural assumption since the moment a wolf mated he could only be enticed by his mated female and never again by another. Something that seriously sucked. It was why he was in no hurry to find a mate. Too much like eating the same meal every night. Who wanted that?

Petra jerked at his hands, looking for the mark that always signaled them when the Fates had chosen their significant other. It was a mark that only appeared on their palms after they'd had sex.

Problem was, he hadn't touched anyone in the last three weeks. Not since he'd seen Aimee.

He pulled his hands away from her. "I'm not mated."

Relief lightened her expression as she reached for his fly. "Then what are you waiting for?"

Inspiration . . . and an erection would definitely help. His cock twitched as she skimmed it with her nails, but didn't do much more than that. Not even her groping was helping.

Fang kissed her and she attacked him.

Still he was cold. Empty. Where was the usual fire he felt? The driving need to be inside her.

He just felt . . .

Nothing.

She sank her hand deeper inside his jeans to cup him as she breathed in his ear. That sent chills over him, but he still had no desire to touch her.

Nipping his ear hard, she pulled back with a curse and slammed her fists into his chest. "What is wrong with you?"

Fang looked at her blankly, wishing he had an answer. Instead, he could only think of one thing. "Parvo."

She screwed her face up in disgust. "Parvo, my ass. C'mon, Fang. I don't want to mate with the rest of these losers. You're the only one I want."

"The mind is right there with you, baby, but the body . . ."

She slapped him. Hard. "You suck!"

Fang wiped the blood from his lips with a grimace. That was the biggest problem with wolfswans. When their hormones took over, they were brutal bitches. Come to think of it, the last time they'd had sex, Petra had bitten his shoulder so hard it'd bled. He even had a permanent scar from it.

She grabbed his hair and kissed him again.

Now his own anger snapping, he pushed her back. "Go slap someone else. I'm not in the mood to be bitten and clawed tonight."

She wrenched at his hair hard enough to pull a handful of it out. "It figures. You would have PMS when I'm in heat." She growled at him. "Fine. I'll go find Fury."

And may you both be mates for all eternity . . .

In hell.

It was what they deserved. Brushing his lips, which were still stinging from her blow, he zipped his pants, then sank down to the ground. He lay on his back to stare up at the dark sky, trying to find some kind of solace.

He heard a scuffle in camp where Petra must have spread her scent around to incite the others. Most likely they'd fight and the winner would take her.

But pleasing a wolfswan in heat was no easy matter.

It often took a whole night and sometimes two or three others would be needed to sate her. Of course that all changed once a female mated. Then she was off-limits to any except her chosen male.

Fang couldn't believe he'd had to turn her down. Even hostile and hormonal, she was one fine piece of . . .

"What is wrong with me?"

Maybe he did have parvo or rabies. Could a Were-Hunter get that? He'd never heard of anyone contracting it, but . . .

Something had to be seriously wrong with him. The scent of a prime female in heat had never failed to stir him before. He should be in there right now, pawing it out to be the one who mounted her.

But as he contemplated that, his thoughts turned to Aimee. The way she'd looked bringing his food out to where he'd been sitting by the bikes. The way his jacket had swallowed her whole as she wore it and smiled up at him.

She'd been beautiful and kind. Gentle and sweet. Even when she'd yelled at him, she'd been . . .

Bingo. He was hard as a rock now.

Fang let out a grateful sigh. *Thank the gods.* At least he wasn't broken. He still worked.

Just not for Petra.

That thought made him physically ill. *Oh, gah, I was better off having parvo.*

"What are you doing here?"

He tilted his head back to see Vane standing a few feet away, looking puzzled by Fang's pose. "Nothing."

"Why aren't you with Petra?"

"Why aren't you?"

Vane sat down beside him. "I can't stand her. She claws like a cat. However, that's never stopped *you* before."

Fang shrugged as he tucked his hands under his head. "There's more to life than sex."

Vane scowled at him. "Who are you and what have you done with my brother?"

Fang gave him a droll stare. "Don't be an asshole."

"All right. I'll leave you alone. But in all seriousness, are you okay?"

"When have I ever been okay?"

Vane laughed. "Good point. I still think it comes from Anya pushing you down that ravine when you were a pup. Definite head injury that screwed you up for life."

"I think it was from you always sleeping on my head when we were pups. Years of nightly oxygen dep do take a toll."

Vane laughed. "Yeah, I probably killed all six of your brain cells before you even reached puberty."

"Probably so. Explains so much, doesn't it?"

His expression sobering, Vane stood up. "By the way, I overheard Markus last night. He was talking about replacing us as his heirs."

No big surprise given his hatred of them. But even so, Markus had always been careful in the past about breaking the clan up with an all-out confrontation. "Why?"

"Because neither of us has mated. He thinks it's a sign that we can't. That we're genetically deficient and therefore unworthy to be Regis."

Fang felt the heat of anger rush through him. He hated his father with a passion so strong, he wasn't sure how he kept from lashing out. "I really wish you'd let me challenge him. Then he'd see just how genetically deficient I am . . . not."

"Don't get so upset. Look on the bright side, at least we're not impotent."

Maybe Vane wasn't, but Fang . . .

"Little consolation," Fang groused as he refused to think about Aimee's hold on him. "Tasting his blood, however, would appease me to no end." He shifted his head to get more comfortable. "So who's he looking at as our replacements?"

"Stefan, who else?"

It just got better and better. Why did he even bother asking? He should have known the answer. "I'm sure Stefan's not championing our cause."

"Nope."

"One day I'm going to rip out his throat and you won't be there to stop me."

Vane froze as he heard the raw animus in Fang's tone. And the anguish. He knew how hard it was for his brother to rein in his fury. How hard it was for Fang to stand down and be subservient to him or anyone else.

It was against everything in Fang's genetic code. And it made him wonder what Fang would have been like had Vane not switched to Arcadian during puberty.

Gods, how terrifying that had been. It'd taken him weeks to even understand what was happening to his body and then once he was sure . . .

Telling Fang had been the hardest part of all. Even though they'd been littermates, a part of him had feared that his brother would attack and kill him for it. Who could've blamed him? The Arcadians were forever attacking them.

And they had killed the only woman Fang had ever cared for.

Instead, Fang had accepted it calmly and vowed his eternal protection. Loyal as a wolf . . . and a brother . . . to the end.

It was a protection that never wavered. Fang tried to hide it from Vane, but he wasn't stupid. He knew how many times his brother stayed awake at night, guarding his secret. How many times Fang had walked away from a fight even though it galled him to do so, so that Vane wouldn't be questioned or outed.

He was his brother's weakness and he hated himself for that.

"I'm sorry, Fang."

"For what?"

For everything. For robbing him of his birthright. Robbing him of his ability to challenge Stefan and Markus.

Most of all he was sorry that his brother had no idea just how much respect he had for him. But it wasn't in their natures to speak of such things.

"For being the thorn in your ass that prevents you from challenging him."

Fang returned to looking up at the dark sky. "Don't worry about it. It is what it is."

Perhaps, but the real question was, what could it be if Vane wasn't around to pull him down? But as Fang had said, it was what it was. There was no changing the fact that he was human and his brother was a wolf.

Sighing, he headed toward his sister.

Fang didn't move until Vane was gone. He lay there listening to the sounds of the insects and wolves while watching the sky above him. The Dark-Hunters had warned them earlier today that there was an enemy pack of Arcadian wolves in town and a group of Daimons who might be looking to augment their life spans by eating a couple of wolves. Their pregnant females were prime Daimon bait.

But Fang didn't fear them. He could hold his own in a fight and he pitied anyone dumb enough to call him out.

If only his father and Stefan would get head injuries that made them even dumber than normal. Oh, to fight them . . .

Closing his eyes, he returned to his wolf form. This was what he needed. It was the only thing that really comforted him.

But as he lay there, he thought of something else that comforted him.

The scent and taste of an ethereal bear.

Put her out of your thoughts. She was as off-limits as anything could be. His father hated him enough. If he ever found out Fang was turned on by a bear . . .

They'd call out a hunt and he'd be slaughtered.

CHAPTER 6

Aimee paused outside of Carson's door, gathering her courage. Even though it'd been a month since she'd last seen the wolfswain, she still couldn't get the taste or scent of Fang out of her mind or her thoughts. It was as if he'd somehow branded her and made her his.

That was the most upsetting part of all.

Since then, she'd been subjected to three more rounds of "find a sex toy, Aimee." And unfortunately, none of the bearswains had stirred anything inside her. Not even repulsion or distaste. She was completely numb to them.

All of them.

What was wrong with her?

She needed to talk to someone and didn't dare speak of her concerns to any member of her large family for fear of it getting back to her parents. Her mother would kill her. Dead. Mutilated. And it wouldn't be pretty either.

But Aimee had to understand what was wrong with her. Why wasn't she finding any bears she wanted to mate with?

Most of all, why was she haunted by thoughts of the most unacceptable male on the planet?

"Aimee?"

She cursed inwardly at Carson's deep voice coming through the door. How could she have forgotten *that* power? He knew anytime anyone came near his office.

So much for indecisive dawdling.

Hold your fishing pole at ready. . . .

Bracing herself, she pushed the door open to see him sitting at the desk where a file was open. His hand, which held a pen, hovered over it as if he'd been making notes.

Tall and muscular, he'd almost pass for a bear. But Carson was an Arcadian hawk. His black hair and sharp features paid tribute to his Native American father and the heritage Carson held dear to his heart.

His features softened to those of fatherly affection for her, which was almost comical since she was about a hundred years older than he, even though she looked younger. "Is something wrong?"

Shaking her head, she entered and closed the door tight behind her. "Do you have a second?"

"For you, always."

She offered him a smile at his sincere answer. The two of them had been friends since he'd first shown up and asked Maman about setting up a clinic in their home—over sixty years ago. It'd been the best decision they ever made. Not only was he the best vet and doctor she'd ever seen, he was a vital ally and trusted friend to them all.

Carson pulled a chair out for her to sit down beside him. Putting his pen aside, he leaned back and folded his hands over his stomach. "So what's on your mind?"

Aimee sat down and tried to sort through her thoughts and concerns. "I've been wondering about something."

When she hesitated, he arched a brow. "Is this a female problem? You want me to get Margie out here for you? Would that help with your embarrassment? You know, Aimee, I am a doctor so there's no reason you can't tell me anything. I may not be a woman, but I understand your bodies and am familiar with your unique problems."

Heat rushed over her face. That was just what she needed . . . a human to give her advice on her animal senses going awry. Margie was nice enough, but she knew nothing about mating rituals. Good grief, this was getting worse by the second. "No, it's nothing like that. It's just . . ."

I want to jump a wolf until we're both limping and I have no idea why.

Why was this so hard for her?

Because you want to jump a wolf and if anyone finds out, you're toast.

True enough. But she had to talk to Carson and find out if this was some freakish problem of hers or if there was a precedent in their species that she didn't know about. Something to make her feel a little more "normal." At least as normal as a werebear with heightened powers could be.

C'mon, Aim. Just say it.

"It's inter-species related."

Carson's other brow shot up. "Are you afraid of insulting me?"

"No . . . at least I hope not." She hadn't even thought about the fact that Carson was half human and half Arcadian. "I'm just trying to understand how it all works. I mean, I understand in your case where one parent is human and the other Arcadian . . . that's almost a natural attraction when two humans meet. Most of the time the human has no idea the other isn't human and so the attraction makes sense, especially since humans tend to have an unnatural attraction to us anyway. I get that. What has me stumped are the ones like Wren's parents. What would make a snow leopard want to mate with a tiger or a Katagari mate with a human?"

There, that should get her an answer without her telling him the real reason she was asking.

Carson considered his answer carefully before he gave her a gimlet stare. "Honestly?"

She nodded.

"No one really knows. There's all kinds of speculation that it's something wrong with the DNA. Maybe a defective gene we don't know about. A birth defect, if you will. Kind of the same thing that makes a human crave inappropriate sexual partners. But . . ." He glanced away.

Great, she had a birth defect.

"But?" she prompted, wanting to hear if he had another explanation that didn't end with her being chromosomally damaged.

"I personally wonder if it's not something the Fates do to us as a continuing punishment."

"How do you mean?"

"Well, look at Wren. Regardless of who he partners with, human or Were-Hunter, he'll most likely be sterile. Anytime a Katagari, male or female, is mated with a human, there's no chance whatsoever of progeny. Even as an Arcadian, I have less chance of fathering children because my father was human. I think it's a way the Fates have contrived to kill off our species."

Aimee hadn't even thought of that. How cruel could three goddesses really be?

Then again . . .

"That makes sense in a very twisted way . . . which would coincide with it being a gift from the Fates."

Carson nodded. "Exactly. It would also explain why it's so common for us to mate outside our species. I think it's why so many Arcadian and Katagaria end up together. The Fates are hoping the women will reject the men and then both are left sterile for the rest of their lives. It's cruel, really."

Yes, it was.

But it still didn't explain her attraction to Fang. "Have you ever heard of a completely out-of-species mating?"

"What do you mean?"

"Like in Wren's case, while they weren't the same species per se, they were both cats. Have you ever heard of, say, a wolf wanting to mate with a hawk or a dragon?"

Or in her case, a bear.

She cleared her throat before she asked the most significant part. "Especially if say one of them was Arcadian and the other Katagaria?"

Carson scowled as if her question was completely preposterous. "No. That's never been done. At least not to my knowledge. Gods, I can't imagine anything worse than that. Can you?"

Actually, yes, she could, lots of things, point of fact. But she wasn't about to say *that* out loud and risk his telling her mother. "Horrifying to the extreme."

And she really did mean that. How could she even think about touching Fang? Like Carson had said, it was unnatural and wrong. It defied everything she knew about her people and their traditions.

Everything.

Yet she couldn't get him out of her mind. He hovered there in the back of her thoughts like a beckoning light, drawing her fantasies to him anytime she left them unguarded. Even now, a part of her wanted to go hunt for him.

I am so broken.

Aimee was about to get up when a sharp, shooting pain went through her head.

Carson leaned forward, concerned as she doubled over from the agony of it. "Are you all right?"

An image of Wren went through her. She could see him outside being trounced by a group she absolutely hated. "Wren's in trouble."

Carson gave her a suspicious look. "He's downstairs busing tables. How can he be in trouble?"

Aimee shook her head as images of him being beaten flashed through her head in sharp clarity. Because of the close friendship they shared, she could almost feel the blows. "He's not inside the club."

Without another word to Carson, she flashed herself to the alley behind the club where they dropped their garbage into Dumpsters.

Sure enough, just as she'd seen in her mind, Wren was there, surrounded by a pack of wolves. It was the Arcadian pack that had been in New Orleans even longer than the bears had. Their leader, Stone, had been at odds with her clan since he'd hit puberty.

All of them hated that little prick.

There was something about him that just chafed her raw. He and his bully squad were always looking for some reason to jump any Were-Hunter who came to Sanctuary—if they were Katagaria, even better. She had no idea why they were so aggressive, but there was no excuse for their behavior.

Wren was trying to maintain his human form, but because he was in the middle of puberty and currently in pain from their beating, his form kept shifting from naked human to tiger to leopard and back again. He was covered in bruises and blood from their bites.

Anger descended on her with a vengeance as she ran at the wolves. "Get out of here! What are you doing?"

They turned on her then. Stone, who was more than a head taller than her and twice her girth, grabbed her and shoved her against the wall. "You're not inside the club, little girl. The protection of Sanctuary doesn't exist out here. Stay out of this or get hurt."

Wren growled as he lunged after one of the other wolves, but he was no match for them. Not while he couldn't control his powers.

The sight of them preying on him disgusted her.

"If those are my only two choices . . . I choose to get hurt." She head-butted Stone and kicked him back, then ran to Wren to try and help him to his feet. Something that would have been infinitely easier if he stopped switching from human to large, heavy cat.

"Can you walk?" she asked him, panting from the strain of trying to lift his body.

"I'm trying."

"Can you flash him inside?"

She froze at the deep sound of Fang's voice in her ear. Looking up, she saw him in human form. Her heart pounded in gratitude as she did what he asked and prayed that Wren's uncontrolled powers didn't interfere with hers for the jump.

Fang turned to face the Arcadians who stared at him in disbelief.

"Well, well," their leader said in a smug tone. "What have we here? A piece of Katagari trash that's taken up refuge with the bears?"

Fang gave him his best shit-eating grin that was designed to anger him. "No, just a wolf who's going to kick your ass back to whatever hole it crawled out of."

Their leader scoffed at his boast. "And you plan to do this alone? You think a lot of yourself, don't you, animal?"

Fang shook his head. "Oh, punk, please. Believe me, when dealing with wusses like you who have to gang up on a kid to feel powerful, I don't need any help."

They charged him. Fang turned into a wolf as he leapt at the leader's throat. He tackled him to the ground. He would have ravaged him more, but out of the corner of his eye, he saw one of the others pull a Taser. As the Arcadian fired it, Fang leapt out of the way. It fizzed on the leader who went down cursing.

Fang dove at the legs of another. Before he could get

ahold of him, Dev and his brothers were there as backup. Not that he needed it, but . . .

The Arcadians scattered like school-yard bullies seeing a principal.

Fang manifested his human form and sneered at their flight. "Yeah, you better run home to your mama. Hide under her skirts until you grow enough balls to stand and fight."

Dev grabbed the one who was still on the ground. "Stooooone," he said, his tone lethal as he dragged out Stone's name. "How many times do we have to tell you not to come here?"

But it was hard to hold on to him since Stone was shifting from human to wolf and back again.

"The tiger started it," Stone growled out the ten and a half seconds he was human.

Dev snorted. "I somehow doubt it. Wren keeps to himself unless he's provoked."

"What about you?" The Dev lookalike with the ponytail sneered at Fang. "Why are *you* here?"

Fang narrowed his eyes as he took issue with the bear's tone. "Back off, Grizzly Adams. I don't answer to you."

"Leave him alone, Remi," Aimee said as she rejoined them. "He allowed me to get Wren inside and send you guys out here to deal with Stone."

Passing an arrogant sneer at Remi that he was sure ticked the bear off to no end, Fang turned his attention to Aimee. Dressed in a simple T-shirt and jeans, she took his breath away. Her blond hair was mussed with a long strand of it falling into her eyes.

Every part of him came to life.

She didn't even look his way as she lunged at Stone.

Remi swung away from him to catch her. "Settle down, little sister."

Aimee struggled against his hold. "Settle down, my heinie. Did you see what he did to Wren? I want to claw a piece of his skin off."

Stone raked her with a repugnant glare. "He's an animal, like you. He deserves nothing better than to be a hide mounted on a wall."

Aimee kicked at Stone, but, courtesy of Remi, her foot just missed him. "You disgusting filth! If you're the ideal of humanity, I'd much rather be an animal." She looked at Dev with her lips curled. "You're right, I hate wolves. They're the most repulsive breed ever conceived. Why Lycaon picked them for his sons is beyond me. I think they should all be rounded up and executed. Filthy dogs! All of you!"

Stunned, Fang felt her words like a blow to his stomach. Dog was the worst insult that could be dealt to a wolf. It likened them to a whipped animal whose only function was to please its master. A mindless supplicant with no power, no dignity, and no sense.

But it wasn't so much what she said, it was the sincere hatred backing those words that cut him the deepest.

She was just like the all the others who hated his species and it was why the wolves did their best to avoid the other branches of their kind. No wonder with all the different breeds living under the Peltier roof none of them were wolves.

It was all crystal clear now.

Making sure to keep his voice even, Fang stepped forward. "For the record, there's a big difference between a dog and a wolf. The main one being, we heel to no one. Ever."

Aimee went cold as she remembered Fang's presence. She froze in Remi's arms as instant regret tore through her. How could she have forgotten he was here?

She turned and saw the anguish he hid behind an emotionless expression. It burned deep in his eyes. "Fang—"

He vanished before she could finish her apology.

Aimee cursed. *How could I have been so stupid?*

The problem was she didn't include him in the same category as Stone and his crew. And up until she'd met Fang and his pack, Stone was the only wolf she'd ever been around.

Remi tsked at her as Dev took Stone inside. "Guess you hurt his little feelings, huh?"

Aimee had to bite her tongue to keep from telling him to shut up.

I can't leave it like this. . . .

Without a word to her brothers, she closed her eyes and zoned in on Fang. He'd manifested not with his pack or brother, but on the lower end of Bourbon Street where he sat on a stoop looking as ill as she felt.

How strange . . .

Fang sat alone outside of a ubiquitous New Orleans row house as anger, hurt, and hatred burned deep in his stomach. He should just go home.

Yeah, right. . . .

Vane was being as moody as a teen Gemini on her period after he'd seen some human he was now pining for. Anya was off with her mate and Petra hissed and growled every time she saw him. Alone and lonely, he'd been wandering around the French Quarter, trying to get his bearings on their latest den.

Somehow he'd found his way back to Sanctuary.

No, it wasn't "somehow." He'd gone there seeking the one thing he knew he shouldn't seek.

Aimee. All he'd wanted was just to catch a glimpse of her. He'd told himself that that would be enough to ease the ache inside him. Just one glimpse and he'd be satisfied.

He let out a tired breath. What had he really expected? That Aimee would fall into his arms, strip him naked, and make love to him?

She's a bear.

You're a wolf.

No, according to her, he was a filthy dog who should be rounded up and executed.

"Fang?"

He looked up at her gentle voice to see her appear on the street in front of him. "How'd you find me?"

Aimee paused at the hostile tone. "Your scent," she lied, not willing to tell him about her powers.

"I don't leave a scent. I know better."

She shook her head in denial. "You leave a scent." It'd been branded into her senses the moment he'd kissed her.

"Whatever." He pushed himself to his feet. "Look, I don't need any more insults from you or anyone else. I'm over my quota for the day. Just go home and leave me alone."

She pulled on the sleeve of his jacket to stop him from leaving. "I didn't mean what I said."

"Don't insult my intelligence. I'm not a dog and I heard the sincerity in your tone. You meant *every* word of it."

She stiffened angrily. "All right, so I meant what I said. Sue me. But it was directed at Stone and his craven bullies. I didn't even think to include you in that category."

Yeah, right. How stupid did she think he was? "I don't believe you."

Aimee wanted to cry in frustration. But the one thing she knew about pigheaded men . . . there was no way to change their minds. "Fine. Don't believe me then." She let go of his sleeve and held her hands up in surrender. "I don't even know why I bothered."

"Why did you bother?" He moved closer to her. So close she was dizzy from it and all she really wanted to do was tuck herself into his arms and feel him hold her.

The scent of his skin filled her head. She could feel the warmth from his body. . . .

Every piece of her sizzled. There was no other word for it. Maman was right, there was no mistaking this. This was the quickening she was supposed to feel—the overwhelming lure to mate. That one elusive sensation she'd been trying so hard to experience with her kind.

And Fang was the only one who made her feel it.

Damn.

She ground her teeth before she answered with the truth. "I didn't want you angry at me."

"Why not?"

"I don't know." But she did know and that was the most upsetting part of all. She wanted him.

All of him.

He reached for her. Aimee stood still, wanting that touch. Needing it.

But she couldn't. *This is so wrong. . . .*

It would crush every person who meant something to her. Everyone she loved.

Stepping back, she bit her lip. "I need to get back and check on Wren. He doesn't do well around other people or animals."

"Neither do I."

She swallowed, then forced herself to vanish.

Fang stood there in the darkness, savoring the last remnants of her scent on the breeze. He wanted to howl over it.

Most of all, he wanted to track her down and ease the pain inside him that wanted to savor every inch of her lush body.

His breathing ragged, it took all his control not to chase after her. But she'd made it clear that she was off-limits to him. He would honor that.

Even if it killed him.

Looking down at the bulge in his jeans, he decided that outcome wasn't as far-fetched a thought as it should be.

"Stone was captured by the bears . . . again."

Eli Blakemore looked up from the book he was reading to pin a menacing glare on his son's second in command. What was his name? David? Davis? Donald? Dreck?

It didn't matter. He was born of lesser stock anyway. Unlike *his* lineage, the Arcadian before him came from some unknown Apollite half-wit Eli's ancestor had experimented on.

Eli's bloodline came straight from the king of Arcadia himself—from the king's *eldest* son, no less. That distinction had been impressed upon him from the moment of his birth. Theirs was a sacred duty to show the plebeians how to behave and to police the animals his ancestor should have slaughtered the moment they were created.

And he'd be damned if a group of Katagaria mongrels was going to touch his illustrious son.

Rising to his feet, he set his book down with a calmness he didn't feel. "Have Varyk come to me."

The wolf gulped audibly. "Varyk?"

Eli gave him a tight-lipped smile. Varyk was the most lethal werewolf ever born. A natural-born killer, Varyk would be the tool Eli would use to destroy that nest of filth that had infested his city. He was sick of those bears and all they represented.

It was time they took back New Orleans for once and for all. Sanctuary was going to burn to the ground.

And Varyk would light the match.

"Yes. Varyk. Fetch him. Now."

CHAPTER 7

Aimee was still shaken by her encounter with Fang as she sat beside Wren's bed. In his tigard form, he lay on his side without moving.

"What happened?"

He blinked twice before he answered. "*I took the trash out and they were waiting for me.*"

"What did you do to them?"

"*Nothing. I think they were waiting for any one of us to come out. I was just the poor asshole dumb enough to be there. . . . Sadly enough, I ignored their rampant stupidity until Stone kicked me in the back. Then it was on.*"

She stroked his soft fur. As was typical, the wolves had been looking for a fight. "I'm so sorry, Wren."

He covered her hand with one large paw. "*Don't be. The gods only know what they'd have done had it been you or Cherise or one of the other females. I'm just pissed off I can't control my powers enough to give them the fight they should have had.*"

She smiled at him as Marvin, his pet monkey, jumped up on the bed to chatter by his pillow. When Wren didn't move, Marvin leaned forward to hug his large tigard head and stroke one of his pointed ears. Now, that had to be the cutest thing she'd seen in a long time.

"I'll let you rest. If you need anything, call."

"*Thanks.*"

Aimee crossed the room and was careful not to shut the door too hard. Wren hated sharp sounds. She wasn't sure if it was from his acute hearing or something bad from his childhood. Either way, she wasn't about to upset him after what he'd been through.

As she neared the stairs, she met her mother who was coming up them with a stern glower.

"Is something wrong?"

Maman curled her lip. "That stupid tigard. I need to ask him why he attacked those wolves."

Aimee was aghast at the accusation. "He didn't. They attacked him."

"So say you and probably him too, but the wolves have a different tale and there are more of them willing to swear to it."

"They're lying."

Maman made a sound of supreme aggravation. "And you would take Wren's word?"

"You won't?"

"No." Maman glared at Wren's door. "He's unnatural. Everything about him, right down to that filthy monkey he keeps."

Then what was Aimee? A Katagari bear who became Arcadian at puberty. One with the tracking powers of a goddess who was currently attracted only to a wolf. You didn't get more unnatural than that.

Which was why she couldn't tell her mother the truth about herself. Yes, her mother loved her, but her mother was an animal and their instincts were to kill anything that was different.

"Whatever Wren is, Maman, he's not a liar. Stone and his group on the other hand . . . when have they ever been honest?"

"They have sent over an emissary. If I fail to give them Wren, they will go before the Omegrion and say that I'm harboring a danger to all lycanthropes. Have you any idea what could happen? We could lose our license *and* our home."

"Then give them Stone back. That's all his father wants anyway. Tell them Wren will be disciplined by us."

"And you rule here, since when?"

Aimee tilted her head down in respect to her mother. "Forgive me for overstepping my bounds. I would just hate to see an innocent punished while the filth of the universe is allowed to dance away freely, especially since they would have jumped any of us who'd been in that alley and that includes you or me."

Her mother's look hardened. "My instincts are to throw Wren to them. He attracts trouble, and we don't need him here. I don't want him here." She let out a long sigh. "However, he was brought to us by Savitar himself." Savitar was the one in charge of the Omegrion. The one being no one crossed or questioned. Ever. "So the human side of me recognizes a degree of leverage so long as I protect him. I will try your way, *ma petite*. But if it fails, he will go to them. No matter what you say."

And I'll go with him to protect him. Aimee didn't say that out loud. Her mother couldn't stand for anyone to question or contradict her—it was the nature of the beast. This was Nicolette's den and they were all subject to her final rule.

"Thank you, Maman."

Her mother inclined her head to her before she reversed direction to descend the stairs.

Aimee followed after her, wondering what was going on in Eli's mind. For years they'd had trouble with that insufferably arrogant jerk and his scouts. But then nothing his clan did had ever made sense to her.

Still, there was a tingle in the back of her mind as if warning her this wasn't his random lunacy. There was something more to what was going on.

Something sinister.

Stone glared at Dev as the filthy bear opened the cage they'd thrown him into. At least he'd finally stopped changing forms. "I take it you've finally come to your senses."

Dev laughed. "If that were true, I'd be hauling you and that cage out to the swamp to feed you to the gators. Unfortunately, your daddy sent over someone to claim you."

Expecting it to be Darrel, he was surprised when Dev opened the door and Varyk stood there in all his savage glory. Tall, ruthless, and pissed, Varyk had shoulder-length brown hair and eyes that were so blue they were piercing and glacial. A derisive smirk was permanently chiseled on his handsome face. And his tough stance always said he was looking for someone to gut.

Stone swallowed as a chill went down his spine. Varyk was only marginally sane. . . .

And that was on his best day.

By the angry glower on Varyk's face, this wasn't one of those better days.

What the hell was his father thinking by sending him here?

Personally, Stone would rather stay in his cage than spend even a second in this man's presence. "Where's my father?"

Varyk growled low in his throat. "You don't speak, boy. Maybe never again." He grabbed him roughly by the neck and shoved him at the door. He turned back toward Dev. "Where's the one who attacked him? I was to escort him back as well."

The bear shook his head in a brazen denial that Stone had to admire. It took guts to annoy someone like Varyk. "No can do. Wren stays here."

"Not what I was told."

Dev flashed him a taunting grin that Stone would respect if it wasn't such a suicidal move on the bear's part. "Well, I just told you."

Varyk gave him an arch stare. "And you don't matter to me, table scrap."

"That feeling is entirely mutual, bear bait. Hell, I don't even acknowledge you as being here. So get out and take your trash with you."

Varyk's deadly gaze turned brittle. "You really don't want to take that tone with me."

Dev crossed his arms over his chest. "Well, I do have several others we can choose from. Contemptuous. Angry. Snide. Aggravated. How about I just settle on extreme sarcasm and we call it even?"

"I want the tigard."

"And I want you to leave. Guess who's going to win this argument? And in case you're even denser than you appear, it's not you."

Varyk seized him by the shirt. "Are you calling me out?"

"I'm calling you slow. Not out." Dev knocked his hands away from him. "Now I suggest you leave. Quickly before I decide that I don't really need to live here anymore."

Varyk lowered his head as if about to attack Dev. Stone held his breath. Varyk was unstable at best. One never knew what he'd do and if he attacked here . . .

They were screwed.

Varyk looked past Dev to the upstairs area. "There will come a time and a place when you won't be as lucky as you are tonight."

Dev laughed evilly. "Come get some anytime you miss your mama and need your ass spanked."

Varyk growled the sound of a wolf on the verge of ripping out a throat. Instead of beating Dev, he turned on Stone and grabbed him by the arm to haul him out of Peltier House.

"Do you mind?" Stone snapped as soon as they were on the street. "I'm not your girlfriend."

Varyk grabbed him by the throat in a crushing grip. "Exactly. I have no reason to not slap you down or kill you." He squeezed hard before he let go.

Coughing to clear his throat, Stone glared at him. "What is your problem?"

"My problem is that I had to suffer the stench of

those animals to save your spoiled-rotten ass. I'm not your father and there's no genetic coding between us to make me want to save you ever again. Tread carefully, boy. Next time I'll leave you there."

"What about my father?"

Varyk didn't respond as he walked down the street and disappeared into the night.

Stone straightened his jacket with a sharp tug. "Yeah, you keep walking, punk. You ever touch me like that again and I'll beat you down." Of course he didn't say that loud enough for the werewolf to hear him. He wasn't completely stupid.

Looking back over his shoulder, he glared at Sanctuary. "Your days are numbered, bears."

And so were the ones for the Katagaria wolves. His father had no idea they were in town. But Stone was going to make sure he was enlightened immediately.

Then they would rain hell wrath down on the whole lot of them.

Fang lay in his wolf's form, sleeping on a soft grassy bed. But even while he dozed, he was alert to everything around him. He'd been that way since he was a pup. More to the point, he'd *had* to be that way since he was a pup. Even though he and Vane were the sons of their patria's Regis, they were subjected to the worst from not only their father, but from those under his direct command, such as Stefan.

Their father blamed them for the fact that their Arcadian mother had refused to complete the mating ritual with him. Her rejection had rendered Markus impotent and hostile.

And her refusal to keep her Katagaria children had made them a target.

So when Anya came near, he jumped awake, ready to fight.

Anya lowered herself to the ground. *"It's just me, Fang."*

He turned human and held his hand out toward her nose. "Sorry, baby. I didn't know."

She came forward to lick his fingers before she lay down beside him and rested her head on his thigh.

He stroked the fur around her ears. "Is something wrong?"

"I couldn't sleep. Orian is out on patrol and I didn't want to be alone."

"Where's Vane?"

"I'm not sure. He's not in his den or camp. I haven't seen him in a while. Have you?"

"He was off helping that Dark-Hunter who lives in the swamp. Talon. I assumed he'd be back by now." Dark-Hunters were immortal warriors who fought for the goddess Artemis. They hunted down the Were-Hunters' cousins, the Apollites, and killed them whenever they turned Daimon and started preying on human souls to live.

It was rare for Dark-Hunters and Were-Hunters to mix, but not impossible, and over the centuries, Fang and Vane had made friends with a number of them.

Anya sighed heavily. *"That's the Dark-Hunter you two fought for the other night, isn't it?"*

"Yeah, Talon and Acheron." Acheron was the leader of the Dark-Hunters and a longtime friend of Vane's.

"I wish the two of you would leave them alone.

Every time a Were-Hunter mixes with one of them something bad happens."

"Ah, don't worry. It was actually fun. Besides, there's a lot of Daimon crap going down and the Dark-Hunters have agreed to help us protect you guys should something happen."

"*So say you, but I don't trust them.*"

"Neither do I, but I do trust Vane and you should too. He would never do anything to cause harm to us or to the pack."

She looked away, shamefaced.

Fang felt guilty about making her feel that way. However, she shouldn't be questioning their elder. Vane would die if anything happened to them.

To think he'd caused it . . .

Vane would never get over that. And yet as Fang sat stroking his sister's ear, he had a bad feeling. He couldn't define it. It hovered in the back of his mind like a specter that wanted his blood.

It's just the concern for Anya.

Was it? Or could it be a premonition? He'd never been particularly precognitive.

But . . .

He wouldn't think about it. Anya was safe. He was here to protect her and Vane would be back as soon as he could. Nothing would change. She'd have her puppies here where their old enemies wouldn't be looking for them. Then once their young were old enough to travel, they'd move again.

That was the way of things. And nothing was going to change. He was going to make sure of it.

* * *

Fang snapped awake at a sharp cry of alarm. In his wolf's form, he was lying beside his sister who'd also come awake at the sound.

"*Stay here,*" he projected to her. "*I'll go check it out.*" He pushed himself up on his paws and trotted over to the main camp where a group of wolves were gathered.

Two were bleeding profusely.

Keegan's older brother, Liam, held his bloody paw up to keep from putting weight on it. His light brown fur was coated in blood. "*It was an ambush. We're lucky any of us made it out.*"

Markus, also in wolf form, glared at him. "*Who?*"

"*Arcadian wolves. They had a trap set for us.*"

Markus cursed. "*Where's the rest of your tessera?*"

"*I don't know. Orian told us to come back and warn all of you.*"

Markus cast his gaze around the pack. "*Gather our forces! I want every able-bodied male.*"

Fang turned human to confront his father. "You can't. What if *this* is a trap meant to call us away from our women and leave them unprotected?" He looked around at the wolves. "Remember what happened before? How many women and pups did we lose to Arcadian slaughter?"

Markus snapped at him.

But Fang saw the indecision in the other's eyes.

William moved forward. "*I think Fang might be right. Some of us should stay behind. Just in case.*"

Markus's eyes glowed in the darkness. He hated to be questioned. "*Fine. Fang and the rest of you women can stay behind. I hunt.*"

The pack divided in half.

Liam limped over to Fang. *"I don't know about you, but I damn sure don't feel like a woman."*

Fang laughed. "Ignore the impotent wonder. So what exactly happened?"

"We were horsing around, hunting after small fowl for practice. One minute we were chasing through the marsh and the next Orian was hit with a Taser, then someone opened fire on us with guns. We lost Agarian immediately with a bullet to his head." Liam looked down at his own injury. *"I got caught on the paw, but it only nicked me."*

Which was why he couldn't use his magick. When they were wounded, their magick was unpredictable and unstable. When used, it could do any number of unwanted things.

Suddenly, Anya cried out.

Turning back into a wolf, Fang ran for her. He reached her in record time. She lay on the ground, writhing.

Terrified, he nosed at her neck. *"Anya?"*

She was sobbing uncontrollably.

Was she in labor already? Fang exchanged a baffled look with Liam who came up behind them. *"What is it?"*

"Orian . . ."

"What about him?"

Anya pawed at the ground as if in utter agony. *"He's dead."*

Fang tried to soothe her. *"No, he was hit with a Taser."*

She shook her head in denial. *"No, he's dead. I know it. I can feel it."*

"You're just pregnant and upset."

She gave him a look so hostile and agonized that it shook him to his soul. *"We're bonded mates, Fang. He's dead. I can feel it."*

Fang couldn't breathe as those words tore through him. Bonded . . .

When two Were-Hunters bonded together, they melded their life forces into one. It was an act of ultimate love and loyalty that meant when one of them died, they both died.

The only exception being if the woman was pregnant. Then her life was elongated, but only until the babies were born. Once the last one was safely delivered, the mother would join her mate in eternity.

Anya was going to die.

Fang struggled to breathe as those words slammed into him with talons that dug so deep into his soul that it was all he could do to remain standing. *"Why would you do such a thing?"*

She lunged at him, biting him hard. *"I loved him, you stupid idiot. Why else?"* She howled, a baleful, haunting sound. The cry of a wolf in utter agony.

Leaning his head back, he joined her and let loose his own pain.

His sister was going to die. . . . And there was nothing he could do.

Anya broke off to continue crying. *"How can he be dead? How?"*

But Fang didn't hear her words. All he could do was see her dead and limp. See her pups as they looked to him for stories of a mother they'd never know.

How could this be?

They would be just like him. They would have that hole deep inside them that nothing ever filled. The question of what it would have been like to be loved. To have a mother who cared for them and nursed them.

Turning human, he pulled her into his arms and held her as his own tears brimmed. "I won't leave them alone, Anya. Ever. They will want for nothing."

Except you and their father.

Those words choked him and succeeded in breaching his control. Against his will, his tears flowed. Embarrassed, he hid his face against her neck and held her for everything he was worth. It·wasn't supposed to be like this. His brother and sister were the only constants in his life.

They were his only solace.

And now to lose one . . . it was more than he could stand.

He held her close, rocking her for hours, unaware of anything else. It was only when Vane returned at dawn that he realized how much time had elapsed.

Vane approached them slowly. "What's wrong?"

Fang grappled with a way to tell him gently. Anya was asleep now, but there was no such solace where he was concerned. He tightened his fist in her white fur and decided there was no way to sugarcoat the truth that would shatter Vane the same way it'd shattered him. "Did you know Anya had bonded with Orian?"

Vane curled his lip as if he found the idea as repugnant as Fang had. "Why would she have done that?"

"She said she loved him."

Vane went stiff all over. "You spoke in the past tense."

Fang took a deep breath and braced himself for

Vane's reaction. Gods, how he wished he wasn't the one who had to tell him. "He died tonight."

Vane let fly a curse so foul, Fang was dumbfounded by it. Normally his brother was much more circumspect. But he understood completely. He mirrored the same emotions.

Vane sank down on his knees beside them and put one hand on Anya. When he met Fang's gaze, Fang saw all the agonized pain inside his brother's eyes that he held in his own heart.

"What are we going to do?"

Fang shook his head. "We're going to have to watch her die."

Vane looked away. It was as if he couldn't face it any more than Fang could. "What happened?"

"A group of Arcadians attacked them and Orian was killed during the fight. What else? Stupid fucking wolf. He should have been here with Anya and not out carousing with his friends."

Vane glanced around the den as if looking for the shadows to come to life and chase them down. "Did they track the rest back here?"

"I don't know. I didn't ask that question. Markus and a group of others went after them."

"And?"

"They haven't returned."

Those words had barely left his lips before the others loped slowly into camp. Some were bloody and limping. But none seemed to be missing.

"Stay with Anya." Vane went to check with them.

Fang didn't move until his brother returned with a steely look on his face. "What?"

"It's the group of Arcadians Acheron warned us about. Somehow they found out we're here and their Sentinels are out for our blood."

That was the story of their lives. No matter where they went, the Arcadians found them and attacked them. Why couldn't their human brethren just leave them alone?

Because the Fates are three psycho bitches bent on completely annihilating your species.

Now his sister would pay the ultimate price for a curse none of them had wanted or deserved. Life was so unfair. But as Acheron said so many times, deserving had nothing to do with anything. Life just was.

Vane sat down beside him. "You look like shit. Why don't you go get some rest?"

"I can't sleep."

"You need to sleep. You're not doing anyone any good if you're too tired to function."

Yeah, but how could he find peace tonight? There was nothing except this sick lump in his stomach that made him want to vomit.

How he wished he could go back twenty-four hours and be oblivious to this future. . . .

Vane gently pushed him. "I have Anya. Go rest. If nothing else, turn wolf for a while."

Fang nodded glumly before he relinquished her over, even though all he wanted to do was hold on to her for as long as he could. But Vane was right. He needed some time in his true form.

And he needed to find some kind of comfort for himself. Something to numb the pain if only for one tiny nanosecond.

* * *

Aimee came awake with a start as pain sliced through her. It was the same sensation she had whenever Wren or one of her brothers was threatened.

Only this time, it was for Fang. She could sense him as if he were in the room right beside her.

And it was the same dread feeling in her chest. The same urgency to locate him immediately and make sure everything was all right.

What had happened?

Closing her eyes, she found him. He was lying on his stomach in his wolf's form. He didn't appear to be injured and yet something about him seemed to be broken. Hurt.

Before she even realized what she'd done, she materialized beside him . . . still in her nightgown.

"Fang?"

Fang froze at the soft sound of Aimee's voice. Opening his eyes, he saw her kneeling beside him. *"What are you doing here?"*

"I-I don't know. I just sensed that you needed someone."

Scowling, he wanted to tell her to leave. To get as far away from him as she could.

Until she placed one gentle hand on his neck.

Fang had always hated to be touched there. Not even Anya could stroke him while he was in his wolf's form. He couldn't stand it.

Yet Aimee's touch soothed him. She ran her hand through his fur, to his ear that she gently rubbed between two fingers. Before he could stop himself, he inched closer to her.

"What happened?"

He choked as he thought of Anya. "*My sister's bond-mate died last night.*"

"Your sister who's burdened?"

He nodded.

"Oh, sweetie . . . I'm so sorry."

Sorry . . . that was a worthless word no doubt uttered out of habit. He hated for people to say that when they had no idea what it really meant. No idea of the pain that was burning deep inside him at a loss he would soon bear that no amount of comfort could alleviate or even dull. How could he go on without his sister here? "*You have your family. You have no idea what—*"

"That's not true," she said, tightening her grip on him. "I've lost two brothers and one of their mates. I know *exactly* how much it stings and how it aches. I know the anguish that no amount of time heals. There's not a day that goes by that I don't remember them and how they died. So don't take that tone with me, buster. I won't tolerate it."

Fang turned human and pulled her into his arms. "I'm sorry, Aimee. I didn't know."

Aimee tightened her grip on him as she bit back the tears she always felt whenever she remembered Bastien and Gilbert.

Worse, they'd died because of *her*. Because she'd shared her powers with them and shown them the location of their enemies. They'd gone after them to protect *her*. The guilt of it. The sorrow . . . there were times even now when it was more than she could bear.

Still, life went on, every aching agonized beat of it.

"It's okay," she whispered, but she didn't mean that.

It was never okay to lose the ones you loved. Life was brutal, harsh, and cold. She knew that better than most.

Her mother's bipolar mood swings were proof of that. While Maman welcomed and protected anyone who was loyal to their house, she was just as quick to kill any she suspected of treachery—hence her unnatural hatred for Wren.

And she was so unforgiving. While Maman loved her, Aimee saw in her mother's eyes the blame that she still had for Aimee even though she'd only been a cub at the time of their deaths.

Aimee sighed. "As Wren so often says, sooner or later life victimizes us all."

"Wren?"

"The tigard you helped me to save. He has a terribly jaded view of most things, but in this I think he's right. We are victims."

Fang shook his head. "I refuse to be a victim. Ever . . . but I can't believe I'm going to lose her and that there's nothing I can do to stop it."

"At least you have time to say good-bye. My brothers were gone in an instant. There was no time for anything, not even grieving."

Fang paused as he realized how much she was comforting him. They were sharing their pain and . . .

What are you doing?

He was reaching out to her and he had no idea why. He didn't trust anyone, especially not strangers. He spurned comfort and always had.

Yet he didn't want to leave her. He wanted to stay like this for a while. To have her stroke him and soothe the pain inside his heart.

Aimee pulled back from his embrace to look at something on the ground. She bent forward and pulled up the scrap of fabric that Stefan had ripped off one of the attacking Arcadians. He'd carried it back for their inspection and Vane had brought it over to him earlier to look at. Unfortunately, the scent was so contaminated, it was worthless for them to even try and use it to track them down.

She frowned intently as she studied it.

He duplicated her scowl. "What is it?"

"I know this patch. It's from a tessera uniform."

His heart stopped beating. "What do you mean, you know this?"

Aimee closed her eyes to use her powers as images played through her head. She could see the wolves fighting, hear them snarling and tearing. See the Arcadians attacking them. But one face was clearer than the others.

It was a face she knew all too well.

"It's Stone's."

Fang tilted his head. "Stone? Why do I know that name?"

"He was the wolf you fought behind Sanctuary."

Fang's breath left him as if she'd hit him hard in the solar plexus. "What?"

"He was the wolf—"

"No." Fang shook his head in disbelief as those words shredded his soul. What had he done?

"Dear gods . . . I'm the one who killed my sister."

CHAPTER 8

Fang was nauseated as reality came crashing down and crushed him. His stupid fight had cost his sister the life of her mate and it would take her from them as soon as her litter was born.

How could he have been such an idiot?

"Fang, you can't blame yourself."

He heard Aimee's words, but he knew the truth. "They wouldn't have even known we were here had I not attacked them." *For you.* He didn't say that last bit out loud, but it burned in his mind like a fiery coal.

What have I done?

"Fang—"

He pushed her hand away. "Please go. Every time you get near me, something bad happens."

Aimee recoiled as if she'd been slapped. And those words stung as much as a physical blow. She tried to tell herself that it was his pain that made him lash out. But it didn't matter. It still hurt.

"I'll go, but if you need a—"

The look he turned on her was harsh, biting, and condemning. "I don't need shit from you or anyone else."

Her throat tightened instantly. Nodding, she took

herself home, back to her bed where she sat stunned by his rejection. It shouldn't hurt at all.

So why did it? And it wasn't just a little ache. Her heart felt battered and stomped on.

He's just a stupid, angry wolf.

True, and she needed to put it behind her. She needed to put *him* behind her. There was nothing she could do for him. She needed to focus on her own future and finding herself a mate who was appropriate for her station. One her family would not only accept, but be proud to bring into their ranks. That was her duty to the ones she loved.

Tomorrow she'd find her a bear and there would be no more thoughts of Fang or any other wolf.

Fang felt like crap. He shouldn't have yelled at Aimee and he knew it. It wasn't her fault. He'd been the one to jump into the fray without thinking. Blaming her was pointless. It was his anger at himself that he couldn't really cope with. Blaming her was easier than blaming himself.

But in the end, he knew the truth.

He was the sole reason Anya would die. His temper and need to fight had caused this. The wolf in him wanted vengeance over that. He wanted to bathe in the blood of his enemies. To wash away his anger and guilt with their deaths.

If only it were that easy.

But his human side knew that no amount of violence would undo what had been done. Anya would die and it would be all his fault for trying to save a bear he shouldn't even care about.

So why did he?

Unable to cope with it all, he returned to his wolf form to lie on the damp ground while thoughts chased themselves through his head.

In the end, he kept coming back to a single reality— how could one chance meeting with one person on a crappy afternoon alter his life so much? How was it possible that a bear had somehow wormed her way into his heart and ruined his entire life?

Eli walked the floor of his dark, immaculate study as he imagined skinning his own son. Yes, the boy was still young, but how could he be so imbecilic? So reckless . . .

Now the Katagaria wolves knew they knew of their existence and they'd be hunting for them. The element of surprise had been lost.

Damn you, Stone.

"You summoned me?"

Eli paused to find Varyk standing in front of his black wood rococo desk, watching him. The hair on the back of his neck stood on end. That man had the creepiest ability to travel completely undetected. He'd never seen anyone more accomplished at hiding their scent or presence.

"We have another mess."

Varyk took the news with complete stoicism. Then again, he took everything that way. "Stone?"

Eli winced. "Of course." There was no need to deny what Varyk could easily verify. "Stone's tessera went after a Katagaria patrol and slaughtered some of their members. I'm sure they're now gunning for us."

To Varyk's credit, he didn't make a face or any indication of emotion. "You wish me to clean this up?"

"I want your opinion on the best way to proceed."

Varyk crossed his arms over his chest and leveled a cold glare at him. "I'd start by killing my son and his crew of idiots before their stupidity spreads to anyone else and infects them." There was even less emotion in his tone than in his body language.

Eli retrieved his brandy from the small marble table in front of him and took a sip before he responded. "Spoken like a man who has no children. I can't do that. I'm not an animal."

"I am."

Eli arched a brow at that. There were times when Varyk did seem more Katagaria than Arcadian, but he knew better. Tougher than hell itself, Varyk was Arcadian.

If only barely.

Varyk slid his gaze over to the fire that was blazing in the ornate Victorian hearth. "You asked my opinion and I gave it. Of course you have to remember that if I'd been on the island with Gilligan, he'd have been killed ten minutes into the first episode. Where I come from, incompetence and stupidity are reasons for justifiable homicide."

Eli snorted. "Well, I should like a plan that doesn't result in the death of my heir."

"Would a good maiming be considered over-the-top?"

Eli shook his head. Varyk was ever persistent. "My city is being overrun by animals. Before Sanctuary brings in any more, I want you to stop them. *All* of them."

"I'm working on it, but you should be aware that taking down Sanctuary isn't an overnight event. Burn the building. They rebuild and Savitar takes revenge on the perpetrators."

"Do you think I don't know that?" Eli caught himself as he ground out those words. He calmed down before he spoke again. "If it were that simple, I'd have had them out of here decades ago. What I want is for *those* bears to be slaughtered."

Varyk arched a single brow at the man's tone and demeanor. There was something insidious. A hatred so raw, there was more to this than what Eli said. No doubt this was worth investigating. . . .

"Why so much venom, Blakemore? What have the Peltiers done to you?"

"That is none of your business," he snarled. "Now go." He gestured toward the door with his brandy snifter. "Do what you have to to get that pack of dogs out and then finish off the bears."

Varyk gave him a mocking bow before he turned on his heel and flashed out of the room, back to his home in the Garden District. It was an elegant antebellum relic that held just the right amount of chill in the air. At four thousand square feet, the house was by no means small, but it didn't quite qualify as a mansion either.

It was, however, a lovely reminder of his solitary existence. And yet he'd lived this way for so long that he could only vaguely recall another life. . . .

He froze in the hallway as he felt a presence he

hadn't sensed in centuries. Spinning around, he used his powers to pin the bastard to the wall.

"Let. Me. Go."

Varyk tightened his invisible hold. "Why should I?"

"Because we're brothers."

"No. We *were* brothers."

Constantine coughed as he struggled to breathe. *Kill him.* The urgent voice inside Varyk's head was hard to ignore. It was what he should do. It was definitely what he owed him.

But curiosity won out. At least for a few minutes.

Varyk released him.

Constantine fell to the floor where he gasped on his hands and knees. Tall and well built, he had coal-black hair and sharp features. It was easy to see the jackal in him. Just as it was easy to see the wolf in Varyk. No one would ever peg them as siblings, which was fine by him.

"Why are you here?" Varyk growled out.

Constantine looked up at him. "I'm being hunted."

"And I should give a damn, why?"

Curling his lip, Constantine pushed himself to his feet. "Since they've already mistaken your scent for mine, I thought the least I could do was warn you."

Varyk scowled at his words. "What are you talking about?"

"How do you think I found you here? A group of jackals came to Sanctuary looking for me. Since I wasn't there, I knew there was only one other person who could smell enough like me to draw my enemies to them . . . you."

He gave Constantine a droll stare. "Wow, you figured that out all on your own too. I'm impressed. You didn't even need to put a quarter in the Zoltan machine. Truly amazing."

"Knock the sarcasm."

Varyk closed the distance between them. "I'd rather knock you."

Constantine tensed, but to his credit, he didn't attack. He merely stood there, taunting him with his presence. "Believe me, I know. Do you think it's easy for me to come here after what happened?"

Varyk grabbed him by his lapels and jerked him hard. "Do you really think I care?"

"Don't you even want to know why I'm being hunted?"

"I truly don't give a shit. In fact, I hope they catch you."

Constantine knocked his hands away from him and stepped back. "Fine, brother. I'll leave you to your solitude."

"You mean exile."

Constantine winced, then paused. He looked back at Varyk over his shoulder. "Mom died last spring. I just thought you should know."

Varyk wanted to be cold and callous. Unfeeling. He wanted that news not to hurt him. Goddamn it, how could it hurt so much after all they'd done to him?

Yet it did. He hated that he'd never had a chance to see his mother one last time.

She'd have only slapped you in the face had you tried.

And right then, he hated himself more for that weakness inside him than he hated them.

"Before I go, though," Constantine said, "I have to ask one question."

"That is?"

"How did a wolf-jackal hybrid infused with the powers of an Egyptian goddess end up as the lapdog of a man like Eli Blakemore?"

Varyk gave his "brother" a snide smirk. "Well, I guess they don't call us jack-offs without a reason."

CHAPTER 9

Aimee looked up from her book as she heard a sharp knock on her door. Closing her eyes, she saw her brother Alain in the hallway with a tray of tea and biscuits. Unlike the majority of her brothers, he had short blond hair and a face that reminded her of a cherub. His blue eyes were always bright and warm, and he kept a small, well-trimmed goatee.

She was warmed at his thoughtfulness. "Come in."

He opened the door slowly—he was always wary of entering a female bear's territory without proper invitation. His mate, Tanya, had taught him well. "It's me. You want some tea?"

"Absolutely." She set her book on the bed and went to hold the door while he came in and put his tray down on her dresser.

Closing the door behind him, she moved back to her bed.

Alain poured them both a cup of vanilla Rooibos tea and brought her the porcelain snack plate that was piled high with sugary biscuits.

She couldn't help smiling. "You haven't done this for me in years."

He drizzled honey into his cup . . . a lot of honey—they were bears after all. He held the plastic bear container toward her.

Aimee took it from him and duplicated the gesture as he licked the sweetness from his fingers. "I feel like a cub, waiting for Maman or Papa to come in and yell at us for breaking curfew—you were always so good at getting me into trouble with late-night tea fests."

Alain laughed. "Maman was never the one who scared me as a cub . . . only as an adult do I fear her."

Aimee hesitated at the odd note in his voice. "Why would you say that?"

"For the same reason you would. I love Maman, you know that. But there are times when I sense something about her that makes me nervous."

Aimee agreed as she set the honey aside. "She doesn't like the others staying here with us. I think she's afraid of them discovering our secret . . . or worse, of them turning on us like Josef did." He was the one who'd led the party that had ultimately killed her brothers.

Like Wren, Josef had been taken into their den as a wounded pubescent cub instead of being left out to die as Maman had wanted. As soon as Josef had healed, he'd turned on them for no reason at all. It was almost as if he'd hated and resented them for having a family when he didn't. And for that alone, he'd tried to destroy them.

His betrayal had scarred all of them—one moment of compassion that had turned into a lifetime of regret—but Maman was haunted more than the others. She blamed herself for not being more suspicious of him. Blamed herself for the deaths of Bastien and Gilbert.

That was why Maman was so hard on everyone now. She kept expecting others to turn on her for no reason too.

Alain stirred his tea with a small demi-spoon. "There are many secrets in this house, *chere*. Sometimes I think too many."

Aimee arched a brow at that. "What are *you* hiding?"

He paused to look down at his palm where the intricate scrollwork lay that declared him mated. It was a mark that was identical to the one on Tanya's palm. "You know my secret."

Her heart clenched at the reminder. Though he was mated to a good bear, his heart belonged to another. It always had.

"I'm sorry, Alain."

He shrugged. "I have nothing to complain about. Tanya's loyal to me. She's kind and we have two beautiful sons. How could I be upset by that?"

"Do you still think about Rachel?"

Ignoring her question, he looked down at his cup as he continued to stir the honey through the dark liquid. "I wanted to ask you something."

"Sure."

He tapped the spoon twice before placing it on his plate. "Have you noticed anything with Kyle?" Kyle was their youngest brother. A little odd at times, he was basically good-natured and sweet even if he did keep to himself more than the others did.

"Such as?"

He hesitated before he spoke. "That he's an Aristos."

Aimee froze in disbelief at those words. "What?"

"He's an Aristos," Alain repeated, his gaze burning into hers. "I'm sure of it."

Aristi were the most powerful sorcerers in their world. Stronger than Sentinels, they were the one thing every Arcadian prayed to be and the one being that made the blood of all Katagaria run cold. "How do you know?"

"We were playing around yesterday, practicing holds, and he took me down with an ease of strength no one at his age should possess. And when he pinned me, I saw it in his eyes."

Aimee felt sick at the news. Aristi were the ones who'd murdered her brothers and they were the one thing their mother couldn't stand. It was also another secret Aimee kept from everyone. She was one too. "Maman will kill him if it is so."

"That's what I'm afraid of."

"Have you discussed this with Kyle?"

Alain shook his head, his eyes horrified by the mere suggestion. "Absolutely not. You're the only one I trust to keep this between us. I would never do anything to cause him harm and I know you feel the same."

Aimee heard the underlying current. There was more to this than what he was telling her. "But?"

"He needs to be trained. Those kind of powers, if left unchecked . . ."

Could kill him. He didn't finish the sentence because Aimee knew that as well as he did. An Aristos required a tutor, especially the males. While a female could adapt better and learn to control those powers on her own, a male couldn't. It was what had saved her, but she couldn't train Kyle without exposing them both. "What should we do?"

"I was hoping you'd have some ideas."

"Not really. I don't even know of an Aristos." That wasn't entirely true, but she wasn't about to share *that* with Alain. "They're too rare."

He nodded. "I know . . . think about it. Let me know if you come up with something. I don't want to leave him alone in this."

Neither did she. Kyle would be as scared by his powers as she was by hers. "You want me to talk to him?"

"I hate to dump it on you, but you're the one he's closest to. He might open up to you. At least more than he ever would me."

Aimee smiled at him. He was right. Kyle kept his brothers in the dark, but for some reason he saw her as another mother. "I'll talk to him tomorrow. See if he knows what's happening to him."

He gave her hand a gentle squeeze. "You're the best."

She snorted. "Go ahead, Etienne, and tell me I'm the best sister you have." Etienne was another of her brothers who was a scoundrel and a charmer. He was forever telling whatever lie he needed to get his way.

Alain laughed again at her insult. "He's such a shit, isn't he?"

"Yes, yes he is. And speaking of excrement, have we heard anything more from the wolves and their threats?"

"You mean Eli's group?"

She nodded.

"Not a word. I think Dev put the fear of Zeus into them when he refused to back down."

"That I doubt. They're pretty stupid."

"Yeah, but even Eli has a smidgeon of self-preservation. He should know by now to leave us alone."

She hoped that was true, but doubted it too. Eli was such a narcissist that the idea of someone actually besting him just didn't seem to be in his scope of reality. "I wouldn't be so sure. They don't call it blind hatred without a reason. I think he's at the point with us that he will cross any boundary regardless of consequence."

He narrowed his gaze on her. "You have one of your precogs, don't you?"

"Yeah, but I can't put a finger on it exactly. I just know he's going to do something we're not expecting. I only wish I knew exactly what and when."

"Then I'll spread the word for everyone to keep their eyes peeled."

"Thanks."

Vane sat off to the side of camp in human form while he listened to the idle conversations around him. Half the pack was in human form while the others were wolves.

Many of the men were restless. There was a disturbing scent in the air. One that denoted trouble, but no one could get a handle on it. Not even he was sure what was causing it.

But he was as edgy as the rest of them. One wrong word or action and he was just as likely to take a life as a Daimon. More so, in fact.

And maybe that was the source of his unease. Ever since he and Fang had helped Acheron and Talon, he'd had a sense of foreboding that he couldn't shake.

Fang walked up to him and offered him a cold beer.

"You want to go patrolling and see if we can find out what's going on?"

Vane popped the lid and tilted his head so that he could see around Fang's body where Stefan and the others were gathering. He shook his head.

If he went out with Stefan in the mood he was in, one of them would end up dead.

"Whatever it is, it's coming this way. I think we should hang close to the women."

Fang laughed at that. "I love the way you think, *adelphos*. Hanging close to women is what I do best."

He smiled at Fang's words. "Yeah, but I haven't seen you doing that lately."

Fang glanced over to Petra who was sitting in wolf form with several other wolfswans. "I've been preoccupied."

"With what?"

"Stuff."

Vane didn't press him. His brother, for all his neverending stream of sarcasm and live-for-the-moment arrogance, could be extremely moody sometimes. Even secretive.

It was a space and freedom that Vane willingly gave him.

"*Vane!*"

Vane choked on the beer as he heard his sister's frantic, scared voice in his head.

"*What?*" he sent back silently.

"*The pups are coming. I need you.*"

"Did you hear that?" he asked Fang.

"I'm on it."

His beer forgotten, Vane shot to his feet and ran for

her. He found her to the side of the camp, near a small outlet of water where she must have gone to get something to drink.

"I've got you, babe," he said gently as he knelt down by her side to help her.

She licked his chin, then whined as more labor pain hit her.

Fang joined them a few seconds later with blankets. "Should I get Markus?"

Vane shook his head. "We can handle it."

As he reached to pet Anya, his cell phone rang. Vane started not to answer it, but the ID showed Acheron, who wouldn't be calling unless it was important. Pissed at the timing, he flipped it open. "I'm busy, Dark-Hunter. This isn't a good—"

"I know, but there's a massive number of Daimons converging around Miller's Well. They're coming for your pack, Vane."

Vane went cold at the news as he looked to Fang to see if his brother had heard the words as clearly as he had. "Are you sure?"

"I'm positive. Looks like they want a supercharge before the Mardi Gras festivities with us so you guys have got to get out of there. Pronto."

How he wished it were that simple. "Anya's in labor. We can't move her. But I'll make sure the others get out."

"All right," Ash said. "Sit tight and I'll have some reinforcements to you ASAP."

The implication insulted every animal part of Vane. "I don't need your help, Dark-Hunter. We can take care of our own."

"Yeah, just the same, we'll be there shortly."

The phone went dead.

Snarling, Vane returned the phone to his pocket. He met his brother's stony gaze. "Get the others mobilized."

Fang nodded, then ran off to spread the word.

Acheron Parthenopaeus, leader of the Dark-Hunters and an immortal Atlantean god under a massive crisis situation, not the least of which was his own brother trying to kill him, cursed as he hung up the phone. This was not good and it was getting worse by the heartbeat. If the Daimons got a hold of those pregnant wolves and augmented their powers, there would be no stopping them and the streets of New Orleans would run red from the blood of its human occupants.

He walked quickly down Bourbon Street toward Canal, which was where his Dark-Hunter was supposed to be patrolling for Daimons out to munch on human souls.

There was no sign of him.

And where the hell was Talon?

The Celt was supposed to be in his swamp, guarding the human, Sunshine Runningwolf, and instead there had been no sign of him when Ash had gone there.

Closing his eyes, Ash sensed the Celt was fine. But he didn't have time to fetch him away from the woman he was protecting. The Daimons were moving fast and he didn't have long before they'd reach Vane and his family.

Then it would rain rainbows and rose petals on them. . . .

Not.

He flipped his phone open and called Valerius who

was still at home. The ancient Roman general was a major pain in his ass on his best day, but in a crisis, there were few better fighters. "Val, I'm on Bourbon—"

"I will not venture down that street of crass iniquities and plebeian horror, Acheron. It is the cesspit of humanity. Don't even ask it."

Ash rolled his eyes at the Roman's arrogant tone. "I need you in the swamp."

Silence answered him. He could just imagine Val at home with his lip curled in repugnance. Not that the general hadn't been in worse places back in the day when he'd commanded a Roman army. He was just cranky in his old age.

"We have a situation, Valerius," he said sternly. "A group of Daimons are after a Katagaria pack and they have women in labor—"

"Where do you need me?"

Ash smiled. The Roman had his moments. Good and bad. Luckily, this was a good one.

"I'll be right there." Ash hung up the phone. He dashed into a nearby doorway where no one could see him and flashed to Val's side in his mansion.

Valerius did a double take at seeing Ash in his living room before the Roman could even return his cordless phone to its pedestal. Dressed in a black Armani suit and black silk shirt, and with his shoulder-length dark hair pulled back into a ponytail, Valerius was the epitome of a privileged, well-bred man.

Patrician to the end.

The only hint of shock Valerius showed was a slight arching of his right brow.

"We don't have time for conventional means of transportation," Ash explained.

Before Val could ask him what he meant, Acheron grabbed him and they materialized close to the Katagaria den.

Val scowled at him. "How did you do that? Are you some odd Were-Hunter hybrid like Ravyn?"

Ash gave a dark half-laugh. None of the Dark-Hunters knew he was a god and he really wanted to keep it that way. The less they knew about him and his sordid past the better. "Long story. The pertinent part is that I have to be careful using my powers around the pregnant Katagaria. If the pregnant wolves are forced into human form by my powers, it'll kill them and their babies instantly. So, I'm fighting strictly hands-on as a human just to be safe. Your powers aren't ionically charged so you should be safe to fight as always."

Val nodded in understanding.

Acheron manifested his warrior's staff, then led Val toward the den.

The camp was in total chaos as the males, mostly in human form, tried to gather up the pregnant wolves and pups and move them without using their magic.

Vane and Fang stood over a pregnant wolf in labor while another male, who bore a striking resemblance to Vane, knelt by her side. The man was quite a bit older than the brothers.

It was Markus.

Ash remembered him well. The ruthless Katagari ruler hated everyone outside the pack.

Then again, Ash amended, as he looked at Vane and

Fang, their father hated many who were in the pack as well. Including his own sons.

"Do us proud, Anya," Markus said sternly. "Know I will raise your pups under my full protection."

The wolfswan whined.

Their father stood up and raked a sneer over Vane and Fang. "This is your fault. I curse the day I ever had werewolf sons."

Fang growled at the insult that implied they were more human than animals, and started for his father, but Vane caught him.

Markus curled his lips. "You'd best protect her young. The gods better help you both if something happens to them." He stalked off toward the others.

Acheron and Val headed toward the brothers.

"What are you doing here?" Vane demanded as soon as he saw them. "I told you we can handle this."

Acheron planted the end of his staff in the ground and eyed him with a patience he didn't really possess. "Don't play hero, Vane. The last thing you need is to fight Daimons off your back while Anya labors."

Vane narrowed his eyes at them. "Do you know anything about delivering a baby?"

Ash nodded. "I do indeed. I've helped deliver more than my fair share of them over the last eleven thousand years. Human and otherwise."

In spite of his earlier words, Vane appeared relieved by Ash's answer.

Vane looked at Val. "What about you?"

Val's answer was as out of character for him as his presence here. "I don't know nothing about birthing puppies, Miss Scarlett, but I can cleave the head off a Daimon without breaking a sweat."

"All right, you can both stay." Vane crouched down beside his sister and nuzzled her snout with his face while the she-wolf panted and whined. "Don't worry, baby. I'm not going to leave you."

Ash sat down by her side and held his hand out for her to sniff him. "I'm a friend, Anya," he said gently. "I know you're in pain, but we're going to stay with you and help you deliver your young."

She looked up at Vane who made wolf noises back to her.

A loud curse sounded.

"Vane!" Fang shouted. "We got gators moving in all over the place."

Ash smiled. "It's okay. They're with me. They won't attack you unless you hit them."

Fang cocked his head in doubt. "You sure? They don't look friendly to me."

"Positive."

The last of the Katagaria pack moved out, except for two. Ash had seen them both before, but he didn't know them. . . .

No, not entirely true. Since he could see into their minds and hearts, he knew instantly that the blond one was Vane and Fang's brother. A brother neither of them knew they had.

The dark-haired wolf was a friend. Liam.

Fang narrowed his gaze at them as they joined the brothers. "What are you doing?"

Fury shrugged. "Wolves don't fight alone."

"Since when do you give a shit?"

Fury glanced quickly to Anya and Ash felt not only his pain, but his longing to be counted among their siblings. It was so raw and deep that it brought an ache to his own chest.

It was also a pain he could more than relate to.

"You two need a level head to help fight." Fury indicated him and Liam. "That's us."

Vane looked up. "Leave them alone, Fang. If they want to stay, let them. The more we have to help protect Anya, the better."

Fang stepped back while the other two wolves gave them distance. They went to stand off to the side with Val and the gators while Ash, Fang, and Vane were huddled over Anya.

The quiet stillness of the swamp was broken only by Anya's pants and whines.

As they waited, Ash felt the grief in Vane's eyes. He remembered a time when he'd listened to his own sister's screams as she birthed her baby. There was nothing more disturbing.

But all that faded when the first cries of the baby were heard. Then the focus became one of joy at the new life that had been created.

"She'll be fine," Val assured the brothers as he noticed their discomfort as well. "We'll get her through this."

"No," Vane said, shaking his head. "All we can hope for is to save her puppies. As soon as the last one leaves her body, she'll die."

Val frowned at him. "Don't be so fatalistic."

A muscle worked in Vane's jaw. "I'm not, Dark-Hunter. She was claimed by her mate. They bonded their life forces. Had she not been pregnant and carrying new life when he died, she'd have died with him. As soon as the puppies are born, she'll be off to join him on the other side."

Ash's stomach drew tight in sympathetic grief as he heard the pain in Vane's voice. He knew how much Anya meant to both of her brothers. He also knew what was about to happen and though he wanted to change it, he knew he couldn't. Fate was what it was and in trying to avert it, he could worsen the outcome for all of them. "I'm sorry, Vane."

"Thanks." Vane brushed his hand through his sister's white coat.

Fang sat off to the side, his gaze haunted as he remained silent. How rare for him not to be making offhand and even asinine comments. That told Ash more than anything just how upset Fang was.

Suddenly, out of nowhere, a horde of Daimons attacked.

Vane shot to his feet to confront them. "I don't know how to birth the cubs," he told Ash. "You stay with her and I'll fight."

Ash nodded and remained crouched by Anya as she snapped and whined.

Fang transformed into a wolf, his stronger form, to fight, as did Liam and Fury, but Vane remained human.

Ash heard the Daimons scream as they found the alligators lying in wait for them.

Anya began thrashing as the fight broke out. Ash kept his attention focused on the she-wolf and only looked up to make sure the Daimons weren't making their way any closer to Anya.

Fang, Fury, and Liam were doing a remarkable job keeping them off in wolf form while Valerius and Vane fought them with knife and sword. The bad thing, though, was that the wolves couldn't use their magic any more than Ash could. Any random shot of their energy could accidently hit Anya and her pups and kill them.

"Vane!"

Ash started at the human noise from the wolfswan. He looked up to see a Daimon about to attack Vane's back. Forewarned, Vane saw the Daimon and whirled around in time to stab the Daimon through the heart and kill him.

Anya lay back.

Ash held her still as the first of her puppies crested. "That's it," he said to her in a calm, soothing voice. "We're almost there."

A Daimon came up through the hedges beside them. Ash sprang to his feet and whirled to defend Anya as Fang caught the Daimon and knocked him away from them.

"Take care of my sister," Fang shot to him in his mind.

Ash quickly returned to Anya.

With the Daimons so close now, he was having to watch the coming cub, Anya, and the Daimons.

It wasn't easy.

"Push," he said to Anya. "Just a little bit more."

The next few seconds happened rapidly and yet they seemed to move slowly through time.

Heartbeat by heartbeat.

Two Daimons rose up from their fight with Fang.

One of them shot Fang with a Taser, immediately turning him human. Fang let out a howl as his body convulsed uncontrollably back and forth between wolf and human.

Vane went after the second one at the same moment the first one aimed the Taser at Vane, who dove at the ground. The Daimon pressed the button and the electrified prongs missed Vane by a fraction of an inch.

They struck Anya instead.

Ash cursed in anger as Anya was transformed from a wolf to a woman and back again. Her screams echoed in the trees and then she fell eerily silent.

Back in her wolf form, she didn't move at all.

Vane ran to her, but it was too late.

She was dead.

Ash let out his battle cry and rushed the Daimon who had killed her. He punched the Daimon hard in the jaw, then used his bare hands to finish him off. He pushed his hand straight into the Daimon's chest, piercing his mark.

The Daimon shattered into a spray of golden dust.

Now that he could use his powers without restriction, Ash made short work of the remaining Daimons.

Fang's transformations had slowed down, but he was still alternating between human and wolf forms as he dragged himself slowly toward his sister's body.

Vane walked stonily toward Anya and sank down beside her. He gathered her wolf's body up into his arms and cradled her as if she were a baby. Tears streamed down his face as he rocked back and forth with her and whispered to her.

Fang let out a fierce howl and turned into a man. His body bare, he laid his head down on Anya's back and held on to her too.

Ash would never forget the sight of the three of them huddled there in their grief. It would haunt him forever.

All too well, he remembered his own past.

Saying good-bye to his sister and her baby . . .

Pain like that never fully healed. He knew it for a fact. Not even eleven thousand years had taken away the bitter burn inside him.

His face grim, Ash took a step toward them. "Do you need me to—"

"Get away," Vane snarled, his voice feral and cold. "Just leave us alone."

Val arched one regal brow. "There might be more Daimons coming."

"And I will kill them," Vane growled. "I will kill them all."

There was nothing more to be done to help them and Ash hated that most of all. The brothers needed time to grieve.

Disintegrating his staff, he turned toward Val who watched the brothers with a troubled gaze. "There was nothing more you could do," Valerius said to Vane. "Don't blame yourself."

Vane let out an inhuman snarl.

Ash pulled Val's arm and led him away from the scene before Vane attacked out of sorrow.

Val's features were still haunted with sympathy. "The innocent should never have to suffer from the battles of others."

"I know," Ash said, his heart heavy. "But it seems to always be the case."

Val nodded. "*A furore infra, libera nos.*"

Ash paused at the Latin quote. *Spare us from the fury within.* "You know, Valerius, there are times when I think you might actually be human after all."

Valerius scoffed at that. "Trust me, Acheron, whatever human part of me that ever existed was killed a long time ago."

Fury watched quietly for hours as Vane and Fang held their sister and wept like children. He remembered a time when he'd cried like that too, but it had been centuries ago.

He'd sent Liam on not long after the fight had ended to tell the rest of the pack what had happened, then stayed behind just in case there was more fighting to be done. Regardless of past battles, snipes, and ill feelings, Vane and Fang didn't need to stand alone right now. Everything they'd cared about was dead. It was a pain Fury wished on no one.

Fury's grief hit him on a different level. While they cried for the sister they'd lost, he cried internally for the sister he'd never know.

It was so hard to watch his siblings embrace like that while he stood on the outside.

Forever a stranger.

But he couldn't tell them the truth. Their own mother and the siblings he'd been raised with had turned on him and tried to kill him. The only woman he'd ever loved had been among those who turned on him. Why then would Fang and Vane ever accept the fact that he was born of the same cursed union that had birthed them?

Besides, now was definitely not the time for a family reunion.

He stepped forward tentatively. Not out of fear, but out of respect. "Guys? We've been here a long time. Since the Taser's worn off, I think we should be going."

Vane pinned him with the coldest dead stare he'd ever seen. He turned that look to Fang. "We need to give her a proper burial. We owe her that."

Fang wanted to scream and curse. He wanted to punch until the impotent fury inside him was quiet. But he didn't know if it would ever be quiet again. Something inside him was shattered. Anya wasn't supposed to die. She was supposed to be here. In all the hell and uncertainty that had been their lives, she'd been the one thing he and Vane had lived for. Their calming influence.

She'd made the wolf human.

Without her . . .

There was nothing inside him now but the wild animal that only wanted the blood of everyone around him.

Fury approached them slowly in human form.

"Where's Liam?" Vane asked.

"I sent him on to tell the others that the Daimons were defeated."

Vane scowled. "Why did you stay?"

Fury glanced to Anya's body. "I didn't think you two were in any shape to defend—"

"We're fine," Fang snarled, and grabbed him by the throat.

Fury covered his wrist with his hand and jerked it away. His turquoise eyes blazed with anger. "Grief or no grief, you ever touch me like that again and I will kill you."

Vane broke them apart. "There's been enough killing here tonight. We need to go."

Fury stepped back.

Fang started to apologize, but the words caught in his throat. Besides, he didn't owe the bastard anything. Fury was probably gloating over this. It would be typical of him.

Dismissing the thought, Fang stooped down to retrieve Anya's body. He stood slowly with Anya in his arms. Her fur tickled his skin. Over and over he saw images of her as a pup, as a teen, and as a woman. Most of all, he saw images of her as his sister and best friend.

Gods, how he'd miss her.

Vane sighed. "You ready?"

No. He would never be ready to say good-bye to her. But they couldn't stay here forever. So he nodded even though he wanted to die alongside her.

Using their powers, they found their pack and where they'd made a temporary den in Slidell. Not too far away since the burdened females couldn't travel easily, but far enough away that they should be relatively safe.

As soon as they appeared, all activity in the camp stopped.

Every eye, human and wolf, turned to them and Fang swore he could hear their sharp intakes of breath.

But it was their father's ashen look that stopped them from moving.

Fang was taken aback by his father's expression.

Was it even possible that the old bastard had feelings for them?

Yet there was no denying the anguish in his weary eyes.

Markus came forward. "Where are the young?"

Vane dropped his hand away from Anya's body. "She died before they were born."

Markus choked on a sob. Stunned by the unexpected show of emotion, Fang didn't move as his father came forward to hug Vane.

At least that's what it looked like he was going to do until his father snapped a small silver collar on his brother's neck. Before Fang could move, Stefan snapped one on him from behind.

Stepping back, Markus looked to the others around them. "It's time for a timoria. Kill them."

CHAPTER 10

Fang fought as Markus pulled Anya's body out of his arms. He didn't want to let her go, but with the collar on, he was virtually human with no powers and no strength to do much more than curse at them.

Stefan grabbed him and with the help of his bastard cronies, he was able to knock Fang to the ground and tie his hands behind his back. He tried to use his powers, but the collar prevented it. And in human form, he wasn't nearly as strong as he was as a wolf.

Vane was on the ground a few feet from him, also bound.

Fury pushed his way angrily through the crowd around them. His face was a mask of disgust as he looked at Markus. "May I speak on their behalf?"

Markus answered his question with a vicious backhand. Fury staggered back from the blow, his lip and nose bleeding profusely. "Only if you want to join them in their punishment."

The raw rage inside Fury's eyes was scorching. He met Fang's gaze and the sorrow and grief there caught Fang off guard. Why in the world would he give a shit if something happened to them?

Wiping his hand across his mouth, Fury stepped back and looked away.

"Sir?" Liam stepped forward this time.

Markus gave him a quelling glare and like Fury, he retreated.

"Is there another one of you bastards who wants to die with them?" Markus cast his furious grimace to all of them.

Fang expected no one to stand up for them and he wasn't disappointed.

Even Petra tucked her chin to her chest and retreated. So much for wanting to mate with him. Cowardly bitch.

Markus laid Anya's body down while Stefan and George hauled them to their feet. "As Regis of this clan, I proclaim Vane and Fang traitors to our people. Vane helped a Dark-Hunter to protect a *human*," he spat the word as if it were the most disgusting thing imaginable.

There was a sharp intake of breath as those words were unleashed.

Fang turned to Petra who refused to meet his gaze. Her cheeks were bright red. And his own anger mounted that she'd betrayed him. Why had he *ever* told her that?

Damn it, I should have known better.

When would he learn that people and animals only betrayed? No one was ever as loyal to him as he was to them.

Markus pointed at them. "Both of them fought against the Daimons to aid Dark-Hunters and both of them have been seen conspiring with those who hunt and kill our cousins, the Daimons. In retaliation for their actions, the Daimons have now attacked our people and threatened the existence of us all." He gestured down to his feet where Anya's body lay unmoving. "My daughter is now dead because of *them*."

The hypocrisy of that statement set fire to Fang's wrath. "Daughter? You've never before claimed her as such. We did nothing wrong! The Dark-Hunters tried to protect us while *you* ran."

"Silence!" Markus threw his hand out and a gag appeared over Fang's mouth. "As the leader and protector of our clan, I command all of you to a timoria."

Markus ripped the shirt from Fang's back while George ripped Vane's.

Fang met his brother's gaze. "*I'm so sorry, Vane,*" he projected mentally to him.

Vane offered him a tentative grin. "*We'll get through it. Don't worry.*"

Fang wanted to share that optimism, but he knew the truth.

They were both going to die tonight.

Fury turned aside as his brothers were tied to a tree and then beaten. Angry and bitter memories tore through him as he remembered their mother's people doing the same to him. Only in his case it'd been their mother who called for his timoria.

The reason for it had been the same as this one. Not that they were a threat to the clan. Not that they'd done anything wrong.

It was the fact that they'd been born to parents who hated them.

Guilt ate at him. He wanted to stop this. To protect them. But how could he?

The pack would turn on him too. And while he and

Liam had tried to speak up for them, no one would speak up for him. It would be as before and he would be attacked and left for dead.

If he was lucky. . . .

So he stood back, his inaction making him as guilty in this as the actual crimes against his brothers.

At least it's not you this time.

The excuse of a coward. Fury wanted to be better. To be as brave as they were and to stand by and take it.

But he wasn't. His fear overrode his bravery and he stood back even though he knew he should act. He tried to ease his conscience by saying that they wouldn't have defended him either.

Maybe it was true.

Fang hated him, he knew that. Since the day Fury had joined their clan, they'd never gotten along. They were too much alike.

And that made this even harder. He saw himself in Fang's eyes. Saw the pain, the betrayal. The brutal hatred.

Most of all, he saw the injustice.

"This is ridiculous," Liam growled beside him. "We should do something."

"Like what?"

Liam looked away, his lip curled. "It won't go well for the rest of us once they're gone. Stefan will be in charge now. Undisputed."

"Then challenge Markus."

Liam snorted. "I'm not strong enough."

And neither was Fury. While he could take Markus on pure animal strength, he was no match for his father's magick. Because he'd been kicked out of his mother's clan shortly after puberty, no one had tutored him on how to control his powers. He could change forms and travel through time and space, but that was about it. And even those he couldn't always control well.

Fury flinched as Fang and Vane were finally cut down. Their bodies were ravaged by the barbed whips to such a degree it sickened him.

They fell to their knees, panting and bleeding. His stomach churned at the sight. To be trapped in human form while a wolf was torture in and of itself. To be wounded while holding that form . . .

He could only imagine how excruciating their pain was.

And still they stood united. Neither was tearing at the other—blaming him for what was happening to them.

That was what Fury envied. It was a pure, loving bond that he'd never experienced or understood.

Vane and Fang were brothers.

To the end.

His hand trembling, Vane reached for Fang, who lay unmoving. His features were contorted by anguish. "Fang?" The torment and fear in that one weak call brought tears to Fury's eyes.

Fang closed his hand around Vane's.

The relief on Vane's face was potent. And short-lived as Stefan and George hauled them to their feet, then retied their hands behind their backs.

There was no pity or remorse on Markus's face. "Take them out to the swamp and leave them for the gators."

Those brutal words told Fury that he'd been right

when he decided to never let his father know he was his son. That lack of mercy. Lack of love . . .

Their mother had been right. Markus was an animal through and through. But then, she was every bit as brutal. Maternal instinct had passed her by so fast, it'd left a skid mark over her intolerant heart.

Fury started to leave until he heard a whisper on the wind. He turned to see Markus speaking into Stefan's ear.

"Hang them from a tree and then summon the Daimons to finish them off and tell them to take their time with it. I want them to suffer."

Stefan bowed his head in submission as anger tore through Fury.

And in that moment, Fury knew what he had to do. . . .

CHAPTER 11

Fang leaned his head back as his entire body ached and throbbed while he hung from a tree branch by a thin wire that cut so deep into his wrists, it sent rivulets of blood down his forearms. The blood dripped from his elbows straight into the murky water below and though he shouldn't hear the sound of it, he swore that he did.

Over and over, he saw the events that had led them here in his mind and he felt like total shit.

"I'm so sorry, Vane. I swear I didn't mean to get us killed like this."

Vane growled as he fell back from trying to pull himself up. Fang could tell his arms ached from the strain of lifting two hundred pounds of lean muscle up by nothing more than the bones of his wrists.

Fang took a deep breath, trying to ignore the severe pain of his own wrists as they throbbed and burned.

"Don't worry, Fang. I'll get us out of this."

Fang heard him, but the words didn't really register. He felt too bad about this situation. It'd been all his fault. Anya's death, their capture. He should have known his father would pull some kind of bullshit.

Why hadn't he seen it coming?

He could have fought harder. He *should* have fought harder. How could he have allowed them to be jumped so easily?

Now he was going to be the death of Vane too. . . .

When was he going to learn?

Vane strained against the sharpened cord that held his hands tied together above his head, secured to a thin limb as he hung precariously from an ancient cypress tree over some of the darkest, nastiest-looking swamp water he'd ever seen. He didn't know what was worse, the thought of losing his hands, his life, or falling into that disgusting gator-infested slime hole.

Honestly, though, he'd rather be dead than touch that stank. Even in the darkness of the Louisiana bayou, he could see just how putrid and revolting it was.

There was something seriously wrong with anyone who wanted to live out here in this swamp. At last he had confirmation that the Dark-Hunter, Talon of the Morrigantes, was a first-rank idiot.

Fang was tied to an equally thin limb on the opposite side of the tree where they dangled eerily amid swamp gas, snakes, insects, and gators.

With every movement Vane made, the cord cut into the flesh of his wrists. If he didn't get them freed soon, that cord would cut all the way through his tendons and bones, and sever his hands completely.

It would be the last mistake his father ever made.

At least it would be if Vane could get their asses out of this damned swamp without being eaten.

Both of them were in human form and trapped by the thin, silver metriazo collars they wore around their necks that sent tiny ionic impulses into their bodies. The collars kept them in human form. Something their father thought would make them weaker.

In Fang's case that was true.

In Vane's it wasn't.

Even so, the collars did dampen their ability to wield magick and manipulate the laws of nature. And that was seriously pissing him off.

Like Fang, Vane was dressed only in a pair of bloodied jeans. Of course, no one expected them to live. The collars couldn't be removed except by magick, which neither of them could use so long as they wore them, and even if by some miracle they did get down from the tree, there was already a large group of gators who could smell their blood. Gators who were just waiting for them to fall into the swamp and make them one tasty wolf meal.

"Man," Fang said irritably. "Fury was right. You should never trust anything that bleeds for five days and doesn't die. I should have listened to you. You told me Petra was a three-wolf-humping bitch, but did I listen? No. And now look at us. I swear if I get out of this, I'm going to kill her."

"Fang!" Vane snapped as his brother continued to rail while Vane tried to manage a few powers even through the painful electrical shocks of the collar. "Could you lay off the blame fest and let me concentrate here, otherwise we're going to be hanging from this damned tree for the rest of eternity."

Fang grunted as he tried to lift himself up too, but he was having even less success than Vane. For some reason he just couldn't manage to lift himself up very far.

Damn them for this. He looked at his brother and

sighed. "Well, not for eternity. I figure we only have about half an hour more before the cords cut completely through our wrists. Speaking of, my wrists really hurt. How about yours?"

Fang paused while Vane took a deep breath and felt a tiny movement of the cord coming loose.

He also heard the limb crack.

Fang panicked at the sound of the crack and at the sight of the gator that was waiting below to swallow them whole. Unable to deal with it, he reacted the only way he could. With words. "I swear I'm never going to tell you to bite my ass again. Next time you tell me something, I'm going to listen, especially if it concerns a female."

Vane growled. "Then could you start by listening to me when I tell you to shut up?"

"I'm being quiet. I just hate being human. This sucks. How do you stand it?"

"Fang!"

"What?"

Vane rolled his eyes. It was useless. Any time his brother was in human form, the only part of his body that got any exercise was his mouth. Why couldn't their pack have left Fang gagged before they strung him up?

"You know if we were in wolf form, we could just gnaw our paws off. Of course if we were in wolf form, the cords wouldn't hold us, so—"

"Shut up," Vane snapped again.

Fang grimaced as he continued to try and pull his legs up, but it was useless. His whole body was going numb and he couldn't stand the sharp stabs of pain the constricted blood flow was causing. "Does the feeling ever come back into your hands after they get all numb like this? This doesn't happen when we're wolves. Does it happen a lot to humans?"

Vane closed his eyes in disgust. So this was how his life would end. Not in some glorious battle against an enemy or his father. Not quietly in his sleep.

No, the last sound he would hear would be Fang bitching.

It figured.

He leaned his head back so that he could see his brother through the darkness. "You know, Fang, let's cast blame for a minute. I am sick and tired of hanging here because of your damned big mouth that decided to tell your latest chew toy about how I guarded a Dark-Hunter's mate. Thanks so much for not knowing when to shut the hell up."

"Yeah, well, how was I to know Petra would run to Markus and tell him you were with Sunshine and that he would think that was why the Daimons attacked us? Two-faced bitch. Petra said she wanted to mate with me."

"They all want to mate with you, dickhead, it's the nature of our species."

"Fuck you!"

Vane let out a relieved breath as Fang finally quieted down. His brother's anger should give him about a three-minute reprieve while Fang simmered for a more creative and articulate comeback.

Lacing his fingers together, Vane lifted his legs up. More pain sliced through his arms as the cord cut deeper into his human flesh. He only prayed his bones held a little longer without severing.

More blood ran down his forearms as he lifted his legs up toward the branch over his head.

If he could just get them wrapped . . . around . . .

He tapped the wood with his bare foot. The bark was cold and brittle as it scraped against the soft top-side of his foot. He cupped his ankle around the wood.

Just a little . . . bit . . .

More.

Fang snarled at him, "You are such an asshole."

Well, so much for creativity.

Vane focused his attention on his own rapid heart-beat and refused to hear Fang's insults.

Upside down, he wrapped one leg around the limb and expelled his breath. Vane growled in relief as the weight was mostly removed from his throbbing, blood-ied wrists. He panted from it while Fang continued his unheard tirade.

The limb creaked dangerously.

Vane held his breath again, terrified of moving lest he cause the branch to snap in two and send him plum-meting into the putrid, green swamp water below.

Suddenly, the gators thrashed about in the water, then sped away.

"Oh, shit," Vane hissed.

That was not a good sign.

There were only two things he knew of that could make the gators leave. One was for either Talon or Ache-ron to rein them in. But since Talon was off in the French Quarter saving the world and not in the swamp tonight, that seemed highly unlikely. As for Acheron, he had no idea where he'd gotten off to.

The other far less appealing option was Daimons—those who were the walking dead, damned to kill in order to sustain their artificially elongated lives. The only thing they prided themselves on killing more than humans were Katagaria Were-Hunters. Since the Were-Hunters' lives spanned centuries and they possessed magical abilities, their souls could sustain a Daimon ten times longer than the average human's.

Even more impressive, once a Were-Hunter's soul was claimed, his or her magical abilities were absorbed into the Daimons' bodies where they could use those powers against others.

It was a special gift to be a "nubby" treat for the undead.

There was only one reason for the Daimons to be here. Only one way for them to be able to find him and Fang in this isolated swamp where Daimons didn't tread without cause. Someone had offered the two of them up as a sacrifice so that the Daimons would leave their Katagaria pack alone.

And there was no doubt in his mind who had made that call.

"Damn you!" Vane snarled out into the darkness, knowing his father couldn't hear him. But he needed to vent anyway.

"What did I do to you?" Fang asked indignantly. "Besides getting you killed anyway."

"Not you," Vane said as he struggled to get his other leg up enough so that he could free his hands.

Something leapt up from the swamp into the tree above him.

Vane twisted his body to see the tall, thin Daimon standing just above, looking down at him with an amused gleam in his hungry eyes.

Dressed all in black, the blond Daimon clucked his tongue at him. "You should be happy to see us, wolf. After all, we only want to free you."

"Go to hell!" Vane snarled.

The Daimon laughed.

Fang howled as a Daimon sank fangs into his shoulder. He tried to head-butt him away. It was worthless. They swarmed over him like ants while he had no way to stop them. He tried to kick and bite . . . anything to attack them.

Nothing worked.

He was powerless to protect himself.

He was powerless to protect Vane. That knowledge washed over him like ice. He'd never known this feeling of utter helplessness. He was a fighter. A soldier.

How could he not be able to protect the very things he loved most? Anya was gone and now Vane . . .

"Get the fuck off me!" he snarled at the Daimons, trying his best to get free.

They sank their fangs in deep, tearing at his flesh. The pain of it was unbearable. He felt like he was being eaten alive.

Vane looked to see a group of ten Daimons pulling Fang down from the tree. Damn it! His brother was a wolf. He didn't know how to fight them in human form. At least not so long as Fang wore his collar.

Infuriated, Vane kicked his legs up. The limb broke instantly, sending him straight into the stagnant water below. He held his breath as the putrid, slimy taste of it invaded his head. He tried to kick himself to the surface, but couldn't.

Not that it mattered. Someone grabbed him by the hair and pulled him to the surface.

As soon as his head was above the water, a Daimon sank his fangs into Vane's bare shoulder. Growling in rage, Vane elbowed the Daimon in the ribs and used his own teeth to return the bite.

The Daimon shrieked and released him.

"This one has fight," a female said as she made her way toward him. "He'll be worth more sustenance than the other."

Vane kicked her legs out from under her before she could grab him. He used her bobbing body as a springboard out of the water. Like any good wolf, his legs were strong enough to propel him from the water to one of the cypress knees nearby.

His dark wet hair hung in his face while his body throbbed from the fight and from the beating his pack had given him. Moonlight glinted off his wet, muscled body as he crouched with one hand on the old wooden knee that was silhouetted against the backdrop of swamp. Dark Spanish moss hung from the trees and wood that jutted out as the full moon, draped in clouds, reflected eerily in the black velvet waves of the water.

Like the animal he was, Vane watched his enemies closing rank around him. He wasn't about to surrender himself or Fang to these bastards. He might not be dead, but he was every bit as damned as they were and even more pissed off at fate.

Lifting his hands to his mouth, Vane used his teeth to bite through the cord around his wrists and free his hands.

"You'll pay for that," a male Daimon said as he moved toward him.

His hands free, Vane backflipped from the stump into the water. He dove deep into the murky depths until he could break a piece of wood from a fallen tree that was buried there. He kicked his way back toward the area where Fang was being held down.

He came out of the water just beside his brother to find ten different Daimons feeding from Fang's blood.

He kicked one back, seized another by the neck, and plunged his makeshift stake into the Daimon's heart. The creature disintegrated immediately.

The others turned on him.

"Take a number," Vane snarled at them. "There's plenty of this to go around."

The Daimon nearest him laughed. "Your powers are bound."

"Tell it to the undertaker," Vane said as he lunged for him. The Daimon jumped back, but not far enough. Used to fighting humans, the Daimon didn't take into account that Vane was physically able to leap ten times as far.

Vane didn't need his psychic powers. His animal strength was enough to finish this. He stabbed the Daimon and turned to face the others as the Daimon evaporated.

They rushed him at once, but it didn't work. Half of a Daimon's power was the ability to strike without warning and to cause their victim to panic.

That would work if, as a cousin to the Daimons, Vane hadn't been taught that strategy from the cradle. There was nothing about them that made him panic.

All their tactic did was make him dispassionate and determined.

And in the end, that would make him victorious.

Vane ripped through two more with his stake while Fang remained unmoving in the water. His panic started to swell, but he forced it down.

Staying calm was the only way to win a fight.

One of the Daimons caught him with a blast that sent him spiraling through the water. Vane collided with a stump and groaned at the pain that exploded down his back.

Out of habit, he lashed back with his own powers only to feel the collar tighten and shock him. He cursed at the new pain, then ignored it.

Getting up, he charged at the two males who were heading for his brother.

"Give up already," one of the Daimons snarled.

"Why don't you?"

The Daimon lunged. Vane ducked under the water and pulled the Daimon's feet out from under him. They fought in the water until Vane caught him in the chest with his stake.

The rest ran off.

Vane stood in the darkness, listening to them splashing away from him. His heart pounded in his ears as he allowed his rage to consume him. Throwing his head back, he let out his wolf's howl that echoed eerily through the misty bayou.

Inhuman and baleful, it was the kind of sound that

would send even the voodoo mavens scurrying for cover.

Now certain that the Daimons were gone, Vane raked his wet hair from his eyes as he made his way to Fang, who still hadn't moved.

Vane choked on his grief as he stumbled blindly through the water with only one thought in his mind . . . *don't be dead*.

Over and over in his mind, he saw his sister's lifeless body. Felt her coldness against his skin. He couldn't lose them both. He couldn't.

It would kill him.

For the first time in his life, he wanted to hear one of Fang's stupid-ass comments.

Anything.

Images flashed through his mind as he remembered his sister's death. Unimaginable pain tore through him. Fang had to be alive. He had to.

"Please, gods, please," he breathed as he closed the distance between them. He couldn't lose his brother.

Not like this . . .

Fang's eyes were open, staring unseeingly up at the full moon that would have allowed them to time-jump out of this swamp had they not both been wearing the collars.

There were open bite wounds all over him.

A deep, profound grief tore through Vane, splintering his heart into pieces.

"C'mon, Fang, don't be dead," he said, his voice breaking as he forced himself not to cry. Instead, he snarled out, "Don't you die on me, you asshole."

He pulled his brother to him and discovered that Fang wasn't dead. He was still breathing and shaking uncontrollably. Shallow and raspy, the hollow sound of Fang's breaths was a symphony to Vane's ears.

His tears broke as relief pierced him. He cradled Fang gently in his arms.

"C'mon, Fang," he said in the stillness. "Say something stupid for me."

But Fang didn't speak. He just lay there in complete shock as he shook in Vane's arms.

At least he was alive.

For the moment.

Vane ground his teeth as anger consumed him. He had to get his brother out of here. Had to find someplace safe for both of them.

If there was such a place.

With his rage unleashed, he did the impossible—he tore Fang's collar from his throat with his bare hands. Fang turned instantly into a wolf.

Still, Fang didn't come around. He didn't blink or speak.

Vane swallowed the painful lump in his throat and fought the tears that stung his eyes.

"It's okay, little brother," he whispered to Fang as he picked him up from the foul water. The weight of the brown wolf was excruciating, but Vane didn't care. He paid no attention to his body that protested carrying Fang.

So long as he had breath in his body, no one would ever hurt anyone Vane cared for again.

And he would bring death to anyone who ever tried.

CHAPTER 12

Aimee dropped a plate as pain tore through her. Trying to breathe, she leaned against the sink.

"Something wrong?"

She looked at Tony, one of their cooks, and shook her head. "Just a weird twinge." Since he was human, it wouldn't do any good to explain to him what was happening with her and her powers.

Fang was hurt.

She could feel it. And more than that, she had an overwhelming need to find him.

Now!

Don't do it. . . .

He didn't want her around him. He'd made that more than clear. And yet she couldn't shake the feeling inside her that said it was imperative to get to him. He was too close to death. Closing her eyes, she zeroed in on him and saw Vane fighting Daimons while a group of them were feeding on Fang. She saw their collars vividly in the darkness and knew that made them helpless in the fight.

They'd be devoured.

Unable to stand it, she forgot about the plate and ran

for Peltier House. Dev had gotten off duty about an hour ago. She flashed herself up to his door and knocked on it.

"Come in."

She opened it to find him sitting on his bed, watching TV while flipping through a motorcycle magazine. "The wolves who saved me are in serious trouble. I can't leave them alone in this fight and I might need backup."

Dev didn't hesitate. "I'll grab Etienne and Colt. You get Alain."

Grateful for his understanding, she left him to go to the next room to knock on Alain's door. Before she could even lift her hand, her cell phone rang. Aimee answered it to find the wolf Fury on the other end.

"Were you serious about offering protection to Vane and Fang?" His voice was deadly earnest.

"Yes, why?"

"Because their father has betrayed them and left them for dead. There was nothing I could do, but I'm hoping you guys are able to save them."

She listened as he filled her in on more details than her vision had provided. Best of all, he gave her their exact location. "Why are you telling me this?"

"Because I owe them, but I can't do anything more. Save them, Aimee, please."

"I'll do my best."

"Thanks and I'll try to keep the pack away. Also, whatever you do, don't tell anyone about this call, especially not Vane or Fang." He hung up before she could respond.

She frowned at his parting words. What a weird request.

Shaking her head, she put her phone away, knocked on Alain's door, and told him what was happening. Like Dev, he shot to his feet to join her.

Once they were gathered together, she took them to where she'd seen Vane and Fang in her vision and to the location Fury had given her. The Daimons were already in flight as they came in.

To her left, Vane held Fang, who was now in wolf form. She ran to them with her brothers right behind her.

"Vane?"

He looked up with an angry snarl until he realized they weren't Daimons. His anger melted under a stern frown of confusion. "What are you doing here?"

She hesitated at telling him the truth. No one needed to know the extent of her powers or of her ability to hone in on other beings' whereabouts with an unerring accuracy. And most of all she didn't want to betray Fury.

"What happened?" she asked, trying to turn his attention from her to them.

Vane shook his head as if trying to wake up from a nightmare. "We were attacked. . . ."

"Look," Alain said, stepping forward. "I don't mean to be rude, but the Daimons are out in force tonight and while most of them are cowards, there's enough Spathi running around that we don't want to be caught out here undermanned. Let's get everyone back to Sanctuary and then talk."

Aimee couldn't agree more.

Vane eyed them suspiciously.

Dev put his hand on Vane's shoulder. "You saved Aimee and my father told you we would welcome you in anytime. We meant that. Now come on. Let's get you both cleaned up and tended to."

Aimee didn't move until they'd all vanished. She looked around the area as the events of the night played through her mind. Vane's and Fang's combined agony lingered here like a phantom wraith that haunted her.

Anya was dead and their pack had turned on them. She winced in pain as she felt for Fang. This wouldn't be easy on him.

Wanting to help, she flashed herself back to Sanctuary. Her brothers had taken Fang to Carson's examining room while they and Vane, who had dressed himself in a fresh pair of jeans and a T-shirt, stood in Carson's office, relaying the events to her brothers.

Carson was inside the other room alone with Fang.

She stood to the side of Dev and waited silently while they talked. It amazed her how much of the horror she'd seen in her visions that Vane left out. But then, maybe not. Admitting your father was out to kill you and your brother for no reason had to be hard on him. Who would want to tell that to complete strangers?

While they talked, she went to get food for Vane. She brought it back upstairs and set it down on Carson's desk.

Vane smiled gratefully. "Thank you."

She inclined her head to him. "Do you need anything else?"

He looked wistfully at the closed door that led to the room where Carson was treating Fang. "Guess not."

Aimee touched his shoulder in sympathy, knowing that the one thing he needed was for Fang to be normal and whole. For him to live through this attack.

And for some reason she couldn't name, she needed it too.

Carson came out of the examining room a little time later, after Vane had finished eating and she'd taken the dishes back to the kitchen.

Vane stood up immediately.

She could tell by the sadness in Carson's eyes that it wasn't good news.

"Well?" Vane tapped his hand against his thigh in nervous agitation.

Carson looked at him and sighed. "He's completely unresponsive."

Vane frowned. "What does that mean?"

"He's withdrawn into himself, probably from shock, and isn't reacting to anything I do."

That news didn't seem to please Vane any more than it pleased Aimee. "What about his wounds?"

"They'll heal, but I'm not sure about his mental state. Bones and scrapes, I can fix. What's wrong with him . . . you might need a psychologist."

Vane pushed past him. "Bullshit." He threw open the door to see Fang lying on the table in his wolf's form. But for the subtle rise and fall of his ribs, it would be easy to mistake him for a corpse. He didn't even twitch.

Aimee moved forward to watch as Vane embraced him.

"Fang? C'mon, buddy. Get up."

Fang ignored him completely.

Vane curled his fists in his brother's coat and tugged hard enough to make Aimee cringe. "Damn you. Get up!"

Fang didn't respond at all. He just lay there, unmoving, unblinking. It was as if he'd left this world and gone somewhere else completely.

Carson went to the opposite side of the table. Gently, he pulled Vane's hands away from Fang's fur. "He's not really here with us. It's like his mind can't handle whatever happened to the two of you and he's retreated deep inside himself."

Vane shook his head in denial. "He's stronger than this. He's always been stronger. . . ."

"Even the mightiest oak can be felled by a whisper of a wind if it comes on the heels of a powerful enough storm."

She swallowed the lump in her throat that burned from the sympathetic emotions choking her. Over and over, she saw Fang as he'd been that day she took the steak to him and he'd waited outside for his pack. There had been no weakness to him. He was raw power and integrity. How could this have happened to him?

She agreed with Vane. It didn't make any sense.

"Is there anything we can do?" she asked.

Carson sighed. "I have no idea. I'd say to call Grace Alexander and see if she can help."

Vane scowled. "Who is she?"

Carson smoothed Fang's fur down from where Vane had tugged at it. "She's married to a Greek demigod and is a licensed psychologist. She's the only one I know who might reach him."

Vane grabbed Fang's head and angled it so that Fang was staring blankly at him. "Look at me, Fang! Damn it, don't do this. I need you lucid. We can't stay here. Do you hear me? You have to wake up so that we can fight."

Carson pulled his hands away again. "I don't think

more violence is the answer. Let him rest tonight. Maybe he'll be better by the morning."

Dev and Alain came forward. "You want us to move him?"

Carson shook his head. "I think it best if he stays where he is for the time being. But I'm sure Vane would like a more comfortable place to spend the night."

Aimee put her hand on Vane's shoulder. "Go on and get a hot shower and rest for a bit. I'll stay here with Fang until you get back."

Vane hesitated. "I don't know."

She patted his arm and smiled. "It's okay, Vane. I'll call you if something changes. I promise."

He nodded glumly. The agony in his hazel eyes was haunting. She wished to the gods that she knew some way to ease the pain there, but there was nothing she could do for him except bring Fang back and right now that looked to be impossible.

Sighing, he pushed himself away and followed Dev and Alain from the room. Colt stayed behind with her while Carson returned to his desk to do paperwork.

Aimee pulled a blanket out of the closet to wrap it around Fang. She ran her hand through his soft fur, stroking it as tenderly as she could.

"I'm right here, Fang," she whispered. "Whenever you're ready to face the world again, you won't be alone. Vane is here and we're here. For you."

If the words reached him, she had no clue. He didn't even blink.

She looked up and caught Colt's gaze.

His gaze was empty and chilling. "I know that stupor he's in. It's the same one I had when my sister was killed."

"I remember," she said, thinking back to the night when Colt had shown up at their door after he and his sister had left them for a year. Their mother had been an Arcadian bearswan . . . her father's baby sister.

Colt and his sister had been born here. And alone he'd returned to them.

Family was family, and they had welcomed him back and kept him safe. He was like a brother to her too.

The funny thing was, whenever he called them cousins or cuz, people thought it an endearment. They had no idea they really were cousins.

Aimee jerked her chin toward the door. "Why don't you go on and rest. I'll be fine in here with him."

"You sure?"

She nodded. "Carson will be just outside."

"If you need anything . . ."

"I know. Thanks."

Aimee waited until she was alone with Fang. Leaning over, she put her face against his neck and held him close. "Wherever you are, Fang, you need to come back to us."

Fang jerked as he heard a soft voice whispering to him. "Aimee!" he called out.

No one answered. There was darkness all around him. It hung thick and heavy like icicles, freezing him as he trudged through dismal water that seemed to cling to his body. His teeth chattering, he had his arms wrapped around himself.

"Vane!"

Still there was no answer. Was he dead?

Was this hell?

It was the only rational explanation. Why else would it be so awful here?

"You're not dead."

He jerked around at the voice that came from behind him.

No one was there either. "Who said that?"

"I did."

He turned again as it spoke in his ear and once more, no one was there. "Who are you?"

"I am Misery."

He saw her then. A thin wraith of a being with flowing black hair that skimmed the palest white skin he'd ever seen. It was so pale, it held a grayish tint to it like ash. Her piercing eyes were dark and large. They seemed to be almost hollow.

"Where are we?"

She smiled wanly. "The Nether Realm."

Fang scowled at her answer. "The what?"

"We are caught in the place between the dead and the living. You were attacked by Daimons and they took enough of your soul that you are no longer alive. Yet you're not really dead. A part of you still lives on in the human realm. You are now trapped in the shadows like the rest of us."

"The rest of who?"

She held her hand up and he saw legions around them. Zombielike, they stumbled and moaned, trudging through the same thick water that clung to him. "We are the forgotten souls who have been relegated here by cruelty."

He shook his head, trying to make sense of all of this. How could he be here? "I don't understand. How did you get here?"

She pulled her arm down and the light faded. "I'm a demon who was trapped centuries ago. My family still searches for me, but they'll never find me. I shall live out eternity here in this slime. Unable to leave without human help. Unable to sleep or to eat real food. There is nothing here but suffering and longing." She sighed. "But sooner or later, your mortal body will die and you will be freed . . . unlike me. Even if I escape, I will never really be free."

Fang shook his head again. "Bullshit. This is just a dream. A screwed-up nightmare."

She laughed. "If only it were so."

Still he refused to believe it. She was lying. She had to be. He turned away from her and slapped himself. Hard. "C'mon, Fang, wake up."

Misery followed after him. "We all go through a period of denial. But it changes nothing. We are here and here we will stay."

"Vane!" Fang shouted as loud as he could, ignoring her and her dire prediction. He focused as hard as he could, trying to reach through this realm to his brother. *C'mon, buddy, hear me!* "Damn it, Vane! Wake me up!"

"The Harvesters are coming! The Harvesters are coming!" Frantic voices called out from the darkness.

Misery grabbed his arm. "Come, we must hide."

"Hide from what?"

"The Harvesters. If they find you, they'll destroy this part of you and you will be trapped here forever as their slave."

He scoffed. "What crap is this?"

She pulled him toward a murky crevice.

Fang started to tell her to stuff it, but bit his tongue. What if this wasn't a warped nightmare? He was a Were-Hunter. Of all creatures, he knew there was a lot more to the universe than a "natural" order.

Better to be safe than sorry until he figured out exactly what was going on here.

He tucked himself deep inside the cramped, craggy space. Out of the obsidian mist he could hear something coming closer. It sounded like human gurgles or nonsensical demonic speech. Eerie and frightening to even the stoutest of heart.

Closer they came.

Closer still, until he could see the outline of their large, twisted bodies. Like Misery, their hair flowed around them. Muscled and tall, they reminded him of ogres or trolls with long, sharp nails.

They closed in on one of the zombies he'd seen. Grabbing her, they tore through her neck with their teeth. She screamed out, then went silent and limp as the Harvesters seemed to inhale her essence. They cast her lifeless body aside as they searched for another victim.

Misery placed her finger to her lips to remind him to be silent.

"*What are they doing?*" he projected to her.

"*I told you, they're taking a part of them and leaving them stuck in this place forever. They are now the Harvesters' slaves and will do whatever they ask.*"

"For what purpose?"

"The Harvesters trade their collected parts to demons and their ilk in exchange for borrowing the demons' bodies so that they can escape from here for a time. They run us into the ground so that they can barter us. But they're not the only ones to be wary of. There are other demons who will try to enslave or torture you. This is a dangerous place for all of us."

Fang didn't move until long after the Harvesters were gone. Misery climbed out first. Hesitant and fearful, she reminded him of a timid rabbit. "They're gone, I think."

Fang was baffled by all of this. "I don't understand how I can be trapped here. I'm a Were-Hunter."

"And I'm a demon with powers far greater than yours, wolf. This is the vortex between dimensions. A hellhole of unimaginable cruelty."

"Then why are you helping me?"

She gave him an insidious half-smile. "Misery loves company."

"You're not funny."

She laughed as she danced around him. "Don't worry, Were-Hunter. Now come, we must be out of the main thoroughfare before the Harvesters return."

Fang wasn't so sure he should follow her, but he had no reason to doubt her. She was right, he knew nothing about this realm or its dangers and inhabitants.

"There has to be a way out of here."

Misery laughed. "Ever hopeful. I like that. But all the hope in the universe won't make a door appear when there's not one. Trust me."

He wished he could. But he wasn't naïve. He'd never

been. Following her warily, he tried his best to see through the darkness. It was oppressive.

Finally, they came to a hole that was cavelike and yet it curved upward toward the dismal black sky. Fang paused at the opening. "What is this place?"

"I call it home. Come, wolf."

Against his better judgment, he entered.

Misery laughed again as she flounced ahead of him. She reminded him of a child as she skipped and danced to a beat only she could hear.

Fang wasn't so enthusiastic and as he topped the narrow walkway, he finally understood his sixth sense. There below were hundreds of demons.

Misery turned to face him with a beaming smile as a large, ugly demon manifested by her side. "Look, Ceryon. I brought lunch!"

CHAPTER 13

Fang tried his best to turn into a wolf, but couldn't. This was so not good, but there was nothing he could do.

Fine. Human he was and human he'd fight if that was all that was left to him. But they were about to learn the one truth where he was concerned.

No one got the better of Fang Kattalakis. Ever.

"Let's dance, punks." He tried to blast them back.

His powers weren't working.

Oh, shit . . .

Misery laughed. "This isn't your realm, wolf. Here you're just a person . . . one with a life force that can feed us all."

Fang tsked at her. "Baby, I'm not worth the indigestion. Trust me." He slugged the first demon to reach him. The demon staggered away. He caught the next one with a blow to his chin that sent him reeling.

But he was seriously outnumbered.

Overwhelmed by the sheer size of their group, he was brought down hard on the cold, wet ground. Cursing, Fang did everything he could to break free.

It wasn't enough.

They pulled him deeper into the cave and strapped him down to a slab of stone.

"That's right, wolf. Fight us with everything you have." Laughter rang in his ears an instant before something hot pierced his thigh.

Fang cried out in pain.

More laughter filled his ears.

Misery came forward to look down at him. "The more you suffer, the stronger we become. We feed on pain. On misery. So give us your best."

A male stood beside her. "It's been a long time since we had one this strong here. How long do you think he'll last?"

"I don't know . . . it should prove interesting and, given his nature, it should be enough to break us out of here and into the mortal realm." She took the dagger from his hand. "In the meantime . . ."

She plunged it down through Fang's stomach.

"Did he eat?"

Vane swallowed at Mama Bear Peltier's question and shook his head. Fang hadn't eaten a bite since the bears had taken them in two days ago.

His brother was dying, and just like with Anya, there was nothing Vane could do to save him.

Impotent rage filled him and he wanted blood for what had happened to them. Not just to Anya, but to Fang as well.

Mama Bear smiled kindly at him. "If you need anything, ask."

Vane forced himself not to growl at her.

What he needed was his brother to be whole again.

But the Daimon attack had left Fang without any will to survive. They had taken more than his brother's blood, they had taken his dignity and his heart.

Vane doubted if his brother would ever be normal again.

Mama turned into her bear form and ambled off. Vane was only vaguely aware of Justin padding by outside in his panther form, followed by a tiger and two hawks. All were headed for their rooms where they could spend the day in their true animal bodies, safely locked away from the unsuspecting world.

If only he could do the same.

"It's a zoo, isn't it?"

He looked up at Colt's voice coming from the doorway. Standing six foot four, Colt was one of the members of the Howlers. Like Mama and her clan, Colt was a bear, but unlike them, he was also an Arcadian.

Vane was amazed the bears had tolerated one in their midst. Most Katagaria packs killed any Arcadian on sight.

He would have.

But then, Mama Lo and Papa Bear weren't the usual bunch.

"What do you want?" Vane asked.

Colt crossed his arms over his chest. "I was thinking . . . you know it would be a lot safer for everyone at Sanctuary if there were two Sentinels protecting the Peltiers."

Vane sneered at that. "Since when does a Sentinel protect a Katagaria clan?"

Colt gave him a droll stare. "That from a Sentinel who's stroking a Katagari wolf's fur?"

Rage darkened Vane's sight at the fact that Colt could see what he'd always kept hidden from everyone else. If it wasn't for the fact that he needed to stay here for Fang's welfare, he'd be lunging for Colt's throat. "I'm not a Sentinel and I'm not Arcadian."

"You can't hide from me, Vane. Like me, you've chosen to hide your facial markings, but it doesn't change what you are. We *are* Sentinels."

Vane cursed him. "I will *never* be a Sentinel. I refuse that birthright. I won't hunt and kill my own kind."

"Haven't you already done that?" Colt arched his brow. "How many Sentinels have you slain for your birth pack?"

Vane didn't want to think about that. That had been different. They'd threatened Anya and Fang.

Colt took a step forward. "Look, I'm not here to pass judgment on you. I'm just thinking it would be easier to—"

"I'm not staying," Vane snarled. "Wolves don't mix with others. Once I'm strong enough to protect Fang again, we're out of here."

Colt took a deep breath and shook his head. "Whatever." He turned around and left.

Vane's heart ached as he left the room long enough to take Fang's uneaten food to the kitchen.

If his brother didn't snap back soon, he didn't know what he'd do. They were both under a death sentence.

It wouldn't be long before their father would send scouts back to determine their fate. Once they found out that both of them had survived, assassins would be coming for them. He needed Fang mobile.

He could fight alone, but carting Fang's catatonic ass around with him wasn't going to be easy and it wasn't something he looked forward to doing when all he wanted was to lie down and lick his wounds too.

Damn Fang for being so selfish.

When Vane returned to his room upstairs, he found Wren just inside the door and Aimee Peltier on the bed beside Fang.

In his early thirties, Wren looked much younger. He wore his dark blond hair in dreadlocks and had yet to speak a word to Vane.

Mama Lo had told him that Wren had been brought to Sanctuary by Savitar himself. No one knew anything about Wren other than the fact that he was a Katagari hybrid and feral as hell.

Aimee was a beautiful blonde—that was, if a man liked his women extremely skinny, and Vane didn't. She was the pride and joy of the Peltier clan and from what he'd seen, she was one of the few truly kindhearted bears.

Vane frowned as Aimee leaned over and whispered something to Fang. She patted Fang's fur, then rose from the bed. She froze as she caught sight of Vane.

"What did you say to him?" Vane asked.

"I told him you were both welcome here. That no one would ever hurt him again."

Vane glanced at his brother. "We're not staying."

Wren gave him a wry smile. "Funny. That's what I said too, yet here I am."

"I'm not you, tigard."

Anger flashed in his eyes.

Vane braced himself for the attack.

Aimee separated them. "Go on to bed, Wren. I know you're tired."

That seemed to diffuse his temper enough that he turned around and left.

Aimee faced Vane. "I know what Carson said about Fang, but . . ."

"What?"

She looked past him to where Fang lay in his stupor. "I don't know. This just doesn't seem like Fang to me. He's not the kind of person to simply withdraw into himself like this and not come out of it."

Vane scoffed. "You don't know my brother. He's not used to anyone getting the better of him. Ever. He took a hard blow to his ego in the swamp, but he'll be fine. I know it." Vane looked over his shoulder at his brother. "He'll be better by the morning."

Aimee didn't respond to that. It was what Vane had been saying since they arrived. She didn't believe it any more than he did.

But she did sense something was greatly wrong. She couldn't put her finger on it. . . .

Yet the feeling persisted.

"Good night," she said, offering Vane a smile before she left them.

Still unsettled, she made her way to her room where she readied herself for bed. As she washed her face and brushed her hair, she couldn't shake the feeling deep inside her. It was like Fang was calling out to her. Like there was something he wanted her to know.

Frustrated, she went to her nightstand and grabbed her cell phone. She'd never dialed Acheron before, but she couldn't think of anyone else who might be able to help her.

He answered on the first ring.

"Hey, Ash, it's Aimee Peltier. How are you?"

"Confused. How did you get my number?"

Aimee raked her hand through her hair as she paced over the Oriental rug in her room. "Dev gave it to me when you gave it to him. Just in case."

"Ah. Sorry for my abruptness. I'm not used to you guys calling me. It's usually one of the Dark-Hunters whining."

She laughed. "Yeah, I guess so."

"So what can I do for you?"

"I . . ." She hesitated at what to say. He'd probably think her insane. How could she explain the feeling to him when even she didn't understand it? "What do you know about Daimon attacks?"

His rich laughter filled her ear. "Not a single damn thing. Why?"

She rolled her eyes at his sarcasm. Yeah, it was a stupid question given the fact he'd been fighting them for more than eleven thousand years. "I don't know if you've ever met Fang Kattalakis, but he was attacked by Daimons a couple of days ago and—" Her words died as Ash appeared beside her dressed all in black. His long hair matched his clothes except for the deep burgundy stripes in it. Though he was the oldest of the Dark-Hunters in age, physically he looked only twenty-one.

"What happened?"

Aimee was too busy gaping at his unexpected entrance in her bedroom to answer his question. Standing a mean six foot eight, the man took up a lot of space in her room and possessed a raw aura of power and an unnatural sexual appeal. "How did you do that? I didn't know Dark-Hunters could teleport."

"Some of us can. Now what happened to Fang?"

She closed her phone and returned it to the table. "He was attacked in the swamp and now he's comatose."

"But not dead?"

"No, he's not dead."

He let out a relieved breath. "Where is he?"

Aimee led him from her room down the hall to where Fang had been given his own room. She knocked on the door and waited for Vane's sharp growl before she pushed it open to find them where she'd left them.

Vane shot to his feet the moment he saw Acheron. "What are you doing here?" His tone was accusatory and cold.

"I heard about Fang. What happened?"

A tic started in Vane's cheek. "It was a timoria. We were left for dead and then attacked by Daimons."

After entering the room, Ash knelt beside the bed to examine Fang's body. He put one large hand on Fang's neck, then he pulled back his eyelids.

Aimee exchanged looks with Vane. "Carson says he's in shock from the attack."

"He says he's dying," Vane added.

Ash dropped his hand and looked up at them. "This is strange. It's like he's already dead."

"Don't say that!"

Ash ducked as Vane would have hit him. "You can attack me all you want to, but it changes nothing."

Aimee put her hand on Vane's arm, trying to comfort him. "Have you ever seen anything like this?" she asked Ash.

"Not in eleven thousand years and I don't get it either. Daimons can feed from humans and Were-Hunters without causing harm. Yet this . . ."

Aimee swallowed. "It's like they took his soul."

"No," Vane said with a sigh. "They took more than that. It's Anya. He can't stand letting her go." He moved back to sit beside Fang. "I don't think he's able to handle the grief of living without her."

Aimee motioned Ash out of the room.

In the hallway, she closed the door tight behind her and hoped Vane wasn't listening. "Do you think it's that simple?"

He shook his head.

"Me either."

Ash glanced back at the door as if he could see inside the room. "Let me check with Savitar. I'm with you. I think there's more going on here than the obvious."

"Thanks."

He inclined his head before he left her alone. Aimee made her way back to her room where she finished getting ready for bed.

The dawn was just breaking when she finally drifted off.

"Aimee?"

"Fang?" Her dreams shifted until she saw him engulfed in a dark mist. He looked tired and pale, but whole. He was dressed only in a pair of bloodied jeans and his bare feet were marked with cuts and bruises.

Running toward him, she tried to reach out only to have him drift away. "Fang!" she called.

"Shhh," he breathed, his voice echoing in the darkness.

"Where are you?"

"I don't know. A cave."

She started forward until he grabbed her and shoved her back against a craggy wall.

"Don't move." His tone was a scarce whisper.

Aimee trembled at his nearness. She'd forgotten just how tall and formidable he was in his human form. But he smelled delectable and looked even better. With a week's growth of whiskers, he had a rugged appearance that only added to his raw sexual appeal.

Wrapping her arms around him, she held him close, reveling in the hardness of his body. Reveling in the fact that he was with her and not dead.

He balled his fist in her hair and buried his face in her neck as if she were a lifeline he clung to. No one had ever held her with such fierce tenderness. Gods, how good he felt and how much she wanted to stay right here with him.

But something wet and warm was tickling her stomach. It was only then she realized what it was. Fang was bleeding profusely from a wound in his stomach. Gasping, she pulled back to see his blood coating her gown. "What on earth?"

He covered her hand with his and pulled it away from his wound. "A group of slug demons attacked me. I got away, but it wasn't easy." He grimaced in distaste. "Look, I don't have long before they find me again, and you can't stay here. If any of them find *you*, they'll kill you, or worse, take you prisoner."

"I don't understand."

He swallowed before he spoke again. "I can't wake up, Aimee. I need someone to find the Daimons who fed from me and kill them."

She scowled. "What?"

"The Daimons . . . they sucked out enough of my soul that they have it trapped inside them. So long as they live, I can't wake up or use my powers—they have those as well. Someone has to kill them so that I can be whole again. Do you understand?"

She nodded. "How will I find them?"

He took her hand in his and held it to his bare chest, just over his heart. The warmth of his skin sent chills over her. "Use your powers."

Closing her eyes, she focused on the night he was attacked. One by one, she saw the faces of the Daimons who'd brutalized him.

He leaned to whisper in her ear, his voice deep and seductive. "I can't do this alone, Aimee. I can't find them from here."

She frowned at his request, which was so out of character. Fang never asked for help from anyone. "Who are you?"

He cupped her face in his hands. "It's me. I swear it."

"No. Fang wouldn't ask for help. Not from me."

He laughed bitterly. "Trust me, this isn't what I want to do either. But I can't fight this on my own. I've tried everything and Vane isn't answering. He thinks I'm a dream and no matter what I try, he won't respond.

You're the only one who's come to me. Please, Aimee. Don't leave me here like this."

Uncertainty filled her. "How do I know it's you?"

He answered her question with a passionate kiss, one that left her breathless and hot. Needy. Trembling. Oh, yeah . . . this was Fang. There was no doubt. No one else kissed like he did. And no one held his scent.

He pulled back, his eyes tormented. "Get me out of here. Please. You're the only hope I have."

She nodded as a fierce screech sounded.

Fang pulled back sharply. "The Harvesters are coming again. Go, baby." He kissed her on the cheek. "Don't come back here. It's not safe for you."

He pushed her away and was gone.

Aimee woke up trembling.

Panicked, she looked around the room to see the sun much higher in the sky as it streamed in from between the slits of her blinds. Squinting, she looked at her clock. 10:00 A.M.

It was just a dream.

Then why was she so haunted by it? Aimee rolled over and tried to go back to sleep. *I need more than five hours . . .*

Still, she couldn't shake the desperate sound of Fang's voice in her head.

He needed her.

She scoffed at herself. "He's in his bed, idiot. Go back to sleep."

She couldn't. No matter how hard she tried, she just couldn't relax or get the sense of urgency to leave her. Berating herself for the stupidity, she got up, threw on her fuzzy green bathrobe, and padded down the hallway toward Fang's room.

"Gah, you look like shit."

She glared at Dev as he met her in the hallway. "At least I have a reason to, bud. Did you break your mirror this morning or what?"

Dev laughed as he kept walking away from her. "I thought you were on the evening shift."

"I am. I'm just going to the bathroom."

He gave her a devilish grin. "I left the seat up."

"Of course you did. At least you warned me this time."

He wrinkled his nose playfully at her before he vanished.

Shaking her head at her brother and his antics, she redirected her steps to Fang's room. She nudged open the door to make sure he was alone, which, thankfully, he was. Vane must have finally gone to his own room.

Aimee slipped into the room and shut the door.

Everything here was quiet. Not even a whisper could be heard.

I am out of my mind. . . .

She had to be.

Moving to stand beside his comatose body, she placed her hand on his soft fur. His breathing was shallow, but steady. There was no sign of violence or of anything.

Fang was fine.

Except for the fact that he refused to rejoin the world. She didn't understand that kind of weakness. He'd seemed so strong and capable. What had happened to make him shatter like this?

It didn't make sense.

But there was nothing she could do for him. Stroking his ear, she sighed. "Sleep well, baby." Then she turned and went back to her room.

Berating herself for being ten thousand times a fool, she pulled her robe off and tossed it to the bed.

As it fell, she saw something strange. . . .

A stain.

A *red* stain.

Confused even more, she looked down at her gown and saw the blood from Fang's wound. And as she caught sight of herself in the mirror, she saw something else that added veracity to her dream. Her face was marked from Fang's whiskers. Her lips swollen from his kiss.

It'd been real.

All of it.

Fang was trapped and she was the only hope he had of coming back. . . .

CHAPTER 14

"What are you doing?"

Aimee jumped at the unexpected sound of Dev's angry tone coming out of the darkness of the hallway while she was trying to slip out without being seen. Why hadn't she just popped outside instead of going to the bathroom like a normal human being?

That'll learn you.

"Damn it, Devereaux Alexander Aubert Peltier, I swear I'm going to put a bell on you if you don't stop sneaking around here without making any noise! What do you do? Wait until I leave my room to pounce on me like a cat with a mouse?"

Narrowing his gaze on her, he crossed his arms over his chest in a tough stance. "You only get angry at me when I've caught you doing something you shouldn't be doing. So what are you up to?"

She tried not to look guilty, but it was hard. "I'm not doing anything."

He raked a look over her that said he knew better. "So why aren't you working tonight?"

"I didn't feel good."

He cast a pointed stare at her white sneakers. "Which is why you're dressed to go out?"

And she would have made it had he not butted in. "I didn't say I was going out."

He snorted. "Don't treat me like an idiot, Aim. I know you better than that. Something's up. It's been up for weeks now with your freaky disappearances. What is it?"

She let out an aggravated breath. He was right. For weeks she'd been searching for the Daimons to no avail. Those little rodents were good at hiding. "You wouldn't believe me if I tried to explain it."

"Try me."

Don't say a word. She saw this train wreck coming and yet there was no way to prevent it. If she didn't answer, he'd nag her until she did.

Or worse, follow her. The bear could be terribly annoying that way.

So with no choice, she opted for the truth. "Fine. I'm heading out to hunt Daimons."

He burst out laughing. "And I'm a flying fat fairy."

"Nice . . . Tinker Bell. Now if you'll excuse me."

He grabbed her arm to keep her by his side. "You're serious?"

"Like Maman about locking the back door."

He shook his head in total disbelief. "Why in the name of Olympus would you go out hunting a Daimon?"

She glanced down to the door where Fang's room was and knew she couldn't disappoint him. "Because if I don't, Fang will die."

He snorted. "Are you high?"

"No."

"C'mon, Aim, admit it. Heavy amounts of drugs are involved here. They have to be."

She shrugged his touch away. "I have to go."

He captured her again. "I don't think so. Last time I checked, we weren't Dark-Hunters and you've got no business going after a Daimon."

And once again, she pulled away from him. "What am I supposed to do, Dev? Vane was thrown out of here this morning and he has his hands full with his pack on his tail and the human he's now protecting. The last thing he needs is to know that Fang is far from safe. That demons are trying to kill him in another realm. It's not exactly something he can focus on right now."

"Aimee—"

"Devereaux," she snapped, mocking his sinister tone. "You know I can't just walk away."

"Why not?"

"Fang saved my life. Now his is threatened and he's asked for my help. You know what will happen if the Daimons keep his soul. Sooner or later, it will die and he will be trapped lifeless and soulless without friend or family—that's something I wouldn't wish on my worst enemy, never mind a wolf who saved my life and yours. I only have a finite time to save him."

Dev growled low in his throat. "*We* only have a finite time."

"We?"

He gave her a harsh stare. "You didn't really expect me to just stand by and let you endanger your life, did you? If you're in, I'm in."

Aimee hugged him. "You're the best."

"No. I'm the worst. Maman will hand me my ass on

a platter if she ever learns about this. I swear to the gods, I have to be the dumbest asshole on the planet to sign on for this."

"No. You're the greatest brother ever born and I will be forever in your debt."

"Oh, goody," he said with exaggerated happiness. "Just what I've always wanted." He let out a tired sigh before he groused, "So what are we doing?"

"Well, the Daimons attacked them in the swamp. That means that they're here in New Orleans . . . somewhere. I say we start hitting their usual haunts until we find them and expire their worthless hides."

"And how will we know when we find them?"

"I'll know. I've seen them."

He made another face of utterly exaggerated thrill. "And how will we know then, Wendy?"

She hated when he referred to her as the Peter Pan character. But she ignored his goad. "Fang showed me. Now let's get started."

He stopped her again. This time his face was dead serious and he was all business. "Showed you how?"

"In a dream."

That went over like a lead balloon. His eyes snapped fire at her. "Should I be banning you from his room?"

She rolled her eyes at his extremely overprotective nature, which was highly misplaced so long as Fang was in a coma. "Don't be ridiculous and we need to get going. Otherwise I'm going alone."

He curled his lip at her in a fierce grimace. "Fine, you pigheaded bear."

* * *

Fang hissed as the demon's blade cut through his side and came out his back. Infuriated, he grabbed the spear and held it in his side with one hand while he rebounded with an upward stroke of his sword that opened the demon's chest.

Screaming out, it died at his feet.

His side throbbing, Fang staggered back, panting from the pain as he wrenched the spear through his tissue and threw it to the ground. Sweat and blood covered him as a chill wind froze his skin and that nasty water lapped at his legs. He was so tired of this place. Of fighting every minute for survival. Part of him was ready to lie down and let them have him, but the other . . .

It didn't know how to give up or give in.

Wiping the sweat from his brow, he lowered the sword he'd taken off another kill and listened to the howling winds that whipped around him. His entire body shook from the cold and agony of his wounds. The storm made it hard to tell if the Harvesters or demons were near and that was the worst part of all.

Twice Misery had stumbled upon him with her crew in tow and while he'd done his best, he had yet to kill that little bitch.

If only he could reach Vane and let him know what was happening. Vane would be a vital ally, but his brother wouldn't believe him. He kept thinking it was a dream or that he was crazy whenever he heard Fang's voice.

Damn you, Vane.

Only Aimee had responded to his call. Only she had believed that the hell he was locked in was real.

Aimee . . .

He sank down by a black tree to rest as an image of her sweet face hung in his mind. He swore he could still smell her. Feel the softness of her skin. And there in the darkness, he found momentary comfort in those thoughts.

Would he ever be able to hold her again?

Gods, to have five minutes where nothing was hunting him, where he wasn't fighting so that he could just hold her close and let her body soothe him.

A screech sounded over his head.

Fang pressed himself closer to the tree as he recognized the Reaper's call. They were taloned and winged demons who would rip apart any creature they found. There was nowhere safe here in this world. Everything was a predator.

Sometimes even the foliage.

But these spindly black trees had proven safe. They alone gave him shelter here. "At least I'm learning to fight as a human." Sickening though it was, he'd become quite accomplished over the months spent here.

Or was it years?

He was having a hard time judging time. But he could hear things from the other side. He knew Vane was mated and he'd heard the times his brother had cursed him for being selfish by not waking up.

As if he wanted to be here.

Only Aimee had continued to whisper comfort to him. *Take your time, Fang. Sleep well.* When nothing else could reach him, he'd felt her gentle hands on his skin.

And that kindness had kept him going and made

him weak as he longed for a world he wasn't sure he'd ever reach again.

But she wasn't there tonight. He didn't feel or hear her at all. And that emptiness was far worse than the horrors that made up this netherworld.

Fang cocked his head as he heard the Reaper approach. Glancing about, he tried to find a better place to hide.

There. To his left was a cave.

He headed for it, hoping there wasn't something worse inside it, waiting to attack. But as he neared the opening, a sharp white stab hit him straight in his chest. The pain was so severe it sent him skittering to the ground where he tried to rise again.

He couldn't. The agony was paralyzing.

The Reaper honed in on him.

Fang cursed. He reached for his sword, but another stab caught him and pinned him to the ground.

Unable to bear it, he screamed out and as he did so, he felt a jolt inside. Warm and fierce, it spread through him like lava.

It was his powers.

Gasping, he threw his hand out toward the Reaper and sent a blast straight at it. The demon screeched as it was fried on the spot.

Fang let out a victorious cry as he realized what had happened.

Aimee had killed one of the Daimons and freed part of his soul. Though he still wasn't whole, he at least had something better than his own two hands to protect himself with. For that he owed her everything.

"That a girl. Baby, I could kiss you!" He held his

hand up and saw the small glow of power emanating from his fingertips. He threw his hand out and blasted the tree where he'd been a few moments before.

It went up in flames.

Clenching his hand into a fist, he had one more thing he was dying to try.

Fang closed his eyes and tried to shift forms so that he could be a wolf again.

Nothing happened.

"Damn it." He was still human.

It was okay. At least he had some of his powers back and right now, that was worth everything to him.

"So you have a helper. . . ."

He spun around to find Misery there. How the hell was she able to do that? It was like she had a beacon on him.

On instinct, he shot a blast at her. She rolled away from it and returned it with one of her own.

Fang twisted away before it struck him and bent down to retrieve his sword. He slashed at her feet, but she was as quick as the wind.

Her laughter rang in his ears. "Cey! We have a new victim!" She smiled brightly at Fang. "By her actions tonight, you've opened the door for us. Thank you, wolf."

Fang lunged at her. "Don't you touch her!"

Laughing, she vanished before he could make contact.

He howled in frustration. "You bitch! Come back here." But he knew it was no good. Misery didn't listen to him.

"Aimee," he whispered. "Please guard your back."

* * *

"Aimee!"

Aimee cursed as Dev snatched her back. "What?"

He pointed to the piece of missing sidewalk at her feet. "You were about to trip."

"Well, you don't have to scream at me. Sheez!" Her heart was pounding from the scare he'd given her. Here they were hunting Daimons and he was afraid she'd trip on a piece of sidewalk?

The bear was out of his mind and had a most screwed-up sense of priorities.

He flashed her a taunting grin. "Yelling at you is what I do *second* best."

She snorted. "I would ask what your first best is, but I don't think I want to know. Man-whore that you are, I'm sure it involves women somehow."

He laughed as he led her down a side street. "I'm not sure we're going to find any more of your Daimon friends tonight. Looks like they're fat and happy and hiding."

She hated to admit it, but he was probably right. They'd been searching for hours. "We're lucky we got the one. There's no telling where the others are."

"How many are we looking for anyway?"

"Nine. Well, eight now."

He gaped indignantly at the number. "Eight? Are you out of your friggin' mind? Nine? How do you propose we find *eight* unknown Daimons?"

She shrugged. "We could always invite them to Sanctuary and kill them out back."

He rolled his eyes at her. "You've gone mental, haven't you?"

"Well, I'm out here with you. It kind of says it all."

He let out a long-suffering sigh as if she were torturing him. "And to think I could be at the door right now, checking out long legs and short skirts."

She gestured toward the street. "Don't let me keep you."

Dev's face went pale as he looked past her.

Aimee turned her head to see what he was looking at, then froze as she saw the shadows stepping out of the walls. These weren't Daimons.

They were demons.

And they were coming for them.

CHAPTER 15

"No!" Fang shouted as he saw images on the cave's wall of Misery and company surrounding Aimee and Dev.

He slammed his fist against the rock, ignoring the pain, as he realized he about to be the death of another woman. It was just like Stephanie all over again. His enemies had found her because of him.

When will I learn? Women were to be protected and he was cursed where they were concerned. It was why he'd tried so hard not to get close to another one.

Aimee shouldn't mean anything to him, but she did, and the thought of her dying tore him apart.

Growling in frustration, he threw his back against the wall so that he wouldn't have to watch her die. But it didn't work. In his mind, he saw what was about to happen and it sickened him.

What could he do? He was trapped here with hardly any powers or much strength. There was nothing here but soul-sucking demons.

Demons . . .

In that instant he knew what he could do to save her. There was one thing a demon and a Daimon had in common. One thing they both needed to thrive and survive.

A soul.

And while he may not have all of his, he had enough of one to entice them.

Fang threw his sword down into the black water. "Demons!" he shouted. "I have a soul for you! Come get some."

No sooner had the words left his lips than the sound of a thousand wings filled his ears. The stench of sulphur and demon body odor invaded his nostrils. He hated this. But he had no choice.

It was him or her and he wasn't about to let it be her.

"Are you out of your ever-loving mind?"

He scowled as a tall, lean man appeared beside him. Dressed in a bloodred cloak that covered black spiked armor, he had eyes so light a blue they were piercing. His brown hair was shoulder length with the front of it falling into those eyes that seemed to hold the wisdom of eternity.

And a cruelty that was unrivaled.

Completely calm against the invading horde, he cocked one finely arched brow. "What are you trying to do?"

Fang refused to answer. "Who are you?"

One side of his mouth quirked up into a hint of a taunting grin. "At the moment, the only friend you have."

"Yeah, right."

The demons came rushing in.

Fang braced himself for their attack. "My soul is—" A muzzle appeared over his face.

The man winced. "Don't even say it, kid. You have no

idea what it means to have your soul sold. Trust me. It ain't pleasant and you really don't want to offer it up to this bunch. Not when you can do so much better with it."

Fang glared at him as he blasted him.

He absorbed the blast without flinching or moving. "Don't waste the energy. It takes something a lot stronger than you to budge me." Turning around, he shot a bolt of fire at the demons.

Screeching, they retreated.

His face a mask of utter irritation, he pulled a small cell phone from his right greave and held it like a walkie-talkie. "Break them down and send them back."

"Do we have to be nice?" a thickly accented male voice asked.

"Hell, no. Make them suffer."

"Thanks, boss."

The man returned the phone to his armor and met Fang's baffled expression. "Oh. Sorry about the muzzle. But it was necessary to protect you from your own stupidity."

It vanished from Fang's face. He rubbed his jaw where it had been while he glared at the stranger who was too at ease with banishing demons. "Who the hell are you?"

The man laughed. "That's a little more astute than you realize. The name's Thorn and as I said, I'm the only friend you have right now."

"No offense, Misery told me that too and you can see how well that's turned out." He gestured toward the wounds that marred him from head to toe.

Thorn took the sarcasm in stride and returned it with some of his own. "Yeah, well, in case you haven't noticed, I'm not Misery. At least not unless you get on my bad side. Then . . . well, let's just say those who go there don't enjoy the experience."

Fang ignored his warning though he could tell by his demeanor that being on Thorn's bad side could be dire indeed. "Then what are you?"

He lowered his cowl. There was an incongruous air around him. One of power and complete cruelty. Yet at the same time, it was as if he kept that under a tight leash. As if he were at war with himself.

How strange.

"Think of me like a governor or a wrangler. It's my job to make sure that the inmates here obey the laws, especially when they go out on parole."

"What laws?"

He smiled evilly and ignored Fang's question entirely. "You've surprised me, wolf, and not many people do that . . . at least not in a good way."

"How do you mean?"

Thorn clapped him on the back. One second they were in the cave and in the next inside a grand obsidian hall. Light glowed from iridescent sconces that were shaped into the twisted faces of gargoyles and skeletal hands. The ceiling arched up a good thirty feet with buttresses that had been carved into the shape of human spines. Opulent, huge, and creepy as hell, it was cold and completely uninviting.

The only thing even remotely appealing here was the giant hearth where a massive fire blazed. A hearth that was flanked on each side by the winged skeletons of two Reapers. Both of which still had a dagger wedged in their rib cages.

Fang grimaced at the sight, wondering if they were real or nothing more than morbid decoration.

Or maybe both. . . .

"What is this place?"

Thorn whipped his cloak off with a flourish. The black armor gleamed in the low light that highlighted the deadly spikes on it. "Stygian Hall. Stupid name, I know, but to my credit, I didn't come up with it. I'm merely the current fool watching over it." A goblet of wine appeared in his hand. He held it out to Fang.

Fang declined to take it.

Thorn laughed evilly. "Afraid I've poisoned or drugged it? Trust me, wolf. I don't need a liquid to do either. If I wanted you dead, I'd be feasting on your meat right now." He took a deep swig of the wine.

Fang was losing patience with all the cryptic bullshit. He'd never had patience for such. "Look, I'm not really chatty and your dramatics are boring the crap out of me. Who are you and why am I here?"

Thorn tossed the cup into the hearth, causing the flames to explode. As those flames curled toward him, his clothes changed from armor into a modern beige suit with a light blue shirt. Instead of an ancient warrior, he looked like a billionaire CEO. Except for his left hand, which was still covered with the metallic claws that had been part of his armor.

"I'm the leader of an elite group of warriors known as Hellchasers."

Fang arched a brow at the name. "Hellchasers?"

Thorn inclined his head. "When demons violate the laws that govern them or decide to skip out on their parole, we're the ones who deal with them."

"Deal with them how?"

Thorn spread his hand and an image flashed up on the dark wall to Fang's left. Misery and her crew were being hauled back into their realm in chains. Bloody and bruised, they looked like someone had used their bodies as target practice. It was obvious the two men bringing them back had been anything but gentle. "In short, we're bounty hunters without a bounty."

"Then why do it?"

Thorn clenched his fist closed and the image faded. "Mostly for shits and giggles. But if we didn't do it, the demons would overrun the human realm and it would quickly look like this one."

"Scary thought."

Thorn inclined his head. "Luckily, we think so too, which is why we do what we do."

"So how do I play into this?"

Thorn approached him slowly as he raked a speculative glance over his body as if judging every molecule of his being, inside and out. "You've got certain talents that appeal to me. A wolf who's survived with demons on his own and without his powers . . . impressive."

That did nothing except ignite Fang's anger. "Yeah, and why didn't you step in before now?"

"Because I thought you belonged here. That you'd been consigned to this realm for past deeds. It wasn't until you started to offer your soul up to protect Aimee that I realized you're here by mistake."

"You're not very intuitive, are you?"

Instead of being pissed, Thorn took the insult in stride. "Let's just say I seldom see the good in others. It's such a rare commodity in the world that I don't even bother to look for it." Thorn spread his arm out and a banquet of food appeared on the table. "You must be hungry."

"Yeah, and I don't eat at anyone's table I don't know."

One corner of his mouth lifted in bitter amusement. "You're wise to think that."

"I also know nothing comes without strings." Fang jerked his chin toward the table. "What's the price of that food?"

"I would say it's a gift to ease my conscience for leaving you here so long when you didn't belong, but I have no conscience and honestly don't give a shit how much you've suffered."

"Then why do you corral the demons to protect the human world?"

Thorn let out a long-suffering sigh as if irritated that Fang had brought the subject up. "So apparently I do have a conscience after all. Damned thing that. I keep denying it, but it won't go away. However, that's not the point. On Mardi Gras night, a few hundred demons were let loose from Kalosis. Ever heard of it?"

"No."

Thorn shrugged. "In short it's the Atlantean hell realm. The demons ate a couple of my men and I now find myself rather shorthanded in New Orleans." He opened his mouth as if he were shocked. "Oh, wait! That's where you're from . . . now do you see?"

"You want me to help gather them."

"Not exactly. More you're to help keep tabs on them and if they step over the line, you bring them back over it . . . or kill them."

"And if I refuse?"

Thorn gestured toward the door where the outside winds howled. "You're free to leave my hall and fend for yourself anytime you want to."

The idea of leaving was less than appealing, but Thorn knew that as much as Fang did. "If I stay?"

"We'll help your girlfriend and her brother hunt down those Daimons and set you free from here."

Fang wasn't quite sold on this. There had to be more than what he was relaying. There had to be. "With all your powers, it seems to me you could recruit hundreds of people to do this. Why do you want me?"

Thorn laughed. "There is a certain breed, a certain tiny handful of people who can do what we do and not get slaughtered three seconds out the gate. It's not about fighting skills or even survival. It's about character."

Fang scoffed at the mere idea. "I have no character."

Thorn sobered as he closed the distance between them. Those ice blue eyes cut through him as if Thorn was looking deep into his soul and psyche. "There you're wrong, wolf. You have loyalty and courage. Unrivaled. Two things that are damn near impossible to find. Have you any idea how many people would have allowed Aimee to die rather than offer up their soul to save her? That, my friend, is the rare, rare quality that I can't teach anyone. You either have it or you don't. And you happen to have it in spades. That ability to sacrifice yourself for someone else. Priceless."

It didn't feel priceless. At times it felt more like a curse.

Thorn held his hand out to him. "So will you join me?"

"Do I have a choice?"

"Of course you do. I would never impose on your free will."

Funny, it didn't feel that way. There didn't seem to be much choice in this at all. He took Thorn's hand into his. "You keep Aimee safe and I'll give you my soul."

Thorn's pupils flashed red so fast that for a moment, Fang thought he might have imagined it. His features stone, he released Fang's hand. "Boy, I need to teach you to take those words out of your vocabulary. Believe me, they're not child's play and neither is what you're about to join."

"Dev?"

He pulled Aimee behind him as he faced the demons coming out of the shadows. "We need to get out of here." He shoved her toward the street.

Aimee started to run, but didn't make it far before another demon cut her off. She tried to flash and couldn't. "Dev? Can you get us out of here?"

"That power appears broken."

She put her back against Dev's as the demons drew so close, she could smell the sulphur on them. "What's going on here?"

"I have no idea. But they don't look like happy demons."

No, they didn't. In fact, they looked like they intended to make nice bear meals out of them.

Aimee manifested her staff. "Any idea how to kill them?"

Dev shrugged with a nonchalance she knew he couldn't possibly feel. "Beheading works on most things and if it doesn't work on these, we are seriously screwed. I'd put away the staff and draw a sword."

"Or you could just stand there and stay out of our way."

Aimee scowled as two men flashed in beside them. Not demons, they appeared human, yet they moved with a speed that belied that designation. Before she could even put her weapon away, they had the demons cuffed and on the ground in nice bloody heaps.

She shook her head as she tried to run through the events, but honestly, it'd happened so fast, all she'd seen were streaks in the air. "What was that action?"

Dev flashed a grin at her. "Chuck Norris meets Jet Li."

The demons growled and thrashed while the men beat them down.

"Shut up already." The taller man jerked the female demon up. "Just once, could I get a demon with no vocal cords?"

The other man laughed bitterly. "At least they're not puking on us this time."

"Small favor that."

And without acknowledging them at all, they were gone.

Aimee exchanged a perplexed stare with her brother. "That is totally out of my realm of experience. And given the freaky stuff we deal with, that says a lot."

"Yeah, I'm trippin' myself."

Aimee shook her head, trying to make sense of all of it. "Did Tony sneak the special herbs into our food again?"

Dev laughed. "I don't think so. But we'll definitely have to ask him when we get back."

"I wouldn't do that."

They separated to find a woman in the alley, right where the others had vanished. Her dark red hair was braided down her back and she wore a skintight black leather halter and pants. She was absolutely stunning and made Aimee feel rather lacking in comparison.

Dev flashed his most seductive smile. "Hello, gorgeous. Where have you been all my life?"

She rolled her eyes. "You are very handsome, bear. But no. You're not my type."

Aimee stifled a laugh at her putdown that Dev took in good-natured stride. "And you are?"

"Call me Wynter."

Dev chuckled. "Nothing like a fire on a cold Wynter's night."

Wynter gave him a droll stare. "Do those cheesy lines work on other women?"

"You'd be amazed."

"If they ever do, then yes, I would be." She walked past him to address Aimee. "Thorn has sent me here to help you find the Daimons who have Fang's soul."

Aimee frowned at the name she'd never heard before. "Thorn?"

"My boss. We don't question his orders. We simply obey. He wants the wolf saved, so here I am."

"We?" Dev asked, looking around to see if anyone else was lurking in the shadows.

Wynter gave him a tight-lipped smile as she ignored his question. "So the Daimons vanished while you were chasing them?"

Aimee nodded. "We think they went into a bolt-hole."

"That could be tricky."

Dev shifted his weight to his right leg as he leveled an irritated smirk at Aimee. "I still say we should hand it over to the Dark-Hunters. This is their job, not ours."

Aimee was growing tired of having this argument with him. "They can't identify the right ones and they can't go into a bolt-hole to flush them out."

"And neither can we. In case you haven't noticed, we're special treats for them and I don't want to end up like Fang, lying in my bed in a coma . . . or worse, dead."

"Then go home, Dev."

" 'Go home, Dev,' " he mocked. "Like Maman wouldn't skin me alive if I left you out here and you came home in a coma. It gets back to that whole 'I don't want to die' scenario that I'm trying so hard to avoid."

"Then back off me, or I'm going to put you in a coma myself."

Wynter sighed. "Do you two fight like this all the time?"

"Yes," they said in unison.

"But she's the one who always starts it."

Wynter rolled her eyes and made a sound of supreme disgust. "Thanks, Thorn. I really needed this and I intend to make you pay for it."

"Fang?"

Fang opened his eyes to find Aimee leaning over him. It'd been weeks or months since he last saw her. Relief filled him at the sight of her whole and unharmed. Somehow Thorn had actually done what he'd promised. "Hey."

She smiled a smile that radiated through every part

of his body and when she spoke, her tone was light and teasing. Most of all, it made him feel almost normal again. "You look a lot better than you did the last time I saw you. Maybe I should leave you here after all."

He laughed even though the very thought of it horrified him. "I'd really rather you didn't. But I don't want to see you hurt either. I'd rather you be safe and me stay here than for something to happen to you."

She took his hand into hers. The warm gentleness of that touch radiated through him. His body ached for a real taste of her.

Oh, to have one minute in the human realm. . . .

"We got three of them tonight."

Fang nodded. "I know. It's why my wounds have healed as much as they have." It was also why he was so much stronger now. "Thank you."

She kissed his hand. "You're welcome. We'll have you back soon. I promise."

Gods, he hoped so. It was hard to stay here, day after day. He felt so alone and out of touch. But at least she was here with him and for that comfort alone, he'd never be able to repay her. "How's Vane?"

"We haven't really heard. He's staying with one of the Dark-Hunters for now to help protect his mate."

"Which one?"

"Valerius."

Fang cursed at the name. Had that bastard done his job in the swamp, Anya would still be alive. Why in the name of Olympus would Vane have gone to him given that? What was he thinking? "The Roman?"

Aimee grimaced and nodded. "I'm sorry, Fang. I didn't think that would upset you."

Yet it did. Not just because of the fact that Valerius hadn't been able to help them protect Anya, but because Fang wasn't there to help Vane when his brother needed him most. He couldn't stand the thought of Vane having to turn to someone who'd already let them down.

"Do you know who in our pack is hunting him?"

"Stefan is the only one we've seen. He's come into Sanctuary a couple more times—no doubt trying to get a shot at you."

Fang cursed. "I've got to get out of here. Vane can't stand alone."

"He's not."

Fang froze at her unexpected contradiction. "What do you mean?"

"Fury's with him."

"Fury?" He gaped in indignation. Obviously Vane had snapped a serious wheel since Fang had been injured. What the hell was his brother thinking? "That guttersnipe? What's Vane doing with him?"

Aimee pulled back as she realized the mistake she was making. What was it with Fang that every time she drew near him, she stuck her foot into something? It was like she couldn't say or do anything right where he was concerned. "I should be going."

He refused to let go of her hand. "You know something." His tone was one of complete accusation.

She hesitated. This wasn't her place. "Fang, I shouldn't be the one telling you this."

"Telling me what?"

Aimee couldn't do it. Vane should be the one to tell him. Or Fury. But not her. "I have to go."

"Aimee," he said in an agonized tone that tore through

her. "Please. I need to know what's going on with him. He's the only family I have left. Don't leave me here not knowing."

He was right. That would be even more cruel and he'd already suffered enough.

Taking a deep breath, she braced herself for his reaction. "Fury is your brother."

His handsome face went white. "What?"

She nodded. "It's true. Like Vane, he changed forms at puberty and became Katagaria. As your father did with you and Vane, your mother called her pack out against him and they beat him down, then left him for dead. Now he's teamed up with Vane to fight against them and to protect Bride, Vane's mate."

Fang shook his head in disbelief. But it was the torment in his dark eyes that tore her apart. She hated hurting him more.

"Fury is my brother? Gah, what's next? Is Mama Lo going to end up being my long-lost sister?"

She rolled her eyes at him. "That's a little far-fetched."

Lying back on the bed, he covered his eyes with his hand. "I feel sick."

Aimee popped playfully at his belly. "Oh, stop the dramatics, Fang. You have another brother. You should be grateful."

Fang was stunned that she'd touched him like that. Anyone else would be missing an arm. But her warm tone actually succeeded in lessening his anger and feeling of betrayal. "And if I said that to you?"

"In case you haven't noticed, my cup is running over with brothers. But you . . . you should be glad to have more family."

Maybe.

"Yeah, but it's Fury." The last creature on earth he'd want to be related to. He couldn't stand that SOB.

Aimee laughed at his dire tone. "We all have a Remi in the bunch. Deal with it, you crybaby."

Fang gaped at her insult. No one ever dared to insult him. Not even Vane. "Crybaby?"

She nodded. "If the term fits . . ."

He reached to tickle her.

She squealed and tried to escape, but he tackled her to the bed and held her under him. She squirmed playfully, her eyes dancing in humor as she reached to return every tickle to him.

Fury went completely still as he realized what was happening. He was locked in hell and Aimee was making him laugh. . . .

Sobering, he looked down into those celestial eyes that seared him to the core of his soul. To that tantalizing dimple that haunted his dreams. How could she make him feel like this? His entire life had fallen apart and yet she made him laugh. Made him forget that he was trapped in a realm with demons who tortured him every chance they got. That he had sold his soul to keep her safe.

How was this even a little possible?

Aimee shivered at the look on Fang's handsome face. His hair fell forward into his eyes while he looked at her with an expression that was hot and deadly.

What was he thinking?

Then slowly, he lowered his lips to hers. She groaned at the taste of him as she wrapped her arms around his body and held him close. She closed her eyes as she inhaled the scent of his tawny skin and let his tongue dance with hers.

This was so wrong. She had no business here. With him. Yet she couldn't imagine anyplace else she'd rather be.

It's not real.

This was a dream. She was only here in spirit. Did that count?

Maybe.

Reluctantly, she pulled back. "I have to go, Fang."

"I know." He nuzzled her neck, sending even more chills through her as his whiskers tickled her skin. "I just needed to feel warm for a minute."

Those words broke her heart. He was still grieving and he was lost in this nether place with no one to trust.

"Here," she said, taking off the locket she never went without. She fastened it around his neck.

Fang scowled at the heart-shaped locket that was engraved with interlocking vines and swirls around a skull. There was nothing masculine about it at all. He should be horrified by its presence.

Yet he wasn't.

Aimee placed her hand over his as he held it. "I'm just a shout away if you need me."

I need you now. . . .

But he couldn't bring himself to say those words out loud. Instead, he leaned in to breathe her lilac scent in one more time. "Be safe."

"You too."

And then she was gone. It was almost enough to

make him whimper. But at least her scent lingered on his skin like a phantom whisper. If only he could hold on to her warmth the same way.

Sighing, he pulled her necklace off and opened it. Inside was a picture of her as a cub with two men he'd never seen before. They were holding the small black bear between them and smiling with pride. These must be her brothers who'd died and that made him think of Anya. It felt like a knife was twisting deep inside his gut.

Even now that pain was raw and biting. Worse was the fact that he knew it would never ebb. He would miss his sister for the rest of his life.

Running his finger over the picture, he realized there was a poem hidden inside as well.

Where I am always thou art. Thy image lives within my heart.

He choked back a rush of emotions that left his eyes cloudy at words that touched him. Blinking fiercely, he cursed the sensation. He was a warrior. A wolf with a capital *W*. He wasn't some old woman to cry at Hallmark commercials.

And yet this one tiny bearswan made him feel like he'd never felt before.

Like he was human.

More to the point, she made him feel wanted.

How stupid was that? His brother and sister had always wanted him . . . well, maybe Vane didn't want him right now because he was useless in the human realm, but Vane and Anya had always been his shelter. They loved him and he loved them.

But what he felt for Aimee . . .

It's wrong, wolf. You shouldn't even think *about her.*

Where I am always thou art. Thy image lives within my heart.

That was exactly how he felt about her.

Closing the locket, he kissed it lightly and returned it to his neck. Yeah, it was girly enough to make him want to puke. Still it was Aimee's and it was obvious she treasured it.

And so would he until he was able to give it back to her in their realm.

Now he couldn't sleep at all. Flippin' figured. It was the first time in months that he'd actually felt safe enough to do more than combat nap as he waited to be attacked. If that wasn't bad enough, he also had the erection from hell. One that was painful and demanding.

Banging his head against the bed, he growled. *Yeah, I am in hell.* But at least he wasn't starving or having to fight the demons off. Plus he was stronger now.

Almost whole.

Soon he'd be back to himself and back in the world where he belonged and all of this would be behind him.

He hoped.

"You're not serious about recruiting that wolf, are you?"

Thorn didn't bother to move as he heard Misery's voice coming out of the shadows behind him. He swilled his wine in the large goblet as he continued to stare into the fire before him—a fire that reminded him of a home he never wanted to claim. "Is there a real reason for this annoyance?"

She came to stand just beside his chair. Draping one arm over the back, she cocked her hip, and looked down lazily at him. "I want to know why you sent your goons after us."

"You broke the law."

She made a sound of disgust before she draped herself in his lap. It was all he could do not to shove her to the floor.

Tracing a fingernail over his cheek, she smiled flirtatiously. "You're not really going to go there, are you? Come to the dark side with me, love. You know you want to."

Yes, he did. The seductive lure was always there and his father continually sent demons like Misery out to help sway him.

But he refused.

He'd made a vow and by the tiny part of him that was decent, he would not be tempted. Using his powers, he flashed himself out of the chair, causing Misery to spill to the floor, so that he could stand by the fire. "Get thee behind me, Misery. I'm in no mood to deal with you."

She pushed herself to her feet. "Fine. But think about this . . . we gutted your last soldier on the ground in New Orleans. Just wait until you see what we have planned for your wolf."

CHAPTER 16

Every day seemed like forever as Fang trained to fight demons in human form and cursed the Daimons who continued to live. At least Aimee was able to bring him up to speed on what was happening out in the real world, but he was tired of being trapped here. He was tired of demon stench.

Most of all, he was tired of being alone. Aimee was the sole contact he had for the world he'd left behind. That was the hardest part of it. Why wouldn't Vane talk to him? Was Fury that much better a brother to him that Vane didn't even remember him anymore?

It was a stupid thought. He knew that and yet it persisted. Probably because he felt betrayed and abandoned by his brother. How could Vane simply dismiss him as a dream and not listen?

How could he not help him when he needed him most?

"Hey, wolf . . . here's something I think you need to see."

Fang paused as Thorn came into the room where he'd been training. He took the staff from Fang's hand as images began to flicker on the walls around them.

Uncertain over what to expect, Fang watched as the images became clear and he saw Aimee Peltier in a club that was under construction. There were ladders and paint buckets everywhere, as well as saws and equipment. But the peculiar part was the fact she was surrounded by Charonte demons while her younger brother, Kyle, was standing with her.

A tall, dark-haired Charonte with mottled blue skin shook his head as sound came in. "There's not a one of us dumb enough to do that."

Aimee flashed him a sweet smile. "C'mon, Xedrix . . . surely one of you is homesick?"

He snorted. "Have you ever actually met the Destroyer?" His tone was acerbic and cold. "You know, there was a time, granted, it was before recorded history, but there *was* a time when she was like a second mother to me. Then the humans had to slaughter her only son, and since the day he was resurrected and she was sent back into her hole, she's been just a little cranky and I had to suffer with perpetual PMS from her for eleven thousand years. No offense, but there's not enough beer, meat, or beignets in the world to make me go back there."

The demons around him sent up a cheer of agreement.

Aimee sighed. "I have to get into Kalosis."

Xedrix gave her an unsympathetic sneer. "Go eat a Daimon."

Kyle laughed. "That won't get her in since they tend to turn into dust when they die and torture doesn't work either. We tried that last night. Little boogers are highly uncooperative."

"And so are we." Xedrix reached for a hammer so that he could return to work.

Aimee turned a pouty look to Kyle that made Fang want to hold her.

Kyle winced, then put himself in front of the demon to cut off his path. "Xed, c'mon. I've done a lot for you guys. Can't you help a brother out? One demon to get us in and out of there. No one has to know."

Xedrix tossed the hammer back into its toolbox. He looked at Aimee. "Why is this so important to you?"

"Fang saved my life. I want to return the favor."

Xedrix scoffed. "Bullshit. People and especially Were-Hunters aren't that altruistic. Trust me. I've been around them since the dawn of time. You little bastards are self-serving to the end. Give me a reason to be suicidal."

Aimee cast a sheepish glance to Kyle before she answered. "He's important to me."

"And my body parts are extremely important to me."

Thorn turned to look at Fang while the images flickered around him. "Your little bear thinks an awful lot of you, doesn't she?"

Fang didn't answer. He was too floored by what she was trying to do on his behalf.

"Please, Xedrix," Aimee begged. "I've lost enough people I cared about in my life. I don't want to lose another. Fang is a good wolf and I can't leave him like he is. We only have one more Daimon to kill to free him. For once I can save someone I care about. I can't live with myself knowing that I failed this close to my goal."

A female demon stepped forward and gave Xedrix a chiding stare. "Look at the poor bear. She loves him . . .

how could you say no to that?" The demon shook her head, then looked at Aimee. "I'll take you."

Xedrix held his hand up. "No, you won't. I won't risk any of you. You have your freedom, you might as well enjoy it. Apollymi will take mercy on me for the desertion—which only means she'll kill me quickly as opposed to torturing me first." He sighed heavily. "I'll take them in."

The demons let out noises of protest.

"You're our leader," another of the men snapped.

"Yeah, head asshole, that's me." Xedrix pulled the towel from his shoulder and handed it to the male who'd spoken. "Enjoy the bar, guys. Remember what Kyle said. Only eat the tourists. No one will miss them." He transformed into his true demon form, complete with black horns and wings. His clothes disintegrated into a loincloth.

He met Aimee's gaze and his eyes glowed a sinister yellow. "Follow me."

Aimee pulled him to a stop. "Thank you, Xedrix. I really appreciate this."

"Really wish I could say the same. Damn bears, getting demons killed. What did we ever do to you?"

Kyle let out a nervous half-laugh. "Well, you did try to eat me."

Xedrix scoffed. "Man up, Kyle. We only took one small bite."

"And it got infected. That bite hurt for a month."

Aimee laughed. "Be grateful it didn't turn into rabies or something worse."

Xedrix arched a brow at her comment. "You know, bear, I'd wait on the insults until after I get you inside and return you. It's not too late yet for my common sense to prevail."

Aimee waved his comments away. "Common sense is seriously overrated. You're a demon. I thought your motto was 'spoils to the victor.'"

"No, our motto is 'everything tastes better with hot sauce.'"

"Then it's a good thing you guys escaped into Cajun country where we have hot sauce on every corner."

Xedrix flashed her a fanged grin. "Believe me, the beauty of that has not escaped our notice." His features sobering, he took them to the alley behind the club and raised his arm. "I really hope Apollymi's sleeping right now. . . ." He cut them a menacing stare. "Shield your eyes."

They did and an instant later a brilliant white light flooded the alley.

Aimee grimaced in pain. Even with her eyes shielded, it was excruciating and blinding. Finally, the light faded. She lowered her hand to see a circle of black hovering in the alley.

Xedrix smirked. "Welcome to bolt-hole hell. The only good thing is that we won't pop into the Daimon central hall at Stryker's feet. We Charonte have a separate entrance." He gave them a hard stare. "Listen to me and do what I tell you or it will seriously suck to be you. We're entering the Charonte domain and they are usually hungry."

Aimee nodded. "We're right behind you."

"Joy of my life," he said, his tone dripping in sarcasm.

Xedrix entered first, slowly. He led them into a dismal black hallway. Raising his arm, he manifested a torch as he continued past doors where they could hear the sounds of demons talking. "What does this Daimon look like?"

Kyle answered before she had a chance to speak. "He's tall and blond."

Xedrix gave him a peeved glare. "Well, that narrows it down to every Daimon here except Stryker. What would that be? Several thousand of them? Could you be a bit more specific and if you tell me he was dressed in black, I'll kill you myself and spare me the agony of dying."

Aimee shook her head. "You're a crabby little demon."

"You should meet my master. She's a true gem." Then without warning, he put his hand on her head and closed his eyes.

Aimee scowled as images poured through her mind like he was scanning her memories by using a fast-forward button. It made her queasy and dizzy.

After a moment, he pulled back. "Cadmon . . . I know where that coward is."

Kyle looked impressed. "So you can like suck out thoughts?"

Xedrix grimaced. "I prefer to suck out guts, but thoughts have their advantages from time to time. Now I suggest you adhere to silence. I'm only one demon among many here and while I . . . well, I really don't care if you live or die but you do, and since we need Kyle to finish off the club . . . yeah, you have to live, so follow in silence."

Aimee stayed right behind him through the winding hallways and then alleyways of Kalosis. She paused at the sight of the huge palace on the far hill. It glistened like polished jet against the dark background and sky. Sinister and awe-inspiring, she had to admire the beauty of it. "Let me guess," she whispered. "Apollymi's abode?"

Xedrix nodded. Putting his finger to his lips, he jerked his chin toward a small building across the street from them.

"I can't be seen here by anyone," he whispered, "or Apollymi will demand my return and death. You two will have to go in and find him."

"How do you know he's in there?"

He put his hand on her and she saw a perfect image of Cadmon asleep in bed with a woman.

"Thanks."

He inclined his head to her. "Good luck."

Aimee hesitated. "Kyle, I want you to stay here with Xedrix."

"But—"

"No buts. You're still new to your powers and this is serious. Stay here and don't get seen."

He nodded.

Aimee slipped through the shadows, making sure to avoid anything that might expose her. Her nerves were completely raw and she did her best not to be afraid. She knew she was powerful and strong, but she'd never had to fight alone before. While she was confident, she wasn't arrogant. This was a dangerous place and she had no idea of the extent of Cadmon's powers.

Keep your thoughts on Fang. . . .

That helped. She cracked open the door, grateful it wasn't locked, and slipped inside the small house. It was so quiet that her mind filled the silence with the thrumming of her heart.

You're about to slaughter a sleeping man.

She hesitated at the thought. All the other Daimons had attacked her, but this one . . .

He was sleeping at home.

Aimee hesitated as that thought washed over her. How could she possibly do this?

He's killed hundreds of people to live. He's not innocent by any means.

He'd attacked Fang when Fang had been tied down and helpless. Powerless. But all of that paled in the face of her conscience. This was murder. Not self-defense. Not justice.

Murder.

She gripped the stake in her hand. *It's too late to chicken out now. Go and finish it.*

How could she?

Stepping back, she bumped into a chair that made the slightest whispered scrape on the floor. Her heart sank.

Still there was no sound.

Thank the gods she hadn't awakened anyone.

Aimee turned only to find the Daimon there behind her. His eyes were dark and greedy as he raked a delighted glance over her body.

"Well, well, what a tasty little morsel you are. While I didn't order delivery, far be it from me to turn down such a thoughtful gift."

Aimee kneed him hard in the groin. As he doubled over, she went to stab him in the back, but out of nowhere a female Daimon grabbed her and slammed her against the wall.

Dazed, she turned to fight only to have three more Daimons pop in. "What was this? An orgy?"

They attacked.

Aimee ducked the first one, and headed for the most important. Cadmon. The one who held Fang's soul. He was the main one she had to kill. The others were simply target practice.

The female kicked her hard to the ground. Aimee flipped the Daimon over her body, then rolled to her feet. One of the men jerked her around. She slugged him hard across the face, her hand throbbing in protest.

Turning, she honed in on her target and slammed her fist into his chest.

It worked. The stake went in and he burst into golden dust.

But no sooner had he gone down than the others swarmed her. Aimee screamed as the female sank her fangs into her arm. . . .

Fang staggered back as he felt the last piece of himself come home to his body. For the first time in months, he took a true deep breath.

Thorn smiled wickedly. "Welcome back, wolf."

But he wasn't back yet and neither was Aimee. He was still trapped in this nether hell. "Can I go to her?"

Thorn grimaced. "That's a little tricky. It breaks quite a few treaties to send you into a realm we don't technically control."

Fang panicked as he watched the scene on the wall. Aimee was losing.

Badly.

"They're going to kill her, Thorn." Then Fang did

the one thing he'd never done in his entire life. He begged. "Please."

Thorn held a hand out toward the wall where the images were displayed. "The doorway's open. Better run for it."

Fang didn't hesitate. He ran at the images, half-expecting to crash into the wall and break his limbs or his neck.

He didn't.

Instead he found himself in the room with Aimee and the Daimons. He grabbed the one who had her fangs still buried in Aimee's flesh and pulled her head back. Manifesting a dagger, he stabbed her straight in the chest and let her dust fall all over him.

Aimee moved to kill the newcomer until her gaze focused on his face. Disbelief filled her.

"Fang?"

He manifested another dagger and put himself between her and the Daimons. He stabbed one and kicked another back. "Get out of here. Now."

"Not without you."

Fang couldn't believe her as she took a post behind him, her shoulders pressed against his. "Aimee, listen to me. We're in ground zero for the Daimons—there's no way we can fight them all off. I need you to get out of here and wake me up. Then we'll both be safe. Now go."

Aimee hated that thought. But he was right. They couldn't fight every Spathi Daimon here and if the Destroyer caught them . . .

As Xedrix said, it would suck to be them.

"Don't you dare die on me, Fang." She ran for the

door and headed to where she'd left Kyle and Xedrix. "Get me home now."

Xedrix teleported them out immediately.

Aimee scowled as she realized she was back in his club and not theirs. "I meant Sanctuary, Xed. Damn!" Growling, she flashed herself back to Fang's room.

There he lay, still and unmoving.

Her heart pounded in terror and guilt for having left him alone to face the Spathi. Was he still alive? "Please don't let those Daimons have gotten to you again." She didn't know if she could hunt them down anymore.

Terrified, she ran to the bed and shook his body to wake him. "Fang?"

He didn't respond. Just as before, he was limp and cold.

Tears filled her eyes as emotions choked her. "Damn it, wolf! Don't you dare do this to me. You better get up. Now! Do you hear me? Fang? Fang!"

Then she felt it. It was like a spark of electricity jolting him as he jerked hard in her arms. One moment she held a wolf and in the next, he was a naked man looking up at her with confused wonder.

One tear slid down her cheek at the sight of him alive and whole.

"Fang?"

Fang looked around the dark bedroom in disbelief that he was really back and that this wasn't another dream that would turn into a nightmare. The scent of Aimee anchored him and held him grounded. He cupped her head in his hand and held on for everything he was worth.

"I'm back. . . ."

She squeezed him and laughed. "I was terrified they'd gotten you again."

His laughter joined hers as he pulled back to show her the bleeding welt on his arm. "They tried." Then he looked her over. "You weren't hurt, were you?"

"Not really. Just the one bite, but it's not too deep. I just can't believe that you're here again." She braced her hands on each side of his face and smiled down at him. "Buddy, you need a shave and a haircut."

Fang laughed. "Yeah, I can imagine."

Her eyes danced with mischief and tears. "You know what this means, don't you?"

"I need a bath more than I need a shave?"

Her smile widened as she teased him. "Well, yeah, that too. But no. You're obligated to me. Big-time."

"Your eternal slave. Always." He leaned his forehead against hers. "Thank you, Aimee." Those words were so paltry compared to the real gratitude he felt.

She'd saved him from an unimaginable hell. Without her, he would have never escaped. . . .

"You're very welcome."

He kissed her on the forehead before he lay back down on the bed and pulled a corner of the duvet over his lap. "I feel like I've been hit by a truck."

"Well, we've been trying to move your limbs while you were a wolf, but sometimes you were so stiff we couldn't."

Fang tried not to think about that. It was probably when he was being attacked by Misery and her crew. But all of that was behind him. He was back where he belonged.

Aimee brushed his hair back from his face. "Are you hungry?"

"Famished."

"I'll grab you something to eat and be right back."

He took her hand as she started away. The warmth of her skin caught him off guard. In the other realm, she'd felt differently. Now he felt the true heat and softness of her body. "Stay with me a little longer."

He'd been alone for so long that he didn't want to be that way right now. He was afraid that if he was, somehow they'd suck him back into that hell realm.

Aimee heard the need in his voice. "I'll summon Dev to bring you something." She helped him tuck himself under the covers while she used her powers to ask Dev to bring food and water.

Fang lay on his side, quiet and still. He had one arm tucked under his head while his eyes danced around the room as if looking at all the shadows to come alive and attack him.

And still he managed to look delectable to her. Even with his shaggy hair and unkempt beard. Even though his body was much thinner, he still sent a jolt of desire through her.

"What are you thinking?"

Those dark eyes met hers and held her spellbound. They also stole her breath. "How grateful I am that you didn't give up on me."

She took his hand into hers and squeezed it gently. "Wolves aren't the only ones who are loyal, you know? We bears have a pretty good reputation in that department too."

Dev knocked lightly before he pushed the door open. His jaw dropped as he saw Fang awake. "Holy shit. The wolf lives."

Aimee got up to pull the tray from his hand and set it on the dresser. "Why did you think I asked for broth?"

"Thought you'd had a head injury or something."

She rolled her eyes.

Dev shut the door and came forward to stand next to Fang's bed. "So when did you get the last one?"

"A few minutes ago."

His look hardened. "Alone?"

"No. Kyle was with me."

That didn't help his glare in the least. In fact, it intensified. "Damn it, Aimee. You risked the cub?"

"He's not just a cub."

"You're right. He's the passenger who fell off the short bus. Damn, Aimee, of all the people to take with you into a fight—"

"Dev!" she snapped, her own anger igniting. She was in no mood for his lecture.

He shook his head. "You know the kid. He doesn't exactly think most of the time. The bricklayer left half his stash at the factory."

Irritated, she pointed at the door. "Get out."

When he refused to do as she said, she pushed him through the door, then slammed it in his face.

"That was really rude, sis," he yelled from the hallway. "You actually hurt my tender little feelings." His voice sounded like a kid's.

"You have no feelings, Devereaux. That bus passed you by a long time ago."

"Oh, yeah. I forgot. Fine. Be that way. I have more important things to do anyway. I have a hangnail that needs my attention."

Aimee rolled her eyes again as she took the broth from the tray to Fang who had been remarkably quiet through their exchange.

"Is he always like that?"

She wished she could say otherwise, but she couldn't. "Basically, yes."

Fang took the bowl from her and sipped from it like a cup. "It's a wonder you haven't killed him."

"Isn't it, though?"

He paused as if he realized what he was doing. He gave her a sheepish look. "I'm supposed to use something to eat this, aren't I?"

That question touched her deeply. That he would be concerned about offending her after all he'd been through. It was unexpected and it warmed her. "Don't worry about it. I know you're starving."

Fang nodded. She was right about that. His stomach ached so badly that it was all he could do not to attack. He downed the soup quickly and then swapped her the bowl for the glass of water. "You know, I could really use a steak right about now."

"Your body isn't used to real food. Carson's been keeping you on IVs and we've hand-fed you liquids all this time. I don't want to make you sick by putting something solid in you until I talk to him."

Fang looked down and realized just how thin he was. "Damn. I'm half my size."

"Not quite, but it will take time to heal."

Still, he shuddered. He didn't like looking like this. Most of all, he didn't like this weak feeling. He was a fighter, not an invalid. "I need a bath."

"Can you stand?"

That question seriously offended him. "I'm not helpless."

"Oh, look!" Aimee exclaimed in an exaggerated falsetto. "Mr. Macho is back in all his glory. Hello, Mr. Macho, it's so not good to see you again. But you know, Mr. Macho, that you've been bedridden to the point that your legs aren't used to carrying your weight and you're not really human. So if you want to get up and fall, gods forbid I do anything to stop it. After all, I live for *America's Funniest Home Videos*. Should I fetch a camcorder now?"

He wanted to be angry at her. At the very least offended, and yet he found her strangely entertaining. "Shut up and help me get to a bathroom."

"Okay, but you might want to put some clothes on before Maman, Papa, or Dev has a stroke. On second thought, we want Dev to have one, but my luck it'll only be Maman or Papa who sees us and that wouldn't go well for either of us."

Smiling at her humor, he dressed himself in a pair of jeans and a shirt. And as he tried to stand he realized just how right she was. His limbs were like walking on damp noodles. But with her help, he was able to get to the bathroom and into the tub. He dissolved his clothes as Aimee turned on the water and adjusted the temperature.

"Should I ask about how at ease you are with me naked?"

She pulled a towel down and set it next to the tub. "I have many brothers."

"That you've seen naked?"

She dropped her hand into the water to test the temperature. "*Bear* naked many a day and more times than I've ever cared for. Plus I help Carson out in the clinic." She folded her arms on the edge of the tall, claw-foot tub and rested her chin on her hands. It was an adorable pose and made him wish he had the strength to pull her into the tub with him and ease the ache in his groin.

"If it eases your ego, you are a very attractive wolf." She handed him a washcloth and bar of soap, then placed a razor, shaving cream, and mirror on the floor within his reach. "However, I do need to leave before Maman or Papa happen to catch me alone with you. Neither of them would be happy and I went through too much to save your life to have them end it now."

Fang really didn't want to be alone again. He'd spent so much time that way these last few months, but he knew she was right. The last thing he wanted to do was get her into trouble.

"If you need me, call."

He nodded as she walked out the door like a normal person. But she wasn't normal and neither was he. They were two animals who had no business interacting with each other.

Sighing, he lathered the cloth and set about cleaning himself up so that he didn't offend his own olfactory glands. Gah, how had Aimee stood being near him? He was disgusted by his own scent.

The shaving was a little harder than the bathing. He'd never quite gotten the hang of it on his best day.

Hissing, he flinched as he cut his chin.

Aimee was there immediately. "What happened?"

Surprised, he frowned. Had she been listening in on him? "I cut myself."

She grimaced at the sight of the pooling blood. She grabbed a piece of tissue and covered it. "Goodness, wolf. Can't I leave you alone for three seconds?"

"I never could do this sh—stuff right."

She took the razor from him and carefully raked it over his cheek. "It's not that hard."

He waited until she pulled the razor away to rinse it before he spoke. "And again, I ask you how it is you're so good at shaving men."

She laughed. "I'm a bear and I have a lot more area to shave than just the face."

He arched a brow at that, then tilted his head to look at her legs as if trying to imagine what they looked like underneath her jeans. "Yeah, you do."

Aimee took his chin in her hand and forced him to lean his head back so that she could shave his neck. Her gaze slid down his ripped muscles to where his erection was plainly visible in the water. Heat covered her cheeks. While she might be comfortable with his nudity, *that* was another matter entirely. And it was something she'd never seen before.

Since she'd never felt the quickening, she'd never mated with a male. Not that she was naïve or uneducated about what males and females did. She knew all the nuances of sex as her brothers felt more than free to share the most embarrassing facts of their premarital exploits, but . . .

She'd never experienced it herself.

And until Fang, she'd never really been all that curious about what she'd been missing. But now she couldn't help but wonder what it would be like to taste Fang. What he would feel like inside her. Even though he was fierce, she knew he'd be gentle. Loving.

Forcing her attention back to his neck, she admired the perfect curves that made up his jawline. He really was a gorgeous man. Even emaciated and worn.

Focus, Aimee.

The problem was, she was focused. Just not on what she needed to be focused on.

Fang licked his lips as she finished shaving him. He tried to keep his hands over the stiff part of himself and he hoped to the gods that she wasn't able to see it. But it was hard and he was in excruciating pain over it.

Pulling away, she put the razor up on the sink. "I know you're not helpless, but do you need me to help dry you off?"

The mere offer of it made his cock jerk in expectation. "Um, no, I think I can do it."

"You sure?"

He felt himself harden even more. "Pretty much. Yes."

"All right. Can you use your powers to take you back to bed while I clean up in here real quick?"

And keep her from seeing just how bad he wanted a taste of her? "Absolutely."

She frowned at the word that had come out as a strange squeak. "Are you okay?"

Fang cursed silently at himself. "Fine." Or at least as fine as a man dying of unsated testosterone poisoning could be.

She gave him a suspicious scowl. "You don't seem fine. You seem a bit agitated."

"Absolutely great." He flashed himself out of there so fast that he forgot to dry off.

He cursed as he realized what a mess he'd made of his bed. Growling at himself, he used his powers to set everything to rights before he conjured a pair of flannel pajama bottoms for himself. But they did nothing to hide his erection that now formed a solid tent at his crotch.

Put her out of your mind.

Yeah, right. Her touch was as branded on his senses as her scent and there was no relief in sight.

Kill me. . . .

He sighed and forced himself to turn over. But the moment he did, he felt a powerful shift in the air. One that could only herald the arrival of an extremely powerful entity.

Ready to battle, he crouched in the bed to find Thorn standing just inside the door.

"What are you doing here?"

Thorn gave him a piercing glare. "It's time for you to earn your keep, wolf. You ready?"

CHAPTER 17

"Earn my keep?" Fang said slowly to Thorn, enunciating every word just so that there was no miscommunication. "Are you out of your fucking mind? I just got back and I can barely stand on my own. What do you want me to do? Bleed on them?"

Thorn laughed. "You sound rather robust to me."

Whatever. The man was high if he thought for even one second that Fang could do much more than what he was currently doing. Sitting. Thorn definitely had to be on something.

Fang leaned back on the bed to glare at him. "What do you want exactly?"

"An end to the mistreatment of small, fluffy dust bunnies. But that doesn't seem feasible at present, so in lieu of that I want you to know that while Xedrix and company may have assisted you and Aimee, they are still demons to be watched and executed if need be."

Yeah, that really sounded like something he was raring to do. Sign him up . . . never. "Why aren't you sending them back to Kalosis if they're such a problem?"

He looked extremely disappointed. "They don't really fall under my jurisdiction. Charonte demons are a different entity and have a separate pantheon they answer to. It doesn't mean we turn a complete blind eye to them, but so long as they take it easy on humanity—which means they're eating the corrupt and not decent upstanding citizens, and their gods keep them in check, we don't worry about them . . . much."

Thorn manifested a five-by-seven photo and handed it to him. It was of a man in his early twenties whose heart had been torn out of his chest. "This, on the other hand, is what concerns us. Or more to the point, *me* and thereby you as default."

While gruesome, it was a scene Fang had seen several times since coming to New Orleans. "It looks like a typical voodoo sacrifice."

"Well, slap my ass and call me Sally if you're not bright. It is part of a summoning ritual for a Grand Laruae."

That was a term a wolfwere didn't hear every day. In fact, he had heard of it never. "A what?"

Thorn's features were completely impassive. "Bad-ass demon with a superiority complex who picks his teeth with the bones of infants. Let's just keep it simple and say he's a demon I want out of the human realm. ASAP."

"And why can't *you* go after him?"

Thorn looked extremely perturbed by his question. "That's a long story for one night when I'm under-the-table drunk. In the meantime, the shortest and simplest version is politics, which really chafes my ass. Believe me, I don't like it any more than you do. In fact, I'd like nothing better than pinning this bastard's warted hide to the nearest tree, preferably an oak one . . . but let's not go there. Unfortunately, I, personally, can't touch him without war breaking out."

He indicated the photo with a jerk of his chin. "Phrixis has taken out some of my best people over the centuries and I'd give anything short of my soul to put him out of commission once and for all."

Fang looked down at the face of the kid in the photo. His features were contorted by fear. Poor kid hadn't stood a chance and that set off his own anger. One thing Fang had never been able to stomach. A bully. Thorn was right. This asshole needed to be stopped.

Thorn pinned him with a lethal stare. "You, my little *loup-garou*, are the best weapon in this battle since our VD maven won't see *you* coming and neither will Phrixis."

"What about the priestess?" he asked since Thorn had brought her up. "What do you want me to do where she's concerned?"

"Her, I'll take care of. There's no treaty where she's concerned so I have free rein to do with her as I will. Bitch going to rue the day she decided to unleash Phrixis on the world."

Fang arched his brow in amusement. Now there was a sentence you didn't hear every day. "Rue the day?"

Thorn shrugged. "I'm old enough to make you look like an embryo. Sometimes it shows. You have twenty-four hours to find Phrixis or I'm sending you back to the Nether Realm."

That threat and his tone hit the wrong nerve. Fang glared at him. "Fuck you, asshole."

Thorn's eyes turned red. A deep, burning red that shimmered like running blood in the dim light. For some reason he couldn't name, an image of Thorn in black armor with wings flashed through Fang's mind. But it was gone so fast, he wasn't sure what prompted it.

"I advise you against taking that tone with me, wolf. While I'm usually good at taming the beast inside me, I don't always succeed. And you definitely don't want to see that side of me. In fact, you should be grateful I'm giving you twenty-four hours. If you were whole and if this wasn't your first target, I wouldn't be so lenient."

"I don't like taking orders."

"And I don't like repeating myself." Thorn glanced at the door where Aimee had walked out before he pinned Fang with a merciless glower. "You offered your soul up to whomever could save Aimee. I answered and now I own you. Lock, stock, and soul. Do what you're told, wolf, or you'll both spend eternity in a place that makes the Nether Realm seem like Disneyland."

Fang's hackles rose. He hated that tone and the threat, but Thorn was right. He'd been the one to make the bargain by his own free will and he would abide by it.

Even if it killed him.

"You seriously lack people skills."

The red faded from Thorn's eyes as a slow, insidious smile curved his lips. "And I flunked anger management the moment I put the counselor through a stone wall. You might want to keep that in mind."

Fang felt the muscle in his jaw working. "I can tell we're going to get along like Batman and the Joker."

"Just remember one thing, wolf. I'm the best friend you'll ever have or the last enemy you'll ever make."

Because he wouldn't live long enough to make another one. Thorn didn't say those words, but his tone implied them.

He handed Fang another photograph and a piece of cloth that held the stench of demon. "That's your target. Make me not regret saving you."

Fang started to flip him off. Had he been stronger, he probably would have. But right now the idea of flying through a wall when he had to go chase down a demon didn't seem like the wisest course of action.

Vane would be proud. The Nether Realm had finally taught him a modicum of self-preservation.

"When does my time start?"

"Ten minutes ago."

Fang snorted. "Thanks. That's real generous of you."

Thorn seemed unperturbed by his sarcasm. "I should probably warn you that I'm not real big on fairness and I have a below-zero tolerance on most things. Do your job. Do it right and we won't have any problems. Fuck up and I'll most likely kill you. Fuck up bad enough and I'll torture you first."

"Anything else I need to know?"

"Just this." Thorn reached out and grabbed him by the wrist. Before Fang could move, Thorn had him on his back in the bed with his palm pressed against his shoulder blade.

Fang cursed as his shoulder burned. It felt as if he were being branded. He tried to fight, but he couldn't move. It was like something inhuman and unseen was holding him down. When Thorn finally released him, he saw that he wasn't far off. The scent of burning flesh hung heavy in the air and on his shoulder was a round circle with ancient symbols.

Reaching to touch it, Fang hissed as he increased the pain of it. "What is that?"

"Protection from the lesser demons and from spells the mavens and warlocks might want to use on you once they realize you're one of mine. Believe me, you'll be grateful you have it."

Maybe when the stinging stopped, but right now he wanted to kick Thorn's ass until that bastard hurt as much as he did. "Will it work on Phrixis?"

Thorn laughed. "You're amusing." He stepped back and handed him a gold hilt. He flicked a ruby stone up and the blade extended three feet out. "This is your sword," he said in a tone implying Fang was less than intelligent. "You press the pointy end into the enemy. Try not to let him make eye contact with you and remember, he spits invisible poison."

"Oh, goody."

Thorn ignored the sarcasm as he pulled out a cell phone. "Call me when it's over. Just press two and I'll answer."

"And if I die?"

"I'll know and I won't be happy. Remember, wolf, I'm one of the few beings who can follow you into the afterworld and seriously fuck you up there. Don't fail me."

"Important note taken. Thank you, Dr. Morbid."

Thorn inclined his head to him before he vanished.

Fang let out a deep sigh as he debated what to do. But there was no decision really. He had to get started chasing the demon and the clock was ticking.

Best to get out of here before Aimee returned.

He picked the locket up from his chest and held it in a tight fist. He would be back.

First, he had duties.

Taking a deep breath, he dressed himself in jeans, a T-shirt, and a leather jacket before he held the cloth to his nose and took a deep breath. With the demon's stench choking him, he left to track it down.

Aimee paused as she entered Fang's empty room. The white duvet was still rumpled and the pillows askew as if he'd just stepped away. "Fang?"

No one answered.

Frowning, she knew he wasn't in the bathroom since that was where she'd just come from. Where would he go? She searched Peltier House and Sanctuary with her powers and still there was no sign of him.

Had he gone to his brother?

She closed her eyes and let her powers wander through the ether until she found him. He was down in the Warehouse District, walking along the street like he hadn't just come back from hell. The antique stores that were housed in the old warehouse buildings were closed for the night as he passed by them.

What in the world was he doing there?

She watched as he paused to lean against a gray brick building as if trying to catch his breath. He had one arm wrapped around his ribs before he pushed himself away and continued down the street. He kept his head lowered and by the predatorial way he moved she could tell he was tracking someone.

Why would he do something so stupid? She'd gone

to a lot of trouble to save him for him to just turn around and get knifed in a back alley when he should still be in bed resting.

"What are you thinking, wolf?"

He was in no shape to be after anyone or anything. And before she could stop herself, she teleported to be right there beside him.

Fang whirled on her with a growl so fierce, she actually took a step back in fear. She'd forgotten just how formidable he could be. Even thin and weak, he was still as fierce as any Slayer she'd ever seen. His long hair fell into feral eyes and the sword he swung came at her so fast that all she could do was gasp and hold her hands up.

The blade paused so close to her that she could feel the tiniest scrape of it against her upraised palms.

"What are you doing here?" Fang demanded, his tone tight with anger.

"Wondering the same thing about you, buster. You know, when last we parted about twenty minutes ago, you weren't exactly in the shape to go out on a walk." She pushed the blade back, taking care not to cut her hand in the process. "Never mind fight something that requires *that*"—she looked down at his weapon—"to get its attention. Do you even know how to use a sword?"

He scoffed at her anger. "It's not exactly hard. They're pretty self-explanatory. You use the sharp end to stab your opponent."

"Yeah, right . . . take it from someone with centuries of experience, they're not that easy to use."

He flicked a slide on the hilt and the blade retracted.

"And take it from someone who's been relying on them for the last few months to stay alive, I'm a real quick study."

Perhaps, but she still didn't want him in the street alone while he wasn't in his best fighting shape. "What are you doing out here, Fang?"

Fang wanted to answer that question, he really did. But how did he explain to her that he'd saved her life by offering up his soul? It wasn't something she'd welcome. Knowing her, she'd curse him for it. The one thing about Aimee, she didn't like people protecting her.

But damn, standing there in front of him with the streetlights reflecting off her pale hair and her brow furrowed by worry for him, she was the most beautiful thing he'd ever seen.

How he wanted a bite of her apple. . . .

Forcing his thoughts away from *that* disaster, he cleared his throat. "I need a few minutes alone. Do you mind?"

She didn't relent in the least. "To do what? And if it's anything nasty like Dev would say to shock me, please spare me the details."

He let out an aggravated breath. "Does everything have to be an argument with you?"

Her face offended, she gaped. "I asked a simple question."

"That has an extremely complicated answer. Now—"

His words were interrupted by a harsh scream. Fang cursed as he realized it came from the same general area where he'd been headed.

It was the demon. He could feel it. The one thing he'd learned in the Nether Realm was how to sense one anytime it was near. The stench and chill were unmistakable. And his new mark was burning like fire.

"Please, Aimee. Go."

As expected, she refused. She even rushed ahead of him toward the scream's origin.

Fang shook his head in disgust as he flashed himself to the demon in a dark alley, narrowly appearing there before Aimee. Wasn't it mules who were supposed to be so stubborn? Obviously someone had missed the memo on bears.

He pulled up short as he caught sight of the mountain of a beast. At least seven feet tall, the demon had flowing black hair and eyes that held no discernible pupil or white in his eyes. They were jet stones set in a face that was contorted by the pleasure he took in causing pain.

The human looked to be in her midtwenties. Pretty and tiny, she was dressed in a blue restaurant uniform. Her face had been torn open by the demon's claws. She sobbed and begged for help while the demon held her there by her dark hair.

As soon as Phrixis realized he wasn't alone, he released her and turned toward Fang.

Extending the sword, Fang flashed himself between the human and Phrixis. "Get her out of here."

Aimee nodded as she wrapped her arms around the hysterical human and carried her away from the danger.

Phrixis laughed as he raked a repugnant sneer over Fang's body. "What pathetic creature are you?"

"*Pathetic*'s really not a word that applies to me."

"No?" Phrixis blasted him.

Fang dodged the blast and swung the sword straight for the demon's throat.

Phrixis laughed. "How weak and worthless do you think I am?" He landed a solid punch to Fang's side. It was so fierce that he swore he felt his ribs crack.

The pain of it drove the breath from his body. Fang fell to one knee, but he refused to go down. He was a wolf and Phrixis was about to learn what that meant. Shifting forms, he attacked.

The demon staggered back as Fang set his teeth into his arm and ripped it open. Phrixis hit him in the head, but all that did was strengthen his resolve as he shredded the demon's arm. In this form, there were few who could take him down.

Phrixis slammed him into the wall with the force of a Mack truck hitting him.

Fang felt his grip loosen under the assault. As the demon moved to grab him, he ran at his feet, skimming between his legs to emerge behind him. Rolling, he changed to human form so that he could grab the sword from the ground.

Phrixis turned to confront him.

The moment he did, Fang stabbed him through the heart. He buried the sword in to the hilt, then snatched it out and stabbed him again.

Phrixis laughed. "Do you think—"

Fang ended his words with a backstroke that severed his head completely from his body.

The demon crumbled slowly to the pavement where he landed in a lump as blood spewed out.

Fang spit at his remains. "Tell me again how great you are, asshole. Nothing like a steel enema to ruin even your best day." His body weak and trembling, Fang leaned back against the wall as he struggled to breathe with his damaged ribs.

At least it'd been an easier kill than the demons in the Nether Realm. Panting, he pulled the phone from his pocket and called Thorn.

"It's done. I killed him."

To his shock, Thorn appeared instantly at his side. "What the hell did you do?"

"Nice attitude, dick." Fang contracted the sword as he scowled at Thorn's angry glower. "I killed the demon like you told me to."

Thorn let out a sound that was a mixture of disgust and rage. His clothes turned from the navy business suit to bright red armor as his hair seemed to become flames. "I didn't say kill him, dumbass. I said to send him back where he came from."

"That's what I did."

Thorn kicked at the demon's body on the ground and cursed. "No. You *killed* him."

Obviously, he was missing a major piece of this puzzle because in his universe, killing a demon wasn't considered a bad thing. Most days, it was considered a public service. "In my world those two things are synonymous."

Thorn sucked his breath in sharply between his teeth. He held his hands as if he were trying to restrain himself from killing Fang. "You know, it's really not that hard to kill a demon, especially with the brand I gave you. Any half-witted preternatural creature can kill their ass. What I needed you to do was to return him to his realm. That's a little more sophisticated and a hell of a lot harder."

"Then why did you give me a sword?"

"Did you look at it before you used it?"

"Yes."

Thorn gave him a doubting glare. "And I repeat. Did. You. Look. At. It?" He snatched the hilt from Fang's hand and held the sword up for him to see the words inscribed there.

Strike hard. Strike fast. Strike thrice. Avast.

Who knew Thorn was a pirate? Fang squelched that thought. *Avast* was simply an archaic word that, no offense to the swordsmith, he hadn't used even when it'd been popular vernacular.

But he couldn't cut all sarcasm from his demeanor. "And in your world, Captain Scary, that would mean?"

"You hit him three times and then you stop. It's in English. Hell, it's in *your* English. You were born then."

Fang gestured toward the demon's now decaying body. "That was my third hit."

Thorn covered his left eye with his right hand as if he had a vicious migraine brewing. "I have a tumor. I know I have a tumor. I just wish I were mortal so that it could kill me."

Frustrated, Fang rolled his eyes at Thorn's anguish. "I still don't understand what's so wrong with what I . . ." His words died under a wave of excruciating pain.

"Wait for it, wolf." Thorn gestured sarcastically at him. "You're about to have enlightenment. It's about to suck to be you, *mein freund.*"

Fang cried out as the most blinding shaft of agony

imaginable ripped through his entire body. It felt as if he were being torn in two. He couldn't breathe or move. "What's happening to me?"

"You're absorbing the demon's powers."

"Huh?"

Thorn nodded. "Yeah. And not just the powers. Your soul is merging with the dead demon's essence. All that he was is now intruding onto what you are. Demons are immortal without souls. When they die, as it were, their life force jumps to the one who destroyed their body and it will try to take you over from now on."

"So what are you saying? I need an exorcism?"

"No. There's no body for him to return to. You're stuck with him. Mazel tov!" Thorn said in an exaggerated voice of happiness. He sobered as his body returned to normal, except for his eyes. They were red with slitted yellow pupils that reminded Fang of a snake's. "And it's why we try real hard not to kill one. Not a pretty reality."

Fang felt his vision changing. It became sharper. Clearer. The scent of blood permeated his head and he could hear it running not just in his veins, but Thorn's.

"What's happening to me?"

Thorn grabbed him by the shoulder and smiled cruelly. "That is the taste of evil flowing thick through your veins. Seductive and inviting, it will entice you from now on. And now you know why I'm a less than happy camper most days. There's the battle I fight every second of every minute of my life. As I said, it now sucks to be you."

Before Fang could stop himself, he vomited on the sidewalk. Gah, the indignity of that. Not to mention the pain of it as his insides felt alive—like they were writhing.

Thorn didn't flinch in the least as he stepped back to give him space. "Don't worry. Your guts aren't coming out even though it feels like it. Your stomach will settle down eventually. However, that need you have for blood and death that is mounting inside you will never go away."

Grimacing, Fang wrapped his arms around his stomach and leaned back against the wall to catch his breath. He tilted his head to look at Thorn. "Why didn't you tell me about this?"

"Honestly, I didn't think in your current frail condition that you could kill him. I figured three whacks with the sword and you'd either be dead or he'd be banished . . . let me go back to the part where this particular demon had taken out some of my best in the past. I should have evaluated your abilities a little more accurately. My bad."

"I hate you, Thorn."

He shrugged nonchalantly. "All creatures do and I really don't care. By the way, your girlfriend is on her way back here to you. Try not to eat her even though the bloodlust is going to be hard to resist. You'll most likely regret it if you do." Then he was gone.

Fang slid down the wall, trying to get his stomach and nerves to settle. But it was hard. He still felt like he was being torn inside out.

Gods, what am I going to do?

Aimee appeared by his side a few minutes later as he leaned back with his head against the wall and his eyes closed.

"Fang?" Her hand was cool as she touched his forehead. "You're burning up."

His only response was to hold her hand against his cheek as the soft lavender scent of her wrist soothed him. But Thorn had been right, he could smell the blood in her veins and he wanted to rip her wrist open to taste it.

"Can you take me home?" he breathed, afraid to try his own powers right now.

"Absolutely." She helped him to stand and it was only then that he realized the demon had disintegrated. There was nothing left except a vague black outline. Would that happen to him too if he died now?

Damn you, Thorn, for not telling me everything.

Aimee flashed them back to Fang's bed and then helped him to lie down. "I'm going to get Carson."

He grabbed her hand and held her by his side. "Don't. There's nothing he can do."

"But, Fang—"

"Aimee, trust me. I just need to rest alone for a little bit, okay?"

He could see the debate in her eyes as he tightened his grip on her hand.

After a few seconds, she nodded. "You need me at all. . . ."

"I will call you. I promise."

She patted his hand before she removed it. "All right. Rest well."

Fang didn't relax until she was out of the room. Only then did he lay back and give in to the conflicting emotions that lacerated him. He wanted to kill something.

Anything.

But he knew he couldn't.

The only thing was, he didn't know how long he'd be able to hold the demon in him at bay. By the feel of it, he was going to turn Slayer. *True* Slayer.

And that, in their world, carried a death sentence.

CHAPTER 18

Fang lay in his bed as a wolf, his mind trapped by the demon powers that were warring inside him as they converted his body even more. He was only vaguely aware of the sounds of the outside world.

He now saw things in infrared while he slept. Every tiny insect in his room. Every creature that walked past his room in the hallway. He was aware of everything on a level he'd never imagined, but unable to respond. He was like an outside viewer who couldn't break through the glass case no matter how hard he struck it.

"Fang?"

Vane. He'd know that deep baritone anywhere. But in Fang's mind, Vane was nothing more than a reddish outline standing beside his bed. There was a woman with him. One who smelled sweet and all human. She stood so close to Vane that she appeared tucked in there.

Fang tried to reach out to his brother, but couldn't. It was almost like he was back in the Nether Realm where only voices could reach him. Only now he couldn't understand the words his brother was saying to him. They were jumbled and malformed as he and the woman said things.

Hanging his head, Fang sighed wearily.

"Aw, what's wrong, little wolfie? Can't you get up?"

Fang went ramrod stiff as he heard the raspy voice of a demon. "Alastor." He didn't know how he knew the creature's name, yet he did.

His body went straight into the demeanor of a lethal predator. Fang lowered his head and watched the demon closely with his peripheral, ready to strike him down with deadly precision when the time came.

Small and wiry, the demon was ugly and gray-skinned. Worse, he stank of sulphur and blood. His hook nose and bald head made him look like a gargoyle. In the darkness of his dream, something silver flashed.

Fang reacted on instinct. He caught the demon's hand to see a dagger held there. Laughing at the audacity, or more to the point the stupidity, he wrapped his other hand around the demon's throat and lifted him from his feet.

The moment he did, he saw Alastor's thoughts in his mind. Heard his own mother telling the demon to kidnap Vane's mate and bring her to his mother's pack so that Bride couldn't complete the mating ritual with Vane. It was a pact his mother had made with the demon to capture all of their mates to prevent them from having even a small chance of happiness.

Or more to the point, to keep them from procreating and spreading their animal natures that his mother despised so much.

Raw fury exploded inside him.

"You rotten bastard," he snarled as his demon's bloodlust ripped through him and the demon inside him roared to life. It wanted him to rip the demon's head off with his bare hands and feast on his entrails. Never had he experienced anything like this.

"I was just doing as I was told." The whine in the demon's voice was like a chair scraping across a floor. It made the hair on the back of his neck rise and did nothing to curb his blood fever.

Before Fang even realized what he was doing, he sank his teeth into the demon's throat so that he could taste his blood.

Stop!

The sound of his conscience succeeded in reaching him. Choking on the thick liquid that tasted like warm metal, he forced himself to step back. Alastor slid to the ground, holding his neck as he pathetically begged for his life.

Part of Fang demanded he kill the sniveling beast at his feet. It was what he deserved. But the part of him that was wolf refused to kill for pleasure.

Katagaria only killed to protect or to defend. They never killed for amusement.

At least not often.

But the wolf in him also couldn't let the demon go while Alastor posed even the hint of a threat to his family—*that* wolves killed over without remorse. "You hunt any of us or those we love again and so help me, I won't stop until I've pulled you into so many pieces, you'll think you've been through a grinder."

Alastor bowed low to the ground as he thanked him for his mercy. "I will never hunt again, master. I swear it." He vanished instantly.

Fang wiped at his lips that were still coated in the foul demon's blood. He cursed at what he'd done. But worse was the desire still in him to cause pain and to kill.

The demon was strong within him and it was hard to resist.

"I won't do it," he snarled at himself.

Ever.

He was a Were-Hunter, not a demon, and he wouldn't cede himself to this hell. He wouldn't become one of them. Not for anything. No matter the temptation or hunger. He would stand strong.

Wake up!

He couldn't. Cold panic consumed him as he staggered through the darkness that had no form or substance, seeking something to return him to his room. Had Thorn relegated him back to hell after all?

No, this was worse than the Nether Realm. There were no caves or anything else here. This reminded him of walking an endless desert that had no sides or borders. The landscape was obsidian and there was no respite.

"Fang?"

He heard Aimee calling to him, yet he couldn't find her in the oppressive black. That was even more terrifying to him than being locked in here. "Aimee?"

"Fang? Wake up, sweetie." That precious, siren voice . . .

If only she could find him again.

"Aimee!" he shouted until his throat was raw, but she didn't seem to hear him this time.

What was going on? How could this have happened to him again?

Something struck him hard in the back of his head.

One moment he was lost in the dark, and in the next he was in his bed with Aimee leaning over him, her features contorted by her fear and worry.

Aimee started to pull away as Fang shifted from wolf to human, but the panic in his eyes riveted her. His breathing ragged, he held on to her hands as if they were a lifeline for him that he was afraid she'd remove.

It made her ache for him. "Are you all right?"

He grabbed her and pulled her into his arms where he held her in a crushing embrace.

She frowned as she realized he was shaking all over. Scared for him, she wrapped her arms around his body to help as best she could. "What is it?"

"Nothing."

But she knew better. Something had happened to him again. Something he didn't want to share.

Fang held her close, letting her scent and arms anchor him back in the world of the living. Closing his eyes, he tried to settle his nerves and his breathing. He felt like an idiot for acting like this. . . .

But the trauma of the Nether Realm was still raw and biting. He never wanted to go there again. He never wanted to go to sleep without having a way to come back.

Shell-shocked and weak, he wanted to feel safe again. But he seemed to have no control over himself anymore. No control over anything.

It was a feeling he hated.

Aimee pulled away to look at him. She placed her hand to his cheek as she searched his eyes with her gaze. "You've been asleep for two days. I was beginning to worry that you were lost again."

He stared at her in disbelief. Two days? Had it really been that long. "What?"

She nodded. "Today is Thanksgiving and you've already slept through most of it."

Fang shook his head as those words sank in. How had that much time passed and he not known it? It seemed like he'd only just lay down to rest.

Aimee scowled. "Did you not hear when Vane and his mate came in to talk to you a little while ago?"

"No," he lied, not wanting to admit to her how close he'd come to slipping back into the comatose state he'd been in before. "Are they still here?"

Both of her brows shot up as she cocked her head suspiciously. "You didn't hear the commotion in the connecting room a few minutes ago?"

"What commotion?"

She gestured toward the wall where a giant mirror was mounted—strange how he'd never seen through that in his sleep; only through the door. "Vane's mate, Bride, beat your mother down in the next room when Bryani came here to kill you. Bride actually caged her during the fight . . . did you really sleep through all that?"

He was aghast at what Aimee described. His mother had come for him?

Was that why he'd seen Alastor?

But the most incredible part was that a human had defeated their mother . . . that took courage and strength. And a giant boatload of stupidity.

"I guess I did."

She shook her head. "I've heard of heavy sleepers before, but dang, wolf. You're special." She stepped back. "Vane and Bride are still downstairs if you'd like to see them before they leave."

That he had mixed feelings about, but his brother needed to know he was alive and back in the world of the living. At least for the time being.

At the rate he was going, he could be sucked back into hell in a heartbeat.

Without a word, Fang dressed himself in a long-sleeved black shirt and jeans before he got up and almost fell again. He caught himself against the bedpost, despising the fact that he was still weak. He needed to be in fighting strength as soon as possible.

She put her hands on him to steady his balance. That innocent touch burned him to the core of his being. Covering her right one with his left hand, he gave a gentle squeeze.

Aimee paused at Fang's uncharacteristic action. Normally he'd be pushing her away, telling her he was fine and cursing her for treating him like he was helpless. That alone told her just how shaken he was from whatever he was hiding from her.

He was a strong wolf and a proud one.

She stepped back to give him space as he made his way to the door and walked out of it. The fact he didn't use his powers was also very telling.

Aimee followed him down the hall to the stairs and to the kitchen that was bustling with activity. One of the few times of the year that Sanctuary was closed to the public, Thanksgiving had always been a celebration for them, a time when they held a massive banquet. All of the Were-Hunters who lived in Peltier House came together to feast and hang out, and this year they also had several of the former Dark-Hunters, and Acheron and Simi, in attendance.

Everyone was laughing and partying. Their cheer echoed into the kitchen where Cherif and Etienne were spooning out more potatoes and meat and adding a lot of barbecue sauce to it—Simi must still be hungry. Smiling at the thought of the Goth Charonte demon who could eat an elephant's weight in food, Aimee returned her brothers' cheerful greeting as she helped Fang to the door.

She paused there while Fang continued into the bar and over to the table where Vane and Bride were sitting together and holding hands. He stood tall and moved fluidly, but she could sense his hurt and unease. His buried anger at the fact that Vane hadn't been there for him.

"Good luck," she whispered under her breath. She hoped everything worked out between them.

Her gaze went to Fury who froze and looked stricken the moment he saw Fang upright and moving. How she ached for all of them and for the family they would now have to piece back together.

A lump in her throat, she scanned the room to seek her own family . . . Alain, who sat with Tanya and their cubs, feeding them honey sticks while trying to keep Zar from playfully stealing them. To Kyle and Cody, who laughed at something Colt had said while Carson pulled a beer away from the twins. Maman and Papa sat to the side, holding hands while they whispered to each other like two teenaged humans wanting to be alone and knowing that they couldn't. Dev, who sat talking and laughing with Remi, Acheron, Jasyn, Quinn, and Simi while Simi plowed through a plate of turkey, stuffing, and ham.

She couldn't imagine not having them in her life. Through everything, family was family, and yet Fang and his brothers were now suspicious of one another.

That broke her heart.

Fang wanted to turn around and leave as he realized every eye in Sanctuary was now on him. Most of them had had no idea he'd awakened and he felt like a freak in a lab where everyone was trying to figure out what had gone wrong in his DNA.

But he wasn't a coward.

Ignoring the cold lump in his stomach and wrapping his arms around himself, Fang kept his gaze on the goal of his brother and his mate. Even though Bride was seated, he could tell she was tall and Rubenesque— just the way Vane liked his women. With auburn hair and eyes so bright they danced with life, she was exquisite. And the love in her gaze as she looked at Vane was something rare. Something that should always be cherished and never abused.

His brother had done well for himself and that only made the lump inside him that much tighter.

Fang did his best to ignore all the other Were-Hunters and Acheron and Simi as he made his way to them. They were the only thing that mattered and as he approached, his anger mounted.

Fang hated what he felt, but he couldn't stop it. Resentment and bitterness swelled inside him. How dare Vane go off and find happiness while he'd been tortured and abused. Images of the demons beating him, of the wounds that had cut him bone-deep, went through his mind. Again, he remembered the unrelenting hunger and thirst that had never been sated. The months of grueling agony.

All the while Vane had been with Bride. . . .

Stamping his rage down, Fang held his hand out to Bride the instant he reached her.

She hesitated a moment before she took his hand into hers and he felt the way she trembled in uncertainty. The scent of her nervousness was heavy in his nostrils and the protective wolf in him wanted to soothe her. It wasn't her fault that he'd been locked in the Nether Realm. She was his brother's mate and he would honor her as that no matter what he felt inside.

"She's beautiful, Vane. I'm glad you found her." He gave her hand a gentle squeeze before he withdrew and met Fury's shocked gaze.

At least the bastard had the decency to look shamefaced. Well he should too. It was all Fang could do not to punch him for replacing him in Vane's affections and loyalty.

But Fury's presence in the room wasn't nearly as shocking to Fang as Stefan's was. Stefan, who'd been the ringleader who beat him and Vane and then chained them to the tree for the Daimons to eat. Stefan, who'd been sent out to kill them. Obviously things had changed while Fang had been out of it.

Now, their father's grand asshole sat at a table looking like someone had beat the shit out of him. No doubt he deserved it.

Stefan refused to meet Fang's gaze.

Vane came to his feet. "Fang?"

Fang didn't stop on his way back to the kitchen. He

was afraid that if he did, he'd attack his brother for abandoning him to the Nether Realm and the last thing he wanted was to taint the happiness Bride and Vane shared. Vane deserved to be happy and Fang had no right to hurt him. He knew that Vane would have moved heaven and hell to get him out . . . had he only answered when Fang had called.

Gods, his emotions were absolutely bipolar and volatile where Vane was concerned.

That pain and hurt were still raw inside him. The months of brutal survival couldn't be undone with a simple encounter. He needed time to come to terms with what he'd been through.

What he'd consigned himself to.

With a hesitant smile on her beautiful face, Aimee met him at the kitchen door. Her T-shirt was a bit tighter on her body today and it caused a vicious wave of lust to consume him. Thank the gods something overrode his pain.

Before he even realized what he'd done, he reached out to her and put his arm around her shoulders. She wrapped her arm around his waist and helped him through the kitchen and back up to his room.

Fang didn't speak the entire way up the mahogany stairs as the lavender scent of Aimee captured him.

Once in his room, he lay back in the huge tester bed while she covered him with a brightly colored quilt.

Her gaze suspicious, she paused by his side. "I know something's wrong with you, wolf. You're never this silent."

Fang snorted at her poor attempt for humor. He probably shouldn't mention any of this and yet he found himself confiding in her even against his better judgment. "If my mother's defeated and Stefan is down there in the bar with Vane and Fury and not fighting them to the death . . ." He didn't finish the thought. He already had a good idea of what that meant.

Someone was now in charge of those two clans.

And it wasn't him.

That stung him deep inside. Things had changed so dramatically and he felt all alone. Disassociated. Stunned. Most of all, deeply betrayed. Maybe he should have stayed in the Nether Realm. It was obvious that no one here needed him anymore. Vane had moved on with his life.

Their entire clan had restructured under someone else's leadership.

What was he going to do now? He felt lost and he hated that sensation.

Aimee felt Fang's turmoil and it made her want to cry that she couldn't help him. She couldn't stand feeling so helpless. Most of all, she didn't want to see their family splintered at a time when they needed one another the most. "You know your brother checked on you every day while you were out of it. Even today, he made sure to come see you. Fury was here too."

"I know."

And still he was so sad.

Without thinking, she curled up on the bed beside him and wrapped her arms around him to hold him close. It was the only way to comfort him that she knew.

Fang closed his eyes as his heart pounded from the warmth of her embrace. No one had ever held him like this before.

No one.

There was nothing sexual about it. It was a hug meant to comfort him. And may the gods have mercy on his worthless soul because it did.

Placing his hand over her much smaller one, he felt something inside him shatter and in that moment, he knew a truth that scared him even more than the demon that was living inside him.

He loved her.

It made a mockery of what he'd thought he felt for Stephanie all those years ago. This wasn't the crush of a young wolf fascinated with a beautiful wolfswan who was coveted by the pack. This was the bloody and bruised heart of an animal that had never really been opened before.

Aimee had come for him and she had stood beside him when no one else had. She alone had fought to save him from hell.

Even now . . .

Gods help me. He shouldn't feel like this. He should shove her out the door and yet he couldn't bring himself to destroy the serenity of this moment with her. The tenderness inside him that her touch awoke.

For the first time in his entire life, he was at peace.

Without a word, she trailed her hand up to brush through his hair. His body was white-hot, reminding him of the fact that it had been literally months since he'd last been with a woman.

And he wanted her with a madness that was consuming. A madness he had to deny for both their sakes.

"As much as I'm enjoying that, Aimee, you're going to have to stop."

"Why?"

"Because I want you so badly I can taste it."

She rolled him over onto his back. Her crystal blue gaze only added to the need in him to have her. Those dainty fingers, so soft and soothing, played over his lips as she smiled at him. Then she did the most amazing thing of all, she lowered her head and kissed him.

Fang growled at the taste of her. At the warmth of her breath mingling with his as their tongues danced together. He surrendered himself to the magic of her mouth.

For a moment, all of his thoughts scattered.

"No," he said, pulling away. "We can't do this."

"I know. I'm sorry." Kissing him lightly on the cheek, she got up slowly and straightened her clothes.

His cock twitched as her breasts were made even more apparent by that action. Damn, hadn't one of her brothers or her parents ever told her not to parade around like that? Her nipples were hard and outlined in a way that tortured him even worse than the demons had.

Gods, to taste just one of those . . .

The wolf inside was salivating.

"Are you hungry?"

Yes, he was, but not for food. "No. I'm all right."

She nodded. "I'll be in my room if you need me."

Naked? He almost groaned aloud as *that* image went through his mind with a clarity that should be illegal. *Damn it to hell, get out of my head.* But the image of her nude body was there and it blistered him.

As soon as she was gone, he placed his hand down to his cock to try and alleviate some of the pain she'd caused. It was no use. He was so hard, he could drive a nail with his erection.

"What am I going to do?"

If he touched her, he would violate all the laws of the Omegrion and her family would mount his balls to the mirror that hung over the bar.

So he would suffer. Whimper . . . none of it would give him what he really wanted, which was to be inside her sinfully delicious body.

"Fang?"

He heard Vane's voice from the other side of his door. Pulling the covers over his lap to hide what Aimee had done to him, he sighed at the welcomed interruption even though he dreaded seeing his brother again. "Come in."

Vane opened the door. "Hey."

Fang would have been amused by his uncharacteristic hesitancy, but right now nothing much could elicit that from him. Not while his body was this hungry.

Awkward silence filled the room as they stared at each other.

Vane leaned against the closed door. "I can't believe you're finally awake. I really thought I'd lost you."

"Yeah, well, you'll have to forgive me for being a selfish asshole." Fang cringed as those words flew out of his mouth before he could stop them.

Vane stiffened as he recognized the quote. "You heard me?"

Fang looked away, unwilling to answer. So he changed the subject. "Why's Stefan downstairs?"

"Markus has fallen and Stefan is no longer a leader. I put Fury in charge of the pack."

Fang couldn't have been more pissed off had his brother slapped him. Then again, that's exactly what he'd done by putting Fury in as their leader.

It should have been *him*.

"He's not strong enough to lead."

"With my backing he is."

And with Vane's backing, Fang couldn't challenge him for leadership. Well, he *could*, but it would break their bond and weaken them before the others, leaving them open to attack. Which was exactly what the other wolfswains would do. Perfect. He'd been completely cut out of his birthright.

Markus would be thrilled.

Vane moved forward cautiously as he watched Fang's solemn contemplation. This wasn't the reunion he'd expected when Fang finally came out of his coma. He'd dreamed of this moment over and over again. Fang waking up, happy to be alive. His brother embracing him. . . .

But something was different now. There was an air around Fang far deadlier than anything Vane had sensed from him before.

His brother was angry and there was a bitterness to him that he didn't understand. Why would he feel like that given what he'd put Vane and Fury through? "You've been out of it for months."

"Believe me, I know." His eyes flashed with brutal malice.

Frustrated, Vane sighed. "What do you want from me?"

"Nothing, Vane, I just want you to be happy."

His mouth might have said that, but his tone didn't.

Vane tried again to ease the tension between them. "I am that. Finally. Bride's better than I ever deserved. And we both have a room for you at our house."

Fang grimaced at his offer. "I don't know. You two are newly mated. The last thing you need is your mentally defective brother spooking the shit out of your woman."

That was a vintage Fang comment. One of the sarcastic retorts that Vane had been craving to hear all of these months past. "Bride doesn't spook easily."

"Probably true if she sees you first thing in the morning."

Vane smiled at his humor. His chest was tight as he realized just how much he really had missed his brother while Fang had been out of it. There was no one else in the world like him. "We want you with us."

Fang shot out of the bed as if he were about to attack. "I'm not your son, Vane," he snarled with an unexpected rage. "I'm not a child. I'm a grown wolf and I really don't think I belong with you guys."

He nodded, but refused to back down. He knew better than to let Fang sense his emotions. It would only make the wolf in him more volatile.

So he tried to change the subject to something safer. "There's something else you need to know about Fury."

Fang scoffed. "He's my brother. Aimee already told me."

That surprised the hell out of him. Just how close was his brother to the bearswan?

That couldn't be good.

"Do you want to see him?" Vane asked.

"Not really. In case you've forgotten, the two of us aren't exactly friendly."

"Yeah, I know. But he's been a big help protecting Bride."

"I'm glad you had him." The tone of his voice belied those words.

Vane scowled at his attitude, which was beginning to chafe his ass raw. He'd been keeping a leash on his temper, but it was starting to slip under the constant assault he didn't deserve.

He was trying, but Fang wasn't making any effort at all.

Instead Fang kept attacking and the wolf part of Vane was getting really sick of it. "Why are you so angry at me?"

Fang simmered inside. His fury was volcanic and he wanted to lash out at Vane in the worst way.

You let me down, you asshole!

But that wasn't the only bane that burned inside him. It was the fact that while Vane had let him down, he'd cursed him for being trapped. That his brother had said things to him that were wrong and hurtful.

And wholly undeserved.

He wanted to feel the same love and loyalty for his brother now that he'd felt the night Anya had died. But it wasn't there anymore and that hurt most of all.

Fang wasn't the same and neither was Vane.

Unwilling to fight anymore when it wouldn't change anything, Fang backed off. "Look, I still don't feel well. Why don't you go and spend time with your mate and Fury?"

"What about you? You're my family too."

Yeah, right.

Funny, he didn't feel like that anymore. "Just pretend I'm still in a coma. I'm sure that'll be easy enough for you to do."

Vane screwed his face up into a look of disgust. "Oh, fuck you, you selfish bastard. You know, Fury and I were the ones who kept you safe while you laid in bed, worthless to us. And now you dare to cop an attitude with me? You are such a bitter shit."

Fang raked Vane with a sneer. "Yeah, like *you* don't know anything about being selfish."

"What's that supposed to mean?"

"You abandoned me to chase tail and then when I didn't rise at your command, you buddied up with a bastard you hate. Don't forget, I know your love of Fury runs about as deep as mine does. Where was *your* loyalty in all this?"

Vane slung his hand out and pinned him to the wall. "You better be glad you've been sick or I'd shove those words down your throat."

Fang blasted him with a wave of his own. It shattered the powers Vane used to hold him and sent his brother reeling as he was released. "You're not the only one who can command magick, dick."

Vane looked up from where he'd landed on the floor against the wall, his features shocked. "How did you do that?"

"There's a lot about me you don't know, *adelphos.* Be grateful that I'm not willing to show it all to you. Now get out."

Vane pushed himself to his feet. No, this wasn't the

same Fang who'd been through a bitter childhood with him. Something was seriously wrong with his brother and he had no idea what.

But if Fang wouldn't tell him, there was nothing he could do.

He wiped his hand against his mouth. "Fine. Sit up here and rot." He slammed the door shut as he left.

Aimee shot out of her room at the sound and paused in the hallway as she saw him. "Are you all right?"

"No, I'm not." Vane glared at the closed door as he imagined splintering both it and Fang's head wide open. "I'm one step away from killing that idiot."

"Fang?"

"Is there another one?"

Her expression bemused, she nodded. "Quite a few under this roof, point of fact, and I'm related to several of them. But why would you want to hurt your brother after all he's been through?"

"After all he's been through?" Vane scoffed. "Pahlease! You sound like him. I'm sorry if laying in bed and being hand-fed because I can't deal with the same reality the rest of us had to face just doesn't relate to what has been happening to me and Fury. We barely survived the hunt. I've had to battle a demon and Daimons and—"

"And you think Fang wanted to be in that coma?"

Vane sneered at her. "You heard what Carson and Grace said. He could have come out of it anytime he wanted to."

Aimee shook her head. "No, Vane, he couldn't. Believe me."

"Believe you? No," he said as his bitterness swelled up deep inside him. How dare she take up for Fang. "I know my brother better than anyone and I know exactly how selfish he is. All he cares about is himself."

"Vane . . . you're wrong. Fang wasn't in a coma. He was trapped in hell. I know because I'm the one who went in and got him out of there. You battled one single demon. He battled *hundreds*."

CHAPTER 19

Fang sat on the edge of his bed with his feet on the floor, his elbows on his knees, and his head in his hands. He was so tired of everything. Tired of trying to hold himself together. Tired of hurting. Of longing for things he couldn't have.

He just wanted one minute of peace.

Why was that one thing so hard to find? Surely it should be simple and yet it was the most elusive target he'd ever known.

Before he could move, Vane appeared there before him in the room. He pulled Fang up from the bed and grabbed him in a hug so fierce he felt his ribs crack.

Fang fought the hold. "Get off me, you fucking perv!"

Vane let go, then punched him hard in his arm.

Grimacing, Fang shoved at him and would have returned the blow with one of his own had Vane not dodged it. "What was that for?"

Vane snarled at him. "For not telling me what happened to you, you *asshole*." That last word was loaded with enough venom to bring down a raging bull elephant.

Completely confused, he scowled. "What are you talking about?"

Vane grabbed him by the shirt and held him with two angry fists. "Aimee told me where you were all the months I thought you were in a coma. What pisses me off most is that you should have been the one who told me. Not her."

Pissed at his tone and hold, Fang shoved him back again. "Yeah, well, you should have been the one helping me get my soul back. Not her."

"I thought I was dreaming."

Fang snorted. "Vane, come help me," he said coldly, using the words he'd tried repeatedly to get his brother's attention. "Not exactly subtle."

A tic worked in Vane's jaw. He gestured toward the rumpled bed. "And when I came in here to see you, you looked comatose. Everyone told me that's what was wrong with you. How was I supposed to know otherwise?"

How indeed. Fang glared at him and his obtuse stupidity. "You should have known better. When have I *ever* laid down and licked my wounds? Really?"

Vane looked away, his features sheepish as he realized the truth. Fang wasn't a coward. He was a fighter through and through. "You're right. I should have known better. I should have thought better of you. But I know how much Anya meant to you. I just assumed—"

That Fang was weak and incompetent. It was what Vane had always thought of him and Fang was tired of being in his shadow. "Look, I don't want to talk about it. What's done is done. Thanks to Aimee and her brothers, I'm back."

Bully that, given the way Fury and Vane had shafted him. But for better or worse, he was here in the human realm.

Come to think of it, he'd basically traded one hell for another. *Tell me again why I fought so hard to get back here. . . .*

Then again, at least here no one was trying to disembowel him.

Yet.

"Let's just forget what happened."

Vane heard those words, but he knew his brother. He'd hurt Fang and it would take a lot of time for both of them to come to terms with what had happened. In all honesty, he hated himself for not being there when he should have been.

But as Fang said, he couldn't undo what had been done. All he could do was make sure that he never let it happen again.

"We're brothers, Fang. You mean everything to me. I hope you know that."

Fang grimaced. "When did you turn into a woman? Gah, if that's what being mated does, I'll do without."

Vane shook his head. "Bride didn't teach me that. Losing Anya did. There are a lot of things I wish I'd said to her before she died. I don't want to make that mistake with you."

Fang made a face. "Yeah, well, please make the mistake. You're creeping me out with the lovey bullshit." He jerked his chin toward the door. "Your woman's downstairs. You shouldn't keep her waiting."

He didn't budge. "We want you to live with us."

Fang still wasn't ready for that. Too much had

changed and living with Vane and his *human* mate . . . he'd really rather not.

"I think I'll stay here for a while. It'll be good for the two of you to have time together without your obnoxious brother intruding."

Vane scoffed. "Is that the real reason?"

"What else?"

Vane looked at the door, then lowered his voice to a low whisper. "Aimee."

Fang snorted, even though his brother was a lot closer to the truth than he ever wanted to admit. "We're friends."

"If you say so. But you have to know that if you're messing with her—"

"I'm not an idiot," he said between clenched teeth. "Wolves and bears don't mix."

"Keep that close. It may be the only thing that saves your life."

Fang rolled his eyes.

Vane clapped him on the back. "If you need me—"

"I'll call."

He shook his head. "I won't let you down again, Fang. I swear it."

"I know." But Fang still wasn't sure if he could trust Vane. His brother hadn't meant to let him down before. Yet it had happened.

Vane held his hand out to him.

Fang took it and let Vane pull him into a tight man hug. He patted him on the back before he left.

Alone, Fang returned to bed only to have someone else knock on the door. He knew instantly who it was. Only one person had that soft, hesitant knock and smelled of vanilla-scented lavender. "Come in, Aimee."

She pushed the door open to frown at him while she held a tray of food. "How did you know it was me?"

"I smelled you."

She tsked. "And to think I waste all that time bathing every day and all my money on soap. Why do I bother when I obviously smell to high heaven?"

He smiled in spite of himself as she set the tray aside. "I like the straight lavender more than that vanilla stuff you have on right now."

She cocked her head in mock offense and rested one hand on her hip. "Oh, I'm being dissed by the wolf who didn't bathe for . . . how many months was it?"

"Not my fault. You could have bathed me."

"Ha! Then you would have been skinned and would have never needed a bath again."

He despised how charmed he was by this exchange. More to the point, how charmed he was by her presence. "Why are you here?"

"I wanted to make sure you and Vane were good."

"Yeah."

She looked at him suspiciously as she neared the bed. "You don't sound sold on it."

"It's not that. I love my brother. I'm just . . ." Bitter. That was the only word to do any kind of justice to his surly mood. He only hoped it was temporary. "It's nothing that I won't get over."

She handed him a beer. "If you say so."

He took it from her and eyed the tray of food she'd parked on his dresser. "I thought I told you I wasn't hungry."

"I figured you were lying."

He laughed. "Thanks for the faith."

Wrinkling her nose at him, she uncovered a plate to show him ham, turkey, dressing, and potatoes. "Do you need anything else?"

You. . . .

Gods, he was such a fool. Her rump was the only roast he wanted to take a bite out of. Even now he could imagine stripping her bare and making love to her until they were both blind from it.

He cleared his throat, wishing he could clear his mind just as easily. "No, and I'm really sorry for the way I treated you earlier."

"You should be, but I understand. I have the same feelings, which really piss me off."

He took a deep draft of his beer. "There's something wrong with us, isn't there?"

"Yes. We're broken."

Setting the beer aside, he pulled her toward him until she was standing between his spread knees. Her scent wrapped around him like a warm cloak as he imagined sliding her T-shirt over her head and freeing her breasts. "I've never wanted a woman as badly as I do you."

She rested her hands on his shoulders as she looked down at him, her gaze scalding hot. "I've never wanted a man until you."

He leaned his head against her stomach while she brushed her hand through his hair, then down to his shoulders. "What are we going to do?"

Her touch sent chills over him. "We have to stay away from each other. I'm my mother's heir. I have to find a bearswain to mate with."

Anger shot through him at those words. He couldn't stand the thought of another man touching her. But he let the heat of her body soothe him until he was calm again. "We can be adults about this."

"Absolutely. We're just friends."

"Friends." Had there ever been a more disgusting word invented?

Aimee looked down at him as he pulled away to gaze up at her. His hair was shaggy and his whiskers were already starting to darken his cheeks again—it gave him a feral sex appeal that was hard to resist. And those beautiful eyes of his . . . she could lose herself to him so easily.

Don't . . .

"I'm going to my room now."

Fang nodded and released her. His heart heavy, he watched her leave even though what he really wanted to do was call her back and run off to a place where no one would care that he was a wolf and she a bear.

"What have I done?"

Made a complete and utter wreck of your life.

It was true. Everything was screwed up and he had no idea how to make it right again.

Sighing, he went to the tray Aimee had brought and sat down to eat.

Aimee tried her best to sleep. But for some reason, she couldn't. It was around three in the morning when she went to the bathroom and saw the light shining from underneath Fang's door.

Against her better judgment, she padded down the hallway to knock lightly on his door.

He didn't answer.

"Fang?" she whispered.

Again he didn't answer.

Closing her eyes, she looked inside the room and found him there. He was pacing the room like a caged animal. Wild. Cold. Deadly.

Something was wrong.

Without considering the danger, Aimee went inside to check on him.

He whirled on her so fast, she couldn't even protect herself. He pinned her to the wall, his hand on her throat as if he would kill her right where she stood.

But the moment he touched her, his gaze cleared and he focused on her face. "What are you doing here?"

"I saw your light and I was worried about you."

Fang pulled back, his features tormented as he raked one hand through his dark hair. "I can't breathe, Aimee. I can't relax. I'm terrified of going to sleep. What if I don't wake up again?"

The fact that he confided that to her told her exactly how upset he was. "You're all right. You're back and you're safe."

"Am I? I couldn't wake up earlier."

She pulled him into her arms and held him close. "It's over, Fang."

Fang wanted to believe that, but how could he? "No, it's not. I can still feel them clawing at me. I can hear the flapping of the Reapers' wings and see the Harvesters looking for victims. They're coming for me. I know it."

She pulled his face into her hands and made him

look at her. "I will stay with you and make sure no one takes you back."

He scoffed.

"Listen to me," she said firmly. "You don't seriously think that I went through months of hell, stalking Daimons and descending into Kalosis to let them have you again, do you?"

Well, when she put it that way. "No."

"Then trust me. I'm not going to let them come for you. If there's one thing a bear can do, it's fight."

Fang nodded. He returned to bed. Aimee pulled the blanket up over him and sat down on the edge.

He took her hand into his and held it close to where Thorn had branded him. But she couldn't see the mark through his T-shirt. He wanted to tell her about the bargain he'd made.

If only he could. The truth was, he was ashamed that he'd been unable to protect her without it.

Most of all, he was scared the demon inside him would manifest and hurt her.

"If I do anything strange, you leave me immediately. You understand?"

Aimee furrowed her brow in suspicion. "Strange how?"

"I don't know. Try to eat you?"

She arched her brows at that. "Ooo-kay. You do that sort of thing a lot?"

"Not really, but who knows after all this. I might even sprout horns and turn into Simi when you're not looking."

"Well, I promise if you come at me with bad juju, I

will tear out your guts. And if you transform into a teenaged female Goth demon, I'm going to laugh my butt off."

"Good."

She laughed. "You're the only one I know who could find that threat a relief."

Fang tried to smile, but his exhaustion was overtaking him. There was something about Aimee that made him feel safe. Before he knew it, he was finally asleep.

Aimee sat there for an hour, watching Fang sleep. It was so strange to see him like that. He reminded her of her nephew who didn't like the dark.

Only Micah was four.

What horrors had Fang been through down there that he was still so haunted by them?

"I wish I could help." But only time could heal what had been broken inside him. All she could do was be there when he needed strength and friendship.

What are you thinking?

She needed to keep her distance from him. Yet it was so hard when all she wanted was to strip her clothes off, slide into bed beside him, and pull his body deep inside hers.

There was something so infectious about him.

What if he's my mate?

Surely the Fates wouldn't be *that* cruel.

Oh, what was she thinking? Of course they would. They'd conspired to have men eat their own children. Mothers kill their babies. There was no one more treacherous than the Moirai.

Her heart heavy, she ran one finger over his grizzled cheek. She loved how he felt. How he looked.

Most of all, she loved his sarcastic, bitter humor.

Letting out a tired breath, she leaned back against the wall. "What's going to become of us?"

Eli looked up as Cosette entered his study. The light-skinned Creole woman was as beautiful as her ancestor, Marie Laveau, one of the most notorious voodoo priestesses in the world. A mere slip of a woman, she wore a white flowing skirt and pale blue peasant top that fell off one shoulder. Her blond hair was pulled back from her face by a red scarf so that the tight curls fell out of control to her shoulders.

But it was her green almond-shaped eyes that were haunting. She reminded him of an untamed cat and swished across the floor with a seductive gait that would draw the notice of any straight man who saw her. That gait also caused unseen bells to chime with every move she made.

Damn, she was gorgeous.

"What can I do for you?" he asked, shutting the planner he'd been making notes in.

"We have a problem, *cher.*"

"And that is?"

"My demon is dead."

Eli didn't move for three heartbeats as those words sank in. "What do you mean?"

"My spirits have told me that a *loup-garou* slew him as he went for the whore I'd sent him to kill. It is hard for me to frame your enemies while my servants are slaughtered before they can carry out their assignment. I just thought you should know."

Eli folded his hands with a calmness he certainly

didn't feel. The demon was supposed to have killed a student and then leave evidence to implicate Kyle Peltier for the murder. The alley of the attack had been carefully chosen since it was a block away from a club the young bear was renovating.

"I'm not happy, Cosette."

"Do I look to be celebrating?" She pinned him with a glower that would make a lesser man fear for his soul.

"Can you not summon another demon?"

She made a sound of deep aggravation. "Summoning one of his strength is not an easy thing to do. I was in bed for three days afterward."

"The details don't really concern me."

"Well, they should."

"And why is that?"

One corner of her mouth lifted into a mocking smile. "The universe is one of careful balance. What you send out always finds a way to return. This *loup-garou* is a hunter, a chaser for another. My spirits have told me to leave him be."

He scoffed at her superstitious bullshit. "You should be careful, *ma petite*. There are things far scarier in this universe than your hunter."

"I know this to be true. But . . . there is something evil brewing here in this city. A convergence of spirits. It concerns me."

"You should be more concerned with failing me. I don't like disappointments." He drummed his hand idly over the black leather as he contemplated her news. "Tell me . . . did your spirits happen to give you the name of this *loup-garou*?"

"They called him Fang."

His hand froze midstroke. Fang . . .

That bastard who was supposed to die. The one who'd laid his filthy paws on his son.

Eli pulled his hand back as raw, unmitigated rage poured through him. "You have no idea how unhappy this makes me."

"There you would be wrong. I do know. But listen to me. My spirits are never wrong. An evil power will emerge here and it will threaten us all. We should beware."

Eli intended to do more than be wary of the trouble. He was going to rely on it and use it. And that was what gave him a brilliant plan.

Why hadn't he thought of this sooner?

Sanctuary laws didn't apply to all species. There was one in particular that they neither protected nor monitored. A species who wasn't bound to follow Omegrion rules.

Forget Varyk and what he was working on. This was so much better. It would be something that the Peltiers would never see coming.

Something that would destroy them forever.

"Cosette, my wily child, I have a new idea for you and your spirits."

CHAPTER 20

True to his words, Fang stayed on at Sanctuary to work as a bouncer. Papa Bear had tried to make him a waiter, but one evening of that had proven disastrous since Fang lacked the proper temperament.

Whenever someone complained about their food, it didn't go well for them.

But for Aimee's intervention, there would still be a tourist in traction. And there was now a hole in the wall being patched by Quinn that was coming out of Fang's next paycheck.

So he worked as muscle when they needed it while Dev stayed at the door and monitored who came and went.

It wasn't the worst job in the world and it left him free to watch Aimee without her brothers tearing his eyes out of their sockets. Better yet, they paid him to keep an eye on her and make sure no one came on to her while she worked. It was definitely a job with perks.

And how he loved to watch her. The way she'd laugh with their regulars or tease the younger humans who'd come in to eat with their parents in the daytime. She always brought them special treats and would even sit down and draw with them if they weren't busy. She loved children of all species.

He couldn't help but wonder how much better she'd be with her own cubs. . . .

There was an unrivaled grace in everything she did and it made him ache just to watch her.

If only he were a bear. . . .

That thought tortured him constantly as they brushed past each other while trying to stay indifferent. It was so unfair, but then he knew that was how life went. And he seemed to be its whipping boy most days.

"Hey, Fang?" Remi barked in his usual distemper. "Give us a hand."

He turned his head to see Wren, Colt, and Remi trying to move the heavy speakers onstage to a new position so Angel, the lead singer of the Howlers, wouldn't bitch again about feedback.

Hernia, here I come.

Aimee paused on her way to the bar to watch as Fang leapt up onstage without touching it. Shoving her notepad into her pocket, she bit the pencil in her mouth at the gorgeous sight of his backside.

The pencil snapped in two.

Spitting out pieces of lead and wood into her hand towel, she scoffed at herself. Yuck! Could anything be more gross?

And it was all Fang's fault.

What am I doing?

Ogling the finest piece of ass in New Orleans.

Well, there was that. She watched as his muscles bulged while he lifted one side of the speaker tower while the group of them slid it across the stage.

"Damn . . . have you ever seen a better sight?" Tara, their human college student/waitress, asked as she stopped by her side. "I love working here. Days like this, I think I should be paying you guys for the privilege."

Aimee laughed. "You know, I very seldom think about it."

"That's because you're related to most of the fine hot meat here. Pity for you. 'Cause to the rest of us . . ." She made a growling noise that belied her human birth.

Aimee shook her head. Good thing Justin hadn't heard that. He'd be on the prowl to make her repeat that sound while naked. Or better yet, make her purr.

Tara sucked her breath in sharply. "That's it, baby. Bend over and pick that up. Take your time with it, honey. No hurry at all. Ooo, mama!"

Aimee laughed until she turned to see who Tara was talking about. Anger snapped as she saw Fang's rear cupped way too tightly by his jeans. Worse, his shirt had ridden up to show a tantalizing glimpse of his lower back and the tight, tawny skin she was dying to taste.

She had a sudden urge to rip the human's hair out for daring to even glance at him. More to the point, she wanted to hang a sign around his neck that read: *Mine. Look at the risk of losing your eyeballs . . . and hair.*

"We need to get back to work."

Tara pouted. "Spoilsport." She trotted off to check on a table while Aimee took another look at Fang. At least he was standing again. But with his weight on one leg and his hands on his hips, he was even sexier than before.

An image of walking up to him and laying her body against his went through her. In her mind, she could already feel him there as he leaned his head back while she trailed one hand over his hard chest, down those perfect abs until she could dip her hand into his jeans and cup him in her hand.

Her body throbbed as she felt herself getting wet at the very idea. Maman had been right. The quickening was almost impossible to resist. It left her hungry and irritable.

And it didn't help that she was going into heat again. It was why her brothers were being particularly careful about letting the humans too near her. They wanted to protect the bloodline as closely as her parents did.

So why didn't she?

Fang's skin crawled as he got the fierce sensation of being watched. Expecting an enemy, he scanned the dark club and was surprised to find Aimee openly staring at him as if she wanted to take a bite out of him.

That was fine by him since he wouldn't mind having a piece of her either.

"Dude!"

He jerked around at Colt's angry snarl. Rushing forward, he grabbed his end and helped to move it. But he could still feel Aimee watching him. It made every nerve ending in his body sizzle and his groin swell to the point he was practically limping.

By the time they'd moved the speakers into their new position, Aimee was gone.

Fang wanted to curse.

It's for the best.

Yeah . . .

He jumped off the stage to find Fury waiting for him

by the bar. Instant rage singed him. The bastard was currently living with Vane and that really didn't endear him to Fang in the least.

"You want something?" Fang asked churlishly as he reached behind the bar to grab a beer. One of the perks of working here. Free alcohol.

"Yeah." Fury turned to face him. "I'm abdicating the pack."

Fang froze and set the bottle down. "What do you mean?"

Fury sighed, arms akimbo. "Look, we both know I'm not strong enough to hold it from anyone who attacks me with magick. But for Vane, I wouldn't have it now. The Katagaria Grand Regis should have been yours anyway. It's only right."

Fang sneered at his "magnanimous" offer that insulted him to the core of his being. "I don't need your fucking charity."

"Then fight me for it."

Fang curled his lip at the asshole and his stupidity. "Don't tempt me. I fight you and I undermine Vane—I don't think so." He drained his beer, then went to grab a towel so that he could help Wren wipe down tables.

Fury followed after him. "Why do you hate me so much? What have I ever done to you?"

You were with Vane when he needed me to help protect Bride. And he was with Vane when Fang needed Vane to help *him*. But he'd never admit that hurt to anyone. It was his to carry, not something to be shared so that they could mock him over it.

When he didn't answer, Fury raked him with a disgusted glare while Fang wiped down a table near them.

"You know what, Fang? I don't even give a shit. You keep being an asshole all you want. I don't care. Stay here sulking with the bears. It's nothing to me, but let me tell you something. I've never had what you and Vane do. I never had a brother at my back, not once. Really, one day you should meet our brother Dare and see what a piece of work he is. Just for the record, he was the first one who came at my back when he learned I was Katagaria. Pardon the pun, but he threw me to the wolves and went for my throat. So if you want to be as human as he was, I'd appreciate a little warning first."

Fang watched as Fury stalked off. He wanted to blast him. To throw him down and rip his throat out.

But they were brothers.

Fury had come here and offered to abdicate as leader. Fang knew the wolf well enough to know that Fury didn't back down easily. It had been a massive knock to his ego to make that offer.

Stop being a dick, Fang. His *brother* was trying to make peace between them.

Fang looked away as he tried to imagine what it had been like for Fury to be in the pack with them all these past centuries, knowing he was family and not saying anything to any of them.

Why? Why would he have done that?

Wanting an answer, he went after him. He caught up to him outside as Fury was unlocking his bike while holding his helmet in one tight fist.

"Tell me something?"

Fury paused.

"Why didn't you ever tell us the truth?"

"I already answered that," Fury said snidely. "The

last time my *brother* found out what I was, he stabbed me and tried to kill me and that was the one I was raised with. The one *I* used to protect from the rest of the pack when they wanted to beat on him for being part Katagaria. Our sister spat in my face and drove her dagger through my ribs—again, this was the same sister I used to protect from our mother and Dare and everyone else. So I wasn't expecting anything better from *you*. Thanks so much for not disappointing me, asshole."

Fang didn't know why, but those words sent him over the edge. Rage descended on him with a vengeance and before he knew what he was doing, he'd launched himself at Fury. Wrapping his arms around his waist, he threw him to the ground and proceeded to beat the holy shit out of him.

Aimee gasped as she saw an image of Fang being hurt in her head. He was fighting outside. All she could see was a blur of body parts and black leather.

Before she could think better of it, she ran to the door where she saw him and Fury across the street, fighting each other with everything they had. The moment she stepped outside to stop them, Dev caught her against him.

"Let me go!" she demanded, tempted to stomp on his foot. If he'd been wearing anything other than his steel-toed biker boots, she would have. But in those, he wouldn't feel anything and she'd bruise her heel.

Experience with Remi had taught her that.

He tightened his hold. "Let them settle this, Aimee."

She stopped fighting to stare up at him. "They're going to get hurt."

"Probably, but you have enough brothers to know that sometimes we just have to beat each other's heads in. It's just a moral imperative."

It was true. She'd never understood that tendency herself, but for some reason, one brother would say something or look weird and then it was on. At least until Papa broke them up.

"Why are they fighting?"

Dev shrugged as he released her and stepped away to return to leaning against the brick wall behind him. He crossed his arms over his chest and bent one knee to rest his foot on the wall too. "I have no idea. But I'm taking odds on Fang."

She wasn't amused by his humor. "Then how do you know this is the best thing?"

" 'Cause I saw the look on Fang's face when he went for Fury. It's the same one I get right before I open a can of whup-ass on Remi."

Aimee ground her teeth in frustration, but Dev was right. She knew that look intimately and had worn it a time or two herself. "Papa always breaks you guys up."

"Yeah, and if they go too far, I will too. But this I think they need to get out of their systems."

"And if they turn into wolves while they're fighting on a public street?"

"We'll deal with it if it happens."

Aimee wasn't so sure about this as she watched Fury lift Fang up off his feet and slam him onto the ground. Fang flipped up and then dealt Fury a blow so hard she swore *she* could feel it. They looked like they were trying to kill each other with their bare hands.

What on earth were they thinking?

* * *

Fang pounded Fury with a lifetime of pent-up anger. Every time Fury had flipped him off or mouthed at him over the centuries and Vane had stopped him from attacking the little prick. Every time he'd wanted Vane in the Nether Realm and had been forced to fight the demons on his own. . . .

Every bit of it came out.

But as he pounded, other images came to him too. Fury trying to stand up to their father when no one else would. Fury staying with them when Anya had died. . . .

Fury fighting by their sides. . . .

Brothers.

He dealt Fury a blow to the chin that knocked him straight onto his back, flat on the ground. He went down on his knee and twisted his fist in Fury's black T-shirt, intending to hit him again. But the sight of Fury's face gave him pause.

There was a cut above his right eye that left blood trailing down his temple. His lips were split, his teeth bloody. Bruises were forming on his chin and cheek.

And even though his eyes were spitting venom, Fury hadn't gone wolf. Human was his weakest form and yet he fought with him as a man.

He wasn't fighting to really hurt him or to win. . . .

Not hurt him. . . .

Fang's dark eyes locked with those eerie turquoise ones. Shame filled him over what he'd just done. He'd attacked Fury as a petty human with hurt feelings.

No, he'd attacked his brother as a rampaging demon.

Lowering his fist, he loosened his hold on Fury's shirt and let him fall back to the sidewalk.

"You through?" Fury taunted as he lay there. "Is that all you got, nancy?"

Fang scoffed at his insult. "You are such a fucking dick."

"And you're an asshole."

Fang sat back on his haunches and started laughing at the two of them on the street, bleeding. He wasn't even sure why he found their patheticness funny, but he did.

As he wiped his hand over his own bleeding lip, he hissed in pain. "Your left hook is impressive."

Fury rolled over to spit blood onto the sidewalk before he sat up. "I could say the same for you."

Fang shook his head as he realized just how sore his ribs were from Fury's punches. For all his lack of Were-Hunter skills and psychic abilities, the little bastard was a good scrapper. "I can't believe of all the wolves in the universe that *you're* my brother."

"Yeah, well, I didn't exactly get the pick of the litter either."

Fang laughed again. "No, you didn't. The Fates seriously screwed you there."

Fury narrowed his gaze as he tested his loosened teeth with his thumb. He spat out more blood. "So are we still enemies?"

Fang hesitated. A part of him kept wanting to hate Fury, but the problem was he didn't know why.

Was he really that human that he could hate without reason? Or was it the demon inside him that wanted Fury's head?

In the end, it was the knowledge that this was his family that won over everything else. For better or worse, they were blood kin. And to a wolf that was all that mattered.

Fang held his hand out to him. "Brothers."

Fury wrapped his hand around his. "*Adelphos*."

Fang pulled him forward so that he could hug him in a way he'd reserved for only Vane and Anya. "But this doesn't mean I like you."

Fury shoved him away. "Don't worry. I don't like you either, dipshit. But I would kill to protect you."

Fang gave him a lopsided grin. "Me too." He pushed himself up, then held his hand out for Fury.

Fury knocked it away. "I'm not your bitch, wolf. I can get up on my own."

Fang spat some of the blood out of his mouth. Yeah, his jaw was going to be sore for at least a week and there wouldn't be any food tonight that required much chewing.

He narrowed his gaze on Fury. "We're way too much alike to ever get along."

"That's what Vane says." Fury picked his helmet up from where it'd landed on the sidewalk when they'd started fighting. He dumped debris out of it before he put it on his head.

"Hey?"

Fury paused.

Fang held his hand out again and when Fury took it, he pulled him into a quick man hug. "The pack is yours."

Fury snorted. "I really don't see you subservient to me. Ever."

"I'm not, but I'm not part of the pack anymore. I'm declaring independence."

Fury flipped his face shield up to scowl at him. "That's suicide."

"No. I'm here." He indicated Sanctuary over his shoulder. "I need some time to get my head straight. If I do, I'll be back. But for now I think this is the best thing for me."

Fury gave him a doubting stare. "If you say so. I'll tell Vane." Lowering his shield, he slung one long leg over the bike and started it.

Fang stood back as Fury opened the throttle and squealed off. It was only then he realized Aimee was standing across the street with Dev, watching every move they'd made.

Suddenly sheepish, he tucked his hands into his pockets and joined them.

"Feeling better?" Dev asked sarcastically.

"Yeah. Thanks for not interfering."

The bear shrugged. "Hey, I get it. Wish someone would let me do that to a couple of my bros."

Aimee let out an exasperated breath as she stepped forward. "You look terrible." She reached up and turned his chin to the side so that she could study his right eye, which was throbbing and stinging. "Sheez. Carson needs to see this."

"I'm not a puss, Aimee. I've had a lot worse that healed on its own. This too shall pass."

She let go of his chin and growled at him. "No offense, but I hate Macho Fang. I really wish you'd put him in a closet, lock the door, and lose the key."

Dev laughed. "Sorry, wolf. We're the reason she has this whole hang-up on men."

"It's all right. As long as she doesn't slap me or bite me, we're good."

Dev sucked his breath in sharply. "Man, wolf sex must be harsh."

"Yeah, well, I don't even want to know what you bears do."

Aimee made a sound of distress. "Excuse me? Boys? I am still standing here, you know?"

Dev grinned wickedly. "Yeah, we know. We just don't care."

In a huff, she turned and left.

Fang started to stop her, but doing that in front of Dev wouldn't be the smartest course of action. And one ass-whipping a night was all he was good for at the moment.

"Why don't you go upstairs and grab a bath? Take some time off. You can help close up at dawn."

"Thanks." Fang went back inside.

Wren paused as soon as he saw him. "Remind me not to get you pissed off."

Fang ignored him as he returned to his room. He was surprised to find Aimee there, waiting for him.

He shut the door fast before someone on the outside caught sight of her there. "What are you doing?"

She held up a bottle of peroxide and a small container of cotton balls. "I was worried about you, Mr. High King Macho." She pulled the chair out from his small desk. "Now sit."

"Aimee—"

"Sit, wolf." It was the sharpest tone he'd heard from her in a long time. "You might have taken Fury, but I can take *you*."

Yeah, right. That was almost funny. However, he knew what she did . . . wolves didn't attack women unless they were trying to kill them or someone they cared about. So she was safe and he was defenseless.

Sighing, he sat down as ordered.

She tipped the peroxide to moisten the cotton pad. "What is it with you males that you have to fight like that?"

"We're damaged?"

"Apparently."

Fang hissed as she touched a particularly tender spot.

She made a sound of agitation. "Stop your whining, you big baby. If you're going to fight, at least act like you can take the wounds."

He glared at her.

She moved to a new spot that was no less painful, but this time he rode herd on his body.

"Would you please explain to me why you two went at it like that?"

Fang shrugged. "There's a part of me that hates him."

"Why?"

"I don't know. Hasn't anyone ever rubbed you the wrong way?"

"Yes. *You* a great deal of the time. But notice I haven't beat *your* head in yet."

He pulled her hand away from his face so that he could stare up at her. "Then why do you keep coming around me?"

"It must be from the rock Remi hit me in the head with when I was thirteen. The concussion must have gone deeper than any of us guessed."

He ran his hands up her sides and pulled her forward until she was straddling his left thigh. Damn, she was the prettiest woman he'd ever seen and all he could think about was ripping her shirt open so that he could taste her.

Aimee let the cotton fall from her hand as he captured her gaze with his. The look in his eyes was scorching and when combined with her heat . . .

He took the bottle from her hand and set it aside. Slowly, he reached up to cup her cheek. She dipped her head so that she could kiss him.

Aimee groaned at how good he tasted as she lowered herself onto his leg. She whimpered as the sensitive part of her made contact with the hard muscles of his thigh. The ache there was excruciating. And as her knee lightly brushed the bulge in his jeans, he growled.

Fang couldn't think as she slid into his arms and he tasted her fully. Yes, it made his swollen and bruised lips burn, but he didn't care. Not when the pain in his groin shoved that minuscule ache away.

By the scent of her, he knew she was in heat. He could have her in an instant. Whenever a Katagari female was in season, her need to mate was all-consuming.

She pulled away from his lips, her teeth nipping before she buried her face against his neck. She laved the skin just below his earlobe. Chills erupted all over him.

"I want you, Fang," she panted in his ear.

"We can't do this."

"I know." She unbuttoned his fly and slid his zipper down so that she could touch him.

In that one moment, he was completely undone. His

eyes rolled back in his head as she stroked him with her soft hand. Gods, how long had it been since a woman touched him?

He bit his lip before he buried his head in her neck to breathe her in.

Aimee shuddered at the feel of Fang's tongue on her flesh. She felt him undoing her pants and when he sank his hand down to touch her, she cried out in pleasure. She lifted herself up ever so slightly so that he could slide one finger deep inside her. No one had ever touched her there before.

She ran her hand down the length of his shaft, letting his wetness coat her fingers as his cock grew even larger. Her body wanted him inside her, but the last vestige of sanity knew they couldn't do that. If he penetrated her, they could emerge as mates.

It was something they couldn't allow.

So she satisfied herself with this bit of intimacy while she reveled in the pleasure of his hand stroking her.

Fang leaned his head back as Aimee ran her tongue from his throat up to his chin. He felt as if he were dying. His body on fire, he showed her how to stroke him.

Damn, she was a quick learner. And the feel of her hand on him while she tongued his ear was more than he could stand.

Fang stood up so fast he barely caught her before she hit the floor. He set her on the desk, knocking the bottle to the floor where it spilled down the vent. But he didn't care. Not when his body was shaking and begging for something that could get them both killed.

But the sight of her there with her pants lowered . . .

Her eyes were dark and inviting as she reached for him. "Please, Fang. I can't stand it. My body is killing me."

He knew that sensation, and the fact that she was in heat made it worse on her. Damning himself for the stupidity, he pulled her pants off.

Aimee felt heat rush over her face as Fang bared her to his hungry gaze. He sank down on his knees as he parted her legs and slid his hands up her thighs to the center of her body.

His gaze held hers captive as he took her into his mouth. Aimee yelped in pleasure. Reaching down, she sank her hand into his hair and held him against her while his tongue soothed the fire inside her.

Fang had never tasted anything better. He ravaged her, exploring every part until her scent was branded into him. And when she finally came, he didn't stop until he'd wrung the last spasm from her.

Aimee lay back against the wall, panting as her body slowly returned to normal. But she saw the pain that was still in Fang's eyes. His body was still swollen.

"You need a hand with that?"

He took her hand into his. "You're not funny, Aimee."

She sucked her breath in sharply as he led her hand down to cup him. He was so large now. That was one of the things she knew about wolves. Their cocks grew larger throughout sex, and when they came it was several minutes before they could return to a normal state.

Fang buried his head in her neck as he thrust himself against her hand. He was like a savage beast and it made her wonder what it would be like to have him deep inside her.

When he finally came, he cried out her name. Aimee held him close, keeping her hand on him for as long as he needed the pressure.

He lifted his head to scorch her with a look of tenderness. "What have we done?"

She kissed him gently. "Nothing. This can't mate us."

Fang wasn't so sure about that. But at least his palm wasn't burning from being marked. At least not yet. Stepping away from her, he zipped his pants up so fast he caught himself. "Shit!" he snarled even though he was grateful for the pain. He needed that to bring the blood back into his brain.

Aimee met his gaze and he saw the tears brimming in her eyes. "I love you, Fang."

He clamped his jaw shut to keep from telling her that he loved her too. That would only weaken him more. "What are we going to do?"

"I don't know. I don't." She scooted off the desk to retrieve her pants and dress.

All he wanted to do was take her in his arms and hold her for the rest of eternity.

Fang pulled her locket off and handed it to her. "We can't get caught. Your mother is the Grand Regis Ursulan and my brothers rule both seats for the Lykos. Us being together would void every treaty Savitar has in place."

She nodded as she fastened her pants. "It would pollute our bloodlines."

He pinned her with a hot stare. "And I really don't give a shit."

Cupping his cheek in her hand, she smiled up at him. "Neither do I."

"Aimee?"

They both looked at the door as they heard Mama Lo's voice in the hallway.

Ah, shit! This was bad.

"Where is that girl?"

"I have to go," she whispered before she vanished.

Fang cursed. But no sooner had she gone than Mama Lo opened the door to his room. He used his powers to camouflage what they'd just done.

At least he hoped he did.

Nicolette scanned the room suspiciously. "Where is Aimee?"

He knew he couldn't deny that she'd been here since her scent would be more than evident to Nicolette's heightened senses and while he could mask most of it, he couldn't remove every trace of her. "I don't know. She brought some peroxide to me and vanished."

Which was true so Nicolette wouldn't smell the lie on him. He just left out some really important details.

Nicolette sighed. "There is another contingency of bears downstairs for her to mate with. I swear, she's never where she's supposed to be."

Fang had to ride herd on his temper at those words as well as the urge to go downstairs and skin a bear. "If she comes back for the peroxide, I'll let her know."

"Please do so."

He caught a strange note in her voice. "Is something wrong?"

"*Non.*"

But he knew she was lying. "What is it?"

"Nothing." She left and shut the door.

Frowning, Fang opened it to watch her leave as Wren

came up the stairs. Nicolette curled her lip at the tigard, but said nothing.

Wren, for his part, made an obscene gesture behind
her back. He paused as he realized Fang had seen it.

"What's the deal with the two of you?"

Wren shrugged. "She thinks I'm a freak. I think
she's a bitch. Nicolette doesn't believe our races should
mix and she hates me for being a mongrel."

"She accepts me."

"I'm a little different from you."

Fang snorted. "No offense, Wren, you're a little different from everyone."

Marvin came running up the stairs with a banana.
He leapt onto Wren's shoulder and chattered at Fang,
pointing the banana at him like a gun. That spoke for
itself. They both were whacked.

"Why do you stay here?"

Wren took the banana from Marvin so that he could
peel it for the primate. "The same reason you do."

"And that is?"

Wren glanced toward the stairs. "She's the only person or animal I've ever met who truly is kind. I don't
have any family and when I was brought here, I didn't
trust anyone. I still don't. Except for her."

Aimee. He didn't say her name because he didn't
have to. She was the only one Wren ever really spoke
with.

"You love her?"

"As a sister and a friend. I'd die to protect her." Wren
stepped closer to him and lowered his voice. "I've seen
how you two look at each other and it scares me."

"Why?"

"Because even though it's frowned on, it's accepted for Katagaria to be with Arcadian. But for the species to blend . . . take it from someone who was crossbred, you don't want to go there. And if not for her, then think if the Fates are cold enough to give you children. The hatred of others drove my mother mad and in the end she hated me for it."

"We're not mates, Wren. You know as well as I do that we have no control over that."

"Of course you do. If you don't sleep together, you don't mate. *That* you control." He broke off a piece of banana and gave it to Marvin. "Trust me, wolf. Stay away from her for both your sakes." Wren left him and headed toward his room.

It was a warning he didn't really need.

Fang returned to his room while those words rang in his ears. The problem was, he wasn't getting hard for any other woman. It already felt like the Fates had mated them. . . .

What am I going to do?

He pulled up short as he saw a shadow in the corner.

It moved forward into the light to show him the last person he expected to see.

Thorn.

CHAPTER 21

Fang moved forward into the room, making sure to show Thorn no sign of his hostility. "What are you doing here?"

Thorn leaned nonchalantly against the desk. He crossed his arms over his chest while he kept a probing stare trained on Fang. "Just checking in with you. Wanted to see if the demon was winning and if we needed to kill you because of it."

"Nice to see you again too. I see time away hasn't made you any more charming."

"Oh, I can be charming. I just choose not to. People start to think you like them, then when you stab them in the back, they take it so personally. Really pisses me off."

Fang sat on the bed and tugged his biker boots off. "Do that a lot, do you?"

"Boy, don't make me smite you." He crossed one long leg over the other.

Fang tossed his boots aside and laughed. "Just how old are you again?"

"You don't need to know anything about me. It's much safer that way."

"Safer for who?"

"Most definitely *you*." There was a deadly undercurrent in Thorn's voice. "There's really only two, maybe three, entities who threaten me. And you're not one of them."

Point taken. Fang leaned back on his arms to narrow his gaze on Thorn. Honestly, he was getting tired of this pointless exchange. "So why are you really here? Do you have another assignment for me?"

"No. Just a warning."

"For what?"

Thorn scratched his chin as if they were just shooting the shit between them and not handing over information that could prove vital. "One of the demon spawn here summoned Jaden out of his hole."

There was a name Fang had never heard before. "Jaden?"

A snide smile curved Thorn's lips. "He's a . . . demon broker. He bargains with the primal source to attain powers and other things for demons. Personally, I hate the bastard and he's not real fond of me either. Since you're new to all of this, I wanted to warn you to stay out of his way."

"Why?"

"Suffice it to say that he's been known to use my people as target practice. He doesn't really think I'm on the up-and-up and so he sees you guys as stupid pawns."

"Does he have reason to think that?"

"Not really. Basically he's just another prick I have to deal with. I think it's emotional scars from his childhood that won't allow him to believe in anything. Or maybe it's post-traumatic stress disorder or simple brain damage. End of the day, don't really give a shit, but he is lethal, so steer clear."

"And how will I know him? Does he by chance wear shirts with his name on them?"

Thorn laughed. "Damn, wolf, I do like your sarcasm. No, his mother didn't sew his name on or in his clothes. But you can't miss him. Tall bastard with one brown eye and one green. Really off-putting. He has a slave collar and an aura of power that smacks of a godhood he doesn't have. He also has demon funk all over him."

Lovely that. Fang could gag already. "Noted and marked."

"Good. Now you need to be on your toes. If Jaden was summoned here, someone is playing with fire and they're after something pretty severe that requires a lot of power to achieve. You are one of three Hellchasers stationed here and I expect you three to play nice and be firemen."

"Firemen?"

"Yeah. When the fires of hell break open, you guys put them out."

Damn, so much for his thoughts that a simple fire hose would work. "Do the other Hellchasers have names?"

"Varyk and Wynter. You've met Wynter already and I'm rather sure you won't like Varyk in the least."

"Why?"

"He's an Arcadian Lykos."

That news hit him like a fist to the gut. For a minute, Fang couldn't focus as raw fury tore through him. "I thought I was the only one you had."

Thorn smiled snidely. "Varyk is a werewolf. You are

a wolfwere. Though to most people there isn't much difference, in our world there is. But if it makes you feel better, you are the only two Were-Hunters I have on tap. Besides, there were politics in the way, which is why Varyk couldn't be utilized against Phrixis."

"You like that word, don't you?"

"Phrixis? Hardly. It's not even an attractive word to say."

Fang gave him a droll stare. "Politics."

"If that's what you meant, why didn't you say so?" Thorn snorted irritably. "And to answer your question, not in the slightest. I hate playing games, but my existence is ever a study of high-IQ chess. We move, they counter, and vice versa. God help us if our enemies ever capture our king . . . and for the record, that would be *me*. Don't let that happen as it would go very badly for you."

"I'll keep my eyes open."

"Good, wolf. And there is one more piece of advice I'm going to give you."

"That is?"

"The mark I gave you will tingle anytime you come near a demon as a warning. The stronger the sensation, the more powerful the demon."

"But don't kill the demon, just smack him with my sword."

Thorn inclined his head sarcastically. "Now you're starting to get it. How are you and your inner demon doing anyway?"

"He hasn't possessed me yet."

"Good. Keep it that way. I'd hate to have to kill you this early in our relationship."

Fang cocked his brow at that. "We have a relationship? Does this mean I get pinned?"

"Oh, I'll pin your ass to the nearest wall. That would actually brighten my otherwise noxious day. Shall we?"

"It's all right. I'm not in the mood and I'd hate to have to make you work that hard."

Thorn shook his head. "Watch your back, wolf. There's a pall over this place and the bears are racking up enemies faster than Wal-Mart rakes in sales. When the time comes, it's going to get bloody."

"I wouldn't have it any other way."

"Don't be so arrogant. Long before I was the debonair sophisticate standing in front of you, I was a warlord. I put more blood on my blade than Madame la Guillotine. The one thing all that battle taught me is that no one walks away without scars. No one."

Fang paused as he realized just how right Thorn was. Vane used to have a similar saying. In a fight, everyone gets bloody.

"Watch your back, wolf, and remember when the time comes to choose sides, make sure you choose well."

At dawn, Fang headed downstairs to help close up and clean. Though Sanctuary was technically open 24/7 for preternatural beings, they closed at 4:30 A.M. and opened at 10:00 A.M. for humans. Mama Lo and Papa were on standby during the off-hours in Peltier House.

Fang entered the bar at the same time Aimee's older brother Zar, who was almost indistinguishable in looks from the quads, was carrying a tray of glasses into the kitchen.

Zar thanked him for holding the door open. "You can help Aimee finish up. I'm done for the night."

Fang nodded as he saw Aimee taking the cloth from Wren and pushing him toward the door. Music was playing at a much quieter level from the jukebox. It was the Indigo Girls, which was one of Aimee's favorite bands.

"Wren, go on. You've put in fourteen hours with only a tiny break. Get some sleep."

Still, Wren hesitated. "You shouldn't be down here alone."

She looked past him to see Fang. "I'm not alone."

Wren turned to see him, then clamped his jaw shut. Nodding at Aimee, he did as she asked.

Fang frowned as Wren flashed out, then he moved over to where Aimee was draping a white hand towel over her shoulder. "I like him, but he's a strange kid."

"I know. Trust me, though, he has reasons for it."

No doubt, given the stories he'd heard. Half the Were-Hunter staff here thought the tigard had killed his own parents. Nicolette couldn't stand him and while Papa Bear appeared mostly ambivalent, he did watch Wren a little closer than the others.

"You're the only one he really talks to."

Aimee moved to pick up a chair, turn it upside down, and put it on a table. Fang beat her to it.

She stood back with a smile. "I love Wren and he knows it."

"Yeah, but he seems like he wouldn't welcome it."

"Sometimes he doesn't. But it's like Cherise says, the hardest ones to love are always the ones who need it most."

He scoffed at her blind optimism. On the one hand, he admired it, on the other . . . she was too kind-hearted. "Do you really believe that?"

She smiled up at him. "Absolutely. I love you, don't I? And the gods know you are definitely not easy to deal with." She stood up on her tiptoes to give him a quick kiss on his cheek before she flounced over to the next table to stack chairs.

How could one comment both warm and offend him at the same time?

But then she was good at that. "Thanks, Aim. By the way I still have a tiny bit of confidence left. Please make sure you stomp on it too while you're at it. Gods forbid it should actually grow into something called self-esteem." Fang continued pulling up chairs.

Aimee laughed as she mopped the floor. "Anytime, wolf. Vane told me I'm not supposed to let you get too big a head."

Papa Roach kicked on next to play.

"Interesting mix you got going there."

"Just wait. Debbie Gibson's on there too."

He froze to look at her as she sang along to the song. "You are joking, right?"

"Nope. I like a wide variety of tunes."

He let out a deep breath. "You've found a whole new way to torture me. Damn, and I thought Misery was bad."

Laughing, she danced with her mop while he admired the fluid way her body moved. It awoke the wolf inside him and made it howl.

How could he be hard again?

This was getting annoying. Trying to distract himself, he looked around the empty bar. Apparently, they were the only two left down here.

"Where's everybody?"

"We never work the humans past 2:00 A.M. just in case something really weird happens the last couple of hours of the night. As for my family, the guys always bail as soon as they can. They think it's funny to leave me here to clean up by myself."

"Why do you?"

"I don't want to hear Maman complain. She comes in like a drill sergeant and white-gloves the place every morning."

The jukebox switched to Badfinger's "Day After Day." Fang paused at a song he hadn't heard in forever. He'd always liked it for some reason.

Aimee danced around while she worked, singing to it.

Enchanted, Fang lost himself in her graceful movements. Before he even realized what he'd done, he was in front of her, holding his hand out for her to dance with him.

Putting the mop aside, she smiled before she accepted. He twirled her into his arms and held her close as they swayed while the music floated around them. They were in perfect synchronization. Her arms felt so good around him as her scent filled his head.

She placed one gentle hand to his cheek. "I give my love to you," she sang, her voice bringing a swell of emotion high in his throat.

He laid his cheek against hers so that he could savor the feel of her in his arms. This was what had gotten him through the hell of the Nether Realm. Her warmth and tenderness.

Her scent.

Aimee twirled her fingers in his hair. "I like your hair longer. It suits you."

He didn't answer as he picked her hand up and led it to his mouth so that he could nibble her fingers. "I want to make love to you so badly I can taste it."

She dipped her hand down to cup him. "Me too."

His cock twitched, demanding she touch him without the denim barrier. It also reminded him of the fact that he had no right to her. That they couldn't be together, no matter how much he ached to have her as his own.

"So how did it go with the other bears?"

She gave a short laugh. "Disastrous. One made a move on me and I coldcocked him so bad for it that they're having to do a testicle retrieval."

"Ow!" Fang laughed, cringing at the mere thought of that. "That'll leave a mark."

"He wasn't quite as respectful of my virgin ears when it happened."

"I'll bet. Want me to go finish what you started? I'll be more than happy to geld him . . . any asshole messing with my girl—"

She silenced his words by placing her hand over his mouth. "Careful, wolf. Anyone hear you say that and you'll be the one gelded."

He nibbled her soft fingertips. "I know. It's just hard on me having to let every hairy-ass bear in the universe come on to you while I can't even make eye contact."

"I know, baby." She kissed him gently on his lips.

Fang leaned his head down and let the peace of this moment wash over him while they danced. He would sell his soul to stay like this.

It's too late. You already sold it to protect her.

Yeah, he should have put another stipulation on that bargain. One that left him in her arms forever.

I am such an idiot. . . .

Trying to distract himself, he changed the subject. "I was briefly talking to Justin earlier tonight and he said something interesting."

"That is?"

"That Dev and your father were trained Strati."

She gave him a look so guarded it could protect national security secrets. "Why is that strange?"

Fang started to divert the conversation, but it was something that had been bothering him about the Peltier bears and it was something he wanted to see if she'd trust him with. "They're Arcadian."

Aimee stumbled at the word. Her heart pounded in fear. How could he know that? No one had *ever* suspected it. "I don't know what you're talking about."

He stopped moving to stare down at her intently. "Don't lie to me, Aimee. I'm not stupid. I've been here long enough to figure it out and I protected an Arcadian too long in my life not to know the signs of one hiding in the middle of a Katagaria pack. If you want me to pretend I don't know, then I will play along. But I wanted you to know that I knew."

And he was placing his life in her hands. If her family ever suspected he'd figured that out, they would kill him without question. Forget eirini and Omegrion law, he would be skinned alive.

He leaned down to whisper. "And I know your secret too."

She trembled as a cold sweat broke out on her body. How had he guessed the one secret she'd been protecting all these centuries? A secret not even her own family knew. . . .

No doubt he hated her for it.

"What secret?"

"That Kyle's an Aristos and you're helping him train his powers."

Nauseated, Aimee started to move away, afraid to hear any more.

"I won't tell anyone, Aimee. I swear it. And it's not because I'm afraid for me. I could care less about that. It's you I would never hurt, not in any way."

And because he was trusting her with his secret, she wanted to give him one back. He had placed his life in her hands. The least she could do was return the favor.

"Are they the only ones you've spotted?"

"I think Zar may be one and possibly Quinn."

Aimee swallowed as fear ran rampant through her. Maybe she shouldn't tell him. What if he rejected her just based on that alone? Arcadians had killed his sister. Granted, they hadn't fired the Taser that ended her life, but she would have died anyway because they killed her mate.

He'd shoved her away before. He might this time too and this time he would have the power to destroy her.

Oh, gods, she wanted to vomit. This was something she couldn't even tell her own mother or father. Yet he had a right to know. It wasn't fair to keep this from him. . . .

Taking a deep breath, she looked up at him. "I'm one too."

Fang pulled away to look at her as those words rang in his ears. No. It wasn't possible. Surely he'd have known if she was one like her brothers. How could she have fooled him so completely?

"What?"

He saw the fear in that clear blue gaze that didn't waver at all from his. "I'm Arcadian. Like Vane, I changed at puberty. It's something I've never told anyone in my life. Not even my family knows."

"Why would you tell me?"

Her eyes turned glassy from restrained tears as she showed him the Sentinel markings on her own face. "I just thought you should know what you're involved with."

Fang cupped her cheek where the ancient Greek design spiraled, marking her as one of the most hated groups to his kind. He saw the fear in her eyes and the fact that she would trust him with this . . .

She did love him. She'd have to because only a fool with a death wish would lay this in the hands of a Katagari who knew how Nicolette Peltier felt about Arcadians. The fact that Aimee had kept it from her mother said it all.

Aimee had laid herself completely naked and open to him. No wonder she was trembling.

"You know it doesn't matter to me."

Aimee choked on a sob as she pulled him into her arms and held him close. "You have no idea how scared I've been all these centuries. I think it's why I've been so afraid to even attempt mating with a Katagari. Can you imagine what they might do to me if they find out?"

Kill her at best. Mutilate her at worst. She was right, it wasn't something to be shared lightly. "You were brave to tell me."

"I trust you that much, wolf."

"And I will never betray that trust. I swear it."

Aimee felt a single tear slide down her cheek. Fang brushed it away.

The tenderness in his eyes melted her. He wouldn't betray her, she knew that. But it still couldn't bind them. This was the most hopeless relationship ever devised by the gods.

"So where does this leave us?" she whispered, too terrified to even contemplate an answer on her own.

His look turned to steel. "Come away with me. Just the two of us. Let's forget about all the differences and prejudices. Let's just leave and be together."

How she wished it were that simple. But it wasn't. "I can't do that, Fang. My brothers died protecting me. But for Bastien, I would never have learned to use my powers. He tutored me when I couldn't trust anyone else. Now I'm the only one who can train Kyle to use his. And Maman would be shattered to lose me too. I'm her only hope at maintaining our legacy. The Peltiers have been on the Omegrion since the beginning. You know how rare that is."

His look turned cold. "Is that really more important to you than me?"

"No, but you can't make me choose between you and my family."

Fang winced as he realized she was right. He was being selfish. "Yeah. It was a stupid idea."

And he was a fool for thinking, even for a second, that she would put him over them. No one had ever done that before. Why should she?

His heart broken, he pulled away. "We better finish cleaning up. As you said, I don't want Nicolette yelling at you."

Aimee watched as he returned to stacking chairs. She'd hurt him and she wasn't sure how. But she could tell there was a wall between them that hadn't been there earlier.

When they were finished, she led the way upstairs. She paused outside his room. "Good night, Fang."

"You too." He didn't even look at her before he vanished and left her in the hallway.

Sighing, she headed for her own room.

Fang didn't breathe until Aimee was back in her room. He stripped his clothes off, grimacing at the soreness he still had from his fight with Fury. That little SOB could punch like a sledgehammer.

He fell into bed, exhausted, but still couldn't sleep for thoughts of Aimee.

In his heart, he knew he couldn't stay here forever. And if she did start mating with other men, he'd have to leave or kill someone. The thought of anyone touching her spun him into the galactic outer rims of pissed off.

I'm going to have to leave. Because every day he stayed here and didn't have her, he died a little more inside.

CHAPTER 22

Weeks later, Fang still hadn't left.

I am a total head case.

No, he was a moron and he couldn't bring himself to leave Aimee. He would rather stay here and be miserable where he could at least hold her when no one was around than leave and be completely miserable without her.

But every day he stayed, it was worse.

Thorn had been right. There was all kinds of shit brewing at Sanctuary. Wren had been thrown out after he'd taken up with some politician's daughter and now the Peltiers and the entire Omegrion were hot after the tigard to kill him over something his own cousin had said at the last council meeting.

Nicolette was convinced the kid was a threat to her precious family and Aimee was hell-bent that it was all a misunderstanding. Mother and daughter had been fighting over it constantly and there had been a time or two when Fang had almost gone for Nicolette's throat over the way she talked to her daughter.

"Please, Fang. Let it go. She's my mother and I love

her." That was all Aimee ever said, but it was hard to do nothing while her mother treated her like shit.

As far as Wren was concerned, Fang agreed with Aimee that it smacked of Wren's distant relations trying to lay hands on his inheritance. But there was no way to prove it. Right now there was a blood hunt out for the tigard and a pack of tigers were stalking him.

Fang felt for him and hoped for the best where Wren was concerned.

Tonight he was on bar duty with Sasha, Etienne, Colt, and Cherif. Out of all the Peltier brothers, Dev was his favorite, but Cherif was a close second. Cherif lacked Remi's nasty attitude. Instead he had a badass aura that said he didn't have to pick or bully to reign supreme.

He simply was, and death to anyone who wanted to knock him off that throne.

Sasha was another Katagari Lykos who stayed here off and on depending on his mood. The last survivor of his pack, he was technically the bodyguard for a goddess. But since his goddess had married, his duties had been light, which meant that whenever he was bored, he'd come hang out with the rest of the animals at Sanctuary.

Tall and blond, Sasha had a nasty temper and a biting sarcasm he could definitely appreciate. All in all, Fang liked the other wolf, but the nature of their species made it hard for them to be around each other too much. Since they weren't in the same pack, they were extremely territorial here.

Kyle's twin, Cody, was sitting at the bar beside Sasha, drinking a Coke. He choked on his drink.

Frowning, Fang turned to see what had set him off.

His gaze focused on Aimee who was wearing a tight string tank top and a pair of cutoff shorts that were way too short.

"Oh, hell no," he said before he could even think not to. "You're not working in *that*."

Cherif agreed. "Hear, hear! Get your ass back upstairs and change before Maman or Papa sees you."

She gave them all a go-to-hell glower. "Were you people born on the sun? It's stifling hot in here and unlike you losers, I'm the one who has to run orders back and forth."

Fang scoffed. "Then be glad we're not putting you in a parka."

She narrowed her gaze at him. "You got no authority over me, wolf." She raked her brother with a curled lip. "You even less so."

Cherif pulled his phone out of his pocket. "I'm calling Maman. Right now."

She hissed at him. "I hate you. I swear one day, I'm going to poison your food." Then she turned her fury to Fang. "And I'm not talking to you for the rest of the night."

That was fine by him so long as she covered herself up. He wasn't about to have her walk around like that with the body she had. They already had enough trouble keeping men and animal hands off her.

Cherif held his beer bottle up toward Fang. "Here's to you, my brother."

Laughing, Fang held his up to tap the bottom of the bottles together in a salute of solidarity against public female fashions that only looked good on a woman you didn't have a relationship with.

"Hey, Fang, you got a visitor."

He frowned at Dev's voice in his earpiece. "Vane or Fury?"

"Neither."

Fang set his bottle down as he frowned. The only other person he could think of would be Thorn, but Thorn didn't usually come in the front door.

His breath caught as a searing pain cut through his shoulder where Thorn's mark was.

What the hell?

Trying not to show the pain, he scanned the room until his eyes fell on Varyk. He didn't know how he knew that, but the name popped into his head like a beacon.

Dressed in a light linen suit and with his hair immaculately combed, he looked as out of place here as Fang would on a billionaire's fancy boat.

Pulling the earpiece out and turning it off, Fang met him in the middle of the bar. "What are you doing here?"

Before Varyk could answer, Sasha was there, looking like he was staring at a ghost.

"You survived?"

Varyk's gaze went to him slowly. Unlike Sasha, his features were completely blank. "Betrayer." There was enough venom in that one word to supply an army of cobras.

Sasha let out a deep, vicious growl. "I betrayed no one."

By Varyk's face it was obvious he didn't believe a word of it. "And yet you survived while the rest of us were hunted into the ground."

"For a dead man, you look awfully hale."

"There's more irony in that statement than you realize, punk. Now get out of my face before I decide killing you is more important to me than Savitar's bullshit laws."

Sasha started away, then stopped. "Lera made her decision based solely on my age."

"And my brother was younger than you and still he was slaughtered. Get out of my presence, Sasha, or lose your life."

Sasha left.

Fang didn't speak until the wolf was gone. "What is up with you two?"

Varyk, obviously one who didn't like to elaborate, shrugged it off. "Forgotten history. You, however, are my present."

"Oh, goody. Do I have to wear a bow?"

His face unamused, Varyk pulled out a scrap of cloth. "Recognize the scent?"

Fang caught the whiff even before he put it to his nose. The stench was unmistakable and it made him see red. "Misery."

He nodded. "She broke out. I can't find her. I've alerted Wynter and now I'm letting you know. I'm sure she's in someone else's body. The question is . . . whose. Keep your eyes open since she has a hard-on for you. We're hoping she makes contact or screws up so that we can find her and send her back to where she belongs."

"I'll be watching for her."

Varyk inclined his head before he turned and left the bar. Fang put his headphone back on and switched it on just as Varyk paused at the door where Dev was standing.

"I feel the need for a bearskin rug."

Dev scoffed. "Funny. I was thinking a wolf's head would look good on my mantel."

"Watch your back, bear."

"You better watch your front. I want to see your face when I take you down."

Varyk flipped him off on his way out the door.

Fang shook his head.

Dev pressed his earpiece in deeper. "What did he want with you, Fang?"

"Nothing. Just wolf business."

Even at this distance, he could see Dev's glare. Ignoring it, Fang went back to the bar where Aimee had returned. Now dressed in a T-shirt and jeans, she still made him hard.

But at least he couldn't complain about this outfit. "Much better."

Snatching her tray up from the counter, she snarled at him, "Shut up, wolf."

"Ouch," Cherif said as she stalked off.

Fang would have gone after her, but he couldn't with half her family watching them. Instead, he projected his thoughts to Aimee. *"Tell you what? I'm going to head over to that table of college girls who've been eyeing me all night like I'm the last piece of steak in New Orleans, and talk to that little redhead. What do you think?"*

Aimee looked at the table and stiffened. *"I'll gouge out your eyes."*

"Then why are you mad at me about you?"

She had the decency to look a bit sheepish as she wiped down a table. *"Because it's different."*

"I don't think so."

She stuck her tongue out at him before she went to take an order.

Fang laughed.

Aimee tried to ignore Fang as she went about her job. They were a little shorthanded tonight, which was why she was down here instead of upstairs reading. Matt had called in sick and Tara was acting strange. Aimee watched her even now as she mixed up orders, which was completely out of character for her.

Aimee went over to her as she headed back to the kitchen with a plate of fried chicken. "Is something wrong, girl?"

Tara shook her head. "I'm just tired and these people are being jerks. Have I ever said how much I hate the living?"

Aimee snorted. "About as much as I do most days."

"I know. It's just . . ." She paused to look at the bar where the men were gathered. "Fang is creeping me out."

Aimee couldn't have been more stunned at that had she thrown the plate of chicken at her. "Fang?"

Tara nodded. "I don't like the way he watches me."

"Fang?" Aimee repeated, unable to believe this discussion. Was the girl out of her mind?

Drugs . . . definitely drugs.

"Yes, Fang." Tara shivered. "His eyes are always on me. Like he's going to attack or something."

Aimee scowled as she looked back at Fang, who had his back to them while he talked to Colt. He didn't seem to have any care or interest in them at all. "I'm sure he doesn't mean anything by it."

"Yeah, right. You know he had a girl upstairs last night."

Aimee's stomach hit the ground at what Tara was implying. Her brothers had built a soundproof room that in theory was a place to put someone who was having trouble with their powers while out here in public view. In reality, it'd turned into a place where any of her skanky unmated brothers could make time with whatever woman caught his eye. "In the closet?"

"Yeah. I heard them."

For a moment, Aimee hesitated. Then she refused to believe it. Fang wasn't some man-whore like Dev. Besides, he'd been with her after everyone had gone to bed last night and she could attest to the fact that he was wound up tight and in need of a "hand" from her.

Stepping away from Tara, she used her powers to contact him. *"Hey, sexy? You been bugging Tara?"*

"Who's Tara?"

"The waitress behind me."

Fang turned around to look. He appeared as perplexed as she felt. *"Bugging her for what?"*

That's exactly what she thought. *"Never mind, sweetie. It was stupid."*

She'd never known Fang to look at another woman. He only had eyes for her and unlike Dev, Etienne, and Serre, he wasn't a player. She knew that.

So then what game was Tara playing? *Maybe she's imagining it. . . .*

That was the most likely scenario.

Putting it out of her mind, Aimee went back to work.

Fang got off work first and headed to his room. He was stiff and sore from all the hours he'd been in human form and needed desperately to be a wolf for a while. He lay on his bed in his true form and sighed.

But even so, he missed Aimee. He could hear her downstairs in the bar and feel her with his soul.

Closing his eyes, he waited for her to join him.

It was just after two when she appeared in his bed. The two of them had been sharing a bed for the last few weeks. She slept as a human while he kept his wolf form. They would "play" in his room since it was far enough away to keep any of her family from overhearing them. But they slept in her room just in case her family knocked on the door.

When they did, Fang would flash out before they entered. It was a dangerous game they played.

One that would mean his life if they were caught, but in his mind, it was more than worth it.

He sighed as she stroked the fur at his neck. Nothing in the world felt better than the way she touched him. Her fingers worked magic on his skin and fur.

Leaning down, she rubbed her face in his pelt and gave a tight squeeze. "I missed you."

Fang turned human and rolled over. Completely naked, he pulled her into his arms to hold her close. "I missed you too."

Aimee sighed in bliss as his lips touched hers. That tight, ripped body was all she needed in her life. And never was the urge to run away with him stronger than it was tonight.

She only wanted to be with him. Reaching down, she cupped him in her hand and smiled at the way he jerked and sighed.

Fang wanted to stay here like this forever as she trailed her hand down the length of his cock. Though they'd done nothing more than pet, he was fast losing patience with it.

He wanted so much more, but he wasn't willing to push her into anything, especially given the hatred his parents had borne each other. If they really were mates, then he wanted her to completely accept him without reservation or doubt.

Relaxing on the bed, his demon sense kicked in. There was a slight rustle out in the hallway.

Worried it was one of her brothers, he tilted his head, then cursed.

It was Wren.

And he was here to kill Nicolette.

CHAPTER 23

"What was that?"

Fang debated telling her. The demon in him wanted to turn the tigard loose on Nicolette and let him kill the bear. It would solve a lot of their problems.

But in the end, Nicolette was Aimee's mother and she loved her. That alone made the non-demon parts of him win the fight. "It's Wren. I think he's after your mom."

Aimee gasped as she looked up at Fang. "You have to stop him."

Now?

Was she out of her mind?

He looked down at her bare breasts that were pressed against his chest. The only thing she wore was a thin pair of pink panties. Panties he'd intended to pull off with his teeth before he licked her until she was begging him for mercy.

But she'd already gone dry on him.

Even more sexually frustrated than he'd been before, he growled. "Let them eat him."

"Fang!"

"All right. I'm going." Flashing a pair of jeans on his body, he left the bed and damned the tigard with every step he took. At this point Wren would be lucky if *he* didn't kill him.

Fang cracked open the door.

In tiger form, Wren was stalking through the upstairs of Sanctuary. It was obvious he was on a hunt.

"Shit," Fang breathed as he realized the tigard was in fact heading straight for Nicolette's room.

As soon as he heard Fang's curse, Wren turned and crouched low as if ready to attack.

Fang had to stop himself from scoffing at the action. Like he could stand up to Fang. "Get your ass in here," Fang snapped. "Now!"

Wren started away from him, which didn't help his mood at all. If he wasn't going to listen to him, Fang was going to rip him to shreds.

Aimee rushed to his side to peep out the door around him. "Listen to him, Wren. Please."

The tigard froze at Aimee's voice. Hoping she wasn't still naked, Fang glanced over his shoulder and realized that one side of her face was red and her lips were swollen from their play. But at least she was dressed.

Before any of them moved, another door opened. Aimee dashed out of sight as her younger brother Etienne froze in his doorway. Tall and blond like the rest of his brothers, the bear was only a few decades older than Wren, but he didn't appear any older in human form.

He instantly flashed to his bear form.

Fang cursed under his breath. "There's no fighting in Sanctuary," he said between clenched teeth, closing his door to protect Aimee as he moved to stand between them. "You both know the eirini laws that govern us."

"He is marked, wolf. Stand down."

Fang paused at the sound of Papa Bear's deep voice. Normally the bear was easygoing and jovial. But this tone was all business and all lethal.

Wren flashed himself to human form to confront the famed Papa Bear. "I did nothing wrong. This is bullshit and all of you know it."

"You've gone mad," Papa Bear said. "You've threatened my cubs and my mate."

Fang had to keep himself silent. Hell, they all threatened the cubs. He'd called Dev an asshole on his way up and had threatened to beat him down.

But obviously Papa Bear wasn't about to cut Wren any slack.

Wren narrowed his gaze at the bear. "No, I haven't. But you can tell your bitch that I'm here for her now."

Papa Bear ran at him.

Fang put himself between them and caught Papa as he lunged. The bear was strong, but the demon inside Fang gave him the ability to hold the bear back and keep him from killing Wren.

Roaring in frustration, Papa knocked Fang aside with one hell of a paw punch and went for Wren.

Wren flashed to tiger form and launched himself at Papa who transformed instantly to a bear. He caught the larger bear about the throat as Etienne attacked him from the back. Wren hissed as Etienne threw him against the wall and laid one leg open with his huge claw.

Dazed, Wren sprang back to his feet only to have his wounded leg buckle.

Fang was trying to rejoin, but his shoulder had been ripped open and blood was pouring down his side. Gah, it hurt and burned.

The bears reared before they started toward Wren. They'd only taken two steps when a bright light flashed in the hallway.

Wren backed up, ready to fight, only to pause as he saw Vane and Fury in the hallway now.

In human form, Vane took one look at Fang's bleeding shoulder and growled low in his throat. "Aubert? Have you lost your mind?"

Papa Bear, or Aubert as he was really named, flashed back to human while Etienne remained a bear. "He is marked for death. We took you in, wolf, when you had nothing. Is this how you repay us?"

Vane's eyes were blazing. "No, Aubert. I haven't forgotten my debt to you or Nicolette. But I will not stand by and see this happen to an innocent. Wren has no clan to back him. Therefore I offer him mine."

Fang was stunned as he heard those words. Was Vane out of his mind? To offer shelter to someone wanted by the Omegrion was suicide.

Papa Bear was every bit as incredulous. "You would back him against the Omegrion's decree?"

Vane didn't hesitate with his answer. His face was grim and deadly. "You're damn straight."

Fang looked past Wren's shoulder and felt the blood drain from his face as he saw Aimee's intent in her eyes. "*Don't you dare get into this,*" he mentally projected to Aimee.

As usual, she didn't listen. "No!"

They all turned to see Aimee in the middle of the hallway behind them. Only Wren and Fang knew whose room she'd been inside.

She swallowed as she looked from her father to Fang.

"Papa, please. Don't do this. This is wrong and you know it. Wren poses no threat to us."

"Are you insane, daughter? He's here to kill your mother."

More doors were opening now. More animals were coming out to investigate the disturbance. This was looking worse and worse for Wren.

"You'll never make it out of here alive," Papa Bear said in warning. "None of you."

Fang looked at Aimee. *"What the hell are we going to do?"*

"Take me hostage."

That sucker-punched him. *"What?"*

"You heard me, Fang. We've got to get Wren out of here before they kill him."

"If I do that, I'll be banned from here. Forever."

Tears glistened in her eyes. *"I know, baby. I know. But if Wren dies, I won't be able to forgive myself. Please help him."*

Fang wanted to scream. She was asking too much of him. And yet when he looked at Wren who was so young . . . and innocent, he knew she was right.

They couldn't let the kid die. And more to the point, now that Vane and Fury were here trying to protect him, they'd be killed too. He had to protect his brothers at all costs even though the demon inside him was laughing at the prospect of watching them die.

Damn it!

A heartbeat later, Fang grabbed her into his arms, manifested a knife in his hand, then held it threateningly to her throat. The irony of this wasn't lost on him. He was about to lose her the same way he'd met her.

"Don't you dare follow us," he warned her family. "I'll kill her if you do." Fang turned to look at the three of them. "Fury, Vane, get Wren out of here."

Wren started to protest, but before he could, Vane grabbed him by the neck and flashed him from the hallway.

Fang leaned his head against hers and wanted to weep at what they were doing. Using his powers, he tracked his brothers and flashed the two of them into a dark room with no windows.

The only light came from two dim lamps on two tables at opposite ends of the room. The modern furnishings were chic and high-tech, not to mention the walls were made of dark gray steel.

This was a boat.

Fang had barely realized that before Aimee turned in his arms and hugged him close.

Vane cursed. "Have you two lost your friggin' minds? Between you and the tiger, we're so screwed."

"No, you're not." Wren tried to flash himself back to Sanctuary. "What the hell?"

"I've got you locked down," Vane said.

Wren knew better than to go after Vane—the wolf was too powerful to take down—but by the look on his face, it was obvious the tigard wanted to try. "Lift it."

Vane shook his head. "No. I didn't just jeopardize my entire clan to see you commit suicide."

"This isn't your fight."

"Yes, it is. I'm not going to sit by and watch an innocent die because some asshole got greedy."

Wren scoffed at Vane's heroism. "Well, thank you,

Mr. Altruist, but the tiger doesn't want your help. So sod off."

Someone started clapping.

Fang, still holding Aimee to his side, saw the Dark-Hunter Jean-Luc entering the room from a door on his right. A pirate in his human life, the immortal vampire slayer still retained much of his old look.

With a small gold hoop flashing in his left earlobe, he was dressed all in black in a pair of leather pants, a silk button-down shirt, and biker boots. His long, straight black hair was pulled back into a sleek queue that emphasized the sharp angles of his face. His eyes were so dark that not even the pupils were discernable and those eyes were dancing with amusement. "Nicely put, tiger."

"Shut up, lapdog, this isn't your fight either."

Jean-Luc sucked his breath in sharply at the insult. "Boy, you better counsel that tongue before you find yourself without it."

Wren took a step toward him, then froze as the human he'd been making time with came through the door behind the pirate. The relief on her face was more than obvious.

The human rushed to Wren's side and threw her arms around him. "I'm so glad they got to you before it was too late. You weren't really going to do something stupid, were you?"

"Oh, no, hon, we were too late," Fury said snidely. "Tiger boy done pissed down the wrong honey tree and got all the bees, or in this case bears, going wild."

Fury glanced to Fang then to Aimee. "Then again, knowing the bears, they'll be gunning for wolf before tiger. Good move, Fang. Making off with their only daughter. Real swift. You know, chocolate is lethal to our kind. I'm thinking if you want to commit suicide, that's the much less painful way to go about it."

"Knock it off, Fury," Vane said, moving over to where Fang and Aimee were standing. "We have to send her back. Now."

Fang contemplated the death and burial of Fury. Brother or not, that wolf still got on his nerves, but Vane was right. "I know."

Tears glistened in Aimee's eyes and they tore him apart as he ached to kiss them away. "I don't want to leave."

Those words shredded his resolve.

Vane looked as sick as Fang felt. "And I thought my relationship with Bride was doomed. Damn it, people and animals, this shit sucks."

Fang couldn't agree more.

Fury snorted. "You're the leader, Vane. Lead."

Vane looked up at the ceiling and sighed. "If I had any brains at all, which obviously I don't, I would never have gotten involved in this. I would hand my brother and Wren over to the bears and just take my wife and go find a nice, quiet place to raise our children."

He swept them all with an irritated glare. "But obviously, I am truly the dumbest man on the planet."

Jean-Luc pulled a long, thin stiletto out of his boot and offered it to Vane. "Here, *mon ami*. Either for you or for them. One cut and all your problems are solved, eh?"

"Don't tempt me." Vane growled low in his throat as he surveyed the lot of them. "Wren, listen close, 'cause,

buddy, your chances are running slim. You kill Nicolette and you're dead. There's no way back from that."

Wren scoffed at him. "There's no way back from an
execution order. Period."

Shaking his head in denial, Fury stepped forward.
"You weren't there when the vote came down. The
council was divided on the order."

Wren frowned. "What are you saying?"

"That you have a shot at redemption," Vane said,
"but not if you kill Nicolette for vengeance."

Wren hesitated as if he were inwardly debating.

Vane sighed. "You give the council proof that you're
innocent of killing your parents and Savitar will re-
scind the Omegrion's order."

Wren scowled at him. "What the fuck are you talking about? They're trying to kill me because I'm dating
Maggie."

Fury made a sound of disgust. "What are you, stupid? Your dating the human is only the catalyst for
why Mama Lo tossed your ass out. The death warrant
is because you murdered your parents."

"Says who?"

"Your cousin Zack."

Wren clenched his jaw shut as if he wanted to kill
something. The demon inside Fang knew for a fact the
tigard was innocent. And outraged. Not that he could
blame him in the least.

But that only pissed him off. Had Wren kept his ass
with Maggie and away from Sanctuary, Fang wouldn't
be forced to abandon Aimee.

Damn that selfish bastard.

"We can help you, Wren," Vane said calmly. "But you have to trust us."

Wren sneered. "I'm not putting my faith or life in anyone's hands. All that ever got me was screwed and my ass is currently sore from it."

Fury curled his lip in repugnance. "Nice imagery there, tiger. Graphic. Ever think of writing children's books?"

Fang popped his brother lightly in the back of his head.

"Ow!" Fury snapped, rubbing the spot where he'd been hit. He glared at Fang.

Fang looked at Vane. "Was I this annoying before my attack?"

Vane didn't hesitate. "Yes, and you still are most of the time. And we have now gotten off topic."

"There's nothing to discuss," Wren said irritably. "You can't keep me here forever, wolf. Putting me on a boat was a nice trick to keep them off my scent, but it won't take them long to figure out where I am. All you've done is drag the Dark-Hunters into our fight and knowing Acheron, I'm sure he won't be amused by this."

Wren paused to let out a tired sigh. "They'll be coming for me and we all know they won't stop. I would rather face them on my own terms than have them attack me on theirs."

Wren headed for the door.

As he passed by Jean-Luc, the Dark-Hunter grabbed him. Before Wren could react, the pirate tranked him.

Infuriated, he growled and changed, but before he could do anything more than that, he collapsed to the floor.

The human's face blanched. "What did you do?"

"Tranked him."

Fury scratched his head as he looked down at Wren's unconscious tigard form. "He's going to be seriously pissed off when he wakes up."

"No doubt," Jean-Luc concurred. "Therefore I suggest we keep him under at least for a day or two until he can heal and you can plan out what it is he needs to do."

Vane looked less than convinced. "Yeah, but if he doesn't listen—"

"Come up with your plan," Maggie said, "and I'll make sure he listens to it."

Fury laughed at her. "Don't be so cocky, human. Wren isn't the kind of beast you manipulate."

Aimee shook her head at him as she exchanged a knowing look with Fang. "No, Fury, you're wrong. With her, Wren is different."

Fury moved over and took Maggie's hand into his. He turned it over to see her palm. "They're not mates."

Aimee looked at Fang and her heart pounded. She loved him with every part of herself. "You don't have to be mated to care deeply for someone. I think Wren will listen to her."

"All we can do is try." Vane moved closer to Wren. "Lend us a hand, guys."

Aimee pulled Maggie aside as the men picked Wren's tigard form up and carried him down the narrow hallway to a lush bedroom.

"Do you really think there's any way Wren can prove his innocence?" Maggie asked Vane as he covered Wren with a blanket.

"I don't know. Hell, I'm not even sure he didn't kill his parents. His cousin made one hell of an argument to the council."

Aimee had to fight the urge to shove Fang's hard-headed brother. Now she knew where Fang got it from. "He didn't kill them. I was there when they brought him in. He was too traumatized by it. He sat in a corner for three weeks solid with his arms around himself, just rocking back and forth whenever he was in human form. As a tigard, leopard or tiger, he stayed coiled up."

Vane frowned. "Was he wounded when he was brought to you?"

Aimee hesitated at the question. Vane wanted to know if he'd been in a fight with his parents. Honestly, he'd looked like hell. But she didn't want them to know that because she knew in her heart and with her Aristos powers that Wren was completely innocent. "He was a little scuffed up."

Vane looked skeptical. "A little or a lot?"

"Okay, a lot," Aimee admitted reluctantly. "But had he been in a fight with two full-grown Katagaria, he would have been a lot more injured than what he was."

"Unless he poisoned them," Fury said. "Zack didn't really say how he'd killed them."

Maggie stepped forward. "I still don't believe it. It's not in him."

Fury let out a mocking laugh. "Yeah, and you are delusional. Babe, news flash, with the exception of you and the pirate, we're all animals here. And we all have a killer's instinct."

Yes, but they killed to protect and for food. They didn't kill for profit.

Aimee sighed as she looked wistfully at Wren's unconscious form. "He did have a really hard time in puberty. He couldn't maintain his forms and he did have extremely violent outbursts over minor things."

Vane arched one brow. "Such as?"

"Well, the first night he was working in the kitchen, Dev startled him and Wren cut Dev's throat with the knife he had in his hands. Luckily Dev pulled back fast enough that it was only a small wound, but had his reflexes been slower or if Dev had been human, it could have been fatal."

Fang still knew the truth. Thanks to Thorn and his "gifts," he had no doubt about what had happened. "That doesn't mean he killed his parents."

Jean-Luc made a noise of disagreement. "It's rather damning. Normal people don't do things like that."

Maybe not in the pirate's world, but Fang knew what it was like to be feral. It'd taken him a long time after Aimee had dragged him out of hell before he'd stopped having night terrors. Before he'd stopped striking out at people in a panicked frenzy. But for Aimee, he'd still be like that. "No, but someone who's been severely attacked and who was powerless to stop it would do it."

Fury shook his head. "I don't know, brother. I think you're projecting what happened to you onto Wren."

No, he wasn't, but he couldn't tell them about his powers or the fact that he'd sold his soul.

Maggie looked at Aimee. "When was the last time Wren ever attacked anyone without them attacking him first?"

Aimee didn't hesitate with her answer. "Just that one

time with Dev, but like I said, he was scared and shaking when it happened."

Maggie nodded. "That's what I thought. Wren is innocent in this. He told me that his parents killed each other and I believe him. Now we just need to put our heads together and think of some way to prove it."

But Fang knew that was easier said than done.

Leaving them alone to discuss the details, he pulled Aimee out of the room and into the narrow hallway.

"What have we done, Aim?"

Aimee reached up to brush his hair back from his face. She could cry over this night. How she wished she could turn back time and just be with Fang in her room again.

But she couldn't.

"Let me go back and see if I can keep them from pursuing Wren."

"I still say fuck them. Let's leave. . . ."

Her family would hunt them down to the ends of the world.

Aimee touched her lips to his whiskered cheek as she placed her locket in his hand. "I will find a way to be with you, Fang. I swear it."

Fang nodded, even though he didn't believe a word she spoke. It had been hopeless before.

Now . . . this was good-bye forever and he knew it.

CHAPTER 24

Aimee took a deep breath as she entered the back door of Peltier House. This was the last place she wanted to be, but she knew full well why she had to return.

Her family would kill Fang and his entire clan if she didn't.

Steeling herself for what was to come, she closed the door and headed for the stairs. She'd only gotten as far as the hall table when Dev came out of the door that led to the kitchen. She saw relief in his eyes a second before it was replaced with anger.

"So you're back."

Aimee shrugged. "It's my home."

He scoffed at her. "I would find another one, if I were you."

She stiffened at the coldness of his tone that bit her all the way to her soul. "I'm being thrown out?"

"You're being warned. You picked your side and it was the wrong one."

"Leave us."

Aimee looked up at her mother's commanding tone. Maman was at the top of the stairs, glaring down at them. Dev shook his head at her before he headed back toward the kitchen.

She flashed herself up to her mother's side. "Don't even think about striking me, Maman. I'm not in the mood for it. And I will hit back this time."

Her mother narrowed her eyes on her. "You would sacrifice all of us for a hybrid orphan without clan?"

Maman was talking about Wren and while he held Aimee's loyalty as a friend, it was Fang's life that mattered most to her. "Never. But I will not stand by and see an innocent condemned for nothing. Can you not see the lie that is being told, Maman? I know Wren. I talk to him. He's no threat to anyone but himself."

Still her mother's face was angry and cold. Her family, and in particular her mother, wasn't stupid. She had no doubt that her mother and father knew she'd left voluntarily with Fang. Given the way he'd been protecting her these months past, they had to know he would have never really harmed her.

"You betrayed us all."

Aimee sighed. "If doing the right thing is betrayal, then yes, I suppose I did. So what are you going to do now, Maman? Kill me?"

Her mother growled ferociously at her, but Aimee stood her ground.

The air around them sizzled an instant before something shattered in Wren's room.

Aimee followed her mother who rushed to the door and slung it open. She half-expected to find Wren there even though they'd told him to stay away until this was settled. She could tell by the scent that it was a tiger, all right, but the blond man searching the room wasn't Wren.

"What are you doing here, Zack?" her mother asked.

The tiger curled his lips as he opened a drawer. "The bastard escaped us. I need something with his scent on it to disseminate to the Strati who seek him."

Aimee arched a brow at that. The Strati were elite Katagaria soldiers who were carefully trained to hunt and to kill. Her brothers Zar and Dev, along with her father, were technically Strati warriors even though they shouldn't have been. But the Peltier clan was all about keeping up appearances.

"You need nothing of his," her mother said to her utter shock as she defended Wren. "Get out of my house."

Zack didn't listen. He moved to open another drawer.

Her mother used her powers to slam it shut. "I said for you to leave."

The tiger turned to confront her. "Don't screw with me, bear. You have as much to lose by this as I do."

"What do you mean?"

But Aimee already knew. Her powers painted a perfect image of what was going on here. "You're the one who spoke out against Wren at the Omegrion . . . you lied."

Her mother jerked her head to look at her. "Do not be foolish, cub. I would have smelled a lie."

Aimee shook her head. "Not if the animal makes a habit of lying. He could easily mask his scent."

Zack took a step toward her only to find his path blocked by her mother.

"Is Aimee telling the truth?"

Zack answered with a question of his own. "Were *you*?" He arched a brow at her mother. "Do you really think Wren's gone mad? Honestly? You just wanted him out of here and you seized on any excuse to expel him. Admit it, Lo. You don't want anyone here but your family and it galls you to have to play nice with the rest of us."

Her mother growled low in her throat.

It wasn't the truth. Her mother would protect most of them with her life, but there were those like Wren her mother didn't trust at all. And those, he was right, Nicolette hated having here under her roof. Thanks to Josef.

Her family was too scarred by the past. By the one they'd trusted who had killed her brothers. And for that, she couldn't blame her mother at all.

Zack narrowed his gaze. "If Savitar ever learns the truth, he'll come for you and all your cubs. There won't be a brick left of your precious Sanctuary."

Her mother seized him and threw him against the wall. He landed with his back against it, but it didn't appear to faze him at all.

Zack actually laughed at her. "What happened to the rules of Sanctuary, Nicolette?"

Aimee caught her mother before she could attack the tiger again.

"Get out, tiger," Aimee snarled. "If I let go of my mother, there won't be enough left of you to worry about Savitar or anything else."

Zack pushed himself away from the wall. He glared at them both. "You have even more to lose than I do. Give me what I need to cover both our asses."

Now it was her mother who laughed. "Are you completely stupid? Wren has never left his scent on anything. Look around you, idiot. There is no personal item here. As soon as an article of clothing comes off his body, he has always washed it or destroyed it. He even keeps a monkey here so that its scent camouflages his own. You will never be able to track him. Face it, Zack, the cub has more intelligence than you and your father combined."

Aimee was suddenly impressed by her mother. Her mother had known that and still she'd allowed Wren to keep Marvin. How unlike her. And it caused a new wave of respect to fill her heart.

Zack's nostrils flared in anger. "This isn't over."

"*Oui*, but it is. You come here again and, code or no code, I will see you dead."

Growling, Zack vanished.

The tension in the air eased considerably.

Maman let out a slow breath as she turned toward her. "Aimee, call your wolf and warn him what has happened. I am sure he knows where Wren is and he can warn them that the tiger is cornered and desperate. In his position, Zack is capable of anything."

She frowned at her mother's sudden reversal. "I don't understand. Why are you being unbelievably understanding? No offense, Maman, it scares me."

Her mother gave her a harsh stare. "I have no love of Wren, this you know. But I respect the predator within him and I do not appreciate being manipulated by another. Nor do I relish being made a fool." Her mother shook her head. "I should have questioned why Zack and his father continually called to check on Wren after he was sent here. I allowed them to plant seeds of doubt in my mind and I saw in him what they wanted me to see. I can't believe I was so foolish."

Her gaze softened as she touched Aimee's cheek. "I give you credit, cub. You weren't blinded. Now we must repair this before the weight of Savitar's wrath comes crashing down on all of us." She urged Aimee toward the door. "Go warn them. You, they will listen to."

"What are you going to do?"

"I am going to speak with your father and brothers. I fear we are on the edge of a very dangerous situation and I want them all prepared."

Aimee took a step toward the door, then paused. "I love you, Maman."

"*Je t'aime aussi, ma petite.* Now go and let us make this as right as we can."

Fang clutched the locket in his fist that Aimee had given him right before she left while he stared at the rain that was pouring down outside. Alone in his room at Vane's house, sitting on his bed with his back against the wall and one knee bent, he could hear Bride and Vane downstairs, laughing.

That sound made him want to put his fist through the wall.

Even though his body kept wanting to shift into a wolf due to the injuries Papa Bear had given him, he refused. As a wolf, he couldn't hold on to this one piece of her. And right now, he needed to touch it.

He pressed the locket to his lips so that he could inhale the scent of her and remember the last sight before she left. They'd been on Jean-Luc's ship. Tears had been streaming down her beautiful face as she'd kissed his lips, then left him alone. Her hands had lingered on him as she pulled away from him and vanished.

The pain of it was more than he could stand.

No wonder he hadn't been able to leave Sanctuary.

His phone rang. He started to ignore it until he realized it was Aimee. Reaching for it, he lost his balance on the bed and went slamming onto the floor. Afraid he'd miss her, he flipped it open and ignored the pain in his injured shoulder and arm. "I'm here."

"Are you all right?"

He ground his teeth to keep from groaning as he made his way back onto the bed again. "Absolutely."

"You don't sound all right. You sound like you're in a lot of pain."

Of all the times for her to be astute. . . .

He looked at the new blood seeping through his shirt and grimaced. "Nah, I'm fine." But, grateful this wasn't on video, he mouthed the words, "Son of a bitch," at the throbbing wound. "Are you okay?"

"Believe it or not, yes. Maman didn't attack. In fact she told me to call you and warn you that Zack is after Wren. As we suspected, he lied to get Wren's money."

"I'll let Vane know."

"Okay . . . I miss you, baby."

"Ditto." Fang held the phone tight in his hand, wanting to keep her on the line, but not knowing what to say. He'd never really been one for chitchat. Snide comebacks were another matter, but actual conversation was beyond him.

"I'll try and slip out in a little bit to see you."

He smiled at the thought. "I'll be here, waiting."

"Okay. I love you."

"Me too."

She gave a short laugh. " 'I love you, Aimee.' You know it wouldn't kill you to say that, right?"

"I know."

"All right then. On that note, I better go. See you later."

Fang winced at the sound of her hanging up the phone. He closed his clamshell and wanted to cry from the pain inside him. But he wasn't that kind of wolf. Tougher than steel, he refused to let anyone know just how much Aimee meant to him.

His heart heavy, he went downstairs to relay her message to Vane, who wasn't thrilled by it. He left immediately to warn Wren while Fang stayed to watch over Bride.

"Is that blood?"

He glanced down at his shoulder. "A little. I'll go clean it."

"Sit."

The sharp command of her tone made him raise a single eyebrow.

Bride smiled. "Sorry. I'm bossy, I know. My father's a vet who works with Carson and I grew up in my dad's clinic. Sit down and let me see what I can do."

He did as ordered while she went to the bathroom to pull out a small medicine kit. He started to pull the shirt off, but the pain was such that he simply dissolved it.

Bride sucked her breath in as soon as she saw the nasty wound. "Did you get bitten?"

"Yeah. By one pissed-off bear."

"Papa Bear?"

He nodded.

Bride pulled out a piece of gauze and soaked it in peroxide. "You're probably lucky he didn't aim lower."

Fang didn't speak as his gaze fell down to the mark on her hand. He looked at his own that was empty. "Is it hard for you living with animals?"

She pulled back. "I don't consider any of you an animal, Fang."

"We're certainly not human."

She took his chin in her hand and forced him to look up at her. "I was raised to respect all life-forms. Hairless, furred, finned, and feathered."

"Yeah, but it has to be hard to live here without your kind around."

"Hardly. You're all my family. My *kind* fills this house."

Fang pulled away as he considered her words. Most of all, he wondered if Aimee would ever really feel that way about him. Love was one thing, but she'd already chosen her family. Apparently his love wasn't good enough.

And that made him sick. Besides, even if she did, he was still in service to Thorn and he had no soul. He had no real freedom.

What could he ever really offer her?

Aimee knocked lightly on her mother's office door. At her welcome, she pushed the door open to see her mother at her computer.

Nicolette leaned back slightly in her chair. An impeccable pose that was sophisticated and authoritative. "Is there something you need?"

Fang.

But she bit her tongue as fear rushed through her. Her mother had been understanding earlier. Would that continue?

"I wanted to talk to you about Fang."

A shield fell down over her mother's face. "There is nothing to discuss."

"You had me warn him."

"As a favor and to right a wrong. You know, daughter, exactly why you and he can never speak again."

Aimee tightened her grip on the doorknob behind her. "And if I can't live without him?"

"You will do as we all do. Your duty. Feelings have nothing to do with our mating and this you know. Look at your brother Alain. Does he pine for his love? *Non*, he has his mate and he has taught himself to be happy."

"I want to *be* happy, Maman."

Nicolette pinned her with a cold stare. "Your duty will make you happy. Trust me, *ma chérie*. In time you will do as you should and Fang shall be forgotten."

Aimee didn't believe that for a minute, but she knew better than to argue. Her mother wasn't about to budge on this.

"Very well, Maman." She opened the door and left.

What am I going to do?

She wanted to thumb her nose at her family and be with him. But would it be worth it?

Flashing herself upstairs, she materialized in the nursery where Alain's youngest cubs were napping in bear form. It was a sparse room that had a fake tree for them to climb on and the walls were painted with a cozy forest theme. The two of them curled together like giant balls of fluff on the thick green carpet, instead of on the bed in the corner. One cub was brown and one black. Beautiful and sweet, she adored her nephews.

Aimee lay down beside them so that she could lift Bryce's paw and play with his claws while he slept. She remembered lying on her brothers in much the same fashion when she'd been a cub.

Pain ached in her breast as she remembered Bastien's face. She missed her brothers more than anything. Time had done nothing to ease the pain or the sadness.

Which made her wonder if she'd ever be able to get over Fang. Or would he haunt her the same way?

Yet as she looked at Alain's cubs, she had to think it was worth it. Had he not done his duty, he wouldn't have such beautiful children.

If she went with Fang, she'd be sterile. A wolf and a bear would never be able to have children.

You could adopt.

That was certainly true. She loved Wren like family and Fang even more so. But an adopted child would never inherit her seat.

Maman would never forgive her for that.

"Why do I have to choose?" she breathed, choking on unspent tears. Why couldn't she have found one single bear to mate with?

I'm so broken.

Sighing, she left her nephews and headed for her own room. But with every step she took, she felt sicker inside.

Eli Blakemore paused beside Cosette as she communed with her spirits. On her knees in the middle of the room, resting in the center of a black cloth with a pentagram and strange writing painted on it in blood, she held her hands up and spoke in gibberish while her eyes were rolled back in her head.

Honestly he hated this bullshit and the stench of her incense offended every olfactory sense he possessed. Most of all, he wanted to swipe his hand across the voodoo altar she had in front of her and send it all flying across the room.

But that would *offend* her. So he waited as she danced and sang and carried on.

It seemed like forever had passed before she finally settled down and opened her eyes.

"Well?" he asked.

"There is disharmony in their home. The daughter is promised to a wolf."

He curled his lip in repugnance. In that one moment, his resolve against the Peltiers was set. How dare they be so unnatural. "That's disgusting."

"Not to them."

"Trust me, it is. But . . ." He let his voice trail off as ideas rushed through his head.

"But what?"

He laughed at the simplicity of the plan that could ultimately ruin them. "The bearswan will be looking for a way to be with him."

"And?"

He smiled wryly. "I think it's time for you to brew one of your potions."

Cosette laughed as she finally understood.

Pleased with himself, Eli folded his arms over his chest. Soon those parasites would be gone and if he played his cards right, he would also eliminate his greatest obstacle of all.

The wolves who had taken his seat away from his family on the Omegrion.

Oh, yes . . . this was about to get good.

CHAPTER 25

Fang couldn't breathe as he lay on the bed in wolf form. His branded shoulder was killing him. The mark burned in a way that made him want to tear his own arm off.

What is wrong with me?

The pain was excruciating as he pawed at the bed, trying to bury himself inside the white and blue quilt. Nothing eased the pain. No position or stretch.

Panting, he felt like his insides were being shredded. *I'm giving birth to the alien in* Alien. . . . Every sound made was too loud for his ears. Every heartbeat tore through his skull.

He wanted to kill something.

The scent of blood hung in his nostrils, enticing him. Calling him . . .

If you kill the bears, you can take their powers and have Aimee.

He scowled at the foreign voice in his head. Was he losing his mind?

What did they really do for you? Nothing. They threw your brother out and left him to fend for himself and his mate. They don't care about any of you. Pay them back for what they did to Vane and Wren.

Death to the bears. . . .

Fang shook his head, trying to clear it of the hostile anger. What was wrong with him? He felt drunk as sounds echoed around him and his vision dimmed.

"Fang?"

He heard Aimee's voice as she appeared in his room. She looked like a sugary morsel, standing in front of his dresser with the light shining in from the window to highlight her pale hair. The shadows played on her skin, cutting angles across her beautiful face. It reminded him of the way she'd looked the first time he'd seen her at Sanctuary.

But tonight, he didn't want her kindness.

The demon inside wanted her blood.

"*Go away,*" he growled at her. He didn't want to be around her while he felt like this. He didn't have control of himself or the demon. It was growing larger and it was seeping through every part of him.

Violent and lethal, he was afraid of himself.

He didn't know how much longer he could hold it off. May the gods help her if it broke free while she was with him. The hatred and desire to cause her pain was ever harsh and demanding.

Don't let me hurt her. . . .

But he wasn't sure he could abide by that. The hunger inside him was too great.

Aimee hesitated at the feral sound of Fang's tone in her head. Something was obviously wrong with him. Uncertain as to what it was, she moved closer and held her hand out to stroke his fur. "What's wrong, baby?"

He turned on her and snapped at her hand as if he'd

gone mad. One minute he was a wolf and in the next human.

He came off the bed, stalking her. Completely naked, his body was covered in a fine sheen of sweat. His cheeks were dusted by whiskers as his damp hair fell into his eyes. Every muscle of his tawny body was taut and corded as if he were pulling back from lashing out.

A new wave of fear consumed her as she backed up. There was a predatory gait to his walk. One that said he was assessing her as prey.

"Talk to me, Fang."

"And say what?" He continued to advance on her until he'd pressed her against the wall and cocked his head. There was a light in his dark eyes that was truly scary. It was a light that warned her to be wary and one that told her this wasn't the wolf she'd learned to love.

This was the one she'd seen that first day in Sanctuary. The feral wolf who terrified everyone.

He buried his face in her neck and inhaled deeply while he stroked her cheek with one hand. "I can already taste your blood."

He sank his teeth into her flesh.

Hissing, Aimee knocked him back with a fierce blow to his solar plexus. "What are you doing?"

He grabbed her arm and pulled her against him in a hold made of steel. "This is what you want, isn't it? Your wolf to attack you?"

Aimee twisted out of his offensive grip. "Who are you?"

"I'm Fang, baby. Can't you tell?"

No. This wasn't Fang. There was something definitely wrong. He didn't even smell right.

Then she saw it. The tiniest flash of red in his eyes. And in an instant, she knew what it was.

He was possessed.

"No . . . ," she breathed as terror consumed her.

Had something followed him back from the Nether Realm?

He tried to bite her again.

Aimee reacted on instinct. Kneeing him in the groin as hard as she could, she shoved him back. He stumbled away, cupping himself.

Please let it only be the demon feeling that and not Fang. Fang she wouldn't hurt for anything. But the demon was a whole other story.

She stood over him, aching for his pain, but not enough that she would be his willing victim. "If you can hear me, Fang, I need you to push this away and come back to me."

His eyes glowed bloodred in the darkness as he straightened up. Without responding at all, he grabbed her roughly.

Aimee whimpered in pain.

That single sound seemed to reach whatever part of the real Fang was still there. She saw the regret flash in his gaze as he released her.

Pure anguish contorted his features as he staggered back. "Run, Aimee. Get out!"

She hesitated, not wanting to leave him here. But she could tell he was holding on to himself by a narrow margin and doing his best not to hurt her. Staying here would only make it worse on him. "I'll get help."

His legs buckled an instant before he fell to the floor where he writhed as if in utter agony. He flashed back to his wolf's form.

Aimee winced, desperate to soothe him.

But first she had to make sure he didn't hurt her. Torn, she knew she had no choice but to leave. It was the best for both of them.

With no idea of what she should do, she flashed herself to Club Charonte—the dance club and bar that Xedrix and company had opened with her brother Kyle's help. Surely a demon would know and be able to tell her how to help Fang with his current dilemma. She couldn't think of anyone else who would have an inkling.

If Xedrix couldn't help her, she didn't know what she'd do.

The club was packed tonight with college students, young locals, and tourists dancing while demons moved through them as staff.

If the humans only knew. . . .

But they weren't what concerned her. Only Fang did.

Loud hip-hop music thundered through the club as lights flashed and danced across the people, demons, floor, and bar. The crowd mingled all around her in couples or in groups while the demons tried to blend in. A few did have their horns showing, but the humans seemed to accept those as fake. Some of them were even showing their real mottled-colored skin, but again, the humans complimented them on the makeup.

Weird.

Aimee stopped a male Charonte with red horns and

orange and red skin as he passed by her with an empty tray tucked under his arm. "Hey, where's Xedrix?"

He gave her a suspicious once-over.

"I'm Kyle Peltier's sister and I need to speak to him."

That seemed to reassure him. He pressed the mic on his headset. "Xed, there's a bear down here for you." He nodded, then looked back at her. "He's on his way."

"Thank you."

The demon wandered off toward the mirrored bar area.

She saw a door open from an upstairs room that must be the office. It had a mirrored window where Xedrix could no doubt look out and spy on his workers and patrons.

Dressed in jeans and a loose blue T-shirt, Xedrix made his way down the steps. Aimee had to give him credit. For a demon, he was damn good-looking. That lean body was ripped and his black hair framed near-perfect features.

But the dismal expression on his face was almost funny as he stopped by her side. "This can't be good for me."

"Nice seeing you too."

"Yeah. What do you need now?"

"Information about a demon."

His features hardened. "Don't piss us off. We don't like that."

She gave him a droll stare. "If someone's possessed by a demon, how do you get the demon out?"

"Call a priest." He started away from her.

Aimee caught his arm and pulled him to a stop. His entire stance oozed impatience. "I'm serious, Xedrix. And this isn't a human. It's Fang. Have you any idea how much damage a demon could do in the body of a Were-Hunter?"

"Oh, a lot." His tone was as dry as the Sahara. "Would definitely suck to be their victim."

She didn't appreciate his humor. "What can I do?"

"I'd leave town."

"Xedrix!"

He lifted his hands in an exaggerated stance of hopeless innocence. "What do you want me to say? Rub his furry belly? I don't even know what kind of demon has him. In case you haven't noticed, there are hundreds of species of us. And you're talking to a demon who comes from one of the nonpossessing kind. We kill whatever gets in our way. Or on our nerves." He gave her a very pointed stare for emphasis on that. "Possession's for . . ." His voice trailed off as he looked past her.

Aimee turned to see a gorgeous blond woman who was eyeing him irritably with her arms akimbo.

"You were about to say?" the female prompted.

"Uh . . . possession's for really great demons who have . . . lots of powers."

It was actually entertaining to watch him squirm. Obviously the blond woman meant a lot to him and he didn't want to make *her* angry.

The blonde offered Aimee her hand. "I'm Kerryna and you would be?"

"Kyle's sister," Xedrix answered so quick Aimee realized that he and Kerryna must have a relationship close enough that he didn't want Kerryna to mistake why he was talking to her. "Aimee. And she was just leaving."

Aimee let go of Kerryna's hand to correct him. "Not yet, I'm not."

"Yes, you are. Adios. There's the door. Doorknob twists to the left. The hinges open in. You should use them. Keep them working. Keep you breathing. We're all happy here."

Aimee sighed at his sarcastic tirade. Ignoring him, she tried Kerryna. "I have to know how to break a possession. Would you happen to have any kind of suggestions?"

Kerryna frowned. "What kind of demon?"

"I don't know. Is there a difference?"

"Oh, definitely. There are those you can kill, those you can drive out, and those who become a permanent part of you. The latter, to quote Xedrix's favorite phrase, really sucks."

Aimee slid a glance at Xedrix, before she returned her attention to Kerryna. "How do I know what I have?"

"Take me to it."

Xedrix made an inhuman sound of protest. "Oh, hell no."

Kerryna gave him a chiding stare. "Xedrix . . ."

He immediately stepped back. "I know I'm Charonte and we defer to our females, but you have to respect the fact that I'm Charonte and we protect our females to the end. You be my female. I be protecting."

Kerryna smiled at him. "Then come with us and stop whining."

"I'm not whining." He looked at Aimee as if he were contemplating her utter dismemberment. "Why is it every time I see you, you make me go someplace I don't want to go? I guess I should be grateful that at least it's not hell again."

"Stop being a baby, demon. Let's go see Fang."

Xedrix screwed his face up in distaste. "What is it with you and that wolf anyway? Can't we just shoot him and put him out of my misery?"

"I'd shoot you first."

"At the rate we're going, I wish you would."

Kerryna smacked him playfully in the belly. "Be nice, Xed, or I'll shoot you myself."

"Yes, akra."

Shaking her head at his sarcasm, Aimee took them back to where she'd left Fang in his room.

It was empty.

Xedrix crossed his arms over his chest. "Where is he?"

Frustrated and worried, Aimee searched the room with her gaze. The bed was still mussed, but the dresser and chest of drawers were perfect. Everything was as it had been, except for Fang's presence. "I don't know. He was curled up on the floor in pain when I left him."

Kerryna went to the spot as if she somehow knew exactly where he'd been. Touching the floor, she gasped. "Oh, this is bad."

Aimee's heart sank to her feet at that dire tone. "What?"

"He's possessed by a primus. A powerful primus."

Aimee wasn't sure what that was, but the tone said it wasn't good. "Can you get the demon out?"

"I don't know." Kerryna stood up again. "If I had my sisters, I could. But alone . . . I just don't know."

"Then what do we do?"

Xedrix was the one who answered. "Kill him."

"Xedrix!" Aimee snapped.

"What?" He gave her a look of innocence that would have been comical had it not been Fang's life they were discussing. "Wolves make good eats. Not as tasty as other things, but they're not bad. And add on hot sauce. I could make do."

Wanting to serve him up at Sanctuary, she looked at Kerryna. "I can track him and find him." Aimee closed her eyes and thought of Fang.

But for once, nothing was there.

Nothing.

How could this be? Her powers were godlike. She could always track. Yet there was no sign of him anywhere. It was almost like he was dead.

That mere thought was enough to make her want to collapse. *You're stronger than that. . . .*

Aimee faced them with a steadiness she didn't feel. "I can't find him."

Kerryna looked back to the floor. "He's a powerful demon. I'm sure he can mask his essence from anyone except a god."

"Then what do we do?"

Xedrix shrugged. His ambivalence was getting on her last nerve.

Narrowing her eyes, Kerryna tapped her chin. "Menyara, I think."

Aimee frowned at a term she'd never heard before. "Is that some kind of funky ceremony?"

Kerryna laughed. "No, it's a person. She lives here in New Orleans and is the one who helped me when I first arrived. I think if anyone can help you, she's the one." She turned a pointed stare at Xedrix. "Since you can't stand her, surely you'll let me go there alone?"

He brought his left fist to his right shoulder and bowed mockingly. "Yes, akra. Your pleasure is ever my misery."

Kerryna snorted. "I'll remember that tonight when you want to come to bed."

He looked horrified by her threat. "It was a joke, baby. I didn't mean a word of it."

She patted him adoringly on the cheek. "We'll see."

Aimee barely had time to focus before Kerryna took her out of Fang's room to a small shack of a bright blue house. Even in the darkness, the blue stood out. Colorful, but ubiquitous in design, it looked like any of a hundred row houses in New Orleans' French Quarter. White lace curtains peeked out from under thick white shutters. It hardly looked like the abode of someone who could defeat a powerful demon.

But if Hello Kitty attacked—watch out!

Kerryna knocked on the door.

After a brief pause, a beautiful African American woman opened it to smile at them. Her long curly hair framed a face that was elegant and exotic. Dressed in a bright yellow sweater that matched the headband she used to hold her hair off her forehead, and jeans, she possessed an aura of fierce power that rippled on the air around them.

There was no doubt that this woman could take on a demon and win.

"Kerry-bell? Who you bring to Menyara's door,

child?" She held her hand out to Aimee. "Come in, *ma petite* bearswan, and make yourself at home."

Eyes wide, Aimee passed a trepidatious glance at Kerryna. "How do you know who I am?" she asked Menyara.

A slow smile curved her lips and wrinkled her nose. "I know much about this world, child. Both seen and unseen. Now come, there's a warm pot of Egyptian chamomile tea waiting with lots of honey."

Aimee followed her into the small house that was decorated like the inside of an Egyptian pyramid. Statues of the gods lined the mantel that reminded her more of an altar. Papyrus paintings lined the walls. Decorated with black, golds, and browns, the house had a homey feel to it. Like walking into a beloved grandmother's house.

Aimee took a seat on the small armchair as Kerryna sat down on the couch while Menyara poured their tea.

Kerryna took a cup from her hand. "I'm sure you know why we're here."

Menyara held the teapot lid as she poured a cup for Aimee. "I do indeed. But there is much in flux right now. Powers aligning and repelling." She handed the cup to Aimee. "You have made a most powerful enemy, *chère*. One who will stop at nothing to see you dead."

"I don't care about that. It's Fang I'm worried about."

She inclined her head before she poured her own cup. "He walks a shadowy line of deceit. But it is not my place to tell you what he has done. Only *he* can do that."

"What do you mean?"

Menyara spread her hand out and a perfect ball of fire appeared in the air in front of her face. "We all create things by our wills." She waved her hand over the fireball to make it grow larger. "Every action we take shapes our creations." She cut the ball in half with her bare hand and it dissolved into embers that extinguished on the carpet. "And it can destroy them."

Maybe she was dense, but Aimee didn't see a connection with that fireball and what was happening with Fang. "That's all fine and good, but—"

"There is no but, child. Fang is on his course. He must see it through."

Well, bully for her, but from what she'd seen, he was having a really hard time of it. "Can't I help?"

"No. There is nothing to be done. Only he can defeat the demon within."

"There's no exorcism?"

Menyara knelt on the floor in front of Aimee and took her hands into hers and held them. "Inside us all are pieces of that which makes the negative." She glanced at Kerryna over her shoulder. "Demons are neither good nor bad. Like you, they have many facets. It is that inner essence, or drive, if you will, that we all have that guides us through our lives. Sometimes those voices that drive us are whispered memories that live deep inside and cause us such pain that we have no choice except to let it out and to hurt those around us. But at other times, the voice is love and compassion, and it guides us to a gentler place. In the end, we, alone, must choose what path to walk. No one can help us with it."

Aimee shook her head. "I don't believe that. Our paths collided with each other for a reason. Like you with the ball. One move and we can take that hate and pain away."

Menyara patted her hand. "Now you're thinking, child. But remember, it is a powerful demon inside him. One who is hungry for blood fire and he will not easily be appeased. Look in your heart and you will see truth."

Kerryna clanged her cup on the saucer at those words. "You told me the heart blinds us."

Menyara laughed at Kerryna. "It does indeed." She pulled a ring from her finger and held it out to Aimee. "Wear this, child. It will protect you."

"From what?"

"When the time comes, you will know."

Aimee looked down at the garnet that was so dark it appeared black. Set in an antique setting of gold lattice-work, it was beautiful. "Your vagueness reminds me of a man named Acheron Parthenopaeus. You two wouldn't happen to be related, would you?"

She laughed. "We are old friends and like me, Acheron knows when the truth will only hurt. You must find your own way in this. By the very laws of the universe, I'm forbidden to intervene."

"Oh, goody. Thanks." Aimee slid the ring on, then paused. "I'm sorry, Menyara. I don't mean to seem ungrateful."

"I know, child. Have no fear. Now it is getting late and you should return home. Your wolf will come to you when the time is right for it to be so."

Aimee nodded, then said good night to the two of them. And here she'd been thinking to spend a quiet early-morning cuddle session with Fang. Instead, she was terrified for him.

Flashing back to her own room, she heard a lot of animated talking downstairs in the foyer. What on earth? It was late and most of the staff should be done for the night.

Curious, she opened the door and went to the stairs. There below was her entire family, along with Jasyn, Max, Colt, Carson, and Justin. As she descended the stairs, she heard their discussion.

"So what did the police say?"

"He was one of three killed tonight. They're thinking it's gang-related, but since Stu is a Dark-Hunter Squire, he knows better. He said it looked more like a demon attack."

Aimee stumbled on the last stair.

"You a'right?" Dev asked.

"Just testing gravity."

Laughing, he shook his head.

Aimee straightened up, then joined them. "What are you guys talking about?"

"Greg, the Arcadian panther who came in two days ago, was found dead in an alley over on Royal Street. There were two more bodies found in Exchange Place. Those human."

Kyle gave her an evil smirk. "They were all drained completely of blood so the cops are thinking vampires."

She scowled. "Daimon kills?"

"No," her father said in a grave tone. "They still had their souls. This was a demon only wanting blood."

And Aimee could only think of one demon new to the city who had been dying for blood.

The one inside Fang. . . .

CHAPTER 26

Fang woke up in a back alley of the French Quarter, his head throbbing as the midmorning sun peeked in through the surrounding buildings to the shadows where he must have collapsed. Every part of his wolf's body ached.

How had he gotten here?

Shifting his weight, he saw the blood coating his fur, but it wasn't *his* blood. Though he was sore, he wasn't wounded. Yet his body was completely saturated with it as if he'd rolled in it. He could even taste it in his mouth.

He turned human so that he could manifest a bottle of water and at least rinse the warm metallic taste out. It was thick on his taste buds and made him completely nauseated.

After sluicing the taste out, he leaned back against the warm brick wall to look up at the latticework of the metal balcony above his head.

What had happened? Fragmented images of the night before went through his mind like he'd been on some kind of drunken bender. He saw Aimee in his room again. But he hadn't hurt her. The other images weren't so clear. They were him with other people . . . one with a Were-Hunter.

A panther . . .

He was fighting the people, two of them . . . or was it three? But he didn't know why. Closing his eyes, he tried to sort through those images. Still, they were cloudy and confusing. There were growls and insults. Fists and swords. Metal flashing as blood poured.

"Did I kill someone?" He remembered a . . . was it a man fighting with him? Maybe it was a demon. The images weren't clear enough to really remember. All they did was confuse him. His head pounded.

Needing something to center him, he manifested a cell phone and called Aimee.

"Fang?"

He let out a relieved breath the moment he heard her soft voice. He didn't know what it was about her, but she soothed him all the way to the core of his being. "Hey, baby, I—"

"Where are you?"

He arched a brow at the sharpness of her tone. She sounded panicked and strange. "I don't know. An alley somewhere."

"What happened to you last night?" Now her words were accusatory. "I tried to find you and couldn't."

"What's wrong?"

"The police are looking for you."

That slammed into him like a fist. Raking his hand over his head, he tried to make sense of everything. "What?"

"They want to bring you in for questioning. Two humans and a Were-Hunter were killed last night. Greg, who only came here a few days ago, went out to hook up with a woman and never came back. They found him late last night with bite wounds . . . someone had ripped out his jugular." She paused before she whispered, "Everyone thinks it was you, Fang."

Of course they did. 'Cause let's face it, in a town riddled with demons, Daimons, and Weres, who else would have done it? Anger sliced through him that *he* of all people or animals would be the suspect. "What makes them think that?"

"A torn T-shirt was found in the alley with his body. It had your scent all over it."

Oh. Well, that was a little more damning than he wanted. Her words also brought back a flash of someone going for him out of the shadows. Of his shirt being ripped off while he fought them, but he couldn't remember anything more than that.

Why had they been fighting?

Swallowing hard, Fang clutched the phone in his hand. "What do you think?"

"I . . . I don't know. You were really out of control when I was with you last night."

Killer. She didn't say the actual word, but then she didn't have to. Her tone more than implied it and it cut through him that she could doubt him even a little after all they'd gone through together. Why couldn't one person, just once, have faith in him?

But no. They always thought the worst where he was concerned.

That was okay, he was used to animals and people

not having faith in him. Why should she? His own brother had thought him weak and selfish. Why should Aimee be any different? "Where were they murdered?"

"The humans on Exchange Place and Greg in an alley on Royal."

Fang looked up at the sign he could see from his own alley.

Royal.

"Shit," he breathed.

"What?"

Fang hung his head as fear went through him. Maybe he'd done it after all. He couldn't remember not doing it and obviously he'd fought with someone over something potent. And someone other than him had been hemorrhaging badly. Bad enough that blood had been in his mouth and all over his fur.

Just like he'd bitten into someone's jugular. . . .

Oh, shit, shit, shit. He was guilty. He had to be.

No, you'd never do something like that.

Or would he? With the demon inside him, he was capable of anything, and last night that demon had been out of control. And it had been blood-hungry.

But he didn't want to tell any of that to Aimee. "Nothing. Do you know what time the murders took place?"

"The humans, no. Greg died about two A.M."

Images of an Arcadian panther flashed as he saw himself attacking one. The guy had been human, then panther, then human again as they clashed. "What was Greg?"

"Panthiras Arcadius."

Double shit.

Maybe her doubt about his innocence wasn't so misplaced after all. It was beginning to look like he was guilty. "I gotta go."

"What are you going to do?"

"I'm not sure."

"Fang. Be careful. Please." That was sincere and it touched him deep.

She might have doubts about his moral fiber, but she still cared about him. "You too."

He hung up and slid the phone into his pocket. Leaning back against the redbrick wall behind him, he raked his hands through his hair as he tried to sort out what had happened. Nothing was clear. All he could remember were the emotions. The rage. The hunger.

What have I done?

Suddenly, he felt as if someone or something was watching him . . . looking around, he saw nothing out of place. Either with his eyes or his senses. At least not until a large raven landed on the black wrought-iron door gate catercorner to him. It angled its head as if watching him intently.

Yeah . . . a bird. A friggin' bird was putting him on edge.

I am definitely losing my mind. And still the feeling of being watched persisted while there was nothing around him to warrant the sensation. The rising sun had even banished the shadows that had been there when he awoke. No one could be watching him from where he sat. Not without being someplace he could see them too.

Except for the bird.

But for the fact there were no Were-Hunters of that

species, he'd think it sentient the way it watched him. *Gah, how pathetic am I that a bird is unsettling me?*

Then he heard the sound of a loud bike thundering out on the street. It had a hell of an engine and he could hear the quickness of the gears changing as the rider accelerated. Someone knew how to drive. The sound grew louder and louder, until it was almost deafening.

Damn, dude, get a new muffler.

At least that was his thought until it came screaming into the alley in front of him. A gleaming 2000 Honda F6C Valkyrie, it had a throaty sound of pure raw power and a customized paint job of flames painted over the glossy factory black.

The rider wore a solid black Aerostitch-armored suit with a jet-black helmet. The only color on his body came from silver vambraces that ran from wrist to elbow and matching silver panels on his biker boots.

He looked at Fang as he shifted into neutral and the engine went into idle. "You might want to run."

"I don't run from shit."

The man shook his head as he turned the bike off, put it on its stand and swung one long leg over it. "Suit yourself."

Then Fang heard it. . . .

A sound that had haunted him every minute of his time spent in the Nether Realm. One that had made his blood run cold. It was unmistakable and clear, and it brought out the rage that was boiling inside of him now.

The sound of a Reaper. . . .

No, not one.

Many.

That sick tug of dread filled his stomach. He'd thought those battles were behind him. But it was obvious this newcomer not only knew of them, he was getting ready to fight them. "Who are you?"

"Zeke." He held his hand out and his motorcycle transformed into a bright oversized sword unlike anything Fang had ever seen before.

The raven flew from the fence. As soon as it reached Zeke's back, it turned into a woman dressed in a tight leather catsuit, corset, and a long black coat. Her short black hair fell in a sleek bob that framed perfect features and coal-black eyes. Sleek and deadly, she was stunningly beautiful.

She snapped her arms down and as she did so, claws and armor covered her hands.

Zeke looked at her over his shoulder. "She's Ravenna and this is your last shot to get out while you can."

Fang shook his head. "I'm in."

Ravenna raked him with a disbelieving stare. "You a fool, wolf. I'd run if I could."

Then all hell, literally, broke loose as the Reapers arrived. Out of the brick walls and street below their feet, they came out en masse. At least two dozen, though it was hard to differentiate among them. They fought as a cohesive unit and their typical strategy was to overwhelm their opponent, knock him to the ground, and then rip him to shreds.

Fang manifested a sword, not the one Thorn had given him, but another. "Can I kill these?"

Zeke ran one through, then kicked another back. He swung a wide arc, beheading a third one in a single stroke. "Abso-fuckin'-lutely."

Fang caught the first Reaper to reach him and sliced it open. It screamed, collapsing on the ground as another came for his back.

Ravenna caught it from behind. "Don't shift forms," she warned before she swung around to confront another.

Fang hadn't planned on it. As a wolf, he was no match for these. He couldn't bite into them and it left him with nothing else to do except run.

And this time, he wanted them dead. All the months of being locked in hell with them and of being bitten and clawed came boiling up through his body. He wanted vengeance and he was taking it out on every Reaper he could reach.

He slung his hand out, intending to blast a demon, but Ravenna caught his wrist.

"That will only make them stronger. Reapers are special. Hand-to-hand only."

At least she told him the rules *before* he made the mistake. *Thanks, Thorn, you bastard*. Fang kicked the next one back as Zeke stabbed another. Their numbers seemed to double for a few minutes, as if they were calling in reinforcement.

At least until Ravenna made a high-pitched screech. Wanting to howl, Fang hit the deck as pain tore through his head. It was excruciating. But he wasn't the only one who felt it. The Reapers shrank back, screaming until they finally vanished.

His ears ringing, Fang pushed himself up to glower at her for that. He wanted to rip her head off over the agony pounding in his skull.

Zeke snatched his helmet off and had a look on his

face as if he felt about the same way. His dark brown hair was spiked up in front from the helmet and sweat, but the rest fell to his shoulders. With two days' growth of beard on his face, he looked lethal in spite of the almost angelic beauty of his features. Pressing one hand to his ears, he glared at Ravenna. "How many times have I told you not to do that shit?"

"They were reinforcing. You want me to let them have you next time?"

"Depends on how long this migraine lasts. Damn it, woman, just stab me through the skull next time." Zeke flexed his jaw as if trying to clear his head.

"Don't tempt me."

Shaking his head to ease his own pain, Fang stood up and surveyed the black birdlike bodies around them. Blood ran thick on the sidewalk as a few of them twitched from death. He dissolved his sword and caught his breath.

Zeke and Ravenna turned to face him. "Nice work," Zeke offered.

Fang nodded in appreciation as he continued to survey the bodies. "What caused this?"

Ravenna patted him on the chest, right over his heart. "You have Phrixis inside you, buddy." She gestured to the demon remains. "They want his powers, which means if they kill you, they get your powers and his. You're the Star of India, baby."

Fang couldn't accept that. It didn't make sense. "How can they be here?"

Zeke held his hand out and shot out a stream of fire to consume the bodies. "They've always been here. You just never saw them until your unfortunate journey into their domain and you had your eyes opened. The doorway between this world and theirs is barely guarded, so coming and going really isn't all that hard for certain species such as these."

Fang narrowed his gaze as he finally understood. "So you're Hellchasers too?"

Zeke snorted as if Fang had just insulted him. "No. We work for the right side of this equation." He all but spat those words.

And Fang didn't? What exactly was Zeke implying? "People, speak a language I can understand because right now, I'm lost. Last time I checked, *I* was one of the good guys."

Zeke shook his head. "You might be one, but the asshole you work for certainly isn't."

"What do you mean?"

"I answer to the archangels Samael and Gabriel. While Thorn is supposedly on our side, he is the blood son of our bitterest enemy and therefore we don't know where his real loyalties lie. He says he's with us, but I don't trust him at all. Given his father and his past, it's just a matter of time before he switches sides and leaves us with our pants down."

"Bitterest enemy?"

Zeke's features turned to stone. "Lucifer."

Fang gaped in disbelief as that reality smacked him hard in his gut. Thorn was Lucifer's son? Why hadn't he seen that?

Because you were desperate. Aimee's life had been threatened and nothing else had mattered to him. No wonder Thorn had been so secretive.

"What have I done?"

Ravenna clapped him hard on the shoulder. "You sold your soul to the wrong side, bud. Congrats."

Fang still refused to believe that. "But he fights the demons."

Zeke let out a long breath. "He has so far. Who knows what tomorrow brings. One thing I've learned while doing this is that people change, people betray, and the only one you can truly trust is yourself."

Ravenna gave him a harsh stare.

Zeke snorted. "Like you wouldn't cut my throat if someone gave you the chance."

She nodded and laughed. "Oh, well, that's true. I really do hate you most days."

Fang ignored them as he tried to understand what was going on. "Wait. Could you explain all this to me? Thorn hasn't been forthcoming with information. What exactly do we do and how do you fit into this equation?"

"C'mon, Fang," Ravenna said as if talking to a toddler who had no higher cognitive functioning. "You didn't really think the Greek and Atlantean pantheons were the only ones still fighting the good fight, did you? Or that the Daimons were the only demons? You know about the Charonte, the gallu, the Dimme, Harvesters, and Reapers. Slug demons like Misery. . . . There are thousands of classes and all of us, regardless of pantheon or power source, have soldiers to fight them."

Fang looked at her suspiciously. "What are *you*?"

"Half human, half Kalios demon."

Kalios were benevolent demons. He'd learned that in the Nether Realm. The only one of their kind he'd met had been torn apart by a Harvester while trying to help him.

He narrowed his gaze on Zeke. "You?"

"Born human. Classified now as a Necrodemian, which loosely translates as death to demons or demon executioner. Unlike a Hellchaser, I have the ability to kill demons without consequence as long as I follow certain protocols, which really, really blow most days."

"While we just send them back."

Zeke gave him a sarcastic salute. "You're getting it."

Fang put his hands on his hips. "I still don't understand how I got dragged into all this."

Ravenna patted him on the shoulder in sympathy. "The last Malachai has been tapped and with it, the oldest dark powers are uniting again to take over the earth. Our soldiers are being rallied and you, my friend, have stepped straight into this battle."

"I was only trying to protect Aimee."

"And that emotion is what has damned many a good soul."

Fang supposed so. But it still didn't lessen the fact that he'd seriously fubarred his life. And all this because he'd wanted a beer. . . .

And ended up wanting a bear.

"So is Thorn evil?" he asked Zeke.

"He's the son of one of the darkest powers ever known. And his father was a trusted soldier for good until he turned. Unlike his father, Thorn has resisted that temptation most of the time." Zeke let out a tired sigh. "In the end, we really don't know. Many members of his army have been known to turn and had to be put down . . . usually after making the same mistake you did when you killed Phrixis. When the demons kill the Hellchaser, they're made more powerful and harder for *us* to kill. Which begs the question, does Thorn fail to warn his Hellchasers about the demons on purpose, wanting the demons to get more powerful for his father? Or is he just that forgetful?"

Ravenna let out a derisive snort. "Or as I suspect, he's just a mentally twisted fuck who likes head games."

Fang would like an answer to that himself. "Bet if I asked—"

"You'd get the same answer we get. He'd either put you through a wall or set you on fire." Zeke smirked. "The fire part really hurts, by the way. I don't know what that bastard has in his fist, but it burns like nothing you've ever felt. For the record, stay on his good side."

Great. Just great. Stay on the good side of a man sired by pure evil. "So I'm no better off here than I was in the Nether Realm."

Ravenna laughed. "Are you insane? Of course you're better off. You can actually sleep here without fear of being brutalized, and there is real food that is worth eating. But . . . you have a crosshair on your back that looks like the mighty Target sign off I-10. Because the demons are all about gathering more power, you're extra-appealing to them. A possessed Were-Hunter . . . you're lucky I'm not trying to kill you."

Fang ignored that last bit. "So how do I get it off?"

Zeke scratched his chin. "Well, my bosses aren't much more forthcoming with information than yours is. We can try to resurrect Phrixis out of you, which could really suck and not work. It could also kill you. Or we could find the one who summoned him and break the chain she used. That should eradicate the little bugger."

"Why didn't Thorn tell me that?"

"I told you, we don't really know what side he's on. You've got to figure either he wants a demon to eat you and get more powerful to fight us. Or he wants you to be more powerful to fight them. Since we don't know if Good Fang or Bad Fang will win, it's a dangerous game he's playing."

"Personally, I want the demon out. How do we find his summoner?"

Ravenna arched a brow at him. "We're in N'Awlins, boy. Any idea how many people here that could be?"

"Well," Zeke said, "there is a third way."

"And that is?"

"An act so purely good and selfless it drives out the demon."

Fang liked the sound of that one. At least it had the most likely prospect of working and not getting him killed . . . maybe. "What is that? Saving an infant?"

Zeke shrugged. "Don't know. The PTB aren't big on specifics."

"PTB?"

Ravenna answered for him. "Powers That Be."

"Great. So what do I do? Just hang out and hope the demon leaves or that his summoner just happens to fling himself under my bike?"

Ravenna let out a sinister laugh. "Fasten your seat belts, buddy. It's going to be a bumpy ride."

"Thanks, Bette. I personally would like something a little more concrete."

Zeke picked his helmet up from the ground. "Well, that's the best we can do for now. Sorry."

Sorry? That was a word Fang would love to make that man eat. "You mentioned a Malachai. What is that?"

Zeke kicked to scatter the dust of the Reapers who'd finally stopped burning. "Easiest explanation is to think of them like an army of fallen angels. Demonic, cold-blooded, and capable of tearing apart anything that got in their path."

"But you said there was only one left."

Zeke nodded. "At one time, there were two armies. The Sephirii, who fought for good, and the Malachai, who were pure evil. Now we're down to one of each. The last Sephiroth is enslaved and the last Malachai vanished. We assumed him dead until a few months back when there was a rupture in the ether."

"A rupture?"

Zeke nodded. "Adarian, the last Malachai, had a son we didn't know about. Somehow the little bastard was born off our radar. When he came into his powers, it made an unmistakable clamor."

"Where is this last Malachai?"

"That's the kicker. We don't know. We're trying to find him, but whoever is hiding him is determined to keep him under wraps and we don't know why."

"I'm sure it can't be good."

"Yeah . . . at any rate, you've consigned yourself to a tenuous post. Watch your back, wolf." Zeke tossed his sword into the air. It transformed back into his motor-cycle.

Ravenna returned to her raven form and flew off while Zeke started the bike.

"I will try to keep an eye on you, wolf. Just be wary of shadows and keep your eyes open for Phrixis to control you."

Disgusted over this new turn of events, Fang waited until they were gone. He still had no clarity about last night or his future, but one thing was sure, he had no intention of allowing the police to question him until he knew more about what had happened.

And most of all, not until he knew more about what was going on.

Over the next few months as he avoided the cops and his family, Fang learned exactly what Zeke had meant about having a target on his back. He felt like he was back in the Nether Realm as demon after demon pursued him.

But the worst part were the blackouts he kept having where he couldn't remember what he'd done.

Where he'd been.

He was still alive, but that was the only thing he knew for certain. And as the blackouts became more frequent, he was afraid to go near Aimee. He would wake up with all manner of injuries that he couldn't explain. Bite marks, wounds, bruises.

If only he knew what they were from.

More people and Were-Hunters were dying and he was beginning to think he was to blame. Every morning, he woke up covered in blood with no explanation for what had caused it.

Fang moved deeper into the swamp, hoping that if he stayed away from everyone, he wouldn't hurt them.

Thoughts of harming Vane or Bride, or most important, Aimee, tortured him.

Why couldn't he remember what he did at night? He wanted desperately to go to Aimee and tell her what was going on, but he didn't dare. For one, he was evading custody. And two, he was afraid he might inadvertently hurt her during one of his blackouts.

He'd come so close that last time he'd seen her. Had she not kneed him . . .

Fang didn't want to think about it. He wouldn't be able to live, knowing he'd hurt her.

What is going on?

"I want you out of me!" he snarled at Phrixis, who was back in his head, telling him to kill.

Why couldn't he have peace?

Worst of all, he wanted to see his nephew and Aimee. He wanted to have a moment of being held by someone who wasn't as suspicious of him as he was of himself. But he wouldn't endanger them.

Not until he knew the truth.

Aimee hung up the phone in frustration as she sat alone in her mother's office. She wanted to crush the worthless device into a billion pieces.

"You still can't get him?"

She glanced up to find Dev standing in the doorway, watching her with a concerned frown on his face. "What are you talking about?"

"I know you're calling Fang."

She started to lie, but why bother? He'd just be able to smell it on her. "I'm worried about him."

"I don't blame you. Body count is mounting and Stu called to say they've set up a special task force to bring him in."

Stu had been keeping them all posted about the killings. Each one had looked like an animal had done it. Like a wolf or a dog.

But the bloodiest kills had been the Were-Hunters, all Arcadians, who'd died. No regular animal would have the abilities to do that. There was another Were-Hunter out there preying on them.

Aimee swallowed the cold lump in her throat as she considered a possibility she really didn't want to think about. "Do you think he's guilty of killing them?"

Dev sighed. "Eight of the dead are Were-Hunters. It doesn't look good for him."

No, it didn't. And the fact he wouldn't talk to her just made it worse. Not to mention, he was no longer staying with Vane. No one knew where he was.

And that made her want to weep.

"Aimee?"

She looked past Dev's shoulder at Maman's call in the hallway. She stood up and moved toward him to make room at the desk for her mother. "Yes?"

Dev stepped aside so that Maman could enter. "A special session of the Omegrion has been called. I think you should attend."

Aimee frowned at the unusual request. "Why?"

"Because it's about Fang."

Her heart sank so fast that she was dizzy. Dev caught her against him. "I'll go with you."

She nodded, grateful for his support. "Thank you, Maman, for telling me."

Her mother inclined her head.

Patting Dev on his arm, Aimee left him and went upstairs to dress herself in a conservative gray suit. She'd never been to the council before and had no idea what to expect.

Dev met her downstairs, dressed in jeans and a dark blue button-down shirt. He stood next to Maman. Aimee paused as she saw them there together. Her mother was so statuesque and exquisitely beautiful. Regal to the marrow of her bones. Her mother possessed such a feminine elegance that Aimee had always felt like an ugly duckling in comparison.

Though they didn't always agree, she loved that woman with all of her heart. And she wished she could be more like her and make her proud.

Dev was his usual kicked-back, charming self. Though he lacked Maman's refinement that had been passed to Zar and Alain, there was something absolutely compelling about his down-to-earth charisma.

"Are we ready, *mes enfants*?"

Aimee took Dev's hand. "We're ready."

Maman flashed them to Neratiti, the mysterious island home of Savitar. It was an island that moved constantly throughout the world as Savitar, a devout surfer, sought the perfect wave. He was a being of a thousand contradictions and mysteries.

And one Aimee had only met a few times in her life. To be honest, he scared the bejesus out of her.

But he wasn't in the room when they arrived. Breathing deeply in relief of that, Aimee took a moment to look around the large circular room. Decorated in burgundy and gold, the room had large open windows that spanned from the top of the gilded ceiling to the black marble floor under her feet. Lushly decorated, it should have been tacky, and yet somehow the elaborate colors and designs worked together to create a beautiful canvas.

A large round table was set in the middle of the room with an impressive throne resting off to the side. She would take a guess that was Savitar's seat.

Most of the Katagaria were already there and seated at the table. Aimee stepped back, somewhat intimidated by them. Dev stayed by her side with a stoic look that made her wonder what he was thinking.

Maman smirked at the vacant seats as she stepped near a tall, dark-haired panther. "Looks like the Arcadians are holding true to form, eh, Dante?"

"Always chickenshits, Lo. They won't face us alone even here." He looked past Maman to meet Aimee's gaze.

Maman smiled warmly as she introduced them. "My daughter. Aimee, meet Dante Pontis."

Aimee extended her hand to him. "You own the Inferno in Minnesota." Though not an official sanctuary itself, it was still a well-known club.

"You know it." He shook her hand, then held it out to Dev. "Good to see you again."

"You too."

Aimee frowned at the brotherly familiarity between them. "How do you two know each other?"

Dante winked. "Scouting bands . . . and other things."

Aimee held her hand up in protest of what he was about to say.

"That was before Dante mated."

Dante tapped his heart. The love in his eyes said it all. "And I wouldn't have it any other way, Dev. One day, I hope you know the joy Pandora brings to me."

"Yeah, that's not what you said when she was pregnant."

Dante laughed.

Fury and Vane entered the room, their faces grim.

Aimee went over to them immediately. "Have you heard from Fang?"

"No." Vane's voice was filled with emotion. "I was hoping you had."

She shook her head as the rest of the members flashed in and took seats at the huge round table.

She and Dev stepped back as two large doors were flung open with primal powers that shook the room. Savitar, dressed in a long flowing robe that reminded her of an Egyptian design, strode in with an aura of power so potent, it made the hairs on the back of her neck stand up.

His long dark hair flowed over his shoulders. Dark-complexioned, he had a well-trimmed goatee, and when he scanned the room, his deep lavender eyes seemed to glow.

Every member stood as he walked over to his throne. He appeared to be furious and there was a noticeable panic emanating from every creature present.

Savitar glowered at them. "Cop a squat, animals and folks. I don't want to be here any more than the rest of you so make it fast and get out of my hair. Let's quickly run down the bullshit pedagogy. Hear ye . . ." He paused as if holding back a desire to hit something. "Who the hell wrote this crap? Welcome to the Omegrion Chamber.

Here we gather, one rep from each branch of the two patrias. We come in peace"—he paused to snort derisively—"to make peace. I'm your mediator, Savitar, and if you don't know that by now, you need to be hit in the head with a jackhammer and replaced because you're too stupid to represent your patria. But in case you're dense and forgot, I am the summation of all that was and what will one day be again. I make order from chaos and chaos from order, which is how I got drafted into this shit. Now let's get on with this before I start splitting your hairs."

His gaze went straight to Maman. "Nicolette, there have been a number of complaints against Sanctuary lately."

Aimee's panic swelled.

Maman, on the other hand, kept her composure. "Complaints? From whom?"

Savitar leaned to the side as he narrowed his gaze on her. "A group of jackals who say you not only refused to help them apprehend a wanted criminal but that you also gave him their location and set him loose on them."

She opened her mouth to speak, but Savitar held his hand up to silence her. "A pack of wolves has said that when one of your Sanctuary staff attacked them unprovoked in an alley outside of Sanctuary, you not only condoned his actions, but refused to hand him over. Likewise, you knowingly allowed Wren to be falsely accused and pursued by this council. And that you personally attacked a tiger in your own home. There have been others who say that you pick and choose who you help and when, rather than welcome everyone in as you've sworn to. What have you to say?"

Maman didn't blink or flinch. "They're lies."

Vane stood up. "I back Nicolette with all good confidence."

Savitar's attention swung to him like a potent laser. "Boy, I haven't even started with you yet. Right now your word doesn't mean much."

Aimee cast a scared look at Dev.

He took her hand and held it while he motioned for her to remain silent.

Savitar pinned Nicolette with a harsh stare. "Did you or did you not have your son warn Constantine that a group of jackals were after him?"

"They attacked my daughter in my own club. They threatened her life."

Aimee looked at the blank seat that was Constantine's. What had happened to him? Why wasn't he here to back Maman?

Savitar gave her no quarter on the issue. "You should have told me, Nicolette. Unleashing their enemy on them is against the neutral code and you know that. And you still haven't answered my question. Did you tell him?"

"Yes. I, not my children, informed Constantine that they were after him."

She felt Dev's hand tighten on hers at the lie. Dev had been the one who told Constantine. Maman was protecting him while offering herself up on the chopping block.

"And when Eli Blakemore and his pack told you, in sworn testimony, that his son and friends were attacked outside your club, did you fail to hand over the attackers?"

Aimee stepped forward.

"*Don't!*" Dev snapped in her head. "*Savitar will kill you.*"

"*This is wrong!*"

"*Aimee, don't embarrass Maman. You know better.*"

She did, but it was hard to stand here and listen to her mother being attacked over things that were exaggerated.

Maman lifted her chin with the dignity of a queen. "I don't trust his pack or the lies they tell."

"Did you fail to hand over their attackers?"

Because of *her* . . . Unshed tears choked her as she realized how much trouble she'd gotten her mother into. No wonder Maman was so harsh at times. While Aimee had known Savitar was unfeeling, seeing this . . .

What had she done? She'd endangered her mother while saving her friend.

And Maman was taking all of the blame on herself to protect them.

"*Oui*, I did in fact."

Savitar shook his head. "And when we stood here and issued a warrant for Wren, did you not lie to the members of this council?"

"No, I spoke what I believed to be the truth."

"Are you sure?"

"*Absolument.* Yes."

Savitar let out a tired sigh while he thoughtfully stroked his chin. "Lo . . . of all the members of this council, you knew better. What were you thinking?"

"What I was thinking was that Constantine, as a Regis of this council, should be warned. His pursuers came in and held a knife to the throat of my only daughter and they attacked my sons. Had I not cared about our license, I would have destroyed them on the spot. Instead, I thought it only fair that I warn Constantine that these people"—she spat the word—"would not honor the laws of sanctuary and for him to not bother seeking one."

Savitar sat forward. "Limani means sanctuary. Telling a marked enemy where to find those out to kill him isn't the code. What about the other accusation?"

"Blakemore is a pig. His son attacked Wren in the back alley and we captured him there, again after he attacked my daughter who was trying to help Wren."

"I have sworn testimonies from ten of their pack members that Wren was the one who hit first."

"Only in self-defense."

"He drew first blood." Savitar's tone was chilling.

Still Maman didn't back down and for that Aimee had a newfound respect for her mother. "And Blakemore would have killed him where he stood had I handed him over. I won't condemn even an enemy to die when he was pushed by bullies."

Savitar rose to his feet, something that made several members of the council gasp. Maman, however, didn't move a muscle.

Savitar moved closer. "If what you're saying is the truth, why didn't you notify me?"

"I didn't think it was worth bothering you over."

Savitar stopped next to her chair. "Your mistake. Effective immediately, your license is suspended for six months. One more violation and it's permanent." Savitar turned to Vane. "And you . . . I told you to bring your brother with you."

It was Vane's turn to show no emotion. "I don't know where he is."

Savitar gave him a cutting glower. "You really expect me to believe that?"

"It's the truth."

That didn't go over with the big guy at all. Savitar looked as if he was about to unleash hell wrath down on all of them. "Very well. I see you need incentive to obey me. Have Fang here in forty-eight hours to stand trial or I'll destroy the Kattalakis pack." He narrowed his gaze on Fury. "Both of them. Adjourned!" He all but roared the last word before he vanished.

Noticeably shaken, the members began flashing out, but not before several made snide comments about Fang and the Peltiers.

Stunned by what had transpired, most of which had been her own fault, Aimee walked over to her mother. "Maman?"

Her mother didn't show even the tiniest bit of emotion. But Aimee could feel it. She knew how hard this was on her. Without the license, anyone could attack them.

They had no shelter. Everything Maman had worked so hard for had been shattered.

What have I done?

Dev sank down beside their mother. "Maman, it'll be all right."

She took his hand in hers and studied it as if amazed by the size of it. "*Non, mon fils.* I want you to go and round up all of our family. Leave and don't come back until the license is reinstated."

Dev shook his head, his jaw tightening with that

look of steely obstinance they knew so well. "We can't leave you."

Maman slapped him. Hard. "Do not question me. You go and do as you're told. Now!"

Dev's features hardened. She could see his desire to strike back, but he knew what she did. Maman was upset and she was acting on an animal's impulse. She had just risked her life to protect theirs.

Without another word, he vanished.

Aimee met Vane's gaze as she went to speak to him. "What are you going to do?"

"What do you think?" he snarled at her.

Horror filled her. "You can't hand Fang over to—" *That monster* was what she wanted to say, but she knew she couldn't. Savitar might hear her and the gods only knew what he'd do then.

"I have a wife and child. My mate is pregnant again, Aimee, and she's human. Am I supposed to give her up for a brother who won't even talk to me anymore?"

Maman came to her feet. She raked a cold, hostile glare over Vane. "This is all your fault. You wolves brought this down on me. Before you came, we had peace and now—"

"Us?" Vane growled. "My brother wouldn't have been involved in any of this had it not been for your daughter! I stand to lose my pack and my mate, and for what? A bear?"

Aimee stepped back as if she'd been slapped by those words.

Vane gave her a hard, cold stare. "You better find my brother and bring him to me."

"And if I can't?"

"You don't want an answer to that question, little bear. Trust me."

Aimee winced as she realized exactly what was going on here. Vane was going to betray Fang one last time, and he wanted her to be the tool to do it.

CHAPTER 27

Aimee stood in her room, packing everything she had. Her clothes, her jewelry, her books. But unlike the rest of her family, she wasn't going into hiding.

She was going to find Fang and they were going to run away from this crap for once and for all. There was no way she was going to be a part of handing him over. He'd been through enough.

A light knock sounded on her door.

"Come in."

It was Dev. He had his hair pulled back into a ponytail and the sleeve of his T-shirt was pushed up, leaving his double bow and arrow tattoo extremely visible. Like him, she'd always found the tattoo funny—though she was sure it irked Artemis since he wasn't a Dark-Hunter.

He hesitated in the doorway, his eyes sad and worried. "Are you going to travel in the SUV with Quinn's mate?"

Becca was pregnant and couldn't travel by her powers.

"No. I'm not evacuating."

Dev shut the door and moved inside. His gaze went straight to her open suitcase. "What are you doing?"

"I'm leaving, but I'm not going with the others."

"Why?"

Aimee sighed as she folded another T-shirt and added it in. "I've endangered everyone. It's only fair I should go."

"Are you crazy?"

That was a matter of opinion and at the moment she probably was. Her mother would definitely say yes. "I should have gone with Fang when he asked me to. Now"—she winced at the memories of everything that had happened—"I've done so much damage here."

"How do you figure that?"

"I was the one who antagonized the jackals and caused them to attack us. It was me who's been on Stone's back all these years."

Dev scoffed. "I'm the one who locked his sorry ass in a cage and threatened him."

"No, I'm the catalyst. You know how unforgiving Maman is. I should go before she kills me herself."

Dev pulled the shirt out of her hands that she was packing and forced her to look up at him. "You are her only daughter. Gods, Aimee, you know how much we all still grieve for Bastien and Gilbert . . . don't make us grieve for you too. You are blood of my blood. For better, for worse, for war, for peace. You are the only little sister I have and I would die if I lost you. Maman and Papa even more so."

Tears blurred her vision at his uncharacteristic speech. "You're always so tough. There's nothing you can't handle."

"Not where you're concerned. Don't make me lose you, Aimee. I'm not that strong."

She pulled him into her arms and held him close. "I really hate you, Dev."

"Yeah, I know. I can't stand you either, butt-munch."

Laughing through her tears, she pulled back to wipe them away. "Gods . . . what am I supposed to do? I love Fang and I don't know if he's innocent. What if he has killed the others?"

"Do you really believe he's done that?"

"No, I don't."

"Then he needs a friend right now. You want me to help you find him?"

"I don't know." She sighed as she thought about it. Fang had been unpredictable the last few times they'd met. But he'd visited here recently. Her gaze fell to the small black teddy bear in her suitcase that he'd left for her on her bed a week ago . . . one that held his scent—he knew she slept best whenever she had something of his to hold. He'd placed it on her pillow with a single rose. Even though he hadn't seen her, he'd still been thinking of her.

But that act of kindness didn't change the fact that he was a powerful Were-Hunter who was possessed by a demon. "He might hurt you."

Dev gave her an offended stare. "I doubt it." He looked over at the picture of her and her brothers that was on her dresser before he spoke again. "Just so you know, Papa, Serre, Griffe, Cherif, Remi, Kyle, Quinn, Zar, and I aren't leaving."

A shiver went over her. "What?"

"We're not about to leave Maman here unguarded. If shit goes down the way we think it's going to, she can't be here alone with the humans."

"Have you told her that?"

"I was on my way down to let her know when I stopped in to see you. Want to come see the party?"

"Oh, yeah. This I definitely don't want to miss." Maman didn't like anyone disobeying her.

She followed him out of her room and downstairs to the parlor where Maman was saying good-bye to the women and children of their family as they left for the Peltier compound in Oregon. It was where they'd lived prior to coming to New Orleans. They maintained a place there and in Nice, France, where her parents had been born. But Nice would be too hard a trip on their pregnant females, so Oregon it was.

Alain, Cody, and Etienne were going with them to watch over and protect them.

Cherif, Quinn, Remi, Serre, Kyle, Griffe, and Zar stood at the bottom of the stairs with their arms folded over their chests. A united front against the world. Never had they looked more imposing. The twins and the quads were barely discernable from each other, but Aimee could tell them apart. Subtle differences that were obvious to those who knew them best.

Remi's perpetual sneer. Quinn's gentle eyes and overt optimism. Cherif, who always stood with his weight on his left leg—an injury from childhood had damaged his right knee and so he always favored his other leg. Serre, who was a hair thinner than Griffe and who always tucked his hands into his armpits. Griffe, whose nails, because he was always tinkering with something, had grease under them.

And then Zar . . . he was Bastien's twin and sometimes it was hard for any of them to look at him without feeling a new stab of pain at the loss. He never really spoke about Bastien, but Aimee had wondered many times how much harder that loss had to be on him. He saw his twin brother's face every time he looked in a mirror.

The two of them had been closer than close. . . .

She couldn't bear the thought of losing another brother.

Ever.

Dev moved to stand with them while Maman kissed the cheeks of her grandchildren.

Once they were gone, Maman turned to the quads. "You will stay safe, *non*?"

"*Oui*," Remi said. "But we're doing it here."

Maman's face blanched as her eyes darkened with fury. "What?"

Zar stepped forward. "Nothing you say or do will change our minds. We're not leaving you, Maman."

"And neither are we."

Aimee turned at the sound of Carson's voice. He came down the stairs with Justin, Jasyn, Sasha, Max, and the Howlers: Angel, Teddy, Tripper, Damien, and Colt.

Tripper Diomedes, who was an Arcadian lion, spoke for the group. "You've given us shelter when no one else would and we're here to stand with you no matter what."

"As am I."

Aimee gasped as she heard Wren's voice. He'd flashed in not far from her brothers.

Maman was completely aghast as she saw him there. "You hate me."

Wren shrugged. "You're definitely not my favorite person, Lo. But your daughter means a lot to me and so I won't stand back and let her family be destroyed. Even if I do think we're all completely stupid for fighting for you."

Maman shook her head as she looked around at all of them. "You do understand how many will be attacking us? How many enemies I've made?"

Remi snorted. "*We've* made, you mean. I think we've all had a hand in this fiasco. Me probably more so than anyone else."

Angel nodded in agreement. "And to that, I say bring the rain. We are here and we won't be defeated."

An amen went up from the others.

Damien flashed a rare grin. "Sanctuary, home of Howlers and stragglers of the Were universe."

Nodding, Teddy clapped him on the back. "Sanctuary forever."

Maman's eyes were bright from her unshed tears as she surveyed the men who were willing to not only protect her home with their lives . . . they were willing to protect her. "Thank you. Your loyalty won't be forgotten."

"And all the free liquor you can hold," Dev said. "We definitely don't want to do this sober."

That broke the tension as they all laughed.

Aimee shook her head. "Yeah, but you're going to get your own drinks, guys, 'cause I'm not running it to you. There's just too many of you."

Maman did what she did best. She took charge. "Very

well, *mes fils du coeur*. We shall keep to our schedules and run business as usual."

Max stepped forward. "I'll be the muscle. Not many can take down a dragon."

"And make sure you ride herd on the humans," Remi reminded him.

He inclined his head.

Maman smiled at them. Gratitude and pride were bright in her blue eyes. "Let's show our enemies and doubters that Sanctuary will stand no matter what they say."

She paused beside Wren. "And you were wrong about me, tiger. I've never considered the ones here as my dupes. I have bent rules for all of you at one time or another. If loving my children above all else is a crime in your world, then you can hang me for that sin as I would have it no other way."

Wren didn't speak until she was gone and Aimee could tell that even now he didn't trust her mother. He walked over to her. "I'm only here for you."

She squeezed him lightly on the arm. "Thank you, Wren."

He inclined his head before he left.

Cherif let out a relieved breath. "Wow, Maman took that better than I thought."

Papa laughed. "She knows how stubborn you boys are and you outnumber her." He stopped in front of Aimee. "You, on the other hand, have to leave."

"I won't go, Papa. This is my home and you are my family. I won't hide while all of you are in danger. I did that once and I've had to live with that cowardice every day since. I won't do it again."

He cupped her face in his large paw of a hand. "They gave their lives for you, *mon ange*. Don't mock their sacrifice."

"I don't, but I'm full-grown now and I will stand and I will fight as they did."

His eyes darkened with sadness as he let his hand fall. "I won't argue. I know you have enough of your mother in you to make it impossible to win."

She smiled. "You would be right."

He scanned the others. "All right then. Let us all prepare for war."

In wolf form, Fang lay in the sun, not far from where Anya had died. He didn't know why he kept coming back here. Maybe it was the part of him that longed for the way things had been prior to her death.

Or maybe it was the need within him for some connection to someone else. Because right now, he felt absolutely alone. His relationship with Vane wasn't what it had been and he'd been staying away from Aimee out of fear of hurting her. The demon was getting worse and more violent.

If anything happened to Aimee . . .

"Fang?"

He lifted his head at the sound of Varyk's voice. The werewolf appeared a few feet away from him. "*What do you want?*" he snarled mentally.

"Savitar has issued a warrant out for you."

Fang was aghast at the order. "*For what?*"

"Murder."

"*Are you serious?*"

Varyk gave him a droll stare. "You don't think I came all the way out here to joke?"

Of course not. Varyk had no sense of humor. "*This is ridiculous. I didn't do anything.*"

"Regardless of that, Vane has been charged with bringing you in or his family and pack will be slaughtered."

Fang jumped to his feet as rage darkened his sight. How dare Savitar threaten his family. "*This is bullshit.*"

"You know Savitar."

Yes, he did. And right now, he wanted that bastard's throat.

Varyk folded his arms over his chest. "And there's more. Sanctuary lost its license."

That was the last thing he expected to hear. "*What?*"

"Because of the complaints of Blakemore and the jackals you attacked, Savitar revoked Lo's license for six months."

Fang felt ill. He'd ruined everything.

Everyone . . .

"And I just found out something you might want to know."

"*Thorn has a conscience?*" Fang couldn't resist asking.

Varyk looked at him drily. "Don't make me laugh." Sadly enough, Thorn had more of one than Varyk did. "I found out something about the Peltiers and Blakemores."

"*They hate each other. We know.*"

"No. Blakemore blames them for the death of his youngest son."

Fang turned human as those words hit him. "What?"

"Yeah. It's a blood feud. Apparently, Junior broke the eirini laws of another sanctuary and was to be banned from them forever."

The eirini were peace laws put in place by Savitar. To break one left the offender on his own for eternity.

"Not long after the Peltiers opened here," Varyk continued, "Junior came running to them for protection and the bears refused to admit him. They were upholding Savitar's laws and I'm sure the fact that Junior Blakemore was a bully and an ass, and that he was being chased by a group he'd provoked, didn't help matters. He and his running buddies were killed out in the same alley where Wren was attacked. Apparently that's why Stone keeps going there. He's hoping to find one of the Peltiers in the same place his brother died so that he can return quid pro quo."

"Then I'm sure the Peltiers are aware of the situation since that would have been . . . what? A hundred years ago?"

"Close, and on the anniversary of Junior's death, Blakemore plans to kill every bear and animal there and to torch that place to the ground."

Fang ground his teeth in helpless frustration. "So what you're telling me is that I can stay and protect Aimee from the psycho and my brother dies. Or I can save my brother and Aimee dies."

"Yeah, basically, you're screwed."

"What else is new?" He met Varyk's gaze as impotent rage scorched him. "I need to know where you stand in all of this."

"Blakemore's my paycheck. Nothing more than that."

"And Aimee's my life . . . if I leave everything I have to you, will you protect her for me?"

Varyk snorted at his offer as his gaze went to Fang's bike and the backpack he carried that held all of his belongings inside it. "What do *you* have to bribe me with?"

"Two hundred million, plus some change."

Varyk choked. "What?"

Fang shrugged over it. Money had never meant much to him. It was as intangible as friendship. "Vane's real good with investments and I don't spend much. You take care of Aimee and I will make sure every cent of it goes to you."

"For that kind of money, I'd do a lot more for you than just guard your woman."

Fang snorted. "I don't want to go there. Just uphold your word." He jerked his backpack up from the ground.

"Hey?"

Fang turned to look at him.

Varyk's face was stoic, but his gaze burned with sincerity. "I will keep her safe. You can count on it. And you don't have to pay me for it."

Fang inclined his head in gratitude before he flashed himself from the swamp to Sanctuary. The one thing he'd learned these past months was how to merge his powers with the demon inside him and use them to his advantage. It allowed him to walk invisible and to do other nifty things—some bloodier than others.

Even with those powers, he'd avoided doing this. Mostly because it hurt too much to see Aimee. Instead, he'd relegated himself to visiting her room just so that he could feel her presence there. Breathe in her scent and remember the nights when they'd been together.

But he didn't want to die without one last glimpse of her. No matter how much it hurt, he had to see her.

Like a whispering breeze, he made his way up to her room. She sat on her bed, holding the leather jacket he'd left behind a few weeks ago. The same jacket he'd wrapped her in on the day they'd met.

Her beautiful blue eyes held so much agony that it carved her pain into his own heart. He hated the torment she caused him. Most of all, he hated the torment he caused her.

"Where are you, Fang?" she breathed.

Unable to stand it, he materialized in front of her.

Aimee gasped at the sight of Fang in her room. He dropped to his knees and laid his head in her lap, then wrapped his arms around her waist. Her hand trembling, she brushed his hair back, amazed that he'd finally come to her. "What are you doing here?"

"I had to see you."

She tightened her hand in his hair, reveling in the softness of it. "We have to run, Fang. I'm ready."

"We can't. I could never be happy knowing I'd cost my brother his mate and child."

"It's not fair."

He pulled back to look up at her. Those dark eyes singed her with sincerity. "I didn't do it, Aimee. I swear I haven't killed anyone who didn't attack me first."

"I know, baby."

He nodded. "I better go."

She held his hand, preventing him from leaving her.

She knew what he was going to do. It was written on his face.

He intended to turn himself in and save his brother.

When he turned to her with a frown, she stood up from the bed and pulled his lips to hers.

Fang growled as her kiss seared him. He twisted his fists in her shirt, wanting her with a need so desperate it tore him apart. But he couldn't stay and he knew it. "Don't start this fire, Aimee."

She answered by lifting his shirt up. Her warm hands skimmed his chest, making him so hard he ached. "Everything is falling apart. But the one thing that hasn't changed is how I feel about you. I won't spend another minute of regret where you're concerned." She removed her own top.

Fang struggled to breathe as he stared at the light blue lace bra . . . his favorite on her. "Are you sure?"

"Absolutely."

Fang pulled her against him as he ravaged her mouth. Nothing had ever tasted sweeter. And for once, he wouldn't be settling for second best. Even if they were mates, at this point, it wouldn't matter. He was about to die and that would free her to find a more appropriate male.

Fang pulled back to look down at her. "How do we do this?"

She arched a sarcastic brow. "You need instructions?"

He laughed. "No, but I don't know what bears do."

She laid her gentle hand on his cheek. "Make me yours, Fang. However you do that."

Dipping his head down to nuzzle her neck, he reached

around her to undo her bra and pull it off. Her nipples puckered, and he moved to give them all the attention he'd been dreaming of.

Aimee cradled his head to her as he played. The one thing she'd learned about wolves and Fang in particular was that he loved to taste and to lick. The one thing he'd always been was thorough.

And as he unzipped her pants and dipped his hand down to stroke her, she knew tonight would be no exception. Her body trembled as he touched her. It'd been so long. . . .

How had he stood it? She had spent night after night aching for him. It felt so good to be touched again.

"I've missed you, Fang." She pulled his shirt over his head so that she could touch him.

Fang felt his powers surge. The one thing about sex and Were-Hunters was that it empowered them. Made them stronger and sharper. And right now, he was more alive than he'd ever been before.

Using his powers, he removed his clothes and left himself bare for her inspection. Not that she hadn't already explored every inch of him. But it had been too long.

"I have done nothing, except dream of you," he whispered, kissing his way around her mouth. He took her hand into his and led it to his cock. He sucked his breath in sharply as she touched him.

Aimee sank to her knees in front of him so that she could take him into her mouth. His knees almost buckled from the pleasure. And as good as it felt, he had to stop her.

"Stop, Aimee."

She pulled back with a frown.

"You do that and this will be over before either of us wants it."

She laughed before she gave him one last lick that sent a shiver all the way up his backbone. It even made his eyes roll back in his head.

Aimee smiled at the look on Fang's face. She loved to tease him and to taste him. The saltiness of his skin made her ache for more, but like him, she wanted for once to know exactly what it felt like to have him inside her.

He sank down in front of her. On their knees, facing each other, he kissed her again. It was hot and demanding as he skimmed his hand down between them to touch her. It made her even wetter as she throbbed.

The quickening inside her rose until it was blinding and her body demanded appeasement. "Don't make me wait, Fang," she whispered, afraid that something or someone would interrupt them again.

Fang kissed his way to her back, making chills spring up all over her body. Holding her in front of him, he brushed her hair from her neck so that he could inhale her scent. Every part of him burned as he ached to be inside her.

He'd waited and dreamed of this moment, never thinking to really have it. He'd almost convinced himself that he could live without ever tasting her again.

But it'd been hard, especially since other females had stopped being appealing to him. Letting out one long breath, he slid his fingers inside her as he positioned himself to take her. He couldn't ever remember a woman being more wet for him and none had ever been more enticing.

Aimee trembled in fear of what was to come as she felt the tip of his cock pressing against her. But this was what she wanted more than anything and at least it wouldn't hurt the way it did for human women. He nudged her knees farther apart as he took her hand again in his and led it to him.

"Guide me in, baby."

With his help, she reached between their bodies and gently slid him into her body. She bit her lip as the thick fullness of him sank deep inside.

They moaned in unison.

Aimee's head reeled as he buried himself in to his hilt. It felt so good to have him there, to feel connected to him like this. She was sharing with him what she'd never shared with anyone else.

Fang pulled her back against him, into his arms as he slowly thrusted against her. He took their weight from her as he laid his cheek against hers and let her scent intoxicate him. In all the times he'd been with a woman, none of them could compare to this. She was so tight and warm. And unlike a wolfswan, she wasn't bucking and clawing at him. Biting.

Aimee was tender.

Most of all, she loved him. In all the world, she alone had tamed the part of him that he'd never allowed anyone else to see. Always fierce and fighting, he only found peace with her. She'd tamed him.

She reached up and placed her hand to his cheek. That one gentle action shattered him. He didn't want to die. He wanted to stay here like this for the rest of eternity.

It was so unfair. His brothers were mated and happy. Why couldn't he be too?

But he knew better. Even if he lived, her family would never accept him. None of their people would. This was unnatural.

And yet it didn't feel that way.

"You are the best part of me," he whispered in her ear as he thrusted and cupped her breasts.

"I love you, Fang." Aimee leaned back so that he could kiss her while he trailed his hand down the front of her body until he could stroke her in time to his thrusts. She could feel him getting larger inside her. Thicker.

She was completely open and exposed to him in a way she'd never been before. She should be embarrassed, but she wasn't. This seemed so right. So perfect.

And as they made love, she wondered what it would be like if they didn't have the world to drive them apart. If they could stay together and be like this. All she wanted was her wolf.

She would give anything to have his children. To give him all the love no one else ever had.

He quickened his strokes, which intensified the pleasure. Her breathing ragged, she returned them with her own until her body couldn't stand it anymore. In a searing burst, she came.

Fang had to bite back a howl as he joined her in release. But it was hard. He pulled her close and kept her weight on his body, knowing they'd be locked together for a while yet as his body continued to release inside her. That was the most difficult part about being a wolf. When they came, it was a lengthy process and if they were separated before he was finished, it would hurt her. And right now his senses were so alert and strong that he felt as if he could defeat an entire pack.

Aimee leaned her head against his chest as he held her so tenderly. "I'm not too heavy, am I?"

"Not at all."

She turned his palm over to look at it. Like hers, it was still blank.

Tears stung her eyes. "We're not mates?"

"It doesn't always show up the first time. You know that."

True, but the way she felt for him . . . she was actually disappointed.

"I didn't hurt you, did I?"

She smiled at his question. "No, baby, you definitely didn't hurt me."

He wrapped his arms around her, making her feel so safe and loved. She fingered the weird mark on his shoulder that he refused to tell her about.

He nibbled her cheek. "Did you know your facial markings are showing?"

"What?"

He reached up to draw the pattern with his fingertips. "Your Sentinel marks are showing."

She used her powers to remove them. "What about now?"

"Still there."

Oh, dear gods . . . she'd had no idea that they would show when she had sex. What if she'd mated with a Katagari bear and they'd come out?

It would have been disastrous.

"I'm sorry I can't hide them."

He kissed her cheek. "Don't apologize. I think you're beautiful."

She tightened her arms around his as those words warmed her to the core of her being.

Fang trembled as he was finally able to withdraw from her. He hated doing it, but he had no choice.

She turned in his arms to kiss him deeply. "Can I go with you?"

"No," he said, his tone firm.

"Fang—"

He shook his head. "No, Aimee."

"I want to be there with you."

"You can't."

She growled at him. "Why not?"

He leaned his forehead against her cheek while he cupped her face with his hand. "Because if I see you there, I won't be able to go through with it and I can't do that to my brother." He looked up at her and the painful torment in his eyes scorched her. "Do you understand? I have to do this alone." He brushed her tears away with the back of his hand. "I love you, Aimee."

Those words infuriated her. "*Now* you say that? Now? What is wrong with you?"

He smiled tenderly. "I never once in my life had good timing. Too late to start now."

She pulled him to her and held him close. "I love you, Fang. Damn you to hell for it!" Then she took her necklace from around his neck and and placed it in his hand. "If I can't be with you . . ."

He clutched it tight and repeated the words that were

engraved in it. "Where I am always thou art. Thy image lives within my heart."

She nodded as more tears flowed. "Mate or no mate, you are the only one I'll ever love."

He kissed her gently before he made himself leave her. If he didn't go now, he'd chicken out completely.

Because honestly, it was hard to justify his brother's happiness and life by breaking the heart of the only woman he'd ever really loved.

It's all right, he told himself. He'd be waiting for her on the other side. One day he'd see her again and there the demon wouldn't have any control over him. He wouldn't have to fear ever hurting her.

She would be safe and there wouldn't be anyone who could keep them apart.

But in this life, he had to do the right thing.

Sick to his stomach, he dressed himself and took one last look at Aimee. Completely naked, she kissed his hand that held her locket.

He bent down to take one last breath of her hair so that her scent would give him strength and carry him to his grave. "I love you," he whispered, then he made himself leave.

"Fang!" Aimee gasped, feeling desolate without him. How would she be able to live knowing he was really gone?

At least in the past there was always the chance that he'd come to his senses and be here.

But now . . .

He was going to die and there was nothing she could do.

Go get him!

The urge was so strong. If only she could. But Fang would never forgive her for that. How could he? She knew the pain of living without her brothers. The unrelenting agony of knowing she'd been the reason they had been caught and killed. They had protected her and given their lives so that she could live.

She couldn't wish that pain on Fang.

No, it would be Vane who would suffer, knowing that his happiness had been bought in blood. Fang's blood.

Besides, Savitar had issued his orders. If Fang didn't surrender, Savitar would hunt him down. He would die anyway.

Heartbroken, Aimee dressed herself and sat on the bed, trying to use her powers to see him.

Savitar wouldn't even allow her that much comfort.

Fang materialized in Savitar's opulent hall where the Omegrion council met.

Completely empty, the room had windows that were open and looking out onto a beautiful sea. Fang closed his eyes as the soft wind brushed his skin and ruffled his hair. The salt in the air was as sweet as the birds that sang outside.

It was a beautiful day to die.

He slid Aimee's locket into his pocket at the same time he felt the fissure of power rippling behind him.

"So you came alone." Savitar appeared in front of him, dressed in a black wet suit. His hair was plastered back from his face and still dripping wet.

"Was I not supposed to?"

Savitar snorted as he wiped some of the droplets off his face. "I didn't know if you'd have it in you or not."

"Guess I'm full of surprises."

He didn't appear to appreciate Fang's sarcasm. "You know the charges against you?"

"I was told murder."

"Fourteen counts. How do you plead?"

Fang shrugged with a nonchalance he most definitely didn't feel. "I suppose most people go down on their hands and knees."

Savitar laughed, then sobered. "But not you."

"Nope. Never." He narrowed his gaze on Savitar. "Honestly, I have no memory of murdering anyone, but if I did it, I'm here for my punishment."

Savitar rubbed his chin with his thumb. "You never flinch, do you?"

"It's not in me. But I expect you to abide by your word and spare my family."

"You've nothing to say on your own behalf?"

"Not really."

"Then prepare to die."

CHAPTER 28

Fang sat in a small cell, waiting to die. He'd assumed Savitar would splinter him on sight, but that apparently was too easy a punishment.

Instead the bastard was making him suffer even more by dreading it. Not that the dread was what tormented him the worst.

It was regret. Those wounds were the ones that tore through him like shards of glass. He wished so many things were different that at this point death would probably be a relief.

He just wished he could see Aimee one more time. Conjuring up an image of her smile, he reached in his pocket to touch her necklace. It wasn't as good as touching her, but it comforted him on a level he'd never experienced before. Even though she wasn't here, he felt her like a tangible angel.

Damn if the words engraved in her locket weren't right. She was in his heart and the knowledge of her out there, thinking of him, being a part of him, made him feel less lonely.

Alone in a tiny spartan cell with only a toilet, he sat on the hard bench with his elbows on his knees. He could hear the sea outside along with gulls squawking. But it was Aimee's face he saw and it would be her scent that he carried with him to the next existence.

"You ready?"

He looked up to see Savitar in a pair of green cargo pants and an open white shirt. The man's face was completely stoic.

Not that Fang expected sympathy from anyone.

"Yeah."

The clear door slid up as Fang rose to his feet. Savitar led him to the sparkling white beach outside and to what looked like an old-fashioned block. It would be almost quaint if he wasn't going there to die. There was even an executioner standing behind it. Dressed in spiked black armor and wearing a helm in the shape of a ghoul's face, he held an oversized sword. He was so still, he looked like a statue.

Fang was both impressed and repulsed by the elaborate display. "You're not just going to blast me into oblivion?"

Savitar shook his head. "Too humane for the crimes you've committed." He raked a suspicious look over Fang. "You gonna turn chicken and jump out and make me chase you?"

"No. I don't want you going after my family."

"Smart wolf. It sucks to have your family pay for your crimes. Take it from someone with firsthand experience." Savitar gestured toward the black stone block that was stained in places by dried blood.

The largest splatter of it was right where Fang needed to put his head.

His stomach churned at the knowledge that soon his own blood would be added to it. And it brought home exactly what was about to happen to him.

He was here to die. . . .

Honestly, he wanted to run. Anything to have one more day. . . .

But he wasn't about to show his fear to anyone, especially not to the one who was going to kill him. Instead, he reverted to the sarcasm that had seen him through the darkest moments of his life.

It was only fitting it should now see him through his death. "You know, you could wash that nasty thing off between uses."

Savitar shrugged nonchalantly. "Why bother? It's not like you're going to catch an infection the last three minutes you're alive."

"Guess not." Fang sank down on his knees in the sand and glanced away from the dried blood. He looked around the beach and the dark green sea whose waves came rushing up, not too far from him, and realized just how long it'd been since he'd really seen the beauty that existed in the world. How many times he'd taken the sun for granted. Instead, he'd spent his life focusing only on the negatives.

But as he was about to die, he realized the world really was incredible.

"Changing your mind?"

"No." He pulled Aimee's locket out from his pocket, which reminded him exactly why he had to do this. "Can I make one last request?"

"For you to go free?"

He shook his head and held the locket out to Savitar. "Would you make sure that's returned to Aimee Peltier?" He reluctantly let go of it.

Why did it feel like he was giving up a limb?

Maybe because she was his heart. . . .

Savitar took it from him and opened it up to look at the photo of her and her brothers. That picture had seen him through hell and he didn't need to look at it anymore. It was as engraved in his soul as her smile, touch, and smell.

He held it out to Fang. "Something you want to tell me about you and the bearswan?"

For the first time, Fang saw that Aimee had added a picture of him to her locket that covered the engraved words, and *that* almost succeeded in breaking him. Hell, he'd forgotten about it even being made. It was one Aimee had shot of him behind Sanctuary one afternoon when he'd been taking a break. She'd come out of nowhere to surprise him and snap the photo.

"Look!" she'd said, laughing, as she showed him the photo on the back of her camera. "I love when you look at me like that. I can see your heart in your eyes."

His hair, which he'd grown out only because she liked it that way, had been windblown and he'd had the dumbest look imaginable on his face—like some lovesick moron. "I look stupid."

"You look gorgeous." She'd given him one of the hottest kisses he'd ever had. "And it makes me want to take a bite out of you."

"That I don't mind. But for the sakes of the gods, delete that thing before you lose your camera again and someone else sees what a friggin' goober I am."

She'd stuck her tongue out at him before she'd danced off, her tight ass teasing him even more than her kiss had.

Gods, to have that one moment back. . . .

Why hadn't she listened to him and deleted the damn thing? Now, in the last moments of his life, Savitar of all fucks would see what a schmuck he really was.

But the important part was that she'd added *his* picture to the locket she always wore close to her heart. Not that he had any doubts about her feelings for him, but that showed him exactly how much he meant to her.

Love and regret welled up hard inside him. In that moment, all he wanted was to run back to her.

Give me strength. . . .

He cleared his throat of the tight lump. "Nothing to say." But he held an image of Aimee in his mind as he laid his head down on the block and waited to die. Closing his eyes, he felt the sword lower slowly down to touch the skin of his neck.

A shiver ran over him. Why wouldn't they just kill him and get it over with?

The blade rubbed against his skin before it lifted up. The demon inside screamed out in panic as it realized what was about to happen.

They were both about to die.

Get up. Fight! Run!

But Fang held steady. This was for his brother and for Aimee. He wouldn't turn craven and risk their lives. Not for anything as worthless as his own hide.

"All right," Savitar said. "Kill him."

In that moment, Fang let out a curse as something

inside him ruptured. It felt like he was being shredded. The pain was excruciating as blood began pouring out of his nose. He was trying to keep his head on the block, but it was getting harder and harder as it felt like acid was crawling up his esophagus and exploding through his skull. The pressure of it knocked him flat on his back.

Savitar and the executioner put their knees on his shoulders to hold him down.

Fang cried out as something hard and painful flew out of his mouth. It shot up, then splintered into a million pieces that fell down over them.

As soon as it did, the two of them released him. Fang panted as the pain subsided and his nose stopped bleeding. Scowling at them, he wiped it away.

The executioner laughed as he pulled his helm off. It was Thorn. "Bet that was some wicked indigestion, huh?"

"What the fuck are you two doing?"

Thorn swung the sword up to rest on his shoulder. "Getting the demon out of you, dumbass. I figured you'd had about enough of him."

Bewildered by the unexpected change of fortune, Fang looked back and forth between them. Was this another head game they were playing with him? Until he knew for sure, he wasn't getting up. "I don't understand."

Savitar dropped the locket on his chest. "The easiest, and I use that word with all due sarcasm, way to get Phrixis out of you required an act of unspeakable altruism. I threatened your brother's life and you came, ready to die to protect him."

Thorn nodded. "The simple love of that one act was

more than the demon could handle and out he came. Since he had no body to return to, he was destroyed. Simple."

"Yeah." Savitar held his hand out to Fang to help him to his feet.

For once, he let Savitar pull him to his feet. He wanted to kill them both, but right now he was too grateful to be alive. "You're both sick, but I appreciate what you did. The bastard was getting a little hard to handle."

Thorn twisted the sword on his shoulder, making the blade flash wickedly in the daylight. "Sorry for the trauma. There really was no other way. Had you had even an inkling, it wouldn't have worked. But if it makes you feel better, we know you're not the one killing those people. That would be Misery and Crew, who you now have to find and kill."

Savitar grinned. "If it makes you feel better, you took it like a man."

"No," Fang corrected him. "I took it like a wolf."

Savitar saluted him with respect. "Touché."

Fang looked out at the beach, grateful that it hadn't been his last sight after all. "Can I go home now?"

Savitar shook his head. "Not quite yet. There's something I want you to see."

The next thing Fang knew, he was back in his cell and this time, his powers weren't working at all.

Thorn sheathed his sword. "Thanks for the assist."

"No problem."

Sick about what had happened, Thorn looked around at the scattered ashes of the demon. "Damn shame Fang couldn't control him. I'd had great plans for them."

Savitar arched one brow. "What kind of plans?"

"You're omniscient. Don't you know?"

Savitar gave him a droll glare. "You know better. I can only see the future after I've impacted it." Which was why he tried to stay on his island, away from the world. Here there was nothing and no one to change.

Life went on without him and he preferred it that way.

Most days.

Thorn shrugged. "I guess we all have a limit to what we can do."

That was supposed to be the law of the universe and yet he'd seen and felt things from Thorn that defied that. "That's not what I've heard about you."

"You going to believe everything you hear?"

Savitar watched as Thorn vanished. He knew that man was playing a game with all of them. He just wished he knew which one.

And who Thorn's real teammates were.

Fang pounded at the clear door, furious over being locked in after what they'd done to him. He'd been put through the wringer and right now he was ready to tear both Savitar and Thorn apart.

"Hold your fur, wolf," Savitar snapped as he appeared in the hallway.

"Why can't I go?"

"Because I think you need to see this."

"See what?"

He jerked his chin toward the wall behind Fang. "Your brother's time is up to bring you in."

What did that have to so with anything? "I brought myself in."

"Vane doesn't know that. I think you should see his reaction."

"You are really sick, aren't you?"

"No. I just know how much in life goes unsaid and hidden. Everyone needs to know, just once, how much they mean to the people around them."

Fang frowned as he vanished. The moment he did, the clear door darkened to black and the wall Savitar had indicated a second ago turned transparent, showing him the council room on the other side.

Vane was already there. Alone.

Savitar strode over to him, again with that stoic expression that gave away absolutely nothing. "Where's your brother?"

"I don't know."

"You couldn't find him?"

Vane's features hardened with determination. "I didn't look."

Savitar's expression turned dark. Lethal. When he spoke, his tone was filled with malice. "Do you understand what you're risking?"

Vane nodded. "My mate and I are bonded. I offer you my life for Fang's, but please, don't leave my children orphans. I know you have the ability to break a bond-mating and I ask you to have mercy. My family is innocent and they pose no threat to you or anyone else."

"You're really asking me for mercy?"

A tic worked in Vane's jaw and Fang knew exactly how hard the next words were for a man as proud as his brother was to say. "I'm *begging* for your mercy, Savitar. I can't hand my brother over to you."

One taunting eyebrow shot up. "You can't or you won't?"

"Both."

"And your mate? What did she have to say about this?"

"She agreed with my decision."

"Even though it means she might not live to see your children grow up?"

Vane nodded. "We understand the consequences. As I said, we're hoping for your mercy. But whatever you decide, I can't live knowing my life was paid for with my brother's blood."

"That's a hell of a thing to hope for. You're not really counting on me to play with a conscience, are you?"

Fang frowned as he heard someone at the door of his cell. He looked back at Vane and Savitar who were still talking.

What was going on?

"Fang? Are you in there?"

His heart stopped beating at the sound of the last voice he expected to hear. "Aimee?"

"Hurry. Get the door open."

Who was she talking to?

"Stand back, akri-wolf! The Simi's gonna huff and puff and melt that door down. And you might not want to be too close when I do it, 'cause melted wolf is tough on the enamel and akra-Aimee might not like it if you turn into a puddle of bloody goo. Besides, burning wolf is kind of smelly to the Simi's delicate nostrils. So stand back."

Fang was stunned. Simi was with Aimee? Ash's demon companion? What the hell was *she* doing here?

What was Aimee thinking?

Knowing better than to argue with Simi, who never took no for an answer unless Ash was the one saying it, Fang did as she said. He'd barely cleared the area when the door literally disintegrated into a molten pool on the floor.

Beaming with pride over what she'd done, Simi wiped her hands together. "That was fun . . . you think Savitar will let the Simi blast through something else? Maybe that curtain over there . . ."

"No, no, Simi," Aimee said, pulling her to a stop. "We don't want to torch the curtains."

Simi's bottom lip jutted out into a strangely becoming pout. "Oh, pooh, you're just like akri. No, Simi, don't be breathing fire around the flammable objects or small children. Except for that black plastic card that's not really plastic. It some metal thing, but the Simi loves it 'cause it let her buy everything she want without limit. He never say no to Simi when she use it. Oh, hello there, Fang. You okay? You looking kind of peaked or piqued or . . . ? Oh, heck, the Simi can never keep those straight."

Ignoring Simi's rant, he looked at Aimee. "What are you two doing here?"

"We're saving you."

"*Aimee,*" he said, stressing her name and the danger she'd placed them both in.

He also stopped as he saw Savitar flash in behind her with a look of extreme fury on his face.

"No buts, Fang. I can't let you do . . ." Her words faded as she caught sight of Savitar standing behind her in the glass's reflection.

Aimee froze to the spot. Her heart sliding into her stomach, she turned around to face what had to be the most terrifying grimace ever conceived.

"Hi," she said, hoping to lighten his mood.

His look only darkened—so much for trying. It'd only made it worse. "What are you doing, bear?"

"By the unhappy glower on your face, I would say making the single worst mistake of my life."

Fang moved to stand in front of her. "She was only trying to help me."

"And going against me in the process. No offense, but that seriously pisses me off."

Simi's eyes widened. "Ooo, you got that throbbing vein like akri gets right before he turns blue. You gonna turn blue too, akri-Savvy?"

Aimee gulped. "No, Simi, I think he's turning redder."

Savitar looked as if he was working hard on not killing her. "Answer me one thing. . . . What were you going to do after you took him out of here?"

Aimee hesitated.

"You didn't exactly think this through, did you?" Savitar looked at Vane who'd just moved into the area to see what was going on. "Wolves and Simi, leave. Now."

Vane passed a sympathetic look to Aimee before he followed Savitar's command.

Fang knew he was about to commit suicide, but he

couldn't obey him and leave Aimee here alone. The protective wolf inside him would never abandon her to anyone's wrath, especially not someone as capricious and lethal as Savitar. "It's my fault she's here. I take full responsibility."

Savitar sneered at him. "Don't make me laugh, wolf. You're out of soul to sell to keep her safe. Take the out I'm giving you before I take your life."

He slowly shook his head, his determination set in stone.

Savitar threw his hand out and blasted Fang so hard it lifted him up and slammed into the wall behind him. "Have you any idea how angry I am right now?"

Fang struggled to breathe. "I think I have a pretty good idea."

"No, I don't think you do."

He slammed Fang to the ground so hard Fang swore half the bones in his body broke.

Simi, who hadn't left yet, went running up to Savitar and whispered in his ear. Savitar's scowl lessened. He dropped his hand as his face returned to its typical stoicism. "Get out. Both of you. But know, little bear, that with this, I've revoked the license on Sanctuary for good."

Aimee gasped. "What?"

"You heard me. Now leave before I kill you both for disobeying me."

He actually didn't give them a choice. One moment they were on Savitar's island and in the next they were in the foyer of Peltier House.

Fang looked around at the dark Victorian furniture, bemused. There was no sign of Vane.

Simi popped in a second later. "Oh, good. Simi was afraid Savitar done gone and been really mean to you. But you okay. That's good."

Aimee frowned at the demon. "What did you say to Savitar?"

"I told him you were Simi's friends and that I didn't want him to make brolf stew."

"Brolf?"

"Bear and wolf, which might be tasty, but not when it's made out of people the Simi likes. Besides, Aimee always feeds me good ice cream whenever I come to Sanctuary."

Aimee hugged the little Goth demon who meant the world to her. One thing about Simi, you could always count on her. "Thank you for your help, Simi."

Simi opened her mouth, but before she could speak, Maman was there, her eyes flaming angry. Aimee's heart flopped at the sight. Never had she seen her *this* mad.

"What have you done?" Maman demanded.

Simi vanished.

Aimee felt the color fade from her face.

Maman would have slapped her had Fang not caught her hand and held it away from Aimee's cheek. That only angered her mother more. "You have ruined us. I want you both out of here. Now."

Wanting to soothe her mother, Aimee stepped forward. "Maman—"

"No," she snarled. There was no reprieve or forgiveness in her voice or expression. "You have endangered every one of us and for what?" She raked Fang with a disgusted sneer. "You are dead to me, Aimee. I never want to see you again and you are no longer part of this family or patria. Get out."

Aimee's vision dimmed. "But—"

"Get! Out!"

Fang pulled her against him. "C'mon. She needs to calm down."

Aimee allowed him to teleport her out of her home to Vane's house.

Vane was in the living room, his face a mask of worry that lifted the instant he saw them. "Thank the gods. I was terrified of what Savitar had done to you."

Aimee barely understood those words as the true horror of what had happened slammed into her.

Her mother had thrown her out. She'd revoked her clan from her and left her abandoned.

Vane furrowed his brow. "Is she okay?"

Fang didn't answer the question. He didn't think Aimee would want him to share what had just happened with someone who, to her, was basically a stranger. "Can you give us a minute?"

"Sure."

Fang waited until Vane had left before he cupped her face in his hands. "Aimee?"

Her tears started then. They flowed silently down her face as her blue eyes were completely haunted. "What have I done?"

He pulled her into his arms and held her close. "It'll be all right."

"No, it won't. Maman will never forgive me."

"You're her only daughter. Once she calms down, she'll be fine. You'll see."

"No, she won't. I know her and I know that tone. She'll never forgive me for this."

Fang bent his knees until he was eye level with her. "You know you're not alone. So long as I have shelter . . ."

Aimee clung to him then, needing that security even though part of her wanted to shove him away and condemn him for doing this to her.

But for him . . .

No. Fang hadn't done this. He'd been there by her side every step of the way these last few years. She'd made the decision to go save him regardless of consequence—even death—and Maman had cut the cord.

The only thing he'd done was try to protect her and Vane and Fury and their families.

And with those thoughts came another realization of something that she'd almost missed earlier. "What did Savitar mean about you selling your soul?"

He stepped away. His demeanor was now closed and reserved.

But she wasn't about to leave it at that. "Fang? Tell me the truth. Please."

She saw the regret in his eyes. The shame. And when he spoke, his voice was tight with emotion. "You've asked me repeatedly about the sign on my shoulder . . . it's a mark of ownership. When you and Dev were in the alley and the Daimons attacked, I sold my soul to a demon to keep you safe."

Aimee gaped at the last thing she'd expected him to say. He'd sold his soul for her. . . .

"Why would you do that?"

He swallowed hard before he answered. "Because I'd rather be damned than see you dead."

Overwhelmed by his devotion and loyalty, she took his hand into hers . . . the hand that should have borne their mating mark, and kissed his knuckles. "All I wanted was to keep you safe and now . . . I've endangered every member of my family. *All* of them."

"We can try to petition Savitar when he calms down. He's not entirely unreasonable."

She gave him an arch stare. Was he out of his mind? Savitar not unreasonable? "He killed off an entire species because they angered him. He's not exactly forgiving."

"I said *entirely*." His eyes turned dark and hopeful. "C'mon, Aim, have faith. Sanctuary is legendary. Your mother is resourceful. Somehow all of this will work out. I know it."

"I wish I could believe that, but I don't know. I have such a bad feeling."

Fang hesitated. So did he, but he didn't want to worry her. Even though he wasn't the most intuitive person in the universe, he knew deep inside that something much worse was going to happen. He just didn't know what.

"Damn, Savitar, that was harsh."

Savitar stiffened as Thorn appeared by his side. "What are you still doing here?"

"Wanted to make sure you didn't skewer my wolf. For all the aggravation, he still belongs to me and I don't want him skinned quite yet."

"Then you better keep him out of my way."

"Noted. But what you did . . ." Thorn shook his head. "Harsh, and coming from me that means something."

Yes, it was, and Savitar already regretted it. But he couldn't have the Were-Hunters second-guessing him. The one thing he'd learned the hard way was that without fear, there was no control. And without control, the Were-Hunters would destroy one another. He had to give them a bigger enemy to fear than one another.

Himself.

But none of that was Thorn's concern. "You know something, don't you?"

Thorn gave him a calculating look. "Did you not see what will happen because of your decree?"

A tic worked in Savitar's jaw at what he had to admit to a man of undefinable loyalty. "Only a glimpse and I was too angry to pay attention."

"Then it's probably for the best."

"Why?"

"Let me just say this. I'm really glad I'm not one of the people who calls Sanctuary home. 'Cause it's about to get seriously fugly for them."

CHAPTER 29

A week later

Fang stood inside Trace's nursery while Vane changed the toddler's diaper. It was so strange to see him doing something like this after all the battles the two of them had fought. Vane's hands were every bit as bloody as Fang's and yet here he was . . .

A loving father.

Squealing with laughter, Trace reached for his dad as Vane picked him up and rubbed his back, smoothing down the yellow SpongeBob shirt. Trace wrapped his chubby arms around Vane's neck and planted a wet kiss on his cheek. Damn if the two of them didn't look just alike.

Except Vane didn't drool as much.

It made him wonder what it would have been like to have that kind of relationship with his own father and it brought home just what had been taken from Aimee. She was devastated over the loss of her birth family. And he couldn't blame her at all.

Nicolette, for all her faults, did love her children.

Vane set Trace down so that he could run to grab his toys. "I meant what I said. You two are welcome here for as long as you need to stay."

"Thanks." Fang watched as Trace grabbed an oversized LEGO and chewed on it. "And not just for this." He indicated Trace with a tilt of his chin. "I can't believe what you were willing to risk for me."

Vane shrugged like it was no big thing, but they both knew otherwise. It had been one hell of a thing Vane had done and Fang still didn't really understand why. "We're brothers, Fang. Nothing will ever change that."

"Yeah"—he indicated Trace with a jerk of his chin— "but I was never that cute."

Vane laughed. "True."

Most of all, Fang couldn't believe that Bride had allowed Vane to go and make such an offer to Savitar, knowing it could have been her life too. Their sacrifice erased any hurt left by his being trapped in the Nether Realm. For the first time since he'd left his bed in Peltier House, he felt close to his brother again. "You know I love you, right?"

Vane pulled him into a tight hug. "I don't ever want to lose you again. Next time you pull one of these vanishing acts, either in this world or the next, I swear I'll kick your ass."

Fang laughed as he shoved Vane away from him. "Man, quit hugging on me. You *are* a perv."

Vane punched him in the arm. "You're such an asshole."

Trace gasped. "Daddy said a bad word!"

Fang picked him up from the floor and laughed. "You tell him, pup. Keep your daddy straight."

But for the first time in years, he felt almost whole again.

Aimee was still hesitant around Bride and Fury's mate, Angelia. Tall and blond, Lia was an Arcadian wolf who'd belonged to Fury's birth pack. They had reconnected last fall when Lia had come to Sanctuary to hunt him down and kill him.

Now the only one Lia would kill was the one who looked askance at Fury.

Yeah, life was anything but predictable.

Lia was staying here with them while Fury was meeting with Sasha to get an update on what was happening at Sanctuary. Aimee couldn't stand the radio silence and Fury had volunteered to be her liaison with her brothers.

"Aimee? Could you set the table?"

As she went for the plates, a flash near the doorway caught her attention. Dev materialized in the kitchen beside her.

Aimee almost dropped the plates. No one from her family had spoken a single syllable to her since Maman had thrown her out.

Dev glanced sheepishly at Bride and Lia before he turned his attention back to her. "Can I have a word with you?"

Handing the pretty blue plates off to Lia, she led him into the living room where they could speak without the others overhearing them. "What's going on?"

He materialized her suitcase. "I wanted you to have your things. I don't agree with what Maman did, none of us do. We're trying to soften her up—"

"But she is Maman."

He nodded as he set the case down beside the couch. "She won't hear us for now. We keep hoping every day that she'll relent and send one of us after you, but it's just not happening. I really miss you and wanted to let you know that you can call on us anytime you need something."

His offer warmed her completely. Unfortunately, she wouldn't be able to take him up on it. Not without getting him into all kinds of trouble and risking his having to join them here at the Kattalakis home. "Maman would be furious."

He shrugged. "I'm a big boy. I can handle it."

Yeah, right. No one was *that* big. Maman didn't like anyone going against her wishes—as was proven by Aimee's current situation.

"So how goes it?" she asked, dying for an update.

"It's tense. There's a lot of riffraff coming in, thinking they can push it since they no longer have to fear Savitar's wrath. But Remi's having a blast since there's no eirini laws in place to restrain him. We've all been getting some of our more predatorial instincts out." It was then she realized just how bruised his knuckles were.

She shook her head, amused and yet worried about her brothers. "How many have *you* killed?"

"None, but there's always tomorrow."

She laughed in spite of herself. "You're so sick."

He smiled with pride—gods, how she'd missed that shit-eating grin of his.

"What about the rest of the family? Are they returning?"

That sobered him immediately. "They're still in Oregon. When the cubs are born, they'll return."

It was what she'd figured. "Then you'll be on the run again. Moving from place to place like we used to do."

"No." Those blue eyes of his cut completely through her. "This is our home. No one's going to chase us out."

Her heart stopped at what he was saying. To continue to run the club without Savitar's backing was suicide. "Is Maman sure?"

"Yeah. After all Dante runs a club that isn't a limani and they haven't had too many incidents."

"Yeah, but—"

"It was a decision we all made," he said, cutting her protest off. "Besides, we've added a few others to our company, including Constantine, who is here to defend us for as long as we need him."

"It's the least he could do."

He nodded in agreement. "The Dark-Hunters are also taking up posts at night to help us out and Kyrian and Talon, hell, even Valerius, are making sure to come by and visit . . . just in case. And of course Nick is there so much, I'm about to start charging the little bastard rent."

She laughed at the last bit, though the news did surprise her. While some of them had been patrons over the decades, she hadn't realized the extent of their loyalty. "Really?"

"Yeah. Since the Dark-Hunters can't be around each other without draining their powers, they swap out each night. So all in all, it's not as bad as you think."

Aimee narrowed her gaze on him. "But?"

"But what?"

"There's a but in your tone."

He tucked his hands in his pockets in a way that reminded her of a bashful kid. "I don't know. I just have a bad feeling and I think Maman has it too. She's really been on edge these last few days."

"Maman is always on edge."

"True, but this is . . ." His voice trailed off as he looked past her shoulder.

Aimee turned to see Fang in the doorway.

There was an instant tension between the two of them. Like two enemies measuring each other up as if waiting for a chance to strike. She hated for the two men who meant the most to her to be this uncomfortable together.

She looked back at Dev to see his gaze drop down to her hand, which was still unmarked.

He cleared his throat. "I better get going."

"Dev, wait." She went to place a kiss on his cheek. "Thank you."

"No problem." He left so fast, she was surprised there wasn't a vapor trail.

Fang came forward, his expression apologetic. "I'm so sorry, Aimee."

She placed her hand over his lips. "Don't ever apologize for loving me, Fang. That's the one thing in my life I would have no other way."

He pulled her against him. "Yeah, but I hate what it's costing you."

So did she, but she would never let him know that. Aimee laid her head against his shoulder. It always felt so good to be next to him. Even at night when he slept as a wolf. He always lay right next to her and half the time she used him as a pillow. He never complained.

Fang closed his eyes as he held her. He didn't understand it, but being with her was like coming home. He'd heard that expression his whole life but he'd never really understood it until now.

And as he held her, his hand began to burn like it was on fire. Cursing, he stepped back.

"Ow!" Aimee snapped, shaking her own hand before she blew cool air across her palm.

The two of them froze in place as reality hit them hard. They knew instantly what it was.

They were mates.

Aimee moved to put her arm under his and hold her hand beside his hand so that they could watch the marks appear together. The highly stylized symbol was similar to Vane's and Fury's, but different enough to mark it as their own.

After all this time . . .

They finally knew in reality what they'd known all along in their hearts.

Aimee placed her marked palm over his and tightened her grip on his hand. "They look like wolf heads."

Fang frowned. "No, they don't."

She turned her hand over again. "Yes, they do. It has ears and everything."

Fang cocked his head as he realized she was right. It did look like a wolf outline. "Are you all right about this?"

"Should I not be?"

Honestly, he half-expected her to wig out at any

second. Not that he would blame her after everything she'd been through. "I don't know . . . I mean, it's cost you everything."

Aimee swallowed. It was true in a way, but in another . . . "It didn't cost me you. I always knew I wouldn't have a choice over who the Fates chose for me and truthfully, I'd have it no other way. I never once dreamed that I'd feel toward my mate the way I feel toward you, Fang. Do you think I'd go stalking through two hell realms for anyone else?"

He laughed. "I hope not."

Aimee held his hand in hers as she walked into his arms until her breasts were pressed against his chest. "How do you feel about it?"

Fang swallowed as he felt his body harden. Damn, she was the most beautiful woman he'd ever seen. And like her, he'd never once dreamed he'd feel this way toward another person, never mind his mate. "Relieved that I'm not a complete freak."

"Fang!" she said in a chiding tone.

He gave an innocent blink. "What?"

Aimee shook her head at him. "We have got to do something about your brutal honesty."

"Like you didn't have the same thought."

Okay, maybe a little, but she'd never admit that out loud.

"Are you two coming to eat?"

Hating the interruption, she looked past him to see Bride in the doorway. "We're coming." When she started to pull away, Fang held her close.

"*I just want to feel you here for a minute longer,*" he projected to her.

Her vision swam at that. He held on to her as if she were the most precious thing he'd ever touched and it made the love inside her well up. Gods, how she loved the way he felt against her. The hardness of his body. The deep masculine smell of his skin. She could stay like this forever.

"Uncle Fang?"

Smiling, Aimee looked down to see Trace tugging at Fang's leg.

"What you need, sport?"

Trace wrapped his arms around Fang's leg, squeezed tight, then ran off toward the kitchen.

Aimee laughed. "I guess he needed the same thing I did."

"Guess so." Fang took her hand into his and pulled her toward the dining room.

Bride pegged them both with a stern frown. "What are you two up to?"

Fang looked at Aimee, then back at Bride. "What?"

"You look like two wolves who found a bone." It was a Katagaria expression that meant the same thing as the cat who ate a canary.

Bride's gaze dipped to Fang's hand. She gasped and almost dropped the salad bowl she was holding. Setting it on the table, she snatched his palm up to look at it. "Oh, gods, you're mated!" Then her eyes really widened. "I really hope it's to Aimee."

Aimee laughed before she held her palm up to show her. "Thankfully so. Otherwise I'd have had to kill me some ho and then beat Fang senseless."

He held his hands up in surrender. "Hey, you know my future sessions are all under your control."

"Dog right, boy."

Vane entered the room and looked around with a puzzled frown. "What's going on?"

"Your brother's mated."

"Yeah, to Angelia."

"Not Fury, sweetie."

It took a second for the news to register. Vane gaped at them before he held his hand out to Fang. "Congratulations."

"Thank you," Fang said, shaking it.

Lia came running forward from the kitchen. "Let me see!" she said to Aimee. She grinned as she compared their marks, which were basically the same except for the colors. Aimee's was blue while Lia's was red. "Welcome to the family. Not that you weren't here already, but now it's official."

In spite of her happiness, those words brought a stab of pain as Aimee realized her birth family would never be this happy for her.

It was so unfair.

But she wouldn't let it taint her joy. At least that was what she told herself. The truth, however, was that it did. No matter what happened, her family was her family and she wanted them with her.

Their absence ached deep inside her heart, but she refused to show that to the others. They were happy for her and she was so grateful for them that words couldn't convey even an inkling of what she felt. So she sat there, choking back her tears while Vane and Bride broke out champagne and they all celebrated.

Even Fury when he returned was thrilled. He kissed her on the cheek and shook Fang's hand.

Aimee excused herself from them and went to the bathroom. The moment she was alone, she shut the door and flashed herself to the alley outside of Sanctuary. It was completely dark. Eerily so. She glanced up at the light that had always been moody on its best night.

When would Griffe get around to fixing it?

Missing her family, she went to the door to open it, then stopped.

They won't be happy. Tears gathered in her eyes as those words cut through her. She wanted to run inside and tell her parents. To have them laugh and congratulate her the way they'd done for her mated brothers. She wanted Dev and Remi and all the others to congratulate her too.

It would never happen.

Go home.

A single tear fled down her cheek. This was her home. . . .

But not anymore. This would never be her home again.

Her home was with Fang as his mate. Forcing herself to let go of the doorknob, she stepped back. As she did so, she caught a glimpse of pink from the corner of her eye.

She went over to it. Her heart sank as she realized it was the body of their waitress, Tara. Just like the other murders that the police had tried to blame on Fang, she was completely drained of blood.

But she still had her soul. . . .

Stumbling back, she realized in an instant what this was.

A demon kill.

Her breathing ragged, she started for the door only to feel an evil presence in the alley with her.

Someone tsked. "You didn't really think you'd be able to interrupt us and then go your own way, did you?"

Out of the darkness stepped not one, but an army of demons.

CHAPTER 30

Fang was laughing with Vane as a rancid chill went straight down his spine. A chill that turned into shredding talons as every instinct inside him went on high alert.

In an instant, he knew what it was.

"Aimee's in trouble."

Fury arched one sarcastic brow as he scoffed. "In the bathroom? What'd she do? Eat the wrong thing?"

He gave Fury a fierce glare. "No. She's at Sanctuary."

Vane frowned at him. "What?"

"She must have flashed there to see her family." Unwilling to waste another second trying to explain it to his dense brothers, he teleported himself out to find her in the alley, surrounded by demons as she fought them back with her staff.

There were easily two dozen, with more appearing to attack as if someone had opened a portal to hell.

Fang met her determined gaze. He manifested his sword to fight them. "Get inside."

For once, she didn't argue. "I'll get help."

After making sure she got inside without harm, Fang

raked the advancing demons with an arrogant sneer. "Ready to dance, punks? It's killin' time."

Aimee ran to the bar where Dev, Remi, Colt, and Wren were, along with her father. They all stared at her as if she were a ghost.

"What are you doing here?" Papa asked.

Aimee struggled to slow her rapid breathing as she felt the sweat rolling down her back. Her entire body was shaking from the battle she'd just left and she was pretty sure her Sentinel markings were showing on her face—especially given the way Remi was eyeing her— but she didn't have time or strength to worry about it. "Tara's dead. Fang is outside in the alley, surrounded by demons. He needs help. Now!"

Dev started forward only to have Maman's sharp voice stop him. "The wolf means nothing to us. They declared war the moment they caused Savitar to revoke our license. We have no use for them. Let the demons have him."

Aimee gaped, then glared. Rage took hold of her as she faced her mother. "He might not mean anything to you, Maman, but he is my mate." She held her palm out to her mother to show her Fang's mark. "And if none of you will help him, then I'll do it myself, and I'll never forgive you for it."

She started to flash herself out, but before she could she saw Blakemore's pack come through the door.

Every member, male and female, was there with a look on their face that said they had come here loaded for bear. They stood shoulder to shoulder in battle formation, heads low, eyes alert.

It was obvious this wasn't a coincidence. This was a well-planned, calculated attack on Sanctuary. Suddenly, everything made sense about the demons outside.

And she knew exactly who was to blame.

Eli.

He'd summoned them up and tonight, on the anniversary of his son's death, he was going to clean bear hide.

Dev grabbed the two swords off the wall above the bar. He tossed one to Kyle and kept the other. "C'mon, cub, let's go save Fang before Aimee hurts us. Remi, the rest of you take out the trash in the bar and make sure you crush it first."

Remi inclined his head before he jumped over the bar and went for the wolves.

The last sight Aimee had before she flashed to the alley was of all hell breaking loose as Eli's thugs attacked the Sanctuary staff. People screamed, guns went off, and bodies entwined in a deadly blur.

But right now, there was one who was fighting alone.

Aimee flashed out to find Fang, who had been joined by Varyk, being overwhelmed by the sheer number of the demons coming at them.

The back door of the club opened and Dev grabbed Fang and Varyk by their shirts to yank them into Sanctuary. "Get in the club and shut the door," Dev growled at her.

Aimee didn't hesitate to obey.

Varyk and Fang shook Dev off them.

"I'm not your bitch, boy," Varyk snarled. "Don't ever touch me like that again."

Dev rolled his eyes at the common wolf complaint. "Next time I'll let them have you."

Panting, Fang pulled Aimee against him and kissed her on the side of the head. Like her, he was sweating from his fight and she could feel his heart thumping wildly in his chest while he held her close.

Varyk looked pointedly at Kyle. "Get some salt. As much as you can find."

"Why?"

Varyk coughed before he answered. "They're slug demons. Put a thick line of it at all the doors and windows, and it'll keep them out."

"You're too late." Wren said, joining them. He nodded toward the front.

"Holy shit," Dev breathed.

Aimee gasped.

It looked like something out of a zombie movie. The last of the remaining humans ran screaming for the door while the Were-Hunters and demons fought. What was most surprising was the fact that Vane, Fury, Lia, and the rest of the Kattalakis Katagaria pack had joined them.

Remi met Aimee's gaze. "I wouldn't blame you if you ran for the door."

"Family forever," she said, holding her hand up to him.

He grabbed her into a tight hug before he pushed her back toward Fang. "Protect her."

"With my life."

They joined the battle. Aimee's heart pounded as she engaged an Arcadian wolfswain. Burly and ugly, he was almost twice her size.

As he reached for her, Thorn appeared, and he

brought with him reinforcements that included Wynter, Zeke, and Ravenna.

Fang gaped as he saw them in the fray. "What's this?"

Thorn winked at him. "One for all and all for fun, my friend. You didn't think I'd let you fight demons all on your own, did you?"

"It wouldn't be the first time."

Thorn laughed as he took the head off a demon who'd made the mistake of getting too close.

"Guess we can kill these, eh?"

Thorn snatched his sword back and gave him a piercing stare. "When your mark sizzles, don't kill them. When it tingles, they're all yours."

So that was the difference in the sensations he felt. "We really need to work on your communication skills."

"Give it up," Zeke said as he caught a demon beside Fang and twisted its neck. "He's just not a people person and we're never going to housebreak him."

Fang head-butted one of Eli's crew. He wanted to turn wolf, his body begged for it, but he had to have arms to fight the demons.

Damn it.

Aimee stepped back from the demon she'd just killed and looked around at the bloody mess. There were just so many demons. Even though Xedrix and crew had come in to help, they were still overwhelmed. Aimee felt like she'd fallen into an anthill. Everywhere she tuned there was a demon or a Blakemore pack member.

We're going to die. . . .

Tears filled her eyes as she fought down her panic. But how could they hold their own? New demons came in, and they were lagging from battle. Her staff was getting heavier by the minute and though her wounds were minimal, they were still aching.

None of them could use their powers since that would only feed the demons' strength. Even Acheron was fighting with staff and sword.

Simi was the only one who seemed to be enjoying this as she ran around with a bottle of barbecue sauce, trying to catch Eli's crew. The rest of them . . .

It's hopeless.

Stop it! We're not down yet.

She was a Peltier mated to a Kattalakis. The blood of two royal Were-Hunter lines was merged inside her and by the gods she would not give in or give up.

Her strength renewed, she tore into the werewolf closest to her. She caught him with her staff, a blow so fierce it lifted him up off his feet and sent him flying into the back of the demon fighting Wren. She lifted her weight up to kick them both back.

Wren laughed. "Get 'em, girl." He flashed back to his tiger form.

As Aimee advanced to finish them off, she caught sight of Eli heading for her mother's back. Maman was embroiled with a demon and had no idea he was anywhere near her.

But the bloodlust in his eyes was unmistakable.

He was going to kill her.

Her only thought to save her mother, Aimee turned into a bear and launched herself for him.

Maman turned at the same time Eli spun on Aimee and dealt her a vicious blow to her side. It sent Aimee flying and made her turn human as she tried to catch her breath through the pain. Naked and bleeding, she tried to focus. How on earth did Fang stay in his alternate form?

She couldn't move. . . .

Gah, it hurts!

Eli went to stab her, but Maman, in her bear form, lunged for his throat, knocking him back. Maman turned back to check on Aimee, who had at least recovered enough to clothe herself.

Her mother placed one large bear claw on her face . . . where she was sure her Sentinel mark was visible. The frightened concern for her in those black eyes brought a trembling smile to Aimee's lips.

"I'm all right, Maman."

Maman went for Eli, but the coward had run off. She pursued him while Fang came running up to check on Aimee.

He helped her up and cupped her face in his hands. "Are you all right?"

She nodded. "Why are you still human?"

"It's the only way to fight the demons and win."

Aimee looked around at all the bodies and the blood-covered combatants and floor. "I'm not too sure we're winning."

He flashed her that taunting grin of his that somehow managed to make her feel better even in the face of possible slaughter. "We're not dead yet."

No, but that was about all that could be said for them at present.

Fang kissed her, then rejoined the fight. Aimee turned to see Remi get kicked back at the same time one of the demons let out a belch of fire. Remi ducked the blast.

The fire went skimming across the polished countertop and caught on the wood of the bar. Flames skimmed across the top and lit the bottles of alcohol.

"Oh, no," she breathed as the fire quickly spread. Her heart in her throat, she ran for a fire extinguisher while Kyle did the same.

"Fang!" she called, needing more help.

Fang turned at the same time Eli went for him.

Aimee froze in painful shock as she realized what was about to happen.

Eli, sword in hand, was going to behead him.

Screaming, she ran at Fang to save him. He turned as the blade was coming down. Aimee died inside as she realized she'd never reach him in time even if she teleported.

Just as the blade would have reached him, Maman put herself between them. The sword, instead of beheading Fang, was buried deep in Maman's side.

"No!" Aimee screamed as she saw the stroke.

Maman fell over Eli, pinning him to the floor as the bear mauled him until he stopped moving. When he was still, Maman tried to leave him, but she stumbled.

Aimee reached her mother, who was shaking and gasping. Blood was everywhere as it flowed from the gaping wound. "Maman?" she choked.

Her mother turned human to look up at her. It was then she saw just how horrific the wound was. Aimee conjured a blanket to cover her mother's naked body.

Carson appeared at their side and shook his head as he saw the wound that had almost cut her in half. "There's nothing I can do. I'm so sorry, Aimee . . . Nicolette."

Aimee grabbed him by the shirt. "Get Talon from the swamp." He could heal wounds like this. "He's her only hope."

Carson vanished.

Maman gasped for breath as she took Aimee's hand and turned it over to see her marked palm. A tenuous smile curled her lips. "My beautiful daughter." She kissed her palm.

Aimee choked on her sobs as her brothers surrounded them. "Hold on, Maman. Talon's coming."

She swallowed. "It's too late, *ma petite.*" Her smile sad, she touched Aimee's marked cheek. "You were always so beautiful . . . you should have told me the truth of you long ago."

Tears stung Aimee's cheeks.

Fang moved to stand behind Aimee at the same time Papa reached Maman's side. His eyes were filled with tears as he sank to his knees.

"Nicolette?"

Tears flowed from Maman's eyes as she reached for her mate. "My precious Aubert. *Je t'aime pour toujours.*"

Her father's hands shook as he gathered Maman into his arms and held her close. "*Moi aussi, ma petite.*"

Maman reached out and took Fang's hand, then pressed it against Aimee's. "Forgive me," she breathed. "May the gods grant you both the happiness Aubert and I have shared, and may you have children as precious as ours." Her lips trembling, she looked out at all the boys who were gathered there. "I love you, *mes enfants.* Take care of each other for me."

Then she turned into a bear. Papa sobbed into her

fur as he held her even closer. His Sentinel marks appeared on his face. "Do us proud, children."

Maman shuddered as her last breath left her. Papa smiled sadly, then laid his head down and joined her in death.

Aimee let out a wail of pain as Fang pulled her against him.

Fang didn't know what to do for her as he rocked Aimee in his arms. She sobbed like a brokenhearted child. Parts of the bar were still burning, but Wren, Acheron, and Max appeared to have most of it under control.

Thorn, Varyk, Wynter, Zeke, and the Charonte had the demons on the run.

Remi let out a feral sound of pain an instant before he turned into a bear. He launched himself at Eli's body, tearing it to shreds. Fang grimaced, grateful that Aimee wasn't able to see the viciousness of his actions.

Not that she didn't know Remi's darker side or probably wouldn't have done it herself had she been more aware. He buried his lips against her hair and rocked her while she let out all her pain. He hated that he couldn't take this from her.

But there was nothing to do except comfort her.

And as everyone realized what had happened and that Eli lay dead, the fighting ceased.

Stone let out his own cry of pain as he saw his father slaughtered on the floor. He fell to his knees sobbing as the rest of their pack stared in disbelief.

"I'll get you, bastards!" Stone shrieked. "I swear it! I'll kill you all!"

Dev shook his head. "There's been enough killing, Stone. Go home, for the sake of the gods."

Stone launched himself at Dev.

The Dark-Huntress Janice caught him and shoved him into the arms of the werewolves behind him. "Boy, you better learn to listen. It's over. Take your punks and go home while you're still on this side of the grave. This is a one-time offer and it's about to expire. Go."

He went, but the promise in his eyes was potent.

He would be back.

The werewolves and demons retreated. Constantine and Varyk passed a look of mutual hatred between them before Varyk, Thorn, and his crew followed after the others to make sure they didn't double back.

Fang swept his gaze around the bar that had been all but destroyed. Tables and chairs along with railings and trim had been splintered. The entire area was charred. Broken glass and weapons littered the floor and were covered in blood.

He'd never seen anything like this.

And as his gaze went to the sign by the door, he felt his heart lurch.

Come in peace or leave in pieces.

The only question was, could they ever pick up the pieces that had been left here tonight?

Dev came forward to pull Aimee away from Fang so that he could hold on to her. Fang started to protest, but realized she needed her family as much as she needed him. While he ached for her, Dev truly felt the pain of the loss. Knowing that pain all too well himself, he released her to her brother.

Dev cradled her head against his shoulder. "It'll be all right, Aim. We're here."

Aimee heard those words, but they did nothing to

ease the ache inside her. All she'd wanted to do was to share her mating with her mother. . . .

Her father. . . .

It was why she'd come here tonight. She'd wanted her parents to be proud of her. To share in her joy.

Now they were gone. Forever.

Had you not been here, they would have been attacked unawares and Maman would have died without your ever seeing her again.

It was true, yet she couldn't stop the pain inside her. The grief that cried out for her mother's love. How could they be gone? How?

It was so unfair and she wanted blood for the loss. . . .

Fang stood back as the bears circled and held on to one another to grieve. They were a family united.

He felt like a total outsider.

Until Aimee and Dev pulled him forward. He hesitated until Remi took his wrist to force him to join them. "You're one of us, wolf." Remi's gaze went to Fury, Vane, Lia, and the others. "As are all of you. Thank you for coming to help us fight. It won't be forgotten."

Aimee reached up to wipe some of the blood off Fang's face before she kissed him. "I guess we're all brolf after all."

Dev frowned. "Brolf?"

Simi huffed at him as if she thought he was completely dense. "A bear and wolf family. Jeez, doesn't anyone understand Charonte English?"

Dev shook his head as he looked around at the hodgepodge of creatures who called Sanctuary home. "This is one fucked-up family."

Fang laughed. "I think it's the nature of all families to be fucked up."

Aimee wiped her tears away. "Simi? What was it you told me once about families?"

"We have three kinds of family. Those we are born to, those who are born to us, and those we let into our hearts."

Aimee held her hand out to Fang as Dev continued to hold her.

Family.

It was all that ever really mattered.

Those we are born to, those who are born to us, and those we let into our hearts.

The ones who were gathered here, they were family and no amount of malice would ever change that. Family could only be destroyed from within.

Never from without.

And tonight they were all closer than they'd ever been before. United in grief. United in spirit.

United in love.

Sanctuary forever.

One week later

Aimee stood in the center of the bar as Quinn and Serre reattached the lights to the ceiling. They were trying to get the bar back up and running as soon as possible, but it was taking awhile to pick up the pieces and reopen.

In true Were-Hunter fashion, they'd cremated their parents and placed their ashes in an urn that now rested in the memorial chapel where Bastien and Gilbert were kept in a special room in Peltier House.

Aimee had visited with them just that morning. She didn't think she'd ever get over the need to see her mother or feel her father's warm hugs.

She would miss them always.

Fang came up behind her and offered her a cup of tea. "Are you all right?"

How could she really answer that?

She looked around at the damage that they had yet to repair. In one night, their lives had all been forever altered. One night that would leave a lasting scar on all of them.

But out of the pain was hope. And like the mythical phoenix, Sanctuary would rise out of the ashes and be every bit as strong as it had been before.

They might never again regain their limani license, but that was all right. That would allow them to pick and choose who they helped and it would give Remi and Dev the freedom to break ass over anyone who crossed the line.

"Yeah, I think I am." She smiled at Fang before he went to help Dev and Xedrix move some of the lumber around.

The bar should be opened again in a couple of weeks. Everything would be back to normal except for two things.

There would be no more Mama and Papa Bear Peltier. That pain burned inside her.

But her brothers had come together and named her and Fang as the new owners of the bar. They would be the two faces that would carry on the legacy her parents had started, especially now that Fang was no longer wanted for what the demons had done. Stu had made sure of that.

For better or worse, Sanctuary would be here. And everyone would be welcomed here equally, so long as they maintained the one law.

Come in peace or leave in pieces.

"Hey?"

She turned at the sound of the unfamiliar voice coming in from the outside door. "Yes?"

A tall blond man stood in the bright sunlight as he skimmed the construction. "When are you opening back up?"

Quinn came down from the ladder. "On the fourth of next month."

"Cool. See you then."

It wasn't until he'd left that they all realized something.

That man had been a Daimon.

And he'd just walked out into daylight.

"Oh, shit," Dev breathed. "You guys think the Dark-Hunters know?"

Fang shook his head. "No, and I think the Dark-Hunters are about to get seriously owned."

EPILOGUE

Two weeks later

Fang lay in bed, completely naked, with Aimee snuggled up beside him. Gods, she felt so good there. . . .

He loved the way she looked when her skin was glowing in the morning light, her hair mussed and her lips swollen from his kisses. There was nothing better.

"Are you ever going to claim me?" she whispered as she traced circles over the muscles of his abdomen.

"I think that's entirely up to you, my lady." In their world, mating was a decision solely up to the woman. A man couldn't force a woman to accept him no matter what.

And if she failed to accept him within three weeks, he was left impotent . . .

So long as she lived.

Aimee lifted herself up to stare down at him. "You haven't mentioned it, so I was beginning to worry."

She was worried? He was the one facing the next few centuries as a poster child for Viagra failure. "I didn't want to rush you. You've been through a lot." And she'd been so sad since her parents' deaths that he hadn't wanted to be a prick by reminding her.

She rose up, showing him the breasts he lived to taste. "Yes, but you only have two more days. . . ."

As if he wasn't counting down to the exact nano-second. . . . He had his watch set to buzz him before it was too late. But again, Vane had taught him that women required a certain degree of finesse. Otherwise, a guy ended up in the doghouse. In his case literally.

"I was hoping you'd be feeling better and willing." He flashed her an evil grin.

Aimee let out a playful sigh at his eager look. Her wolf could be impossible at times. But she wouldn't have him any other way, and the thought of not having him at all hurt her on a level she didn't even want to think about.

Fang would be hers forever.

She would make sure of it.

Sliding her body over his, she straddled his hips. He was gorgeous, lying in her bed, his tawny skin offset by her white sheets. He had a day's worth of whiskers on his face that made him look as feral as he was. And his longer hair had an adorable wave to it.

She took his hand into hers so that she could nibble the pad of his fingers. He hardened instantly.

Fang looked up at her, his breathing turning ragged. "Are you sure?"

She nipped at his knuckle as she released his hand. "Don't be silly. I've been waiting for years for this moment."

His eyes turned dark, sincere. "I've been waiting a lifetime for you."

Those words touched her. She held her marked hand up. Fang placed his palm to hers, their marks joined as he laced his fingers with her so that they could complete their mating ritual. She was so nervous, and she wasn't even sure why. It wasn't like they'd never had sex before and yet . . .

This would bind them forever. She would belong to him and he would be hers exclusively. It was a major responsibility to be a part of someone else's world.

But she would have it no other way.

Their gazes locked, Aimee lifted herself up and set herself down on top of him.

Fang bit his lip as her body closed around his. He wanted to thrust against her, but it wasn't part of the ritual. This was her time. She would set the pace and she would dictate what they did.

And when she started moving against him, the wolf inside wanted to howl in pleasure. With their marked hands locked, he ran his free hand down her back as she moved in short, torturous strokes.

She brushed her hand against the mark Thorn had placed on his shoulder. He would still have to fight demons for him from time to time, but Varyk had explained to him how his life was basically his own.

Then again, as he looked into Aimee's eyes, he realized his life would never again belong to him alone. Aimee was his life now.

She tightened her grip on his marked hand. "I accept you as you are, and I will always hold you close in my heart. I will walk beside you forever."

Fang smiled as she whispered the words that bound them together in a ceremony that went back to a time before recorded history. He repeated them back to her and then added one more statement. "I would gladly give my life for you, Aimee."

"You are my life, wolf, so you better take damn good care of yours."

He started to answer that with a quip, but the thirio came upon him so suddenly that he couldn't do anything except hiss as he felt his cock harden even more. Pain exploded in his mouth as his teeth elongated to sharp fangs and a raw bloodlust came over him that made a mockery of the one he'd known when Phrixis had lived inside him.

The thirio was the urge to bond their life forces together and to make them one for all eternity.

In life and in death. It was what her parents had shared. What Anya had had with her mate and what his brothers had done with their mates.

Once put in place, it was unbreakable by any other than Savitar.

Fang ground his teeth to keep from biting her.

Aimee cupped his face in her hand as she stared down at him. "Let's finish this, Fang."

Searing joy tore through him, but he didn't want to take this step lightly. "Are you sure?"

She gave him an unamused smirk. "I have been through hell for you . . . twice. Do you really think I want to be in this life without you?"

Those words touched him deep. Fang sat up underneath her, pulled her close, then sank his teeth into her skin.

Aimee let out a small cry of dismay as her own teeth elongated. She felt her powers soaring as their blood was mingled. Brushing his hair back from his shoulder, she bit him.

The room around her swam as every sense she had sharpened and burned. In that one instant, she could feel Fang's heartbeat as if it were her own. The two of them were truly united.

Forever.

They would never again have to live without each other. It was the greatest gift.

And the ultimate curse.

But she would have it no other way.

Locked together, they came in unison. Aimee pressed her cheek to Fang's as he held her close and she listened to his heartbeat slowing.

"I swore I would never bond to anyone," Fang whispered in her ear. "I thought only fools did this."

"And now?"

His dark gaze locked with hers. "I'm the happiest fool on the planet."

She kissed him then and couldn't agree more. She too was the happiest fool on the planet.

Coming soon…

Look for the next Dark-Hunter® novel from

#1 *New York Times* Bestselling Author

SHERRILYN KENYON

NO MERCY

ISBN: 978-0-312-54656-4

Available in August 2010, in hardcover,
from St. Martin's Press

SherrilynKenyon.com

Dark-Hunter.com

officialsanctuary.com

Coming soon…

Don't miss the exciting new young adult series
from publishing phenomenon

SHERRILYN KENYON

INFINITY
The Chronicles of Nick
ISBN: 978-0-312-59907-2

Available in June 2010, in hardcover,
from St. Martin's Griffin

www.chroniclesofnick.com